P9-EES-350

"Take Care of Yourself. Come Back Safe!" She Murmured Huskily.

He brought up her face to kiss her mouth. For a long, tremulous moment he held her matched to his body, and she knew that he'd slept last night as poorly as she. If he'd come to her, she might not have been able to remember she belonged to Shea, for she loved this man, too, and in this time of parting her anguished flesh cleaved to his.

"Marc!"

He bowed his face to her hands, then quickly took the reins Belen offered. His eyes went over her as if to fix her image forever in his mind. "God keep you, love."

"Come back," she said. "Please. Come back."

He bent to brush her cheek with his fingers. "I'll have to. You're my woman."

She watched through tear-blinded eyes as he rode into the rising sun. Like Shea. Like John Irwin.

Now all her men were gone.

Books by Jeanne Williams

Bride of Thunder
Daughter of the Sword
Harvest of Fury
A Lady Bought with Rifles
The Valiant Women
A Woman Clothed in Sun

Published by POCKET BOOKS

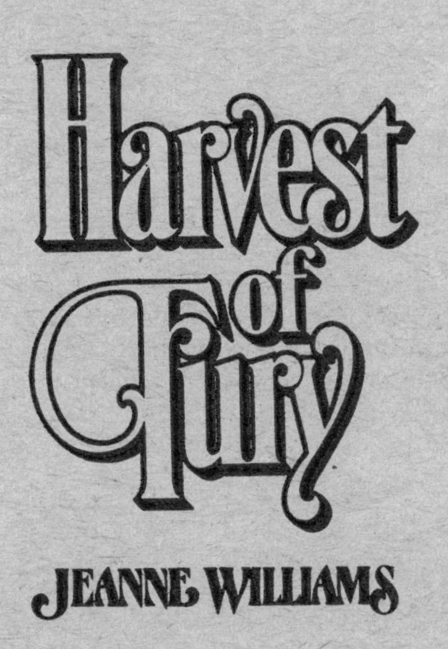

JEANNE WILLIAMS

PUBLISHED BY POCKET BOOKS NEW YORK

Distributed in Canada by PaperJacks Ltd., a Licensee of the trademarks of Simon & Schuster, a division of Gulf+Western Corporation.

This novel is a work of fiction. Names, characters, places and incidents are either the product of the author's imagination or are used fictitiously, and any resemblance to actual persons, living or dead, events or locales is entirely coincidental.

Another *Original* publication of POCKET BOOKS

POCKET BOOKS, a Simon & Schuster division of
GULF & WESTERN CORPORATION
1230 Avenue of the Americas, New York, N.Y. 10020
In Canada distributed by PaperJacks Ltd.,
330 Steelcase Road, Markham, Ontario.

Copyright © 1981 by Jeanne Williams
Map copyright © 1981 by Don Bufkin

All rights reserved, including the right to reproduce this book or portions thereof in any form whatsoever. For information address Pocket Books, 1230 Avenue of the Americas, New York, N.Y. 10020

ISBN: 0-671-82537-2

First Pocket Books printing August, 1981

10 9 8 7 6 5 4 3 2 1

POCKET and colophon are trademarks of Simon & Schuster.

Printed in Canada

ACKNOWLEDGMENTS

On the Border with Crook by John Bourke, a humane and educated officer, makes fascinating reading and covers the main part of the Apache wars (Bison Books, University of Nebraska Press, 1971). *Life Among the Apaches* by John Cremony (Rio Grande Press reprint, 1969) has interesting detail. Other helpful books were *Adventures in the Apache Country* by J. Ross Browne (University of Arizona, 1974); *Arizona Territory* by Jay Wagoner (University of Arizona, 1970); *Cycles of Conquest* by Edward Spicer (University of Arizona, 1972); *History of the Cattle Industry in Southern Arizona 1540–1940* by J. J. Wagoner (University of Arizona, April 1952); *Historical Atlas of Arizona* by Henry Walker and Don Bufkin (University of Oklahoma Press, 1979); *The Cowboy at Work* by Fay Ward (Hastings House, 1976); *Western Horse Behavior and Training* by Robert W. Miller (Doubleday Dolphin, 1974); *Verde to San Carlos* by William Corbusier (King, Tucson, 1971); *Mules, Mines and Me in Mexico* by Morris Parker, edited by James Day (University of Arizona, 1979); *Teresita* by William Curry Holden (Stemmer House, 1978); *Joe Hill* by Gibbs M. Smith (University of Utah, 1969); *Western Apache Raiding and Warfare* by Grenville Goodwin, edited by Keith Basso (University of Arizona, 1973); *Frontier Military Posts of Arizona* by Ray Brandes (King Globe Az., 1960); *The Apaches* by Don Worcester (University of Oklahoma, 1979).

I owe special thanks to two friends whose books were of tremendous help. For the Camp Grant Massacre I leaned heavily on Don Schellie's *Vast Domain of Blood* (Westernlore, 1968), a meticulously researched account of the event, giving all sides in the trial's reconstruction. For the Cananea strike, C. L. Sonnichsen's *Colonel Greene and the Copper Skyrocket* (University of Arizona, 1974) carefully sifts the evidence from participants and historians. Dr. Sonnichsen also kindly lent me *La Huelga De Cananea* by Manuel González Ramírez (Fondo de Cultura Económica, Mexico, D.F., 1956).

The following *Smoke Signals*, published by Tucson Corral of the Westerners, gave good background: *The Desert Dream of the South* by James Lee Neeley, Fall 1961, No. 4; *Aftermath of Cibecue* by

Sidney Brinckerhoff, Fall 1978, No. 36; *Alamos . . . Sonora's City of Silver* by Rachel French, Spring 1962, No. 5; *The Military Posts on Sonoita Creek* by James E. Serven, Fall 1965, No. 12; *Clabazas of the Rio Rico* by Bernard Fontana, Fall 1971, No. 24.

The Arizona Historical Society was my help and refuge. Tracy Rowe and C. L. Sonnichsen gave many useful leads, and Don Bufkin supplied the map. Particularly useful was the Charles Morgan Wood Collection. I drew from his *Camp Grant Massacre* and also found *A Letter from Crittenden* by Petra Etchells (July 1872), a vivid recreation of life along Sonoita Creek in those troubulous times.

The *Bisbee Review* kindly allowed me to go through back issues and make notes of the summer of 1917. Dr. Evelyn Hu-Dehart sent me some material on Santa Teresa de Cabora and encouraged me with her interest. Julian Hayden, chief Pinacateño, is always inspiring.

Also helpful were Dr. James W. Byrkit's Ph.D. dissertation "Life and Labor in Arizona, 1901–1921, with Particular Reference to the Deportation of 1917," and *Yoeme*, a collection of Yaqui tales and folklore by Mini Kaczkurkin (Sun Tracks, University of Arizona, 1977).

Joe Hill's songs have become part of America's folk-song heritage, but they were first printed in the Little Red Song Books published in various editions by the Industrial Workers of the World. I have allowed myself the anachronism of letting Johnny sing "I Dreamed I Saw Joe Hill Last Night" before the song was written in 1925 by Alfred Hayes. Earl Robinson supplied the music a few years later, and it has helped keep alive the mythic story of the executed leader.

My husband, Bob Morse, watched out for my natural history, especially details about birds. I would also bless and thank my agent, Claire Smith, ever supportive, empathetic, and resourceful; Meg Blackstone of Pocket Books for her sensitive and constructive ideas; Martin Asher, also of Pocket Books, for his interest and help; my excellent and painstaking typist, Leila Madeheim, who is so much more than that; my son, Michael, for reading with attention to military and weapon detail; and my daughter, Kristin, an indispensable critic.

Jeanne Williams
Tucson, Arizona
March 1980

For George Papcun,
who lived for his dream
of a better, brighter world

Arizona 1861–1917

". . . Mines without miners and forts without soldiers are common. Politicians without policy, traders without trade, store-keepers without stores, teamsters without teams, and all without means, form the mass of the white population."

—J. Ross Browne *Adventures in the Apache Country*
(Harper and Brothers, 1969).

"All Indian men of that [Apache] tribe are to be killed whenever and wherever you can find them . . ."

—General Carleton to Colonel Kit Carson
Oct. 12, 1862

"Hostilities in Arizona are kept up with a view of protecting the inhabitants, most of whom are supported by the hostilities."

—General E. O. C. Ord,
Jan. 22, 1870

"I believe that it is of far greater importance to prevent outbreaks than to attempt the difficult and sometimes hopeless task of quelling them after they do occur. . . . Bad as Indians often are, I have never yet seen one so demoralized that he was not an example in honor and nobility to the wretches who enrich themselves by plundering him of the little our Government appropriates for him."

—General Crook,
quoted in *On the Border with Crook*
by John Bourke (Scribner's, 1891)

". . . But the meat of the cocoanut, and the bone of contention, was contained in the remark of a Mexican laborer to another, who said, 'Yes, that is all true, but why don't the company pay the Mexicans the same wages they pay the Americans?' "

—W. B. Kelly, *Bisbee Review*, June 2, 1906
as quoted in *Colonel Green and the Copper Skyrocket* by C. L. Sonnichsen
(University of Arizona Press, 1974).

"Of all the crimes of the Porfirio Díaz regime the most monstrous was against the village in the sierras of western Chihuahua, Tomochic. . . . Apart from the heroism of the men of Tomochic . . . there was a singular and extraordinary factor. This was the inspiration of a nineteen-year-old girl, Teresa Urrea, whom they called La Santa de Cabora. Her name was their battle cry, and was on the lips of the Tomochitecos unto the death of the last man."

—Mario Gill, *Episodios Mexicanos*
(Mexico, 1960)

"The IWW appealed to rootless, voteless, womanless, alienated men. It embodied and made dramatically tangible the beliefs, dreams, hopes and visions that promised to the victims of industrial capitalism an escape from the futility of their lives."

—The IWW In Wartime Arizona by James W. Byrkit,
in *Journal of Arizona History*, Summer 1977

"How it could have happened in a civilized country I'll never know. This is the only country it could have happened in.
As far as we're concerned we're still on strike!
. . . I'll forget it when I die! I'll forget it when I die!"

—Peter Watson, one of the Bisbee deportees, on
tape to Dr. Robert Houston, Feb. 12, 1977,
Journal of Arizona History, Summer 1977

Who's Real

As in *The Valiant Women*, the historical background is as accurate as I could make it. Though my main characters are fictional, many others are drawn from life. Among actual military men were Captain John Irwin, Lieutenant Colonel Baylor, Captain Sherod Hunter, and Generals Sibley, Carleton, and Crook.

Prominent Arizonans were Granville and William Oury, Sylvester Mowry, Solomon Warner, Sam Hughes, Peter Brady, the Penningtons, Tom Gardner, Esteban Ochoa, and Governor A. P. K. Safford. Pete Kitchen was very real. For fictional purposes, I have him and Doña Rosa remain at their Santa Cruz Valley stronghold though Apache ravages forced even this doughty pioneer to move to Magdalena, Sonora, during the Civil War.

Eskiminzin, Mangus Coloradas, Cochise, and other Apache leaders lived, of course. The Camp Grant Massacre happened as detailed. However, the Papago youths who'd killed for the first time were not killed during their purification vigil as are the ones in this book.

In the third part of the novel, Santa Teresa lived and worked her healings, and Cruz Chavez and his valiant men died at Tomochic. Colonel Greene played his part at Cananea, and Sheriff Harry Wheeler supervised the deportation in Bisbee.

While weaving the lives of my fictional people into the fabric of history, I've tried to give a fair and valid presentation of actual people and events.

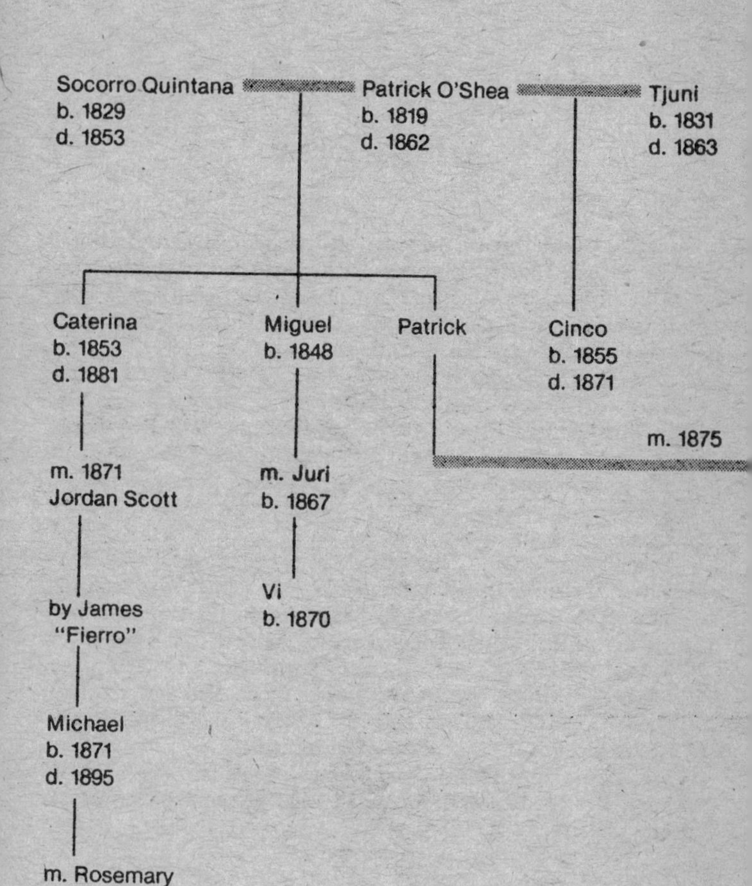
Socorro Quintana
b. 1829
d. 1853
Patrick O'Shea
b. 1819
d. 1862
Tjuni
b. 1831
d. 1863
Caterina
b. 1853
d. 1881
Miguel
b. 1848
Patrick
Cinco
b. 1855
d. 1871
m. 1875
m. 1871
Jordan Scott
m. Juri
b. 1867
by James
"Fierro"
Vi
b. 1870
Michael
b. 1871
d. 1895
m. Rosemary
Santiago "Sant"
b. 1891

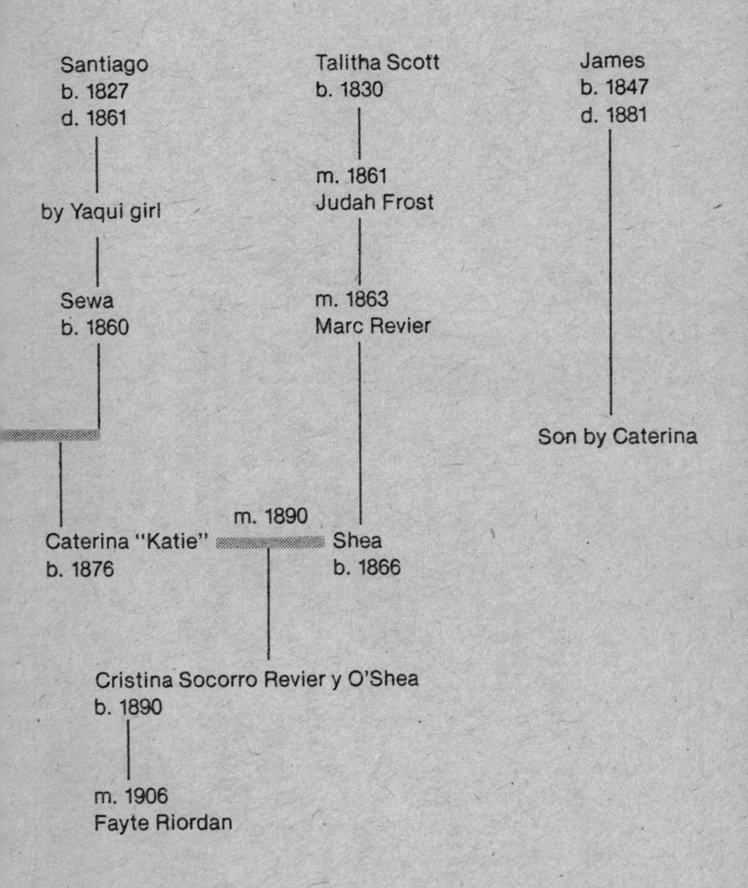
Santiago
b. 1827
d. 1861
by Yaqui girl
Sewa
b. 1860
Talitha Scott
b. 1830
m. 1861
Judah Frost
m. 1863
Marc Revier
James
b. 1847
d. 1881
Son by Caterina
Caterina "Katie"
b. 1876
m. 1890
Shea
b. 1866
Cristina Socorro Revier y O'Shea
b. 1890
m. 1906
Fayte Riordan

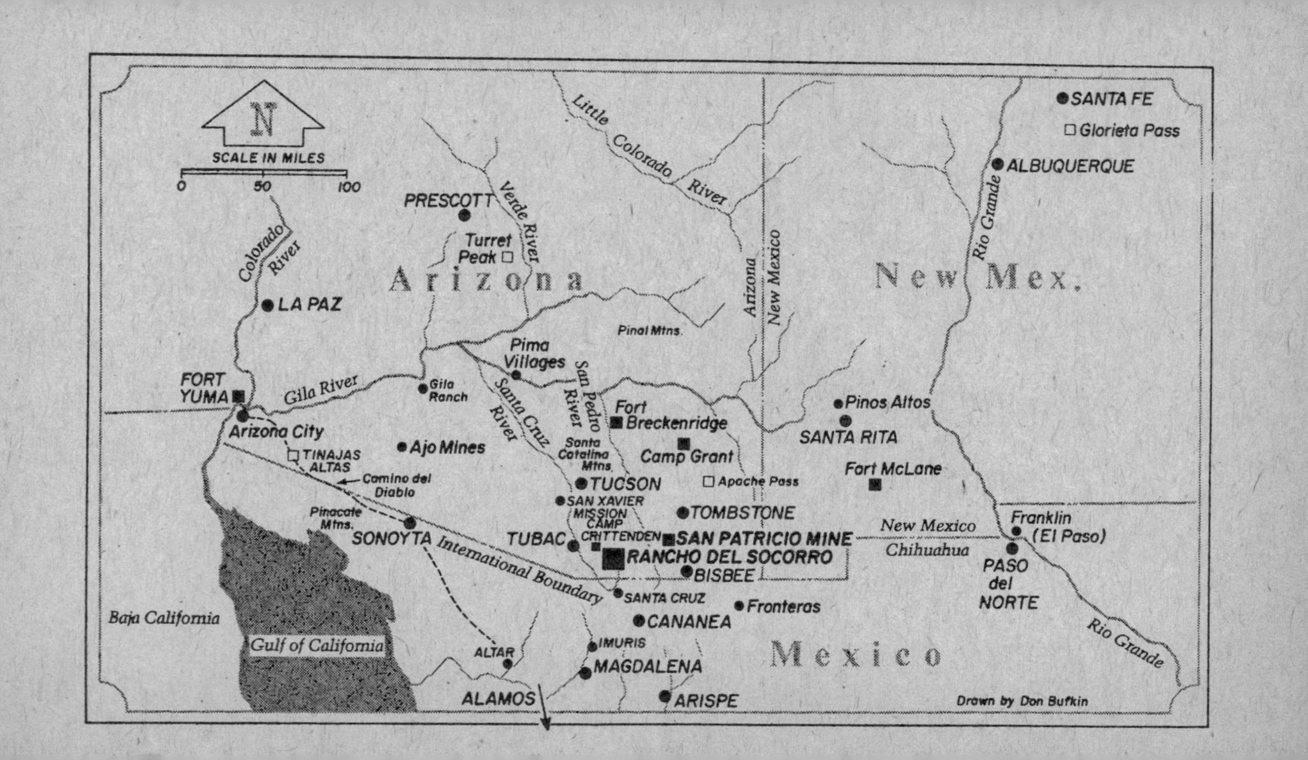
N
SCALE IN MILES
0
50
100
SANTA FE
Glorieta Pass
ALBUQUERQUE
Rio Grande
New Mex.
Little Colorado River
Arizona
New Mexico
PRESCOTT
Verde River
Turret Peak
Colorado River
LA PAZ
Pinal Mtns.
Pima Villages
FORT YUMA
Gila River
Gila Ranch
San Pedro River
Santa Cruz River
Fort Breckenridge
Pinos Altos
SANTA RITA
Arizona City
Ajo Mines
TINAJAS ALTAS
Camino del Diablo
Santa Catalina Mtns.
Camp Grant
Fort McLane
TUCSON
Apache Pass
SAN XAVIER
MISSION CAMP
TOMBSTONE
Pinacate Mtns.
SONOYTA
International Boundary
TUBAC
CRITTENDEN
SAN PATRICIO MINE
RANCHO DEL SOCORRO
BISBEE
New Mexico
Chihuahua
Franklin (El Paso)
PASO del NORTE
SANTA CRUZ
Fronteras
CANANEA
Baja California
Gulf of California
ALTAR
IMURIS
MAGDALENA
Mexico
Rio Grande
ALAMOS
ARISPE
Drawn by Don Bufkin

Harvest of Fury

PART I

La Madama

1861–1862

I

Talitha cleared the supper dishes from the oak table before she turned to confront the young, redheaded Irish doctor from Fort Buchanan.

"John, it's kind of you to take this trouble, but I can't leave. The cattle, the horses, the land, everything Shea and the others worked for—it's up to me now to hold it together."

"Shea's gone to fight the very army he expected to protect his family and ranch," John Irwin said grimly. "He'd never dream of wanting you to stay now that all the troops in Arizona—not that there were ever that many—are pulling out." He glanced from the twelve-year-old twins, dark, lithe Miguel and tall, wiry, flame-haired Patrick, to seven-year-old Caterina, who was rocking little Tosalisewa, just past her first birthday. "He'd value these children—and you—above the ranch and the whole damn boiling!"

Shea's last words when he rode away had been to tell Talitha to take care of the children for him—and to take care of herself. Not a word about the ranch. He couldn't have guessed that within a few months the federal government would abandon this region that already called itself Arizona, though it was legally part of Doña Ana County of the Territory of New Mexico. The Overland Mail had stopped running in April; and now, in July 1861, the troops were pulling out of Fort Buchanan, only about four miles from the ranch, and Fort Breckinridge, about fifty miles northwest of Tucson. Laughably small forces to oppose the swift-raiding Apaches, but now even they would be gone.

Looking at the children, Talitha saw in them their parents who'd braved scalp hunters, Apaches, and the fierce country to reclaim this old Spanish land grant in 1847 after it had been deserted for over twenty years because Mexico had been unable to defend its northwest frontier against Apaches.

Caterina flashed a smile from those startling gray-blue eyes, otherwise looking so much like her mother, Socorro, that even after nearly eight years Talitha felt a rush of grief and need for the kind and lovely woman who'd been her foster mother. Socorro's looks were echoed, too, in Miguel, but Patrick was the image of what Shea must have been as a boy, blazing red-gold hair and eyes the dark gray of a thundercloud. Though he liked John Irwin, the boy glared at him now.

"We can't let the ranch go to pieces! And Mangus is our friend. Isn't he, James?"

Talitha's half brother, born of a blond Mormon and her Apache captor, Juh, frowned, his dark blue eyes shocking in his lean brown face. At fourteen, he was a head taller than his sister, his sinewy body hard and spare from his years among the Apaches. From the time he was seven until his return a few months before, he had lived in the camp of Mangus Coloradas, great chief of the Mimbreños.

"Mangus will do what he can. But the soldiers have hunted the Apaches since they came to these parts five years ago. Miners and other whites have swarmed in. The Apaches are angry. When the soldiers go, the Apaches will want to drive out the rest of the whites. That's why Mangus sent me to you. To try to protect you if there was a raid. I will do that."

"See?" cried Patrick triumphantly. "Miguel and I

can shoot as well as Belen and Chuey. And so can you, Tally," he added kindly. "If Apaches or bandits hit Socorro, we'll make them wish they hadn't!"

"Apaches aren't too likely to ride up to the house while we're all together and behind walls," Talitha reminded him. "We'd probably be scattered around and be picked off one or two at a time."

She thought briefly of alternatives. Her father, Jared Scott, who, with Cooke's Mormon Battalion, had marked a southern route to California in the winter of 1846–47, had stayed in California to pan gold until, three years ago, he had come to see Talitha. Wistfully, for Talitha had been only six when he rode off with his battalion, Jared had offered her a home and any help she might ever need. Though he was resettling deep in Apache country, two hundred miles north on the Verde River, he'd thought he would have the usual Mormon friendship with Indians.

No word had since come from him. He might be dead, or gone to join the United States Army as he'd done before. Besides, if the Apaches decided to drive out all the whites, Jared's place would probably be no safer than Socorro. Talitha wouldn't have gone there herself in any case. She meant to stay at the ranch. But she wished there were some safe place to send at least Cat and Tosalisewa.

Meeting John Irwin's worried gaze, Talitha sighed. "There's no safe place in Arizona, New Mexico, or nothern Mexico, John."

"There's Santa Fe. The troops would escort you there."

With a pang, she remembered that little adobe village high in the mountains. That was where the Mormon Battalion had left its weaker members and most of the women and children. Talitha's mother, uncles, and grandfather had started out to follow the battalion at a slower pace. Talitha still blanked out the way her uncles and grandfather had looked, full of arrows, bound to their wagon wheels and burned, when she and her mother were taken captive.

Judith had died of fever brought on by James's difficult birth. One of Juh's other wives grudgingly nursed James for a few months. After that, Talitha kept him alive by feeding him piñon nuts, finely ground and mixed with water and honey. He'd been less than a year old when Shea had ransomed him by proving to Juh his bravery, taking a second brand on his cheek to go with the one the army had given him.

Talitha had worshiped Shea since that day, though after his beloved Socorro died his grief and resultant drinking had deepened her love with compassion. Only the night before he left to join the Confederate forces mustering in Texas had he at last permitted himself to treat Talitha as a woman. That one sweet night, ever to be treasured! He'd promised to marry her when he came back, start a fresh new life with her.

A thrill at once of rapture and of loss ran through Talitha as she straightened. She must be here when he came, hold the ranch for him and these children.

Meeting the young captain's eyes, she smiled and shook her head. "Santa Fe's where I started, John. I'm not going back. None of us have kin in the East, anyone who could be trusted to take care of the children. Even with the danger, they're better here with me."

"We're not children, Miguel and me!" snorted Patrick.

Cat, still rocking Sewa, took James's brown hand and pressed her soft cheek to it. "James loves us, Captain Irwin. He's part Apache. He won't let them hurt us."

Dropping to one knee beside her, James laughed. Great closeness had grown up between the two of them since his return, a closeness which made Talitha, who'd mothered them both, feel shut out.

Talitha had longed for years to have James back, but in those seven years he'd changed from the brother she'd kept alive among Juh's hostile wives to an

Apache youth inured to hardship, almost old enough to go on his first raid when he would act as a servant to the older men and his family would pray that he'd bring back many horses and cattle. Only when he played with Cat and Sewa could Talitha see flashes of the little brother who'd so loved Chacho, his princely black cat who had gotten hydrophobia and given it to Shea. It was in taking Shea to a Tarahumare hermit for curing that Socorro had gone into premature labor and hemorrhaged to death. Guilty because he'd lied to protect his stricken cat, James had gone with Mangus from Socorro's grave.

Irwin's jaw squared. "Even Tucson would be safer than this. By God, if this territory were under martial law, I'd pack you up there whether you liked it or not!"

Talitha stiffened. "How fortunate for our friendship that you can't!" Her mind had been grappling with the formidable situation, though, and she added persuasively, "It would be wise to bring the El Charco people to the main ranch, to provide more protection for all. I'll give them the alternative of going deep enough into Mexico to get away from Apaches; but if they stay, that'll give us four more men—five, if Güero comes."

"I don't like Güero," Patrick said. "He's mean to horses."

Talitha didn't like Pedro Sanchez's older son, either, the way his green eyes seemed to burn through her clothing, but she shrugged and said, "Gracious, John, that gives us more good shots than the presidio at Tubac often used to have when they were supposed to protect the whole Santa Cruz Valley!"

He slammed his fist into his palm. "Damn it, Talitha, don't you understand? It's going back to the way it was when the ranch started, maybe even worse."

"Sylvester Mowry's Patagonia mine is like a fortress," she reminded him. "Pete Kitchen has his ranch so well fortified that the Apaches don't try to take his house anymore; they just run off stock and kill his pigs."

"And men, when they catch them."

There was no answer to that. Irwin stifled a growl of frustration. "You'll at least move the El Charco vaqueros up here?"

Talitha laughed. "I'll surely invite them, most heartily." She crossed the room and put her hand in the captain's. "It's kind of you to worry about us, John. I hate to see you go. Especially when—" She bit her lip.

"When I'll fight for the Union, while Shea joins the rebels?" Irwin supplied gently. "I hate that, too, but that stubborn Irishman has it in his head that the Union's like England, always pushing weaker countries around."

That was true. The brand of desertion on Shea's cheek had seared into his spirit, along with the death of his brother. He'd hated it when Americans had started coming into the Arizona country, though he'd become friendly with some of them, including this Irish-born young surgeon.

"Come see us as much as you can before you leave," Talitha urged.

"I'll do that." He bent to kiss Cat and Sewa, then shook hands with all three boys, who suddenly seemed taller and older, sobered and challenged by what lay ahead. Then, with a teasing grin, he swept Talitha close.

"If you're not afraid of Apaches, you shouldn't be afraid of me!"

He gave her a quick, light kiss, picked up his plumed hat, and went out into the warm July twilight.

Standing in the door, watching her brother and Shea's children follow the officer through the opening between the boys' quarters and the granaries, Talitha hugged Sewa close and in the baby's warm, soft sweetness found some comfort for her sad heart. She had to choose for all of them. If they suffered for it, were slaughtered as so many others had been—

But this had always been dangerous country. Shea had left them in that knowledge. It wasn't as if she were willfully plunging the children into this threat. The only other choice was to flee like refugees, abandoning these children's heritage, all their parents had worked for.

The peaches that grew in the courtyard were ripe, though the pomegranates were only faintly tinged with crimson. Talitha reached up for a peach she'd noticed earlier that day, rubbed the fuzz off on her skirt, and took a bite, savoring the mellow richness as juice filled her mouth.

She loved this place—so painfully made by the courage, patience, work, and faith of its founders. It was home, where Shea, her love, would return. If she hoped to prove worthy of him, no matter how young, unsure, and frightened she was, she must somehow be as valiant and enduring as Socorro.

But she had had Shea! Talitha wailed silently, then had to admit, to herself, *Not at first she didn't. Not when she was left alone in the desert with all her people dead. She was younger then than you are, so let's have no excuses!*

Even so, trying to emulate Socorro seemed an impossible challenge. Sighing, Talitha savored the fruit and straightened her shoulders. With all her strength and will and devotion, she would hold this ranch. That was all she could do; she could do no less.

When she said after breakfast next morning that she was going to El Charco and to San Manuel, the Papago enclave of Tjúni, the fourth of Rancho del Socorro's partners, James said he'd go with her. At that the twins clamored to ride along. Cat, torn, finally decided that Anita was capable of looking after Sewa for the day, and the five began the ride southward. Patrick was on coal black Thunder. Miguel's Lightning was a creamy gold. Caterina bobbed along on Mancha. James would never love another horse as he had his gray Tordillo, killed one hard winter to feed women and children among the Apaches, but he'd picked a tough, angular roan, Alacrán, or Scorpion, and they respected each other, moving as one.

On the hill behind the ranch buildings were the crosses raised for Santiago and Socorro, and on the far side of the hill in a small grotto were buried the scalps of many Papagos and Mexicans whose hair had been taken by white scalp hunters hungry to collect the bounty that had been offered for Apache scalps by the government of Sonora, the most northwestern state of Mexico, of which the Gadsden Purchase, presently part of the territory of New Mexico, was a portion. Now that civil war had engulfed the country, Apaches might well reclaim the great expanse of mountains, plains, and river valleys.

But not, if Talitha could prevent it, Rancho del Socorro. As Patrick, hair gilded by sun, rode close to Cat, laughingly calling some big-brotherly tease to her, Talitha thought they must look much as their parents had at the same ages. Patrick O'Shea, known as Shea, had left Ireland during the potato famine of 1845 with his twin, Michael, and joined the U.S. Army, which was preparing to go to war with Mexico. Coming to feel more sympathy with the Catholic Mexicans than with the overbearing sergeant who constantly harassed them, the brothers had swum the Rio Grande and joined the famed San Patricio Battalion, formed of deserters from the U.S. Army. The survivors of the battalion had been court-martialed by the conquering U.S. Many were hanged. Shea and Michael were branded and flogged but escaped, heading for California. Michael died of thirst in the desert, and Shea, a parched-leather skeleton whose gashes couldn't even bleed and whose tongue was shriveled to a hard lump, had been brought back to life by Socorro.

Socorro had been in desperate straits herself, though she'd found a life-giving natural cistern, or *tinaja*, in the desert rocks. She was traveling to California to marry her cousin when Areneños killed her father and her escort, plundered their wagon, and left her to die. The *tinaja* saved her, but such a gently reared girl would probably have died a slow death from exposure or hunger, or a swift one from more Areneños, if she hadn't rescued Shea, who, when he had regained his strength, walked her out of the desolate cinder cones and lava flows to a ranch where they found only Santiago left alive after a scalp hunters' raid.

When Santiago was able to travel, they'd taken two hundred cattle, loaded mules with whatever they could salvage, and started for an abandoned ranch which Santiago remembered from driving cattle to sell in the presidios of Tubac and Tucson. On the way they'd found Tjúni, intent on avenging the scalp hunters' slaughter of her family and village.

A chill always shot down Talitha's spine when she remembered the Place of Skulls. That was where Tjúni and Socorro, picking berries, had come upon the scalpers raping and killing the women of Mangus's camp. Tjúni had brought down three men with arrows, Socorro killed one, but the fifth escaped.

Judah Frost. Talitha still had nightmares about him, with his silver hair and ice-crystal gaze. She'd been thirteen when he caught her bathing in a hot spring not far below the Place of Skulls. He'd said then he meant to have her when she grew up. Through the years, as he was welcome at the ranch and became Shea's partner in freighting and mining, Talitha had felt stalked by a giant cat, unable to tell that Frost was one of the scalpers because he was an expert shot who'd surely have killed either Shea or Santiago had they challenged him.

He *had* killed Santiago only last year, when Santiago returned from years of slave labor in a Mexican mine where Frost had sold him while telling the O'Sheas that their friend had married a wealthy Mexican widow and had stayed in Mexico to manage her holdings. Freed by Yaquis rebelling against the government, Santiago had been nursed and loved by a Yaqui girl he had married when he learned she was with child. He'd come back to confront Frost, who'd shot him, wounded Shea, and taken Talitha hostage. Before he released her near Pete Kitchen's ranch, he'd done what he'd intended since that first day they met.

She'd thought she'd never be clean of that, but Marc Revier's tender loving had cleansed her. Marc, the Freiburg-trained engineer, who'd taught her to read and write, brought her books, waited for her to grow up. She thought of him with pain and loss, for she loved him in her own way.

"He's god to you," Marc had said bitterly of Shea. She had refused to marry Marc a year ago. Was he still at the Tecolote mine south of Yuma Crossing?

At least Frost was dead. Shea and the pursuers had found his horse dead and a man's corpse dangling head downward over a fire that had split the skill and charred the face past recognition. Talitha forced the thought of him from her, assessing with a practiced eye the cattle grazing along a dry wash or streambed that would become a torrent when the rains started, as they should within a few weeks.

In spite of the weeks of dry heat, the cattle were holding flesh well. Over the years the scrubs had been butchered or sold, the best kept for breeding. The starting herd of "black" Spanish cattle, not necessarily black, had been mixed with curly-haired, beefier animals from Texas and some heifers acquired from an Illinois drover headed for California.

That spring the vaqueros had collected about five hundred *senales,* the bits of ear cut off while earmarking and branding. For each calf there were probably four older animals, which meant the ranch was running close to twenty-five hundred head.

Not all of these carried the S brand and belonged to the O'Sheas. At the beginning, before there was money to pay the vaqueros, each was allowed to mark every twentieth cow for himself. Shea, marveling at this vast country, so rich with opportunity in spite of its dangers, had wanted those who worked with him to share his good fortune.

Living at El Charco, fifteen miles south of the main ranch, the Sanchezes, who worked for Shea, had, in effect, possessed their own small kingdom. Would Pedro consent to leave it, move to the Socorro? Once before, when he was a boy, Apaches had driven him from this place. Pedro, now fifty, might well decide that this country would never be safe, take his herd and family, and depart with the aim of going far enough south to be out of the way of Apache raids.

No one could blame him. But Talitha, mechanically noting the age of the cattle she passed by the rings around their horns, the wrinkles around their eyes, and the condition of their tails, prayed he would be steadfast.

The Sanchezes were at dinner. Plump, motherly Carmencita scattered grandchildren to make room at the rough table, and soon all were relishing her perfect tortillas, tasty beans, and stewed wild turkey. Carmencita exclaimed over how the twins and Cat had grown and gave thanks to God that Talitha's brother had returned from the devil Apaches.

James showed his teeth. "*Señora,* I myself am a devil Apache."

"Your poor mother was a captive. That is not your blame."

His hard grin widened. "No blame indeed to be the son of a great warrior and the foster son of Mangus."

Carmencita crossed herself at the feared name and hastily asked how little Tosalisewa thrived. After the health of all the children had been discussed, Talitha glanced up and down the table. The Sanchezes' tall, quiet daughter, Juana, beside her mustached husband, Cheno Vasquez, his brother, skinny Francisco, on the other side. Next were the youngest Sanchez son, Natividad, his broad, friendly face looking younger than his thirty years, and his Papago wife, Mársat, a pretty girl with luxuriant black hair who laughed a lot and jingled her shell earrings flirtatiously. Güero, the oldest son, wasn't there. Talitha didn't inquire after him; if there'd been good news of the Sanchez black sheep, poor Carmencita would have been bursting with it. Though every man was needed, Talitha was relieved that he wasn't here to watch her with his hot green eyes.

All the men seemed made of rawhide, weathered and tough. Trained to horses and their woven leather ropes, or *reatas,* they knew every cañon and wooded thicket on the big ranch, every watering place, and if and when it would go dry. Even if new men could be found, it would take them years to learn the country as these vaqueros knew it. They were part of the place. Yet they must be given their chance to leave it.

She told them the army posts were being abandoned, the troops pulled back to fight in the war between North and South.

"Ay," said Carmencita, shaking her head. "That same war to which Don Patricio felt he must go, may the Virgin protect him!"

Talitha nodded. "The Apaches don't understand about the war. They just see troops leaving, the overland stage stopped, and think they've driven them out. This will look like their chance to get rid of all the settlers. I won't blame you if you want to take your cattle and look for a safer spot in Mexico."

Pedro's dark eyes studied her from his wrinkled, wise-monkey face. "And you, *señorita?*" His gaze flicked to the O'Shea children sitting on the floor amid Vasquez and Sanchez youngsters. "You will refuge in Tucson with Don Patricio's family?"

"We stay at Rancho Socorro."

"*Bueno*. So do we." He glanced at his son-in-law. "You, of course, Cheno, must decide for yourself, you and Francisco. Natividad?"

"With you, Father," returned his younger son, grinning as happily as if he'd just been invited to a dance.

Cheno caressed his mustache, then exchanged a look

with his brother Francisco, whose prominent Adam's apple bobbed as he swallowed. Cheno shrugged, speaking for both of them. "What's the difference? When one gets far enough south to be out of reach of Apaches, there are rebelling Yaquis and usually the last governor of Sonora is leading armies to unseat the present one. I can't see that the Yanqui soldiers gave much protection anyway. Don Pedro Kitchen has the right idea. Fortify a ranch and have enough men to fight off attacks."

"If you're agreed to stay, that's what we must do," Talitha said. She explained that she wanted them to move to the main ranch.

After Pedro's first dismay, he made a gesture of assent. "Behind walls and with provisions and water, all of us could stand off a raiding party that could overwhelm either group taken separately." He puffed out his cheeks. "A good plan, *señorita.* You should have been a general."

Every one laughed at that, though Carmencita looked with sad resignation about the adobe that had been her home for thirteen years. "We'll build you another house," Talitha promised as they embraced in farewell. "Maybe it won't be too long till you can come back here." Till Shea comes back from that wretched war. . . .

Carmencita smiled and patted Talitha's cheek and then kissed Cat in a way that made Talitha sure she was remembering that horrible day eight years ago when Shea, Santiago, and Talitha rode in with Cat, born that dawning, and Socorro, dead from that birth.

"If one has life, health, and love, a house doesn't matter," the older woman said. "Besides, it will be good to be near my Anita and her children. They grow past all knowing between one visit and the next." Carmencita's glow faded, and she gave Talitha a sharp look. "You'll take the news to Tjúni?"

"Yes." Talitha gave a rueful chuckle. "Though the

last time I took her a warning, she let me know plainly that her *ranchería* is prepared to look after itself."

It still was. Tjúni herself came to meet them, followed by three little boys, the two smallest dark and naked. The oldest, perhaps six, paler of skin and with a cast of red to his long hair, wore loose white cotton trousers.

He was Shea's son Cinco, born the fifth day of the fifth month of 1855. Tjúni had always loved Shea. After Socorro died, she had hoped to be his wife. When he refused this, the Papago woman had angrily taken her infant son back to the Papago settlement at San Manuel, her part of the ranch, and vowed to give him a Papago father. She had, returning gifts Shea sent to the boy. Probably it was better that Cinco be reared purely Papago, but Talitha felt stabbing pain as she looked from Shea's sons to their half brother, who was ignoring them to stare in fascination at Cat.

She smiled bewitchingly at him. "Who are you, little boy?"

He stared at her, eyes wide with puzzled worship. "My son no speak Spanish," Tjúni cut in. She gave Talitha a hostile look. "Why you come? With *these?*" And she stared at the children of the man she'd adored and the woman she'd envied.

The twins remembered Tjúni, of course; and they had been seven when Cinco was born and knew, with a vague knowledge, never discussed, who had fathered him. Flustered, their usual outgoing friendliness withered under Tjúni's cold gaze, they reined back with James. Cat's eager smile faded. Never in all her life had anyone watched her like that, with dislike and bitterness.

"It's hot," Talitha said. "Surely you'll offer us some water?"

Grudgingly, Tjúni led them to an adobe-plastered hut with a thatched roof supported on poles protruding from the front of it. They tied their horses to several mesquite trees and sat on the hard earth while Tjúni poured water from a clay jar into gourd dippers. She was nearing thirty but moved as lithely as a girl and her short-nosed catlike face had a sullen beauty.

"Now," Tjúni said with the air of one who had been wronged. "Why you come?"

Her face changed only once, when Talitha said Shea had gone off to fight. For a moment the firm-set lips softened, looked vulnerable. Only for a flash. When Talitha finished, the Papago woman made a scornful sound.

"Before I tell you. We have always a watchman. Our cave in the mountain has supplies and water. We go there if Apaches come."

"But—"

"Apaches raid Papagos for three hundred years. We still here."

No arguing with that. "The El Charco people are moving to the main ranch," Talitha said, rising. "Would you like to set up your *ranchería* there?"

Suddenly Tjúni's face changed. Lowering her voice, she sounded almost fearful. "You see *her?* She still watch rancho?"

A primeval chill ran through Talitha before she sternly told herself that even if Socorro could come back, she would protect, not harm. "I've seen nothing," Talitha said matter-of-factly.

Sometimes, though, she'd felt an almost palpable presence, a steadying reassurance. And, at the very least, Socorro had left an example that inspired while it discouraged, for who could hope to equal her?

"She there," Tjúni insisted.

"You saw her?"

"Plain as you stand there." Tjúni shivered in spite of the heat. "Night, but much moon. Black hair move in wind. Beautiful. Smile like always."

And where had Tjúni been? In bed with Shea?

"Did she say anything?"

"Not words." Tjúni frowned, puzzled. She went on gropingly. "At first I was afraid—think her angry. But she—somehow she make me know she not." Old resentment and humiliation tinged the Papago woman's voice. "She want me to be good to Shea, help raise children. She want all happy."

"But you left," Talitha said. She didn't mean it as an accusation, but it sounded like one.

Tjúni's eyes flashed. "Shea no marry, I no stay! Let ghost cook for him, sleep with him!" With a curl of her lip as she looked at James, who was standing out by his horse, Tjúni said, "You keep *tigres* at the ranch, too, now you pet Apaches?"

Angered past speech at this slur on her brother, Talitha shot a furious glance at the woman and said in a choked voice to the children, "Let's go!"

Cinco had slipped away but now came back, running. He reached Cat as she was clambering into the saddle and pressed something into her hand.

Tjúni spoke harshly to him in Papago, but he paid no heed, eagerly watching Cat, who smiled in delight at a little wooden blue bird.

"Thank you," she told him. Impulsively, she unfastened the gold crucifix Shea had given her one Christmas and handed it to this darker-skinned half brother. "For you."

With a smothered sound of rage Tjúni snatched for the keepsake, but Cinco eluded her. It was clear that he had no fear of his formidable mother who doted on him.

Pulling back beside Talitha, Cat pressed the bird to her cheek. "Isn't it dear? I'll have it above my bed." She handed it to Talitha, who balanced it in her fingers.

"It's so light it must be made of yucca root."

That was all she could think of to say. She was troubled by Cinco's immediate and rapt devotion to Cat. Had he sensed his true father's blood in her? If that kinship was the answer, why hadn't he fixed on Patrick or Miguel?

"I wish he could come to live with us," Cat murmured. "After all, he's father's son."

"Tjúni doesn't want that," Talitha said. "She has the right to raise the boy as Papago if that's her choice."

James rode close to examine the small azure bird. "I can make you a hawk or eagle," he said disdainfully. "Much better than this."

Cat made a face at him. "I won't let them get my pretty little blue bird!" She turned to wave at the small figure that stood alone at the edge of the settlement.

James's young mouth hardened. Again Talitha felt a flash of warning. Cat had always been loved by everyone around her and had loved freely in return. What would happen if her loves conflicted?

Talitha shrugged her foreboding aside and began planning where and how to best accommodate the El Charco folk. She felt weighted down, totally unfitted for the responsibilities that were now hers; but she must not show that to the ranch people who had so bravely chosen to stay and help her.

Socorro would have . . .

Oh, would the day ever come when she could stop that fatal measuring? In the years since Socorro's death, she had become almost a saint among the vaquero families. Sometimes they prayed to her for a sick child or other woe. Swiftly it was being forgotten by Anita, Carmencita, those who'd known her, that she'd never learned to make properly thin tortillas and sometimes stormed at Shea for a redheaded burro. Human she had been. Which made it harder for Talitha, who knew better than to attribute supernatural powers to the vibrant, compassionate woman whose children she must mother, whose husband she longed to have for her own.

Straightening in the saddle, Talitha threw back her head. She was not, could never be, Socorro. But she'd work to be the best Talitha possible and pray that would be enough.

II

John Irwin said his good-byes the night of July 20. Talitha clung to him involuntarily when he kissed her. Accepting that her love lay elsewhere, he'd been her good friend these past five years, filled some of the void left by Marc Revier's refusal to play the part of family friend. Grinning down at her, Irwin lowered his red head and kissed her again.

"Can it be?" he teased half seriously. "Now that I'm leaving, you realize what a treasure I am? Suddenly see that I'm really the man you love?" He shook his head and sighed comically. "Better late than never."

"John, you shocking flirt!" Talitha had to laugh and felt better, though tears made her blink. "I'll miss you terribly. We all will."

"Yes," assented Cat. "Even if you are a Yanqui. Captain John, you won't fight my daddy?"

"I'll certainly pray not to," he said gravely, looking at Talitha.

He told her then that Confederate Lt. Col. John Baylor was gathering men at Fort Bliss, Texas, evidently intending to march into New Mexico and seize it for the South. It was altogether likely that Shea was in this group, and though it was something over three hundred miles away, it was near Mesilla, where the closest federal law officer and courts had been, and seemed much more real than if he were joining some command back in the States. Talitha's heart felt as if it were shriveling into a tight, dry ball.

"Be sure if there's any way I can ever help Shea, I will, short of treason," Irwin said softly.

He bent to meet Cat's hug, took a third kiss, long this time, from Talitha, shook hands with the boys, and strode away for the last time. When the hoofbeats had faded, Talitha stepped outside, full of desolation, and wept.

Next day the boys rode over to watch the dragoons leave Fort Buchanan. Even Patrick returned sobered. The Stars and Stripes, so briefly flown over that region, were hauled down, and the troops moved out to solemn drumming while all the supplies and equipment they couldn't carry smoldered in the fired buildings.

"The troopers weren't even out of sight when Papagos swarmed in to pick up whatever they could use," Miguel said. His brow furrowed. "Isn't it strange? Soldiers were here so long. Now, just in a day, they're gone."

"White men are like that," said James.

Belen took a wagon over next day and salvaged a few wheels, iron, and other useful things. The rest of them worked on three new houses for the El Charco families. Till the homes could be finished, the boys yielded their little house, once Tjúni's, to Juana and Cheno. Pedro and Carmencita had Shea's old room, and Natividad and Mársat used the *sala,* or living room. Carmencita assumed control of the kitchen, helped in turn by Juana, Anita, or Mársat. When Talitha offered, she was shooed out.

"You must manage the ranch now, see to all for Don Patricio," Carmencita admonished. "Leave the house to me!"

The responsibility weighed on Talitha, especially when she looked around the kitchen at mealtimes and counted ten other adults and thirteen children, if James could be called one. It lightened her mood to reflect that to Belen, Chuey, and Rodolfo, who'd taught her to ride and work cattle, she must seem almost a child, too. But she wasn't. In addition to running the ranch, she must serve as a parent for the twins, Cat, and Sewa. James seemed past needing anyone.

She also assessed their numbers according to who could shoot. Shea had insisted that Anita learn, but she was a poor markswoman. Carmencita and Juana couldn't shoot at all. But Patrick, Miguel, and James were all good, better than any of the vaqueros except Belen.

Twelve rifles against not only Apaches but roving bands of marauders from either side of the border as well! At least they had the rifles, Sharps breech-loading carbines; and there were enough Dragoon Colt revolvers to go around. Besides the supply of ammunition Shea believed in keeping, John Irwin had brought over boxes of cartridges.

"The commander's orders said he could leave the fort's 'improvements' with loyal Unionists," he'd said with a laugh. "For today, Tally, I'm assuming that's what you are."

The arguments between North and South meant little to Talitha. She remembered being hustled across the icy Missouri River in the middle of a February night to escape Illinois mobs that were destroying Mormon property and threatening to serve all the men as they had Joseph Smith and his brother Hyrum, done to death in prison by masked men. It was on the way west to settle in Utah out of reach of Gentile persecution that Jared Scott, Talitha's father, had been assigned as one of the five hundred men of the Mormon Battalion that marked a wagon route to California. It was while Jared went with Lt. Col. Philip St. George Cook through deserts and mountains, even passing through Tucson, that Judith Scott, trying to follow with her children and kinsmen, had been captured by Apaches. Talitha had no fond memories of the United States, and the issues that rent it seemed confusing and far away.

What was real to her was the Santa Cruz Valley and the lands along Sonoita Creek, Rancho del Socorro. To defend these, she'd been grateful for the U.S. Army's cartridges.

The day that she'd ridden to El Charco and San Manuel with news of the soldiers' withdrawal, she'd sent Belen to the San Patricio mine forty miles east with the same message. Somewhat to her surprise, the miners, all from Sonora, had chosen to stay. When Irwin surprised her with his bounty of ammunition, Talitha decided to share it with the miners, and a few days after the abandonment of Fort Buchanan she set off with two loaded pack mules and Belen. She'd turned a deaf ear to Pedro's urging that she take a larger escort and to the twins' eager wish to ride along.

"We need to keep enough people at the ranch to stand off a raid. Remember, all the daylight hours we need a watch. Paulita and Cat are old enough to help with that." Talitha wrinkled her nose at the twins. "It's a good job to take while you rest from laying adobes. See how much you can get done while we're away."

They groaned and would have argued, but Belen said firmly, "Listen, boys. I no longer call Talitha *doncellita,* little maiden. Now she is *la madama,* the mistress. We do not dispute with her."

Both boys gaped for a moment. James looked grimly amused, and Cat blinked. Then Patrick sank to one knee and kissed Talitha's work-toughened hand.

"Madama, a sus ordenes!" His blue-gray eyes laughed up at her.

She gave his thickly curling hair a tug. "My orders, you rascal, are to get Carmencita's house built."

However they might joke about it, she was in command. Her decisions could mean life or death for two dozen people, including all those she loved except for Shea and Revier. Her father, Jared, ranching up on the Verde? She had loved him as a child, when he carried her on his shoulders or danced by the campfires with her mother on the trek from Iowa, but now she did not know him.

As she and Belen rode southeastward toward a gap in the sharp-toothed mountains, Talitha remembered that the mine had been the reason for Socorro's and Shea's coming to Mangus's camp. When the captive Talitha had asked Socorro to take her and her infant brother away from the Apaches, Juh had at last consented to let his son go with the whites till he was seven or eight, provided Shea proved his courage by taking the second brand.

Along with the children, the O'Sheas got Mangus's promise not to raid the mine which Santiago's uncle, Don Narciso, wished to reopen in partnership with the O'Sheas provided such a guarantee could be won. Shea bought Don Narciso out after the 1854 Gadsden Purchase and continued to give the Apaches ten percent of the goods brought up from Mexico in pack trains which supplied the mine. Don Elizario Carvajal still managed the San Patricio, apparently with as much honesty as could be expected from someone operating at a distance from the owner. Talitha was surprised that the miners had chosen to stay, but pleased. The freighting business had collapsed after Frost's death, and Shea, detesting railroads, had refused to buy stock in them; but even if the cattle were run off, income from the mine would buy new herds, keep the ranch going.

They spent that night on the San Pedro River, then threaded their way through narrow, steep mountain passes. Early in the afternoon white thunderheads began to boil up from the horizon, and as they descended a stomach-tightening narrow trail winding down from a butte into the great basin where the camp lay, the storm burst, torrents of slicing bladelike rain, scudding gravel from under their feet, making the treacherous rocks even more slippery. The mules stopped, hunching against the downpour, but when

Belen located an overhang, they trusted him and moved into it, as did the led horses.

"Too violent to last long," Belen said cheerfully.

They drank from canteens, John Irwin's gift, and chewed a few mouthfuls of jerky. After about twenty minutes the deluge dwindled to a steady rain. Belen studied the completely darkened sky.

"It's not good to go down the cañon in this, *madama.*" That name that meant she was his mistress, no longer a girl to be shielded. "But this looks like going on for hours. Shall we put our trust in God and make our way to the bottom while it's still light?"

Talitha tried to laugh, though her mouth felt stiff. Heights were her one really irrational fear, and she had ridden much of this day with her face turned toward the inside of the trail, not daring to glance down at the dizzying gorges below.

"I don't see what else we can do." She shrugged, setting her hat more firmly on her head. "We'll lead the horses?"

"Yes. And the mules will lead us."

It was a harrowing descent. Even the surefooted little mules, cumbered by their nearly three-hundred-pound loads, slipped now and then, sending rocks scuttling downward. Talitha kept as close to the cañon wall as she could, looking straight ahead, never into the jagged chasms. Twice she slid to one knee, and the second time Ceniza almost crowded her off the ledge, but Belen reached back and checked the well-trained mare till Talitha could clamber to her feet.

All the way down, for several hours that seemed eternities, the rain plastered their clothes to them, but it perversely began to ease when they reached the gentler slope winding into the basin.

"Coffee will be good," Belen encouraged. "And I hope there's a rich meat stew and plenty of fresh tortillas!"

But though it was time for supper as they came in sight of the clustered adobes and ramadas, no smoke rose from any of the houses. There was no barking of dogs, no children playing, no laughing or calling of women, no miners coming home from their work in the flank of the long humped mountain to the north.

Belen checked. His broad swarthy face lost its gleam of anticipation. His gaze swept the basin, scanned the surrounding mountains, the pass to the south through which pack trains carried silver ore to Mexico and brought back supplies.

In the soft, nagging, persistent rain, nothing moved. A tight knot formed in Talitha's chest. "Maybe they decided to go into Mexico after all," she said in a voice that husked out little more than a whisper.

"Wait here, *madama*."

Talitha didn't answer but nudged Ceniza alongside Belen's rangy sorrel. The vaquero gave her a grim, weighing look, then got down to hobble the mules. So he didn't think there'd be anyone at the mine to need the cartridges.

By the time they contoured around the slope and started into the basin, the rain had pattered to a stop. Sun blazed on creosote and cholla, striking diamonds everywhere, and the air seemed washed with liquid gold, pungent and clean with the gratitude of the recently parched earth. These things reached Talitha's senses, though dread was building in her at every inch they traveled.

During the close to two years she'd lived among Apaches, she'd seen a small *ranchería* wiped out in Mexico, several luckless wayfarers brain-roasted or filled with arrows as her uncles and grandfather had been. That was a long time ago, almost as long ago as the Mormon temple gleaming whitely at Nauvoo, or Winter Quarters in Iowa, or the foreign-seeming little city of Santa Fe. Talitha had helplessly tried to keep Socorro from bleeding to death and hadn't been able to help Santiago at all when he crashed sideways, felled by Judah Frost's concealed derringer. She had seen death, but always she had prayed never to look on it again. As they neared the silent houses, she hoped most desperately that the people had decided to abandon the place till more peaceful times.

Her heart lifted as she saw mules and horses grazing along the stream that spilled down from the mountain to water the broad bowl. Apaches would never have left them. And then Belen reined in, waving her back.

"No farther, *madama.* You cannot help. It isn't good to see—"

But she had seen enough. A human rubbish heap, bones gnawed and scattered by beasts and vultures. In that sickened glance before she gripped the saddle horn and turned away, she saw that a number of the tumbled skulls were small, those of children and babies. Tufts of hair and patches of weather-baked skin adhered to a few, and scraps of clothing stuck to arm and leg bones.

Rain had scoured the skeletons on top, splashed mud on those sprawled on the ground. It must have happened several weeks ago, shortly after the message of warning.

Ceniza shied at a little skull that had lodged in a tangle of rotting cholla joints. Without her warm brown skin, soft hair, and big eyes, Sewa's head might look like that. Talitha began to shake.

"Why did they kill the children?" She meant: How could they? Though she knew bitterly well that all the warring peoples of that region, Pima, Papago, Apache, Mexican, and Anglo, had killed each others' babies, murdered the defenseless.

"Bandits don't burden themselves with little ones," Belen said. "These didn't even bother with mules and horses."

"Who do you think they were?"

"Probably some gang from Sonora. Lots of them are on the prowl, looting whatever they can now the soldiers are gone." Belen picked up a shovel leaned against a nearby wall. "While I dig a grave for these poor bones, *madama,* you might see if there's anything of importance left in the headquarters."

Reining her mare far around the scattered human ruins, Talitha rode to the long main building which served as office, store, and Don Elizario's quarters. Hitching Ceniza to a post, she saw many bullet holes scarring the adobe; percussion caps and spent cartridges lay about. The marauders had been well equipped, which argued for their being Americans, riffraff run out of California or Texas.

At least they'd met with a stiff fight here. Talitha pushed open the door hanging awry on leather hinges and sucked in her breath. Part of what had been the bearlike hulk of Don Elizario was staked to the wall, half skeleton, half mummy, ravaged by beaks and talons. The hip joints dangled loosely, while the leg and foot bones were scattered about the floor, gnawed by coyotes. Two other skeleton remnants lay near the small windows where they'd fallen.

Talitha hadn't liked the mine manager. His sly little eyes had lingered knowingly on her even when she'd been a child. But she hoped he'd been dead, or nearly so, when he was hung up like this.

Swallowing, she went into the storeroom. Bolts of cloth, blankets, boots, saddles, and tools had been dragged to the floor, grain, corn, beans, and other supplies spilled on them, and the whole set afire. Waste for the joy of it. The weapons had been taken, and the strongboxes which held the gold and silver received for the mine's ore had been blasted open and emptied.

In Don Elizario's rooms, as luxurious as the place allowed, carved wooden furniture had been hacked and fired, along with the huge mattress and pillows. A costly mirror lay shattered. The glazed windows were broken. Talitha went out the door and rode back to tell Belen there were more to bury.

Resting on the spade, he wiped sweat from his brow and frowned at the crimson sunset. "We'll have to stay the night in the basin, *madama.* Let's go unpack the mules and make camp. Another night won't matter to these poor dead ones."

To try to sleep near this place of death? Talitha shuddered, but she knew it was impossible to go back up the cañon in darkness. "Why don't you dig till you're tired?" she suggested. "I'll find a good spot near the stream and unload the mules."

He nodded. "The more I dig now, the sooner we can be out of here in the morning."

Talitha collected the mules and led them down to good grass growing along the stream. Undoing the lashings, she lifted off first the boxes of cartridges on top of the pack frame, then the boxlike leather aparejos fitting to either side, praising the sturdy little gray-brown beasts, scratching them between their ears. They went quickly to water, but the ground was too wet for a refreshing roll, so they began to twist up satisfying bites of the lush grass. After unsaddling Ceniza, Talitha got out the coffeepot, tossed some jerky and pinole into the frying pan with enough water to soften them, and began to gather wood. A fire was always a dangerous signal, but she believed that she and Belen needed hot coffee and hot food tonight.

She was breaking a mesquite limb across her knee when long arms closed around her.

"Let me do that."

Even through startled panic, she knew that deep, ever so faintly accented voice, though she hadn't heard it for over a year.

"Marc!" Turning, she threw her arms around him, joyously searching the squarish face with broad cheekbones, the old saber scar across his left cheek and eyebrow. The lines at the corners of his blue eyes were deeper, like those edging the good-humored mouth, and a few gray hairs were mixed among the thick brown ones. With laughter that changed to a sob, she buried her face against him. "Oh, Marc!"

"Why, I believe you're glad to see me," he teased, stroking her head and shoulders, her friend, who'd given her her first glimpses of the world beyond. He'd taken her to her first dance, that wonderful Christmas celebration at Colonel Poston's mining headquarters in Tubac. That was when he'd first betrayed that he loved her as a woman. She'd seen him only a few times in the years between then and last summer, when he'd joined the party trailing Judah Frost and then brought Shea, wounded, back to the Socorro.

It was then, driven by a desperate need to be cleansed of Frost's use of her body, that Talitha had asked Marc to make love to her. She loved him as much as she could anyone except Shea, found comfort and healing in his strength and passion. But when he learned that she still wouldn't marry him, he'd ridden off in anger to the Tecolote mine southwest of Yuma Crossing near the Devil's Highway.

He brought her face up, brushed her mouth with his, then moved back, steadying her. "Prettier than ever, Talitha! Don't you know that women who don't marry are supposed to dry up and look like sticks?" When she didn't smile, he turned to look across the basin toward the settlement. "Where's Belen? Why are you here instead of at the camp?"

He heard of the outrage in silence, the muscles in his cheek going taut. When she'd finished, he gave her a little shake. "My God, Talitha! Surely this will persuade you to at least move in to Tucson!"

"You stopped at the ranch?"

"Of course. That's how I knew where to find you."

"Then you saw that the El Charco people have joined us."

He glanced through the twilight at the devastated village. "There must have been—what?—fifty miners here? With weapons."

"They must have been taken by surprise. For the silver and gold. We have no big amounts of them at Socorro."

"Raiders won't necessarily guess that—or care. Apaches don't hanker after coin, you know. They prefer stock and captive women and children."

She turned away. "I *was* glad to see you."

He caught her to him in exasperation. Even in the dimming light, his eyes blazed. "Damn you, Talitha! Can I love you and applaud your bullheadedness?"

"You don't have to applaud," she said through her teeth.

"Shea wouldn't want you to stay now that the soldiers have gone."

The way he spoke strangled the hope she'd had, that he'd come to stay with her, help run the ranch. Gripped with disappointment and bone-weariness, she tried to wrest free of him.

"I suppose you're going to join the army, too—the Union one!"

"You know how I feel about slavery, Talitha. And this country gave me hope and faith after I saw the start of freedom strangled in Berlin." Pleading against her averted face, he said with that inexorable firmness she knew nothing could shake, "I owe my new country much, Talitha. I must pay what I can."

"Pay," she thrust. "But don't try to frighten me out of paying a debt myself!"

With a rough intake of breath, he forced her against him, set his hand at the back of her head, and kissed her till she was weak, desirous, clinging to him, her softness yielding to the hard demand of his body. He started to sink down with her on the grass.

"No!" she choked out as his fingers hurried to find and caress her breasts. "No, Marc!"

"You want me, Talitha."

She didn't try to deny it, only put away his ardent, warm hands. "I—I'm engaged to Shea."

"What?"

"I think you heard me."

"But—there was only Socorro for him."

Stabbed deep, Talitha struggled for calm. "I'm not a fool. He can't love me as he did her; I don't expect it. But he's promised to marry me when he comes back from the war."

Marc released her and strode off a distance. His

voice was strange. "To win this astonishing concession, you must have somehow tricked him into your bed."

Talitha yearned to slap him; she had to clench her hands. "It's none of your business, but *that* came after the promise!"

After a moment he faced her. "I'm sorry, Talitha." There was sadness in his tone, a compassion that was harder to bear than his scorn. "As you say, it's none of my business."

"Don't sound like that!" she said fiercely. "As if you were sorry for me."

He sighed, pushed back his hair. "You'll think it's jealousy, and I'm damnably jealous! But I *am* sorry. For you. For what you're getting in return for such total, terrible love."

"And what do you think I'm getting?" she taunted, cruel in her hurt.

"You're beautiful. Shea has a man's needs. And of course he loves you—as a daughter, a child he protected. So he'll take you with his body and be ashamed of that, feel he's wronging you."

She put her hands over her ears, trying to shut out his relentless words, suppressing flashes that betrayed what Shea must have felt in spite of their physical rapture that last long night.

"I'm not his daughter, not a child! I'm his woman."

"No," said Marc. It was like being forced to hear some true depth of her own self speaking. "You may be his pleasure, his last sweet flower, but his woman was Socorro."

"She's dead! Eight years she's dead!"

"That has nothing to do with it." He took her hands again and held them against his heart. She felt the pounding of his blood, powering the sure, massive strength she'd always found in him. "Talitha, my own dear love, you're my woman. Whether we marry, whether we ever lie together again, whatever happens. That's why I know how it must be for Shea."

She bowed her head. His words echoed those she'd

cried despairingly at Shea when he'd tried to persuade her she was mistaken in the nature of her feeling. *"But I have loved you! All these ways and all these years."*

"Perhaps you're right," she said miserably. "But I want Shea, want to make him as happy as I can. And yet—oh, Marc! I'm so mixed up! I love you, too. But it's different—"

"I know," he said, with a soft, bitter laugh. "I'm only a man. Shea has always been your god."

Small use to say that it had been Shea's devastation, his loneliness approaching that of a bewildered orphan, that made it impossible for Talitha to leave him. She might not be his woman, but he needed her. And when he came home . . .

Lifting her head, Talitha kissed Marc's cheek. "Please, Marc. Be happy."

"Oh, I will be." He got out flint and steel and knelt by her tinder, grinning up at her in the gathering night. "I still have the sun. And so do you, Tally. Remember that."

Belen came up while Marc was coaxing the fire, delighted to have a friend to share their camp in that haunted basin. Marc had been given a parcel of tortillas by Carmencita, and these served as scoops for the pinole stew. They sweetened their coffee with chips flaked off a piece of hard brown sugar and talked of the war.

"The United States simply abandoned us," Talitha accused. "We can't be blamed for siding with the Confederacy if they'll offer any sort of protection against things like this." She jerked her head toward the mining camp.

"The Gadsden Purchase has been a funny case from the start," Marc reminded her equably. "There've been very few real settlers. Buying and protecting it has been pushed by a bunch of Texas railroad men and mining interests financed by speculators from both coasts and Europe, helped by an expansion-minded Democratic administration. You could say Arizona was developed mostly because of the Democrats' increasing need to add western states to their balance of voting power."

"Marc!" How could he put it that coldly?

Talitha thought of her friend Larcena Pennington, recovering from lance thrusts whose scars she'd carry to the grave; of doughty Pete Kitchen and his refusal to budge from his fortress on Potrero Creek; of Socorro's grave, and Santiago's. Surely this was how a territory was made, through the lives, courage, and suffering of its people. In the flickering light, Talitha looked at Marc defiantly.

"Whatever the government does, some of us will stay. And it's to us the land really belongs, not to those boards meeting in San Francisco or Ohio or New York."

He raised his tin cup in wry salute. "The Apaches think it's their country. Papagos, Pimas, Maricopas, and Yumas say the same. Notwithstanding, the federal government has poured a lot of money into securing this southern link between East and West. Ten million for the Gadsden Purchase, hundreds of thousands on boundary commissions and railroad surveys. There was the wagon road built from El Paso to Fort Yuma, the exploration of the Colorado River, and the establishment of forts. Starting in 1858, the government subsidized the Overland Mail to the tune of six hundred thousand dollars yearly." Marc spread his hands. "For all of this, Arizona's remained a no-man's-land. Even after this war's over, it'll be a long time before it's a place to live in in any safety."

Belen shrugged heavy shoulders. "Don Marcos, in my country, the boundaries of which were sung by angels and Yaqui prophets, and the eight cities located by sacred visions, there is no safety. The *yoris*, the Mexicans, would take the fertile lands decreed to us by God. So there is fighting. So there will always be till we're left in peace. What is safety?" He spat into the dust.

They were all weary and soon unrolled their blankets. The men put Talitha between them, and though she was distressed at having hurt Marc again and disturbed by his assessment of how Shea felt about her, she was still grateful to have him close in this valley of death, to know that she could reach out and touch him.

Comforted, she slept.

They were up before sunrise. Marc helped Belen dig the long common grave and Talitha collected stones for heaping on top, not that there was enough left on the bones to tempt scavengers. By midmorning the pitiful fragments of what had been men, women, and children were decently covered, and the three of them heaped on rocks and stones. Don Elizario lay among his workers.

Belen made a cross and fixed it among the rocks. "God pity them," he said and bowed his head.

Marc and Talitha did likewise, though she had her old angry feelings that if God was all-powerful and good, He wouldn't allow such things to happen; if He wasn't all-powerful and good, there was little use in praying. And still she prayed. At the limits, a mortal must cry for help.

Marc insisted on going with them to the ranch. "It'll ease my mind to know you got home safe from this journey," he said. "Besides, if I cut northeast and hurry, maybe I can catch up with the troopers. It's not healthy to ride alone through Cochise's and Mangus's prime territory."

Talitha fought down a longing to beg him to stay. One man wouldn't make that much difference to the cause of either North or South. It made a difference to him, though, and so she couldn't plead.

They reached the Socorro late one afternoon. Next morning before sunup, he was on his way. After he'd said his good-byes to the rest of the household, Talitha walked with him to the corral.

She was sick of this. Sick of seeing the men she cared

about go off to kill or be killed, and for reasons that had nothing to do with the dangers here. Pressing his hands to her face, she murmured huskily, "Take care of yourself. Come back safe!"

He brought up her face to kiss her mouth. For a long, tremulous moment he held her matched to his body, and she knew that he'd slept last night as poorly as she. If he'd come to her, she might not have been able to remember she belonged to Shea, for she loved this man, too, and in this time of parting her anguished flesh cleaved to his.

"Marc!"

He bowed his face to her hands, then quickly took the reins Belen offered. His eyes went over her as if to fix her image forever in his mind. "God keep you, love."

"Come back," she said. "Please. Come back."

He bent to brush her cheek with his fingers. "I'll have to. You're my woman."

She watched through tear-blinded eyes as he rode into the rising sun. Like Shea. Like John Irwin.

Now all her men were gone.

III

It was early in August when Cat, who was standing watch from a perch on the corral, called that there was a horseman coming. "He's wearing a serape and sombrero and seems to be alone," she reported.

"Ring the bell twice," Talitha said.

That was the signal for all in hearing to make for the houses and arm themselves, just in case the announced visitor wasn't friendly. Three rings meant raiders, positive danger. So, when the bell sounded, there was always a heart-stopped tension while waiting for that dreaded third peal.

Taking up a rifle, Talitha peered out the window, sighed with relief as she thought she recognized the rider, but waited a few more minutes till she was sure.

"It's Pete Kitchen," she told the twins, who'd dashed inside and grabbed weapons from the rack by the door. "Tell Cat to ring once."

An isolated sound of the bell after an alarm meant there was nothing to fear and work could be resumed. The twins lingered, though, eager to see the man whose prowess as a fighter and determination to hold his ranch against raiders of any color had made him almost a legend.

With a smile of thanks, Kitchen turned over his reins to Miguel, who led the horse off for watering. Lean and erect, of medium height, Kitchen took off his sombrero and bowed with Southern courtliness.

"I'm sure glad to find you all right, Miss Talitha." His blue-gray eyes twinkled in his ruddy face as he noticed the rifle she'd leaned against the wall. "Glad you keep a sentry posted." He tweaked one of Cat's black ringlets. "Is this your bell ringer?"

"One of them." Talitha was fond of this rough, kindly, indomitable man. It was to his house she'd stumbled after Judah Frost's assault, and it was his gentle wife, Doña Rosa, who had helped her bathe and made her rest. Doña Rosa lit candles on the graves of the marauders, red and white, who were buried in front of the ranch they'd tried to despoil. "Come in, Mr. Kitchen, and stay for dinner. How are Doña Rosa and all those pretty nieces?"

"Fine. Or were when I left for Tucson last week." He grinned. "Sixty-eight of us voted an ordinance of secession. Elected Granville Oury to be territorial delegate to the Confederate Congress and petitioned Jeff Davis for troops. Colonel Baylor's taken Mesilla and proclaimed the Confederate Territory of Arizona! He's the governor, of course. Some doings!" Kitchen sobered. "But Tubac's finished, Miss Talitha. That's why I rode over here, to see if you were still at the ranch."

"What's this of Tubac?" Belen asked.

Since everyone had come in, Carmencita and Juana began to set out the meal, and it was while eating heartily that Kitchen told how Apaches were ranging up and down the Santa Cruz, plundering and killing. Among their victims were the superintendent of the Sopori ranch and the innkeepers at Canoa. The few men left at Tubac had defended themselves stoutly, however, and got a message for help through to Tucson, where Granville Oury hurriedly collected twenty-five volunteers.

Kitchen winked. "Since I was going that way anyhow, I figured I might as well have the benefit of an armed escort. We sure surprised those heathens! They lit out, and so did a gang of about seventy-five Mexicans who'd come up from Sonora to rob and loot. That bunch stopped at Tumacácori, though, and stole everything they could carry off. Killed a harmless old man even the Apaches hadn't bothered."

"Everyone's left Tubac? Colonel Poston?"

"Oh, he's been supervising the Heintzelman mine down south, but while he was off looking for new sites in the Papago country some mean Sonorans talked the laborers into killing Poston's younger brother and two Germans who worked at the Heintzelman. Poston buried them and took off for California."

So debonair Charles Poston, who'd offered open-handed hospitality to all who passed through Tubac, who'd married couples free and thrown in a festive wedding feast, whose Christmas parties had been attended by officers from the fort and ranchers from as far away as Magdalena and Sopori, the one touch of glamor in Talitha's life—Poston was gone.

"Now it's really going to be Tucson, Tubac, Tumacácori, and to hell!" Kitchen went on. "Though we can hope the Confederacy will send us some troops. I have to tell you, Miss Talitha, that I reckon you sure ought to get out of here while you can. Be glad to send over a few dozen of my men to help you move."

The abandonment of Tubac was even more shattering to Talitha than that of Fort Buchanan. It had been where she'd learned to dance, had thrilled to the knowledge that men admired her in the lovely gowns Judah's sweetly beautiful wife, Lenore, had had made up for her. But she could remember earlier years when the presidio had been deserted, when Apache raids had emptied the Santa Cruz Valley.

Straightening her shoulders, she smiled at Pete Kitchen. "It seems strange, Mr. Kitchen, but I lived here before you did, before the mining companies came, and the soldiers. If the O'Sheas could start the ranch when they did, we should be able to hold it now." The grizzle-mustached man looked so worried that she ventured a tease. "At least there aren't any scalp hunters these days."

"Only because no one's paying for hair," growled Kitchen. He glanced at the children, who were eating at a second table. "I hate to think of you over here without O'Shea, but your men are trusty and you have good thick walls and a well inside them. Mostly Apaches choose the most gain for the least risk. If it looks like they're going to lose a lot of men, they'll hunt easier pickings." Slowly, he got to his feet. "You got plenty of ammunition?"

"Enough for a small war," Talitha assured him, then inquired with wicked innocence, "By the way, when are you moving to Tucson?"

"Me?" His mustache fairly quivered. "Doggone it, girl, I—" At the vaqueros' chuckle, he broke off and scowled a moment before he laughed, gripped her hand, and shook it as he would have a man's. "Good luck, Miss Talitha. I'll get over once in a while to see how you are. If I can do anything, send for me."

"You're very kind." They both knew the chances of getting a message to him in case of a raid were pitifully slight. "Give Doña Rosa and her nieces my love."

"I'll do that." He sighed gustily. "They'd enjoy a visit from you, but I reckon we're still years away from when folks can go see each other for the plain fun of it."

Patrick had fetched his ewe-necked but serviceable horse. Donning his serape in spite of the heat, Kitchen snugged down his sombrero, waved, and jogged off westward, toward abandoned Tubac and often-despoiled Tumacácori, though he'd swing south at Calabazas, also deserted, heading for his ranch on Potrero Creek.

"He doesn't look all that wild and deadly," grumbled Patrick.

"We aren't bandits," Talitha reminded him. "Come

on, now, let's see if we can't finish Carmencita's walls today."

As she helped lift and stack the heavy bricks she wondered if Shea was with Baylor, if there was any chance of his being sent nearer home with some detachment. He'd been gone over two months. She couldn't even be sure that he was alive, that he'd ever reached a Confederate post to volunteer. The only way he could get a letter to her was through a traveler, and travelers along the Sonoita were going to be mighty few.

I won't even think he might be dead, Talitha told herself. *He has to be alive. Has to come back to me—to all of us.* She recoiled from the very thought of a world without Shea, and her desolation at it made her really understand for the first time Shea's agony at losing Socorro, and why he had tried to blunt it with drink and Tjúni.

Come back, love, and I'll make you happy. Talitha vowed it across the miles, willing him to hear, to believe. But she felt no response.

Tubac abandoned, and Fort Buchanan. San Patricio destroyed. Shea gone, then John Irwin, then Marc Revier. In all that region south of Tucson, which was seventy miles away, only, besides the Socorro, Pete Kitchen's ranch and Sylvester Mowry's Patagonia mine were left.

In spite of her brave words to Kitchen, this isolation was altogether different from that of her childhood. Then, like Cat now, she'd trusted the grown-ups. Shea, Socorro, and Santiago had borne the weight of decisions, of risking other people's lives. It was that responsibility more than physical labor that exhausted Talitha. Of course, after what she and Belen had found at the San Patricio, she'd given the vaqueros another chance to leave. They'd all stubbornly chosen to hold on.

"We weren't harassed during the siege of Tubac,"

Chuey pointed out, riding squealing little Tomás on his foot while braiding a new rawhide rope for six-year-old Ramón. "It must be that Mangus's protection still carries authority. Besides, *madama,*" he added fatalistically, "there's no safe place in all this region to ranch. But we are vaqueros; what would become of us, huddling in town?"

So August turned to September. The new adobes, roofed by mesquite rafters covered with bear grass, wheat straw, and adobe, replaced the old ramadas, making a solid enclosure around the small courtyard with the well and granaries, the pomegranate and peach trees.

Red-streaked mesquite beans dried on the roofs to be stored in the round adobe granaries. Talitha, the twins, James, Paulita, and Cat made forays along the mountain slopes and draws, returning with squawberries, hackberries, chokecherries, wild currants, grapes, and acorns which, ground, made a tasty flour. The ranch had irrigated fields of melons, beans, corn, and wheat, but Talitha had been taught by Socorro and Tjúni to garner wild foods in their seasons.

Because of rushed work on the houses they'd missed jojoba nuts that summer, but November's harvest of the planted fields would signal time to gather black walnuts along the creek and go into the mountains for the small but very rich and nutritious piñon nuts.

In mid-February, the first timid greens had appeared. March had offered cholla buds, the plump curving fruit of yucca palmillo, and agave hearts roasted to a sweet syrupy brown mass. May had been tender young cattail shoots, and June had brought their rich golden pollen, so good in soups and breads.

Late summer rains had also produced large round puffballs, some white, some brownish, and these succulent treasures were carried home to be sizzled in bacon grease or sliced into stews. The smaller ones could be confused with a kind of deadly mushroom, but Talitha had learned from Tjúni to cut the ball across.

The mushroom showed its developing gills and shape, like a bird growing in an egg, but if the inside was smooth, creamy white, the ball could be eaten with gusto.

They celebrated Cat's eighth birthday the twentieth of September. Chuey and Rodolfo woke her by playing their guitars and singing "*Las Mañanitas*" outside the window.

"On the morning you were born,
Were born the flowers . . ."

Oh, God, thought Talitha, rousing. Had they forgotten? Of course they hadn't. No one who'd known and loved Socorro could forget that she'd died in a rush of blood in the dawning Cat was born.

Socorro, valiant and tender, Shea's miracle, adored by both him and Santiago, to all of them the human, sometimes hot-tempered embodiment of the dark madonna blessing the *sala*. A madonna from the ranch where everyone but Santiago had been slaughtered by scalp hunters.

Blessing and tragedy, kindness and courage, horror and treachery. Cat living out of her mother's death; James begotten by the hated Juh. Wondering at the tangled, inexplicable threads of fate, Talitha dismissed fruitless musings and crossed the room past Sewa, who lay drowsily smiling at a sun mote, to kiss and embrace Cat, who was just springing out of bed.

"Happy birthday, Caterina Katie-Cat!"

"Oh, Tally! Don't call me that baby name!" Running to the window, she leaned out, laughing, honey-golden cheeks flushed, and thanked the vaqueros, gracious as a queen. They departed, happy at her pleasure, and she spun dancingly across the floor. "See, they know I'm growing up! They never sang for me before. I'm not a *young* child anymore."

"No," agreed Talitha gravely. The vaqueros must have made the flattering gesture to make up for Shea's absence, for the lack of presents obtained from the San Patricio pack trains or at Tubac. "You're not a *young* child. Will you bring Sewa in? I want to start the panocha for your feast tonight."

"Panocha!" sang Cat, still whirling. "My favorite!"

"That's why!" Talitha laughed. "And there's nut candy, Anita's special tamales, and all your favorites. I hope, ancient one, that you're not too dignified to enjoy them!"

Cat trilled with pure glee, hugged Talitha in a last caracol before she began to dress, and started to sing to the baby. May she always have a bright spirit, Talitha thought. Dressing quickly, she hurried to the kitchen and began grinding the dried, sprouted wheat.

There was wild turkey, and beef barbecued outside by the vaqueros, who would later savor by themselves the pit-roasted head, or *tatema.* Steaming tamales stuffed, as only Anita could do it, with spiced shredded meat, and chilis, tortillas, beans, corn soup, acorn bread, roast corn on the cob, currant and grape preserves, nut and pumpkin candies, and the panocha, a sort of pudding, made extra rich for the occasion by doubling the number of raw sugar cones. Sewa, who at fifteen months couldn't chew most of the food, loved the panocha, and it was a mark of Cat's love that she didn't grudge the astonishing amount of pudding that the tiny girl devoured.

After supper came the gifts. Miguel gave her his best sombrero trimmed with silver coins. Patrick had cut down a silver-buckled belt she'd long coveted. From the vaqueros and their families came a fringed jacket of softest buckskin and a new *reata.* Talitha, with Anita's help, had fashioned a gay red dress out of material in the storeroom.

Cat rejoiced, putting on all her presents, not sure whether to mince to match the dress or swagger for the hat, belt, and jacket. Then, without a word, James gave her his gifts.

There was a quiver of mountain-lion skin lined with red flannel and filled with arrows winged with turkey feathers, and an arced bow, a leather wrist guard, and a hawk carved from polished mesquite. It perched on a knotty crag, talons painstakingly carved, beak realistically hooked. In spite of its crudities, it captured amazingly the proud, free essence of the bird.

"Why, James!" cried Talitha. "I didn't know you could carve like that."

He didn't answer but said to Cat, "This is a red-tailed hawk. His feathers are very good for arrows, but I didn't want to kill him so I used some from a turkey. The bow's of wild mulberry."

"Oh, James!" Throwing her arms about him, Cat gave him a resounding kiss. "The hawk's wonderful! But I won't let him catch my little blue bird. Will you teach me how to shoot?"

"And us, too!" clamored Patrick and Miguel.

"I'll teach anyone who wants to learn," James promised expansively.

Talitha watched her brother in surprise. Happiness softened the proud set of his mouth, and there was a glow about him. It came to her that he wasn't as haughty and scornful as she'd thought.

"It was with bows that Tjúni and Socorro killed the scalp hunters and won Mangus's friendship," Talitha said slowly. "I'd like to learn to shoot, James."

He nodded approval. "An Apache may have two good revolvers and a rifle, but he always has his bow. It makes no sound to alarm enemies when a sentry is killed, and half a dozen antelope can be killed in a herd before the rest notice and run. It's easy to carry and can be relied on when a weapon jams or there's no ammunition. Guns are good, but if I had to choose, I'd have a good bow and arrows feathered from the red-tailed hawk."

And so it was that when the twins' thirteenth birthdays came the fifteenth of October, work stopped early to give time for target shooting before the festive meal.

Of the vaqueros, only Belen had chosen to make a bow, and Talitha overheard Chuey reminding Rodolfo that their older companion was, after all, a Yaqui and thus had an affinity for uncivilized weapons.

"What about me, Chuey?" she had teased, stepping out from behind the door.

"I—uh—" Chuey strangled a moment, gulped, and then said forthrightly, "*Madama,* with your pardon, who can explain gringos?"

It had been fun to make the equipment, hunting for branches of wild mulberry that were straight and without knots, then stripping them of bark and working the green wood into shape with the arched center to be hung for drying.

Arrows were more tedious. Fortunately, there was plenty of the proper sort of cane growing along the creek. After these were cut, they had to be smoothed and the joints leveled out by running them back and forth across the bottom of a heated skillet. Much easier, James explained, than heating and using a grooved stone arrow-smoother.

Belen, who did the ranch's blacksmithing, forged tips from steel salvaged at the fort. These were fitted into notches cut in the hardwood foreshafts which were then tied on with sinew. The next step was to settle down amid the canes with supplies of quail and turkey feathers, wet, softened sinews, and charcoal and an earthy reddish mineral that Talitha remembered from Marc's geology lessons as hematite.

The part of the shaft where the feathers would go was colored red and black and covered with piñon pitch so the charcoal and hematite patterns, varied so one person's arrows could be told from another's, wouldn't rub off. This was polished by rolling the shaft in a doubled-over yucca leaf. James scraped the split feathers carefully so that they'd fit close to the shaft.

"You must take parts from three different feathers so they'll point the same way," he explained. "If you tried to get two parts from the same feather, they'd face each other and the arrow wouldn't travel so true and fast."

After cutting the nocks, he showed how to bind the feathers, starting the nock end with one or two held in place with the fingers. After a turn or two of the wet sinew, he clamped the end in his teeth and wound the rest of the sinew by rolling the arrow. Then the third piece of feather went on the same way. The three lower ends could be tied on all at once before they were trimmed to the right size.

"I'd sure hate to lose one of these after all this work," Patrick grunted, frowning with concentration as he tried to get the sinew started while holding the feathers.

"Oh, well"—James grinned—"it's a good way to pass winter evenings." To Cat, who was struggling determinedly, teeth tucked over her lower lip, he said indulgently, "You hold the feathers and let me wrap."

The men and boys were hunting now, cutting most of the meat into strips for drying into jerky. At James's instruction, they took the sinew from the deers' backs and the back of the hind legs. For each bowstring, strips of this were dried. James then showed how to wet the ends and join them into one long string, which was looped around a stick and twisted. James chewed down the bumpy places while Miguel held the stick.

The damp string was fastened to the bow, barely tightened, and left to dry. Then it was tightened two more times before it was ready to try.

Talitha had been too young to pay much attention to Apache weapons when she'd lived among them. Now, appreciating the work and accumulated experience that went into making an outfit, she used her bow with respect and tried to practice daily, learning to reach easily over her right shoulder for an arrow in the javelina-hide quiver Belen had made for her, and then nock the arrow with the first finger above the nock, the second and third below, while the shaft rested on the side of her thumb, which was braced up against the arc of the bow. Drawing back the string, she sighted along the arrow and let it go, with varying degrees of success.

Belen had used a bow in his youth and was soon as good as James. Patrick and Miguel quickly became proficient, Patrick doing better when aiming quickly, Miguel best when deliberate. Cat, bound to make James proud of her, practiced till Carmencita said despairingly, "Ay, *niñita,* what kind of wild Indian are you set on becoming? If your mother—"

"My mother used a bow," Cat reminded her pertly, but she hugged and kissed the grandmotherly woman. "Don't scold. I'll defend you if bad people ever come!"

She did very well at the twins' birthday celebration, several times hitting the ball of cedar bark placed varying distances away, while Talitha hit it only once. The twins made equal scores but couldn't hit the ball when tossed in the air, though James and Belen could.

Next there was a roping contest. Talitha wouldn't let animals be used for sport, so the vaqueros and boys spun their *reatas* at rawhide bags yanked by on a pulley or at pieces of wood waved tauntingly at them.

James, taught long ago by his godfather, Santiago, was still good but no match for the vaqueros, who used their ropes almost every day of their lives. Talitha, a competent roper, was happy to watch the others and applaud when Chuey was judged the most expert.

For weeks the twins had been loudly declaring that they were grown up, nearly, and didn't expect presents. Nevertheless, after a feast similar to Cat's, they had begun to look the slightest bit disappointed until presents appeared from all sides.

Quivers from Belen, Patrick's of gray fox skin, Miguel's of mountain lion; embroidered leather vests and trousers from the ranch families; fringed leather gauntlets from Talitha; handkerchiefs painfully embroidered with their names from Cat; and from James, leather war clubs.

Carmencita and her daughters regarded the last with distaste. James explained that a long stick was stuck through a peeled cow's tail and a rock sewed up in hide was fastened to the end. The cow's tail was left to dangle from the handle.

"Good for close quarters," Belen decided, hefting one. "A hard blow to the head should kill."

James nodded. "They can be used against bears and lions, too."

"I would prefer," said Belen dryly, "not to be that close."

The branding began, Talitha and the boys helping. Since they had to comb the hills, arroyos, and mesquite and oak thickets of the thousands of acres of the ranch, they took turns working the most distant stretches, going out in a group of four and camping till all the unmarked yearlings were earmarked and branded, and most of them gelded. This last went against Mexican custom, but Shea had said it was the best way to improve the stock.

While the small group was branding, the other vaqueros worked in signaling distance of the house, branding and starting to cull out the cattle destined for market. Pete Kitchen had sent a messenger to say he was driving a herd to Tucson and would be glad to take some from the Socorro if a couple of vaqueros would help his men. Talitha had accepted gratefully.

Belen, as was his long custom, brought Talitha the *senales* from each twentieth calf to which he, as one of the ranch's first vaqueros, was entitled to as part wages. As she added the hairy bits of hide to those already in a chest, James looked at them thoughtfully.

"Talitha, my sister, you have many cattle."

Surprised, for she never thought of them as hers, separate from Shea's, she nodded after a moment.

"But half of mine are yours, James. And Santiago would have wanted his godson to have at least some of his share." When she married Shea, James could have all her cattle, but no one at the ranch knew how things had changed the night before Shea left. She was almost afraid to talk about their intended marriage, as if the hope of such happiness might tempt fate.

James glanced at Sewa, who was edging about the room, moving from object to object till her precarious balance would lapse and she'd plunk down on the floor.

"I wouldn't rob her," he said, then chuckled. "It sounds funny, to *own* cattle. Apaches steal and save the trouble of raising them."

They hadn't talked of what James was ultimately going to do, make a life with the whites or go back to the Apaches. Mangus had sent him that spring to parley in case of Apache attack on the Socorro, to remind raiders that these people were friends of the greatest of all Apache chiefs. But no chief, even Mangus, could compel other Apaches to obey him. When they did, it was from free will and the force of the huge Mimbreño's personality.

Thinking of the giant who had called her Shining Girl, Talitha realized he must be well into his sixties. He couldn't live forever. It was not to be hoped that his protection could last from the grave; in fact, it would be a miracle if it held now, what with the Apaches seeing in the troops' withdrawal a chance to drive out the intruders whose towns, mines, and roads had begun to spread in the past few years.

Looking up at her brother, for he was taller now than anyone at the ranch except cadaverous Francisco Vasquez, Talitha said carefully, "The Apaches can't go on raiding forever. This war will end. When it does, no matter which side wins, there'll be troops, miners, merchants, probably a railroad."

"You'll be glad of that!"

"Not really. Though I'd be glad not to live under

constant fear of bandits or Apaches. The thing is, James, it will happen; it's the world you'll have to live in."

His young mouth twisted and his blue-green eyes were brilliant in his dark face. "And what will happen to my people?"

Stabbed at the *my,* Talitha couldn't keep a harsh note from her voice. "Your father's people will have to learn to own cattle instead of stealing them, and how to raise more food."

"Your words rattle like dried chick-peas on an old rawhide," James said rudely. "What's happened to the Gileños and Mescaleros who've tried to farm and live peacefully as their agent advises? Often there's no food issued, or not enough. Settlers and troops in that part of New Mexico have crowded out or killed the game, stolen the Apaches' horses, sold them bad whiskey, and killed them even when they were camping near the forts."

Talitha knew it was true. Dr. Michael Steck, as agent, had tried since 1854 to get reservations for the Gileños and Mescaleros where white men couldn't go, and to provide them with farming implements and seed as well as rations. The government never supplied enough food, however, and the Indians often had to steal or starve. Seeing what had happened to the groups that had tried to live according to the white man's way was certainly no argument for convincing Mangus and Cochise that they should do the same.

"I know the whites have often been as cruel as Apaches," Talitha said. "But the whites are going to keep coming. Nothing will stop that, James. So the Apaches must manage to live with them, somehow, or be killed out."

"There are always the mountains of Mexico where white-eye soldiers can't go."

"For heaven's sake, you have 'white eyes' yourself! And the Mexican government will surely help the

United States ferret out Apaches in the Sierra Madre if they can't spare troops to do it themselves."

The conversation was turning into an argument. The last thing Talitha wanted was to push her brother into stubbornly siding with the Apaches. She clamped her teeth on other undeniable facts and went to wash off the smell of dust and cattle.

IV

Talitha dispatched three hundred head to join Kitchen's herd at Calabazas. The Vasquez brothers and Rodolfo, two of them bachelors and eager for a town, were to help Kitchen's men to get the cattle to Tucson, but the other vaqueros rode back after the rendezvous.

In about ten days, while those at the ranch harvested beans, melons, and the last crop of corn, the trail riders returned. They hadn't been bothered by Apaches, and the townspeople had been delighted to buy beef. It would be needed that winter, what with the outlying food-producing places abandoned and those who'd lived on them refugees in the little city. Colonel Baylor had proclaimed Mesilla the capital of the Confederate Territory of Arizona and himself the governor, but he was going to be fighting for control of New Mexico. Beleaguered Tucson could expect little help from him.

Most of the ranch's money was in a San Francisco bank. Talitha hoped to leave it untouched till Shea's return, though there'd be no income from the mines unless they could be protected. The ranch, however, was almost self-sufficient, and had supplies of cloth and other purchased necessities, though she had told the vaqueros to fetch back sugar and coffee.

So the gold and silver she put in the chest that held Shea's *senales* and the gold nuggets her father had left with her would go mostly for wages, which she kept track of and paid on request. She suspected there'd be few chances to spend money as long as the war lasted.

Now that the ranch force was in full strength again, Talitha went on a piñon-nut expedition with James and the twins. Cat, in spite of her entreaties and tempers, was left behind.

For years, first with Socorro and Tjúni, more lately with the twins and a vaquero, or Shea, if he was in the mood, Talitha had gone into the mountains above the Place of Skulls to collect the small, tasty nuts. She knew where the largest stands were. A steep trail contoured up the mountain and led along the ridges through piñon and juniper with pines towering higher.

It was only midmorning when they reached a place where the horses could graze while they picked up the fallen nuts from beneath the gray-barked trees. By sunset they'd gathered several leather bags full and sat down to eat their jerky and pinole, not risking a fire.

Suddenly James stopped chewing and listened intently.

"A horseman."

In a few seconds the rest could hear, too: hoofs muffled by the fallen leaves and needles. "Shod," whispered James. So, unless the intruder rode a stolen horse, it was no Apache. Rising soundlessly, James took his bow and arrow and crept back along the trail behind a dense growth of manzanita.

Talitha and the twins picked up their bows, nocked arrows, and waited. They all had rifles and revolvers, too, but the flight of arrows wouldn't give them away as bullets would.

"Belen!" James exclaimed.

The boys and Talitha hurried along the trail. Belen looked at them in great distress. "She isn't with you? Caterina?"

"Cat?" cried Talitha. James made a sound in his throat, and the twins went pale. "She—she's not at home?"

Belen shook his head. "Paulita had the watch at

noon. When Caterina didn't come for dinner, we thought she was with her friend, but when Paulita came down without her, and Mancha was gone, we knew she must have followed you."

Talitha's mind raced. If her horse had slipped or any ordinary accident befallen, Belen should have found the evidence. Oh, Cat! Wicked, beloved, willful little Cat! Had Apaches got her, or bandits?

Of the two, Apaches were preferable. They wouldn't ravish the child or really hurt her—but Caterina Teresa O'Shea y Quintana to be an Apache drudge, as Talitha herself had been?

James was asking if there'd been any signs of struggle. Belen had observed none, though he admitted he'd come in a hurry, anxious to be sure she was safely with the others.

"Of course, at the places where you left the horses and gathered nuts, there was much confusion, many tracks." His eyes widened. He said quietly, "There were moccasin prints among the others, but I thought them James's." For James preferred his Apache footgear.

James went back to kneel by his saddlebag. He got out pinole and jerky, then took a long, deep drink. After a moment's thought he took a serape, not for himself, Talitha was sure, but for Cat. He had his knife, his rifle and his revolver, and his bow and his quiver, filled with thirty arrows.

"It's almost dark," Talitha protested, catching his arm.

He shrugged. "Maybe I can hear something. Or smell. Anyway, I can't stay here."

"Let us go with you!" Patrick urged. Miguel was already collecting necessities.

"No." James's voice was bleak. "You'd be heard. I'll do better alone." To Talitha he said, "If I don't come back, try to get word to Mangus. He'd return Caterina, no matter who took her, for her mother's sake.

Apaches don't usually think much of women, but he revered Doña Socorro for her valor and sweetness."

All Talitha could do was nod. She had delivered the twins, just as she'd delivered Cat, but the boys had had a living mother. Talitha had carried the newborn girl home while Shea rode with the dead woman in his arms. Cat had been to Talitha both daughter and younger sister, loved as dearly as James, though less fiercely, since no one had threatened her until now. Now both were in danger.

It would have been a relief to follow James, but he was right. Apache trained, he was the one to trail them, or anyone else. But how, how, to get through the night?

"I'm not sleepy," she told the others. "I'll keep watch and wake you later."

The boys grumbled but were asleep almost as soon as they rolled up in their blankets. Talitha huddled in hers, leaning against a tree. She felt as if she were shriveling inside with icy dread.

Did Cat sleep tonight? Was she alive? It was strange to pray that Apaches had her, but far better they than white men who'd abduct a child.

"*Doncellita.*" The old pet name spoken in Belen's gruff voice was as comforting as a touch. "Can you not rest?"

"Later. You sleep now."

He settled against a nearby tree, wrapping his own serape about him. "There's no use for us both to stay awake," Talitha protested. Belen said nothing. Gratefully, with a rush of love for the aging Yaqui, she understood. He would not leave her to endure alone the terror of that night.

"Do you think there's any chance James may find her in the dark?" she asked.

"There might be a fire. Or noise." Amazingly, he said, "Let me tell you a story, as I did when you were small."

"Oh, Belen—"

"Try to pay attention. It is good to have stories in a time of trouble. They remind us there is more than now.

"When I was young and the Mexicans tried to break up Yaqui land, tax us and make us live like them, I fought, as you know, under our great general, Juan Banderas. He was executed in 1833, and that's when I came north. But I remember those tales we told around our fires to hearten us in the nights of fear." He chuckled. "There are some I will not tell you."

But he told her of the time it was so dry that even the Río Yaqui dried up, the mountains were hazy with heat, and rocks burned like coals. The desperate people sent first a boy and then a swallow to Yuku, the thunder god, but though he promised rain, he didn't send it.

Then the leaders of the eight pueblos asked Bobok the toad if he'd carry their message. Bobok agreed and borrowed some bat wings with which to fly up to Yuku. Again Yuku promised rain; but Bobok, instead of going home, dug under the ground near Yuku's door. When Yuku sent a storm to destroy the importunate toad, it couldn't find him and hunted all the way to earth, raining as it tried to kill him. Bobok flew down to the top of the rain cloud and sang loudly, "Bobok, bobok, bobok!"

The storm tried to find and kill the toad and rained even harder. He led it to the land of the Yaquis, and it rained till there were hundreds of little Boboks all singing gladly because the rain couldn't kill them. That's why toads still come out singing after every good rain. So the earth was saved, and Bobok went back to his pleasant muddy lagoon.

Talitha drowsily smiled at the story. She'd heard the toads so many times, great choruses of them when the rain had spread like a sheet over the broad grassy valley. She was getting sleepy. She should get up and move around. . . .

"Did I ever tell you about my mother's brother who went into the Red Mountain near Torim?" Belen continued. "He was hunting one day when suddenly he was stricken with *chictura.* This is when one becomes lost, even knowing a place very well, and can't tell north from south, east from west. The cure is to make a cross of spit on the ground and sit on it with head hanging down for a few minutes. My uncle did this; and when he stood up, he knew his directions again, but he found he was very close to Sikil Kawa, the Red Mountain. Within is Yo-Ania, an enchanted place where no Christian should go, and he started to walk fast toward his pueblo. But it was exactly noon, and as he passed a little cavity in the hill he heard music so beautiful that he simply had to hear it better. My uncle was a musician, but not very good with his flute because he didn't practice.

"He squeezed through the little opening and found himself in a big room where a bearded man greeted him and gave him into the charge of the loveliest girl he had ever seen. She took him deeper into the mountain. By magic she showed him all the richness and marvels in the world, all that delights the heart and body. Then she brought him into a cavern of ferocious wild animals, lions twice the size of any he'd ever hunted, huge bears with claws like steel. These pressed against him, showing their teeth, growling. He smelled their tainted breath but managed not to flinch or walk faster.

"'You must be tired,' the girl said, smiling at him with very red lips. 'Sit down on that log a moment.'

"He did as she said. The log began to move, coil up around him. It was the king of all the animals, a huge snake that entwined him in a horrible embrace and licked his face, darting its forked tongue about his eyes and nostrils. My uncle stared into those ancient evil eyes but managed to stay quiet.

"'*Bueno!*' laughed the girl. The snake unfolded itself, and my uncle was brought to where the things for dancers, musicians, hunters, and vaqueros were displayed. He could have picked any gift he wanted and walked out of the cave, the best at whatever talent he chose, except for Christian things, a *matachini, maestro,* or *fariseo.*

"He passed the rattles and masks of the pascolas, the headdress of the deer dancers, the *reata* and gear for vaqueros, the hunters' weapons, and out of the drums and other instruments he took a flute.

"'That is your *don,* your gift,' agreed the girl. 'Now your soul belongs to Yo-Ania. Since you are young, you have twenty-one years to play the flute better than anyone. At that time, no matter where you are or what you're doing, you'll vanish from the world and come to live in our Red Mountain.'

"Well, my uncle didn't think that such a bad fate if he could spend eternity with the girl, and not the king snake with his clever, licking tongue. He took his flute and squirmed with great difficulty out of the mountain, for the hole was only big enough for his head. He came back to Torim and was very famous. People suspected what he'd done, but it was his soul and they were glad to have his wonderful music at fiestas.

"In the twentieth year, he began to drink a lot, dreaming of giant snakes. In the twenty-first year he went off hunting and never came back again."

Talitha's spine tingled. "I hope the girl met him, not the snake."

"If you lose your soul, what matters?"

She would have made such a bargain to have Shea. Perhaps in a way she had, refusing Marc and John Irwin, waiting insistently, offering what she knew Shea desired, though his conscience forbade it. But if there was a way to barter with the powers, she'd do it now, trade her lifelong dream of being Shea's love for the safe return of Cat and James.

Belen told other stories, then: of the naked Ku bird who begged feathers till he became the resplendent parrot, always gabbling boastfully of his splendor; of the talking tree that long ago foretold the coming of the white men; and of the clumsy pascola who became graceful and witty after his encounter with an enchanted goat.

Lulled by the familiar deep voice, Talitha kept jerking awake. The next thing she knew, there was gray light filtering through the trees.

Then everything came flooding back. How could she have slept? Scrambling up, she saw with fresh guilt that Belen had folded his blanket around her when he had evidently settled her beside the tree. She wrapped the rough wool around him now, saying reproachfully, "You tricked me! Belen, you kept watch all night!"

"I told myself stories," he teased as he smiled at her.

"Sleep awhile now," she commanded.

He stood up, offering her a piece of jerky. "I'm refreshed. I'll follow James. Perhaps he needs help."

Or perhaps he's dead. "I'm coming with you."

Belen started to object, but she hushed him with a glance. "The twins can wait for us today. If none of us return, they can go home tomorrow, and maybe Pete Kitchen can help get a message to Mangus for help in freeing Cat."

"What's that about the twins?" yawned Patrick, stretching.

Belen raised a hand. They all listened. In a moment Talitha could detect the sound of shod hoofs, the occasional *ting* of metal striking rock. Talitha started to run forward, but Belen checked her.

"Hide, you three. I'll see who it is."

Talitha shooed the reluctant twins behind a matted thicket of manzanita and waited, her heart feeling wedged in her throat, as Belen left the faint trail and vanished in the juniper and piñon.

It was only minutes before she heard his voice, full of joy and relief, though she couldn't make out the words. With the boys she ran toward the voices, hearing Cat's now.

Cat slid down from Mancha and ran to Talitha, almost leaping into her arms. "Oh, Tally, I was bad to follow you!" There was a bruise on one cheek, but otherwise she seemed unhurt. "That man caught me! I was so scared. And—and James had to kill him—"

James, on foot, looked exhausted. "Tulan had her. He's a Mimbreño who doesn't live with the people anymore because on a raid he ran and didn't help his companions. He had made a fire, and that was how I found them."

"He was going to kill Mancha and eat her," Cat went on in a trembling voice. She was shaking all over, though Talitha had wrapped a serape about her and held her close. "I—I tried to stop him. I bit him, hard. He knocked me into the bushes. That was when the arrow went into him. All the way through his chest."

"Tulan was always a glutton," said James. "If he hadn't been so eager for roast horse that he risked a fire, I might not have found him till after daylight." James looked ready to drop. His mouth contorted. "He was a coward and an outcast, but I wish the first man I killed hadn't been Apache."

Pulling away from Talitha, Cat ran to hug him, but he didn't bend so she could reach his neck and she caught his hands, pressing them to her face, kissing them. "James, I—I'm sorry! Sorry you had to kill the man—"

"I'm not." James sank on one knee to hold her while she sobbed. "I'll never be sorry for anything I do for you. I just wish an Apache hadn't been my first kill. Stop that crying, Catarina! You need to go to sleep now."

He picked her up and set her on Mancha, but as she clung to him for a last instant she murmured against his cheek, "I love you, James! Best in the whole world! I'll always love you."

Though the sun was up, it seemed to Talitha to be suddenly muted. Fear gripped her. The adoration in Cat's eyes as she smiled down at James, the passion of her whisper, were altogether too much like the consuming way Talitha had, from a slightly younger age, worshiped Shea. With James fixed on being Apache, what could come of that but grief for them both?

Cat, Belen, and James slept that morning while the others gathered nuts. At noon Belen took the child home. After two more days of piñon collecting, the rest came down. James had been moody and silent, but when he showed them where Mancha had been led off from a mass of confused tracks marking where they'd stopped to gather nuts, he apparently decided it was time they had some lessons in tracking.

He searched till he found where a footprint had flattened the grass, then carefully pressed the marked grass down and examined it. "See the moccasin print?" he invited. "A white man's boot or shoe would crush the plants. The grass is discolored, which shows the print isn't fresh." He broke off a few pieces and showed them there was still juice inside the stems. "But since the grass still had moisture inside, I know it hasn't been a long time since a Mimbreño walked here."

A little farther on he picked up a piece of dung, broke it open, and showed them the residue of grama grass. "If it were sacaton, we'd know the horse came from where it grows. Barley usually means Americans, but maize would probably be Mexicans, or travelers from there. If you study droppings, you'll soon be able to tell how old they are from the amount of moisture left." He pointed to where Mancha had urinated. "A mare goes like that, behind her rear prints. A stallion or a gelding shoots his spray forward toward his front feet."

Intrigued, Patrick and Miguel begged him to take them tracking and he said he would, his spirits higher than since he'd returned with Cat. "Now I'm going to run down the trail a way and hide myself." He grinned, including Talitha in the challenge. "You try to see me! I'll be in easy sight, but I think you won't find me."

"Bet we do!" scoffed Patrick.

They proceeded carefully, scanning every thicket, every outcropping or pile of boulders. Suddenly the grass beside the trail heaved upward. James grinned at them, brushing away the remains of his disguise.

"That's one way. Now, watch."

Scrambling into a slide of rocks, he hunched over and lay so perfectly still, so much a part of the landscape, that though they looked straight at him, it was hard to believe he wasn't just another boulder. He took his gray blanket, wrapped himself in it, and huddled down, sprinkling a few handfuls of earth on top, and became a hunk of granite that an unwary traveler would pass within a few yards without suspicion.

Talitha shook her head disbelievingly. "I wonder how many Apaches I've gone past without noticing!"

"Probably a fair number," James said. "Apaches watch a lot more than they attack and usually study a party pretty thoroughly before they come down on it. If a group's armed and looks like it can fight, often it's not bothered. Apaches like careless groups that offer plunder without much trouble."

"That doesn't sound very brave," observed Miguel.

"Brave?" James raised an eyebrow. "Apaches have fought on with two or three mortal wounds. But they think it's crazy to take unnecessary risks. A man who charges into danger without thinking is considered simply a fool. No one would want to follow him on a raid or warpath."

As they rode he told the boys how warriors prepared for war. The night before, all the invited men danced, showing how they'd fight and get the enemy's property. Then women joined the dance till dawn when twelve men, each of a different clan danced in turn and sang of some occasion when he'd proved his courage. The last of the twelve sang about death, reminding the warriors that it came sometime to everyone.

After that, the warriors were provisioned with mescal, ground seeds, and corn. The war chief told two old men who'd be staying home how many days the party would be gone and gave them a rawhide cord. The old men, now in charge of the camp, were to tie a knot in the cord each day so they'd know when to expect the warriors' return. On Mexican raids, they were usually gone thirty to forty-five days, going in the spring and fall when there was water.

"The leaders plan to reach enemy country in the full moon so the party can travel at night and see well to run off stock," James added. He frowned regretfully. "I should have gone on my first raid this fall, though I couldn't do anything but gather wood and water, cook, and take care of the horses, and see how things are done."

Patrick's eyes shone. "It really sounds exciting!"

"Yes, it's most interesting for the Mexican herders, like our own men, who get killed," said Talitha sharply. "And for the women and children who're brought back as slaves!"

"Some of the best warriors were born Mexican," James pointed out. "And none of the women taken to wife by Apaches have ever wanted to go back to their families, even when they had the chance." He slanted an arrogant smile at her. "I have seen such women shoot arrows into Mexican captives and laugh to watch them die."

"I have seen it, too." Something in Talitha's throat tasted like warm, thick blood. "But your mother, James, hated her captivity. I—I was so glad to get you away from Juh, so you wouldn't grow up like him—" Her voice broke. What would become of him, this brother of hers?

The blue-green eyes met hers with hostility. "If I weren't Apache, Caterina would still be with Tu-lan."

That was unanswerable. It was also true that it was good for the twins to learn all that James could teach them. It might save their lives. But James's insistence on his Apache identity was a twisting knife in her, a deep, sad aching. Though she told herself that Caterina was safe and had learned a valuable lesson, when she thought of the way Cat had kissed James's hands a great dread gripped her.

But perhaps it was a good thing. James loved Cat; if their devotion turned from almost that of brother and sister into that of lovers, wasn't there hope that, for Cat's sake, he'd stay at the Socorro, reconcile himself to his white blood, and live that way?

Let it be, Talitha entreated her circle of gentle, loving powers—Socorro and her own mother, Judith. *Please let it be.*

As they forded the creek and started for the ranch Caterina came running out to meet them. Straight to James, who swept her up in front of him and teased her, laughing, as they rode toward the corral.

The Roof Feast fell in mid-December, a private thanksgiving for those of Rancho del Socorro. It commemorated the day in late 1847 when the founders of the ranch—Irish Shea, Spanish Creole Socorro, Papago Tjúni, and Santiago, who was mixed Opata, Apache, and Creole—had feasted to celebrate the completion of the roof that would shelter them from winter storms.

They had been thankful, too, for the wild foods they'd garnered, the two hundred head of cattle brought safely up from Santiago's despoiled home, and Mangus's friendship. Here the four of them, all homeless, without family or friends, had begun to build a home and were themselves almost a family, albeit a strange sort of one. Each had narrowly escaped death; each had despaired to extremity. Here in the broad valley watered by the clear, pleasant little Sonoita, surrounded by mountains near and distant, they had begun to live again.

And it was at that first feast that Shea and Socorro

had stood in front of the dark Madonna of Guadalupe who smiled down on them from her niche in the *sala* as they pledged themselves to each other. Six years they'd had, loving each other with passionate tenderness.

Talitha still couldn't think of Socorro's death without rebellious grief, especially when she reflected that she'd only been twenty-three when she died, a scant two years older than Talitha was now. To die so young, leaving twin sons, a new baby, a husband who loved her as Shea did! But perhaps such a loving spirit never truly died. Though Socorro's body must long be dust in her grave next to Santiago's on the hill, Talitha sometimes seemed to feel her presence as a comforting strength, and she felt it tonight, mingled with the madonna's smile, as Socorro's children and those of the vaqueros feasted with hilarity at their table while their elders occupied that rough hand-hewn table made so long ago by Shea and Santiago.

There was venison, turkey, beef, and ham, Anita's succulent tamales, many kinds of stew, bread, grain dishes, nut cakes, candies, and panocha. When everyone had eaten to satiety, the dishes were cleared, the youngest children put to sleep on Shea's bed, and Chuey and Francisco got out their guitars.

They sang *corridos* they had composed: "The Valiant Women," about Socorro and Tjúni killing the scalp hunters; "The Double Branding," about the price Shea had paid for James; and "The Return of Santiago," which recounted his death at Frost's hands and how Frost had perished in the desert, his brains roasted by Areneños. Mixed in with these stories of the ranch people were funny songs for the children and, of course, love songs.

"If some day you pass my house,
Do not forget ever that I was your lover.

Because, anyhow, in this world there are other lovers;
As I loved you, so I can hate you."

All the vaqueros except Belen could play, so the guitars circulated to accompany songs doleful and gay, bitter and hopeful.

"Your horse is wounded,
Your spade is broken,
Your deeds are strange,
And there's no end to your loves!"

"A man after my own heart!" chuckled someone in Spanish.

No guard was kept after dark, except on moonlit nights. Taken entirely by surprise, the vaqueros sprang up, then relaxed as Carmencita ran to the door and embraced the golden-haired, green-eyed man who lounged there, laughing at their discomfiture.

"Güero!" the plump little woman cried, patting his face and muscular shoulders as if to assure herself of his reality. "Oh, my son! How glad we are to see you!"

No one else looked in the least glad, especially not Natividad, his half brother, Anita and Juana, his half sisters, and Pedro, who'd accepted and reared some white man's careless sowing. Though he was expert in all vaquero skills, his cruelty to horses and his flaring temper left everyone but Carmencita glad that he'd taken to wandering after his first trip to California with a Texas trail drive over ten years ago.

About thirty now, he was in the prime of vital bull-like strength. Over his mother's graying head, he looked around the room as if he owned it, a sardonic curl to his lips.

Talitha stiffened as his eyes locked with hers. It was as if his big, square hands had closed on her, pressing life and air from her lungs, stopping her heart. She sat frozen, like a rabbit in the shadow of the hawk.

That angered her. Angry, too, for Carmencita, of

whose love he was so contemptuous, she gave him the hard, proud look of *patrona* to hireling.

"You're late for the branding, but doubtless there are other things you can do for your winter's keep."

"To be sure," bubbled Carmencita. "And it's good to have all the men we can, to discourage attacks. Sit down, my son, and eat. How lucky we've been feasting! There are all the things you like."

"Yes, *mamacita.*" He allowed her to seat him on a bench. His eyes weren't on the food she bustled joyfully to bring, but on Talitha. "There's everything I like."

He shrugged when asked where he'd been since his last visit a year or more ago. "California. Several claims I had shares in finally proved out. Nothing wonderful, but I've enough to buy my own ranch."

"Your own ranch!" Carmencita beamed with prideful wonder. "Ay, my son a ranchero! To think of it!"

"You may come and cook for me," he said indulgently.

"My wife stays with me." Pedro's wrinkled little monkey face was grim. "And I am not leaving this ranch where Don Patricio has been more than generous, allowing us to build our own herds."

Güero stared at him before deftly scooping up stew with a tortilla. "I have heard Don Patricio rode off to that gringo war. One hopes for his safety, of course, but there's the chance he may not long require your loyalty."

"Then his children will, more than ever," cut in Talitha. He seemed a terrible, unnamable threat, and not because of his idle tempting of Carmencita. "It's a poor time to go into ranching, with thieves and Apaches running wild from Tucson to Magdalena."

"You're right, *señorita.* I shall buy now only the land, while it's cheap, but I won't stock it till the Apaches are calmed." His mocking gaze rested on her throat. She felt naked as the pulse leaped. "So, for the time, I am very much at your orders."

Go away, she wanted to tell him. *Go away and never*

come back. But just one more good shot could make the difference in a siege. Besides, how could she dismiss Carmencita's beloved son?

"Another man will be welcome," she said.

It was like going down a steep-walled cañon river, convinced there were deadly rapids ahead, but having no way to escape.

V

Güero gorged himself, mostly on meat. Between bites, he confirmed that Pete Kitchen was still holding out, as was the Patagonia mine where he'd had dinner. The dozens of mines and smaller number of ranches in the Santa Cruz Valley and the surrounding mountains had been deserted, plundered by Apaches or bandits. Rumors were that a Confederate general was at Fort Bliss in Texas, raising forces to complete Baylor's conquest of New Mexico and push north and west to take California and Colorado. If Shea was with Colonel Baylor, which seemed likely, perhaps he'd be sent this way and could get a few days' leave. Heartened at that thought, Talitha felt her peculiar fear and distrust of Güero ebbing and was able to applaud his singing when he borrowed a guitar and gave them, in a rich tenor, the boisterous song of a vaquero in from the mountains for a wedding.

The godmother, too, if she suits me,
I can also carry along:
And a godfather is no problem,
Caught here where my ribs are strong . . ."

Talitha laughed with the others when he had finished the song of bragging *machismo,* but she couldn't smile when he sang about the man who'd finally possessed a woman who'd long resisted him.

"'As the pears fell from the tree that held them,
So you fell, into my arms, my darling!'"

Then, smiling at Talitha, he gave the response in a coquettish falsetto that made even Pedro grin and clap.

"'Don't talk to me like that, you impudent devil!
Even though you see me thus, I've always been decent!'"

Talitha didn't laugh. "It's time you were in bed, Cat," she told the girl, who was speculating on the newcomer. "I'm tired, too. Good night, everyone. It was a lovely feast."

"Yes," said Güero, rising with a bow as she collected little Sewa and shooed Cat to the door. Chusma, her old tabby, got down from a warm *banco* by the fire to follow them. "Most lovely, *señorita.* I'm glad I came home."

She didn't answer but swept her rebozo about herself, the baby, and Cat as they hurried through the cold to their room. After the children were tucked in, Talitha got quickly under the covers.

If Güero had to come back, she wished he hadn't appeared on the night of the Roof Feast. She knew that was foolish. An extra man would be useful. Just because he watched her as he did didn't make him a menace to the ranch. If she encouraged him, doubtless he'd try his luck; but she couldn't imagine, if she treated him with the icy courtesy she intended, that he, a vaquero raised in spite of his recent fortune, would dare lift a hand to her.

Even so, though Chusma curled warmly against the

back of her knees, Talitha felt very cold and shivered for a long time.

As days passed into weeks the edge of Talitha's fear dulled. Güero attended to his duties, even helping grind corn and wheat in the little mill that was powered by a stream diverted from the creek, and for the first time seemed to fit easily in with his family and the other vaqueros. She'd been foolish, Talitha told herself. He'd only seemed different at first, dangerous, because he'd been away and naturally wished to swagger a bit over his travels and comparative wealth. Still, she couldn't relax or joke with him as she did with the other men, and his green eyes, when she caught them fixed on her, had the power to make her turn quickly away.

They celebrated Christmas and the Day of the Three Kings twelve days later, the smaller children receiving gifts each time, since by now Mexican and American holidays were hopelessly scrambled at the ranch. They celebrated St. John's Day, June 24, with roping, fancy riding, and barbecue; and on November 2, the Day of the Dead, the vaqueros and their families took food and flowers to the graves on top of the hill so that the returned dead could feast with them. This custom had distressed Shea, though he hadn't forbidden it, and Talitha had never gone.

Shea was always at the back of Talitha's mind, and Marc Revier came to her thoughts almost as often. Yes, in addition to Shea, who'd had her worship since she was seven, she remembered Marc and prayed for his safety, though she pushed away memories of his loving, which disquieted her lonely flesh. She and Marc had made love every night for a week after her abduction by Judah Frost, and after the first cleaning, Marc had sweetly, fiercely, taught her delights. When her deprived body dreamed its way to release, he was the man.

That disturbed her, though she could scarcely control

her dreams. Shea was her dearest love, but she couldn't remember much of what had happened the night he'd finally taken her, except that it was ecstasy, shared loveliness past knowing.

Mostly, when she thought of Marc, she saw him smiling, saying with an ironic twist to his long mouth which had dealt so wildly and yet so sweetly with her body, "I still have the sun."

So have I, thought Talitha, holding those bare, proud words like a talisman. But she wanted more: a life without constant threat and Shea home again, Marc safe.

There had been no word from either of the men. Talitha had hoped, though not expected, that they might be able to send a letter by some traveler who could leave it in Tucson till Pete Kitchen got to town and picked it up.

Pete did come by early in March with the news that a company of mounted rifles under Capt. Sherod Hunter had ridden into Tucson February 28 and run up the Confederate Stars and Bars, while his commander, General Sibley, was marching up the Rio Grande, promising the inhabitants to respect their religion and give them a "strong and lenient" government.

"I—don't suppose you heard anything about Shea? Or Marc Revier?" Talitha almost whispered.

The keen gray-blue eyes watched her with sympathy. Awkwardly, he patted her hand. "No, Miss Tally, I didn't hear any particulars, except that Captain Bascom—you remember he got in that wrangle with Cochise last year at Apache Pass—was killed at Valverde in a battle."

The then lieutenant had come for dinner at the ranch once with his friend John Irwin. Talitha remembered him as a pleasant, serious young man only a few years her senior. Dead now, that eager life wasted in a battle where he'd fought on the opposite side from Shea's.

Would the whole war be like this? Hearing of battles, but not knowing if Shea or Marc—or John Irwin, was in them, if they'd been hurt? Wrenching away from that agonizing prospect, she asked Pete if he thought the Confederates could give the Santa Cruz Valley any protection.

"Those hundred men can't do much but garrison Tucson and scout around a little." Kitchen shrugged. "There aren't many Unionists left in Tucson, but Hunter gave them a choice of swearing allegiance to the Confederacy or having their property confiscated and leaving the territory."

He named several of them. Solomon Warner, who'd opened his store in 1856 just a few days after the last Mexican troops withdrew, stocking his shelves with goods brought in by mules from Fort Yuma. Leaving his painfully developed business in rebel hands, he was on the way to Sonora. Sam Hughes, born in Wales, a cook, hotelkeeper, and prospector in California, had come to Tucson in 1858 and prospered by supplying grain and meat to the Overland Stage Company stations. Staunchly for the Union, he'd set his face for California.

Gone from the territory, too, was Peter Brady, who'd visited the ranch with Andrew Gray's railroad surveying party in the spring of 1853 when the German artist of the expedition, Charles Schuchard, had painted for Socorro the picture of the ranch house that hung in the *sala*. Brady, after the survey, had gone into ranching and mining and had most lately been post trader at Fort Mojave, where Beale's wagon road crossed the Colorado. Gray himself had gone to fight for the Confederacy.

"And Don Esteban Ochoa, the merchant," Kitchen went on. "When he wouldn't swear loyalty to the South, Hunter gave him just time to get his horse, weapons, and a few rations and leave town or be shot."

Except for Brady, Talitha knew the exiles only by reputation, but they were all decent, honorable men. She hated that they'd lost everything achieved through such risk and persistence. It didn't seem fair that real Arizonans should be dispossessed by military forces of either side; but perhaps that was what war was all about: property and power.

It was a relief, after Pete had jogged off, to pick up little Sewa and carry her out into the bright sunshine. Always, when she was sad, Talitha found that the warmth of that honey-brown skin and the playful mischief in the big dark eyes were good antidotes. Holding Talitha's neck with one proprietary arm, the child pointed up the creek where two hawks were soaring.

"*Deelicho!*" She used the Apache word. Then, chuckling, she added in Spanish, "*Gavilán.*"

"Yes," agreed Talitha. "And 'hawk,' too. We'll have to ask Belen for the Yaqui." Sewa spoke well for her twenty-one months. The main trouble was sorting out her Spanish, English, Apache, and Yaqui.

The red-tails had made their nest for several springs now in a big sycamore and didn't bother the smaller birds who nested close by, though Talitha had several times seen a group of robins chasing one of the hawks, pecking at the big bird, which made no effort to retaliate. Once, when ravens were after it, Talitha had marveled to see the hawk turn over and offer its talons, at which the ravens retreated, cawing as they flapped away.

The hawks rose in great circles, crossing one another's arcs till they almost touched, becoming small specks in the blue brightness. Then one dropped at great speed till Talitha could see it had partly folded its wings. When it seemed about to crash into the trees, it opened its wings and climbed high again, seeming to hang above its mate. Wheeling and plummeting, the birds passed out of sight as riders came into view.

All three O'Shea youngsters were learning how to track, how to fade into the landscape, and constantly increasing their skill with bow and arrow. Several times the twins had startled Talitha by speaking suddenly from behind piles of rock where they wore crowns of oak and brush that made them look like scrub growing behind the boulders. The boys could spear targets now with long lances of sotol, tipped with bayonets salvaged from the fort. The lances entered the cedar-bark targets with a force that made Talitha wince, for she had seen them used on people. If the boys were to live in this country, though, it was best they learned to use every possible weapon.

James was holding something bundled up in Cat's serape. As he came closer, Talitha saw a sharply hooked beak, open to show a pink tongue, and golden eyes that held some of the fire of the sun.

"*Gavilán-hawk-deelicho!*" squealed Sewa, reaching toward it.

"Don't touch," warned Talitha, putting her down. "The hawk doesn't want to play. Goodness, James, how did you get it?"

"It's been shot with an arrow, which has dropped out except for the point lodged in the wing," James explained, dismounting with great caution as Cat sprang down and took Alacran's reins. "It's a Chiricahua point. I think it was shot a good distance away, probably by someone wanting arrow feathers. The hawk could fly for a while, but then its wound swelled and the point worked in till the wing's lame."

"We're going to get him well," Cat said. "Aren't we, James?"

"We'll try. Can I make a nest for him in the old granary, Tally?"

She nodded. "No one goes in there. Can I help you get that arrow point out?"

"Yes, but take care. His talons are like knives."

"*You* be careful, James!" hissed Cat.

"*You* take the baby inside," he retorted.

Miguel, who had a rabbit tied to his saddle, led the horses off to the corral while Patrick, obeying James, fetched heavy gauntlets and restrained the hawk's head as James got out his knife.

"I think we'd better douse the wound with mescal," Talitha said. She asked Anita, who was staring from the door, to bring some.

"Hold the wing back," James said. "And keep that serape tight!"

Pus wept out as he edged the sharp blade down the side of the arrow. In spite of the restraining hands on him, the bird struggled convulsively. James worked to the front, tugging at the flint while he pried upward with the knife.

The point came in a welter of corruption that oozed down the hawk's white underbody and rust-speckled flanks. James took the gourd of mescal Anita offered and poured it over the wound, holding the angry flesh open so the harsh cleanser could reach deep.

Swaddling talons and beak, James carried the bird around the house to the granary, where Cat had already lined a large willow basket with straw and Miguel waited with the rabbit.

"All of you stay outside," James warned. He tipped the hawk into the basket and stepped back quickly. It flopped over on its back, holding up its fearful claws. "We'll give you something to hold, K'aak'eh." K'aak'eh meant "He was wounded," and also sounded quite a lot like a red-tail's cry.

Drawing his knife again, James cut up the rabbit, leaving on the fur, and proffered a haunch on the edge of the knife. The talons gripped, Talitha heard the sharp snap of a bone.

Putting the rest of the luckless rabbit within the hawk's reach, James shut the door. "All we can do now is feed him. He's young, not a year old, though he's beginning to get his red tail feathers. He'll molt all summer and by fall will have his adult plumage."

Cat skipped in excitement. "He'll stay with us, won't he, James?"

James glanced at her in surprise. "No. Not after he can fly again, hunt for himself."

"But, James, I'd love to have a tame hawk!"

"Hawks aren't for taming," he said sternly. "I'd kill one that hung around people waiting to eat their leavings. It would be like the Apaches around the forts in New Mexico who've given up their pride for some moldy corn."

The disgust in James's tone made Cat's mouth tremble. It was probably the first time he'd ever refused to indulge her. But her puzzled hurt passed before they reached the house and she held to his arm, chattering on about how handsome K'aak'eh was and how they'd soon have him well.

The young hawk did mend swiftly. After a few days he stopped threatening James, who nonetheless kept a respectful distance from the vicious claws and beak. But soon James began to wrap his arm and hand in folds of rawhide and let the hawk clamber on, taking him out into the sun and air.

The hawk's wonderful plumage, a rich rusty brown on the back, with the red of the tail becoming more marked, breast and underbody white with speckling at belly and flanks, ruffled in the breeze that stirred James's dark hair. Boy and hawk had a savage beauty that sent an ache through Talitha. James *was* Apache. Like the bird, he had to be free. But she prayed he could make peace with his white blood, not have to live like a hunted animal as Americans spread over Apache lands.

It was at the Agave Feast that Güero sang again, his eyes green flames in the firelight. A dozen agave hearts had been put to bake about noon the day before, after the fire had died down on the stones lining the round pit dug about ten feet wide and a yard deep. Covered then with bear grass and a layer of earth, the hearts were done tonight, mushy golden-brown. Carmencita didn't approve of eating such heathen food, so there was barbecue, too, and a big pot of spiced beans.

After the meal, the vaqueros began to play their guitars, but the others stopped when Güero began.

Truly he had the best voice, deeply resonant. He sang a nonsense song, imitating birdcalls, that had the children laughing, struck a few chords, and swung into the boisterous "Best Vaquero" in a way that soon had the other men clapping and calling out "Eee-ha!" in time to the song.

When he came to the end of that swaggering canter, his gaze rested full on Talitha. He sang a love song, and though she wrapped her rebozo tighter about her, it was as if his eyes and voice penetrated her garments, lingered on her flesh.

> *"Pardon me if my caresses offend you.*
> *Pardon me if my songs offend you . . ."*

Their eyes met. A fiery chill shot through Talitha. She took Sewa from Cat and off to bed and didn't return to the fire. But dimly, though the window was shut, she could still hear Güero's voice.

> *"They say because of your love some evil will follow me.*
> *I don't care if it's the devil, I also know how to die."*

Now that it was spring, maybe he'd go away. She hoped he would, then was angry at herself for that coward's thought. The ranch needed all the men it would get, she reminded herself.

She thought of Shea and Marc, trying to blot out Güero's questing stare with their faces, but they kept going faint and vanishing. Were they still alive? Would she ever hear again of either of them?

It had been a long time since she cried, but that night she did, hard and bitterly, with a kind of despair.

A few days later Miguel, on lookout, reported horsemen. At the signal bell, every adult in hearing except for Carmencita grabbed a rifle and took a position.

"Americans," called James after a few tense minutes. "Most are in gray. They ride like soldiers."

"Maybe they're from Tucson. Let's wait till we're sure." Talitha kept her voice steady, even though her heart raced as she couldn't repress a crazy, flaring hope that Shea might be in the little group of perhaps a dozen men.

Opening the door, rifle in view, Talitha called, "Who are you?"

A young man in the lead swept off his gray hat, exposing long blond hair, and bowed from the saddle, motioning his men to wait as he rode forward. "Lieutenant Todd, ma'am, of Hunter's Rangers. We're foraging."

"Apaches and bandits have been down the Santa Cruz before you," Talitha said dryly. "I doubt they left much."

The officer flushed and straightened his shoulders. "I trust, ma'am, that you're not a Union sympathizer. My orders are to confiscate any cattle and usable goods of such persons."

"I sympathize with North *and* South since I have friends on both sides. This ranch is owned, sir, by a man who's off fighting for your Confederacy. Perhaps you've met him. Patrick O'Shea."

"An older man?"

"Shea's not old!"

The lieutenant grinned, looking very boyish. "Well, ma'am, older than I, with red hair and a badly scarred cheek?"

Talitha's heart leaped. She could only nod.

"I saw him at Mesilla," Todd said. "He went up the Rio with Sibley and would surely have been in the Valverde fight. They moved on to take Albuquerque, and we've just heard they've secured Santa Fe and run up the Confederate flag. Is Captain O'Shea your husband, ma'am?"

"No." She didn't want to explain with all the listening ears. "But I'd be most grateful if you could learn anything about him, or get a message through."

"I'll try my best, but don't count on anything, ma'am. Things are in an uproar, what with Union troops moving toward us from California and a bunch of Coloradans coming down on Sibley. To top all that, President Davis just removed Baylor from the governorship of Arizona."

"You have a lot of news, Lieutenant," Talitha interrupted. "Won't you and your men come in for dinner and rest yourselves?"

He was happy to accept. The vaqueros took the horses off for grain and water while the rangers lounged on the long front porch. Only the officer came in to eat with the family, but the women served the others with generous baskets of tortillas, stewed meat, and beans.

Hunter and his hundred men were doing all they could to impede the advance of several hundred California volunteers who would soon be crossing into Arizona. Constantly moving, Hunter was burning all thc hay stored for Union use at the old Butterfield Overland Mail stations, and early that month he had gone to the Pima Villages northwest of Tucson on the way to Fort Yuma to arrest the miller Ammi White, a federal purchasing agent who'd been buying supplies for the California troops. Hunter destroyed the mill and distributed the fifteen hundred confiscated sacks of wheat to the Indians, since he had no way to get it to Tucson.

"A Union captain with a squad of cavalry rode up to the Pima Villages, expecting to make a building where they could store Ammi White's wheat and flour, scout for more supplies, and then jog down to Tucson to capture or wipe out Hunter's command." The lieutenant chuckled. "Well, ma'am, I'd like to have seen that Yank captain's face when the man he thought was Ammi White turned out to be Capt. Sherod Hunter,

C.S.A.! The captain, his nine men, and Ammi White were all brought prisoners to Tucson."

"But if there are thousands of Californians and only a hundred of you . . ."

A somber look crossed the young face, but Todd shrugged jauntily as he reached for another tortilla. "We'll give them a mighty good run for their money. If Sibley wins the showdown in northeastern New Mexico, he can turn on the California column General Carleton's put together out in Los Angeles."

He went on to say why Col. Baylor had been relieved of his command. Jefferson Davis had been horrified at an order sent by Baylor to Capt. Thomas Helm, commander of the Arizona Guards in Tucson.

"Governor Baylor said to lure the Apaches in with whiskey and gifts as if to make peace and then kill all the adults." Talitha gasped sharply and put out a hand to James, whose eyes blazed. The lieutenant, sopping up meat juices, didn't notice. "The children were to be sold to pay for the expense of killing their parents. A nasty business. Helm never acted on it, thank heaven!"

After the lieutenant went his way with a gift of ten steers that Talitha thought Shea would want her to make, she sought out her brother, who was holding K'aak'eh on his swaddled arm and staring at the mountains.

She said gently, "James, Baylor lost his command."

"You gave those soldiers beef."

"Yes. Out of my animals."

"Once you said some of those were mine."

"As many as you need."

"Next winter, then, in the hungry time for my people, I want to take them thirty or forty or fifty head. If they can eat, maybe they won't raid so much."

Talitha certainly didn't love Apaches, but she was sickened by the thought of cold-blooded slaughter of the sort Baylor and a good many others advocated. "The cattle are yours," she told her brother. "James, if the Apaches would stop raiding, the soldiers wouldn't bother them."

"Tally, my sister, you know that isn't true. They'd be killed for their reputations, as has already happened with those who tried to keep peace in New Mexico. Besides, if they don't raid, they starve."

"They've got to learn to grow their food."

With a harsh laugh, James said to the hawk who watched him with unblinking golden eyes, "You hear that, K'aak'eh? Will you till the soil with your talons, drop seed with your beak?"

In a wave of despairing fear and anger Talitha cried, "James! Men have brains. They can change and choose. Even Apaches . . ."

"Though they aren't quite human?" James finished smoothly. "They should be grateful for a bit of earth when they've roamed and ruled most of what you call New Mexico, Arizona, and Sonora?" He offered a squirming mouse to the hawk, settling it on the granary roof to tear and devour its prey. "For nearly three hundred years Apaches have fought Spaniards, Mexicans, Papago, Pima, and sometimes Navajo. You know that while the bluecoat soldiers were here they could do nothing."

"But when they come again, it'll be different." Talitha caught her brother's sinewy brown hands. "James, you know it'll be different."

He looked past her into the mountains. "I know," he said at last. "But that can't make a difference to me."

He wouldn't look at her at all. At last she had to leave him with the hawk and the wind.

VI

Talitha woke one April morning to music and listened in drowsy pleasure for a moment till she recognized the song, the voice, the day. She was twenty-two; and Güero was singing "*Las Mañanitas*" for her, "The Beautiful Little Mornings."

"I wish I were a sunbeam to enter your window
To wish you good morning, lying in your bed . . ."

Talitha got up quickly. Impossible to lie there with his singing on her as light as the air and as inescapable, as enveloping.

Sewa and Cat were still sleeping. Talitha covered them both, smiling at the way Cat lay, like a swimmer collapsed in the middle of a stroke. She sleeps violently, Talitha thought and wondered what life would bring this girl, who loved violently, too. Sewa, in contrast, was curled in a ball, knuckles pressed to her rosy mouth. She'd be two years old in July, the sweetest age for children. If only Santiago could have seen her! Glancing back at Cat, Talitha realized that neither little girl could remember a mother. Of course, she'd done her best to act as one. She was sure she couldn't love her own children more.

For a moment she allowed herself the luxury of

imagining what her children and Shea's would be like. Surely there'd be one boy with red-gold hair and eyes the darkest blue of the sky. She smiled at the imaginary child, then sighed. Sometimes she thought she'd never have children of her own. Here she was, twenty-two! And yet, beginning when she was six, with James, she'd been a mother all her life.

Güero was surely gone by now. A glance through the window showed the small courtyard empty. She stepped out into the bright morning and started as Güero stepped from behind the pomegranate tree by the window. He bowed, hair the color of tarnished raw gold tumbling over his forehead.

"Let me be the first, *señorita,* to wish you a happy birthday."

She was sorry that he was, but there was nothing for it but to thank him perfunctorily. As she moved swiftly toward the kitchen Güero easily matched her stride. "I've been breaking that pretty little chestnut mare the *señorita* remarked on, gentling her for a lady. Perhaps it would please you to try her this afternoon?"

Hc addressed her with the formal *Usted,* your grace, as was proper, but his tone couldn't have been more familiar had he used the intimate *tu,* thou.

Talitha had already planned her private celebration. She'd go in the warm part of the day to the hot spring below the Place of Skulls, wash her hair, and have a long, luxurious soak in the hollowed stone that formed a deep natural tub, constantly renewed by the sparkling water bubbling out of the cliff. She had liked the dainty chestnut mare, thinking her like Castaña, Socorro's horse, who was her grandmother. But the knowledge that Güero had been taming the filly made her speak almost rudely.

"I'm too busy to ride today. Thousand thanks for your trouble, but I've decided that mare doesn't suit me. When I need to spare Ceniza, I'll use that black gelding, Azufre, that Belen's been working."

Güero stiffened. "The *señorita* prefers geldings?" he asked in a soft, scornful voice.

Talitha slashed back. "It's not for you, vaquero, to question my preferences."

His mouth twisted. He stepped in front of her, blocking her way. "But I must, *señorita.* Tell me plainly, *por favor.* Is it that you will not ride with me, this day or any day?"

"I will ride with you when we are working cattle."

"But not alone, for company?"

"No."

He colored hotly. Sorry for his humiliation, warned by instinct that to flout this man was dangerous, Talitha tried to soften the refusal. "It wouldn't be proper. I am engaged."

"Engaged?" Clearly, he didn't believe her. "To whom?"

"To Don Patricio."

"The *patrón?* Your foster father?" The green eyes narrowed, the handsome face turned ugly. "If you must lie to me, *señorita,* do better than that!"

"It's true! We agreed the night before he left."

"And he was drunk, perhaps?" Güero spat near Talitha's feet. "I've heard no whisper of such a thing! Everyone knows the *patrón* loves only that dead one on the hill."

"All the same, when he comes back, we'll marry."

"That old man?"

"Even if he were old, I'd choose him over anyone in the world. Now that you understand, *por favor* let me pass."

He did so, bowing ironically. "Yes, *señorita.* Finally, I understand." He spun on his heel and strode off with a jangling of his sunburst-roweled spurs.

That beginning left a taint on the day, though Talitha was touched by the handkerchiefs Cat had laboriously embroidered for her with her brand, T, and by her other gifts. From James and the twins there were a dozen new arrows, and from the ranch families buckskin trousers and vest, fringed and ornamented with silver conchos.

These were bestowed after the noon meal. A few hours later, while the sun was still high, Talitha took her new clothes and some powdered orris root, telling Carmencita she was going to the hot springs.

"Is that safe?" worried the older woman.

Talitha laughed. "Nothing can happen to me on my birthday!" She gave the plump, motherly woman a hug. "I'll take my weapons and be back before dark. I'm just so tired of taking quick little baths in the tub!"

"It's enough to bathe on Saint John's day," Carmencita grumbled.

Talitha grinned. "Not if you've been working cattle."

For weeks she and the men had been riding the expanses of the ranch to see how the cattle had wintered, treat any screwworms, and help young heifers who might have trouble dropping first calves. With a kiss for Carmencita, she went out to the corral and whistled up Ceniza, giving the ash-gold mare a piece of bread and rubbing her velvety muzzle before saddling her. Ladorada, this mare's mother and Talitha's first beloved horse, was eighteen now, retired to graze. Chusma, the cat Santiago had brought from California, matriarch of the dozens of cats that routed mice and snakes from around the ranch, was ten. That was the sad thing about loving animals. Their lives were so short beside a human being's. Even when they were colts or kittens, you knew you'd see them die.

Ceniza tossed her head and snorted at some rustle in the brush, a trait Shea had said she inherited from her grandmother Castaña. Her rather melancholy trend of thought checked by the persistence of a mischievous spirit, Talitha sent the mare into an easy lope, watered her at the creek, and after a half hour's ride unsaddled her to graze, hobbled, in a grassy meadow, while

Talitha made her way up the narrowing cañon, over rocks and boulders washed down by heavy rains.

This was the dry season and there was only a trickle of water flowing along the watercourse. New leaves were coming out and wild cherry was starting to blossom. A gray fox vanished like a shadow into a hackberry thicket, and the red-tailed hawks soared in their dizzying circles while a bluejay chattered saucily at an acorn.

Drinking in the fresh new smells of spring with the underlying scent of dead leaves and pungent pine and cedar, Talitha reveled in the dappling of sun that managed to reach her through the trees, feeling how good it was to be alive. When she undressed and climbed into the big rock basin, she shut her eyes and lay back, lulled by the warm water, the sound of it gurgling out of the rocks above.

All her fears and worries seemed to loosen and float over the basin's edge. Sun kissed her through the glimmering ripples. Wonderful to have unlimited amounts of heated clean water, room enough to stretch out full length and let the water lap against your chin.

This was a special place to Talitha. She'd found it herself when she was thirteen. Although the Place of Skulls where the scalp hunters had whitened lay in a grassy little park not more than half a mile onward, and though this had been where she'd first met Judah Frost, these unpleasant memories weighed little beside the many refreshing baths and hair-washings she'd had here.

Sitting up, Talitha rubbed the powdered orris root into her hair, making suds. They made their own soap at the ranch with wood ash and fat, but it was harsh yellow biting stuff, and Talitha feared it might be bad for wild creatures to drink. The orris root left no traces when its bubbles dissipated, and it was used by both Indians and Mexicans.

When her hair was so clean it squeaked, she stood up

and shook it about her, fanning it with her hands till it started to dry. Then she washed her body.

As she touched her breasts, she thought, with a pang, of Shea. Would he remember at all that it was her birthday, or was he in a situation where such things didn't matter? Shutting her eyes, she tried to reach him with her thoughts, tell him how she loved him, make him think of her, see her as she was now.

Holding out her arms, offering herself, she murmured softly, "Shea. Oh, my dear love—"

"He can't hear you, but I can."

She froze, then started to reach for her clothes as Güero stepped out of the manzanitas but checked when she realized she couldn't get to them. Disdaining the frantic impulse to at least try to cover herself with her hands, she threw her hair back and stared at him. She had often quelled a devilish horse by showing no fear and speaking steadily. That was all she knew to do now with the man who came toward her, eyes like green flame.

"You were to comb the southern bounds of the El Charco *sitio* today. Go back to your work and I will pardon your discourtesy. No doubt you saw my horse and wished to be sure I was safe."

He made a dismissing motion with his hand. "The time for nonsense—and singing—is past, *señorita.*"

His avid gaze ran over her. She could see the pulse hammering in his temples, the whitening groove behind his nostrils. "I've tried to woo you, to have you in sweetness. Since you've spurned that, I'll have you as I can."

Another long step brought him within reach of her. His sweaty male odor was strong and frightening. It took all of Talitha's will not to run, to try futilely to escape.

"If you touch me, your own brother will help hunt you down."

"That fool Tivi? What do I care for him, or old monkey-face Pedro, who got horns from my French father?" Güero deliberately cupped her breasts, stroking the nipples with his thumbs. "How white you are where you're hidden from the sun! I've always wanted a white woman, but those I had in California were whores."

"So would anyone be who slept with you."

His lips peeled back over square white teeth. "Is that what you'll say of yourself when you hold me in your arms?"

"I never will."

His hands ran along her waist, curved over her thighs and belly. "But you will, *patronita.*" His eyes smiled into hers. "For you won't let the Socorro go the way of the San Patricio miners' camp."

She was already numb with horror, but as she slowly understood him she felt encased in freezing, immobilizing ice. "You—you were with the bandits?"

"More. I led them. It's a loose gang, scattering around Sonora between raids, but it wouldn't take me long to gather them, and plenty more." He kissed first one breast, then the other, sucking hurtingly as he caressed her flank, all the time watching her. "You could hold us off a day or two, but the end would be the same."

Her mind dodged this way and that. "What's your proposition?"

"You will name me foreman, I will be your lover, and all will be safe and serene at Rancho del Socorro."

"Your family," she said wonderingly. "Your mother, who loves you so. Do they mean nothing?"

"Less than nothing. I hate them for stupid Mexicans who were diddled by a Frenchman. I hate that Frenchman, too, for causing me such a life out of an hour's amusement."

Sickened for Carmencita, who, taking for granted her dutiful children, had loved this one best, grieved for Pedro, who'd been a father to him though he knew the truth, Talitha said coldly, "And if I don't make you foreman?"

"I'll take you away with me now, gather my comrades, destroy the ranch, and keep you as long as I choose." Reflectively he added, "One of our men fancies young girls. He'd let Caterina and Paulita live a little while."

She had to kill him, that was all. Had to find some way. Her rifle leaned against the boulder where her clothes were spread, and there were her bow and arrows, tantalizingly close; yet even if she could reach them, no use unless she could put a little distance between herself and Güero.

"I'll have you now," he said, laughing as he swept her into his arms. "Perhaps seeing how much man I am will help you decide."

She already had. She must agree to make him foreman, agree to be his woman, and then, when he wasn't expecting it, kill him. Belen would help her sneak the body to some place where it would never be found. Better for Carmencita to think her son had drifted off in his erratic way than to know the truth about him.

It was no use to fight. She would not give him that satisfaction. But when he tossed her clothes on the ground and lowered her upon them, pressing her down while he worked at his own clothes, the dread she'd kept at bay exploded. Kicking, writhing, she buried her teeth in his wrist and hung on as he swore. A blow loosed her hold, sent the world dark for a second. He was opening her mouth with his, forcing her knees apart.

A meaty thud, grinding on bone. A warm torrent drenched her. Red. Red everywhere, in her mouth, her nose, her eyes. She coughed, then struggled aside as Güero collapsed, blood pumping in jets from the side of his neck.

She looked up into the chill silver eyes of Judah Frost. But he was dead! She shut her eyes. He was still there when she looked up, cleaning the edge of a small ax before he tucked it into his belt. His thick silver hair gleamed, and as he stooped beside her she could see the black whisker stubs on his close-shaven jaw and chin.

"What, my darling?" He smiled, though no warmth lit those wintry eyes. "No thanks for rescuing you?"

"You—you— They found your body along the Devil's Road."

He shook his smooth head. "*A* body. Some prospector the Areneños had already waylaid. Roasting his head so his face charred was ingenious, wasn't it? He was about my build and my clothes fit. A shame I had to kill Selim, though, to clinch the identification. That was a fine horse."

The former scalp hunter had no doubt had more qualms about killing his valuable mount than in slaughtering women and children at Santiago's former home and in Tjúni's village.

Stunned, Talitha lay there, heedless of her nakedness, the dead man's blood drying on her. The brief fear she'd had of Güero was nothing compared to the horror she'd felt for this man since the time she'd met him, here, at this very spot, nine years ago.

"Full circle, love. When I saw your horse in the meadow, I was delighted to think we could have so poetical a reunion." He grimaced at the slumped figure of the dead man. "Then I found his horse a little way up the cañon and I did you wrong, Talitha. I thought you had a lover. However, what I heard pass between you corrected that notion. Now, my sweet, wash that hideous mess away and give me thanks and a proper welcome."

She might have known he was alive. The devil never dies. She felt unable to move, unable to accept his reappearance.

"Get up," he said impatiently. "You'll have to wash your hair again, too."

"Why have you come back?"

"Now, why do you think?"

She moaned and turned away, hiding her face. It was

as if time had turned back a year and he were going to rape her in that shallow arroyo west of Pete Kitchen's ranch. She shrank away from him and tried to cling to the ground as he lifted her.

"I'm fastidious, my dear. You'll have to cleanse yourself before I kiss you."

He set her in the basin. When she only stared at him dully, he made a smothered sound of exasperation and splashed her face, throat, and shoulders, then forced her head down and rinsed her hair.

"There, that's better." He pulled her petticoat from beneath Güero's knees and dried her as much as possible. Slowly he drew her against him, set his hand at the back of her head, and lowered his mouth to hers.

It was like being enveloped by dark, heavy water, deprived of air and light. She could not see or feel or smell anything but him. He was filling her senses, drugging them.

Suddenly, amazingly, he let her go, supporting her when she would have fallen. "We have plenty of time." The words, when she comprehended them, struck at something vulnerable beneath her frozen shield. "I don't want you when you have all the animation of a cedar post. Get dressed while I haul this carrion into the brush."

Before he tugged at Güero, he got Talitha's weapons and kept them with him. "An enterprising man," he said regretfully, returning from dragging the body into a tangle of hackberry. "I could have used him if he hadn't wanted you so badly."

"You have much in common," Talitha agreed, scrubbing blood from her skirt before she slipped it on over the damp petticoat. She was beginning to recover, to see Frost as an actual man, not an almost eerie superhuman. "You both have killed harmless, helpless people and have enjoyed inflicting yourselves on women who don't want you."

"I assure you that's not my usual pattern," Frost said, unmoved. "Most of my women are all too willing.

They cloy, like Leonore, my poor, lamented wife. Perhaps that's why you've been an obsession with me since I met you as a spitfire child."

She didn't answer, a great helplessness washing over her as he kicked dust over the dark, soaked earth. Shea was gone, and Marc. Who could help her against this man? She knew him too well to hope he'd come back without some means of bending her to his will. He motioned in front of him and waited till she started down the rocky way.

"What are you going to do?" she asked.

"Why, my love, I'm going to take you home. By the way, do you want that body found?"

Talitha winced as she thought of Carmencita and rejected the impulse to let Güero's disappearance remain a mystery. It would be best, probably, if the mother knew her idolized son would never be able to return to her, if she gradually healed and turned that wasted, tragic love on her good children and grandchildren. "Yes," she told Frost. "Better he's found, or at least his horse goes home without him."

So, when they reached Güero's horse, Frost quickly searched the belongings tied behind the silver-mounted saddle, took out a leather bag full of gold and silver, and appropriated the rifle before he slipped the bridle off the animal and gave it a slap on the flanks.

"Now it'll look like murder for robbery. I'll hide the rifle till I'm going somewhere where it can be sold."

"Everyone at the ranch knows you killed Santiago and kidnaped me," Talitha said. "Even if I wanted to protect you, which I don't, Belen, for one, would kill you."

"For Belen's sake, I hope he won't try," Frost said gently. "Now listen, Talitha, while I explain why you're going to marry me and why your precious ranch people had better be glad you are." His next words sliced into her derisive laugh. "The Confederates won the battle at Glorieta Pass southeast of Santa Fe late in March. But some Coloradans under a Bible-thumping preacher,

Major Chivington, burned the Reb supply trains and bayoneted hundreds of horses and mules. An army can't fight without food. Sibley's on the run for Texas, and so, if he's alive, is your Irishman."

As Talitha stared, Frost said brusquely, "Of course I stopped in Tucson to learn what I could. You might have shown some sense and moved in there. But no. I heard that Shea had gone off a year ago to get in some licks at the government that branded him years ago, and that, at Pete Kitchen's last report, you were forted up at the Socorro." His even, rather small white teeth flashed. "The Confederates are done for in Arizona and New Mexico, Tally. I was with the Union troops when Hunter's men were whipped a week ago at Picacho Peak near the Pima Villages. They'll have Tucson within a month, and you can bet that my good friend Colonel Carleton will declare martial law."

"Your friend?"

"The best. Because I know this country, he's relying on me to help him identify traitors."

Talitha remembered the Union men who had forfeited their property when Hunter banished them. "A traitor in this war," she said, "is just someone on the other side. And you, Judah Frost, you never had any side but your own."

"Which sends me to Dante's deepest hell, doesn't it?" He smiled at her approvingly. "That's better, darling. Anger puts color in your cheeks, which have been, till now, distressingly pale. But the point is that at a word from me Carleton can and will confiscate all that Shea owns. I'll buy it at a ridiculous price. Your defeated hero will come home to find himself as poor as he was when he left Ireland."

"He had even less, barely his life, when Socorro found him in the desert."

"And you think you could play Socorro to him?" Frost shook his gleaming head. "Shea's in his forties now. The war won't make him any younger. I'm astonished that you'd dream of letting him come home to the loss of all he's built up. Especially when you've braved Apaches and bandits to hang on." His mouth quirked and a dark eyebrow lifted. "Am I more fearful to you than Apaches, Tally?"

She said nothing. The truth was that she feared him more than death, more than torture, more than anything she'd seen Apaches do. He threatened what her mother and Socorro would have called her soul.

Amused, Frost probed deeper. "I think we can assume that I daunt you more than all the Pinals, Coyoteros, Mimbreños, and Chiricahuas combined. But, on a more personal note, would you have preferred that golden-haired half-breed to me?"

"Yes!" she said without hesitation.

"Oh?" The brow above those gray-silver eyes furrowed. "Can it be you had a tenderness for him that led to his violent declaration this afternoon?"

"No. But I'd rather him than you." Exhausted by this cat-and-mouse game, she confronted him as they reached their horses. "I'd rather anyone than you—the grossest, filthiest bandit, the cruelest Apache!"

His smile faded. He threw her down. Though she remembered that he needed resistance to keep him potent, she couldn't stop fighting, struggling in panic, throwing her body one way and the other, till at last, clamping her with knees and hands, he took her savagely. When he fell away, he lay with his arm over her, breathing heavily.

"You feel close to virgin," he said at last. "Almost as you were when I took you for the first time. Can it be there's no one else?"

Aching, poisonously soiled by his spilling within her, Talitha knew that, strangely, she had the power to hurt Frost and took bitter comfort in doing so now.

"After you had me, I got another man to make love to me as fast as I could. Often. I had to get rid of the feel of you."

"Now I wonder who that was?" The look on his face as he raised himself on an elbow made her wish she hadn't taunted him. He must never know about Shea, and she didn't want him to suspect Marc, either.

"He's gone," she said wearily.

"One of the officers? That redheaded surgeon who was always paying you court?"

She shook her head. "John was just a friend."

"Well, if he's gone, it scarcely matters," Frost said, offering her a surprisingly clean handkerchief as he rearranged his clothes.

When Talitha had cleaned herself the best she could, he helped her into the saddle, then got on his own horse, a beautiful light gold creature with a mane as silvery as its owner's hair. Even in her misery Talitha admired it.

"What's it to be, Tally?" In the setting sun, on his pale horse, Frost in his severe, cold beauty looked like an angel of death. "Will you let Carleton confiscate the Socorro and the mine, or will you take me home and explain that, whether those who remember Santiago like it or not, I'm the only person who can save their home?" Reading her mind, he laughed softly. "No, love, it won't serve to have me quietly ambushed. I left a list of prosperous rebels with the colonel's adjutant, to be opened and acted on in case of my death. Guess whose name ranks even higher than Sylvester Mowry's, that ex–West Pointer with his Patagonia mine?"

"Even so, I think Belen will kill you."

"Not if you explain things properly. That Yaqui adores you. He'll place your present good above revenge, though I don't doubt he'll hope to finish me when times are more auspicious."

"Tjúni knows you were with the scalp hunters who killed her people. She owns her land, the San Manuel *sitio,* and she'd probably even be glad if Shea lost the rest of the ranch."

"Love turned to hate?" Frost grinned. "It's a pity to dash your hopes, but I stopped by San Manuel on my way here. They had just buried Tjúni. Seems she slipped and broke her neck up in the mountains."

"Did you—?"

He spread his hand like a man greatly put upon. "You'd like to blame me for everyone that dies, but that's hardly realistic, my dear. I won't deny, though, that I went there meaning to make sure that woman would make me no trouble."

Poor little Cinco, more so than the other children, for they had a living father. Talitha would have to get over as soon as possible and see if there was anything she could do.

Though she'd never liked Tjúni, the Papago woman had demanded respect. She had been one of the all-powerful adults of Talitha's childhood. Knowledge of her death brought shock, a sense of loss. Of the four who'd begun the ranch, only Shea lived. Could she let him come back to find it gone, his faithful vaqueros scattered, the graves of Santiago and Socorro neglected?

"What is it you want?" she asked Frost.

"You. For good, for my wife."

"That could hardly be for good."

"For life, then, let's say." He was unruffled.

"I can stay at the ranch? Look after the children?"

"If I said no, that'd end our chance of a bargain, wouldn't it?"

"Yes. The children matter more than the ranch."

"Then you may stay with them for the foreseeable future. I have business to attend to all the way from Los Angeles to St. Louis. It would be difficult for you to travel with me even if you longed to." He laughed.

"And when Shea comes home?"

"You and I will remove to one of my properties. I swear that I won't kill him unless he forces it." Frost touched her cheek. "Take heart, my love. With great luck, he might make you a widow."

She looked at this man who had stalked her since she was thirteen and now, at last and finally, had her trapped. "I'll pray for that."

His eyes dilated for a moment, black spreading over

the crystalline pupils. "Out of all the women I've known, I wonder why it's you I must have? When I saw you first in Mangus's camp you couldn't have been more than six, but even then I knew it."

"You probably wanted my scalp."

"Have a care, Tally. I'm not always amused by your tongue." He gave her the bow, arrows, and rifle, knowing she dare not use them. "Well? Do we go to the ranch and tell the good people our happy news?"

With an effort, she pulled herself erect and turned Ceniza toward the ranch.

PART II

Shea

1862

VII

There had been Valverde, the Texans Shea commanded yelling like fiends as they charged through grape and canister with double-barreled fowling pieces and revolvers. After the Yanks retreated to Fort Craig, there was a truce while both sides buried their dead in the trampled, bloody sand beside the Rio. A Confederate victory, even though General Sibley halfway through the battle had been "sick" and gone to an ambulance behind the lines, where, it was suspected, he treated his ailment with more of its alcoholic cause.

He'd decided not to besiege Fort Craig—the Yanks had hoaxed them finely with those painted log cannon! So they'd rushed up the river to Albuquerque, short on supplies, to find the Unionists gone and most of the matériel destroyed by the quartermaster. Lucky they were able to get medicine, arms, and three thousand rounds of ammunition out of the federal depot at Cubero.

If we'd had enough supplies, Shea thought, stumbling through a rocky cañon, trying to encourage his thirsty, starving men. Lack of fodder, food, and ammunition, not enemy fire, had defeated the Confederates in New Mexico. When they'd pushed on to Santa Fe, thinking that seizure of the federal stores there would save them, they found the Union quartermaster had sent his two hundred and fifty thousand dollars' worth of supplies to Fort Union and burned the vacated storage buildings before the whole Union force retreated to the fort. "Poor New Mexico!" the people said. "So far from heaven, so close to Texas!"

A reeling boy whose blistered feet would carry him no farther sank down in a heap, lank hair plastered with sweat to his freckled forehead. Couldn't have been more than a few years older than the twins. Poor kid, when he'd volunteered it must have seemed high adventure to him, glorious to fight for the South.

But after the flush of occupying Mesilla and the victory at Valverde, there'd followed that long spring marching up the Rio, not enough forage for either horses or men, few reinforcements, rumors of a big army coming from California and another heading down from Colorado.

It was those blamed Pikes Peakers who'd doomed the Confederate cause in New Mexico, sneaking around to destroy the supply train and kill those horses and mules. Crippled without supplies, there'd been nothing to do but retreat. They'd veered west of the Rio to cut through the San Mateo Mountains where they'd be less harassed by the Federals. Here they'd had to abandon everything they couldn't carry through the rugged gaps and passes; and though it hadn't happened yet, Shea knew that soon the lame and wounded would be abandoned, too.

He knelt by the boy and shook him. "Come on, son. I'll help you."

Tears streaked the young, sunburned face. "Cap'n, I . . . I cain't. Feet's plumb raw."

"Want those Dog Canyon Apaches to get your hair?"

Fear opened the blue eyes. "Lord Jesus, Cap'n! Got to be scalped, druther it was by Comanches! They're Texas Indians, anyways!"

"Get up, then. Here, put your arm around me."

And so they walked, Shea supporting most of the lad's weight, thinking grimly that it was a good thing the kid was starved down or he couldn't have held him up. Had he cared to hang around Sibley, he'd have got more food, maybe even a horse to replace the one shot under him at Glorieta; but though Shea had done his share of heavy drinking, he had no use for a general who stayed so drunk that he couldn't lead his men or plan for them.

Shea had already been at the rear to urge on the flagging, while Lt. Rip Harris exhorted from the front of their company's remnant. Rip was sound. If anything happened to Shea, he'd keep the men moving.

Poor Rip. He'd have to leave the ones who couldn't walk anymore, leave them in order to save the rest. Shea wasn't brave enough to do that. Duties and command be damned, he couldn't leave this boy, or any man, to the Apaches.

The scarecrow clinging to him kept buckling at the knees. Shea stopped and gave the young soldier the last of his water. They were far behind the others. The clear cold knowledge came to Shea that only a miracle could get them out of this, and his miracle, Socorro, was dead.

Still, you went on as long as you could. You tried. As he plodded on, now mostly carrying the boy, he thought of Talitha.

He sucked in his breath. In the play of light on pitiless rock and barren earth he saw the shine of her hair, the brilliance of her eyes.

With a wrenching of his guts, he remembered her sweetness that last wild night, her soft warmth that changed to tremulous ecstasy, the passionate tenderness he'd never dreamed he could feel again after Socorro.

Not that it was the same. Socorro had been his soul. But Talitha was a rare woman.

Scarred in heart and body, twice her age, he didn't deserve her love, but he hadn't been able to make her see that. He'd begun to think maybe he could make a new life with her, since she was set on it. But he knew he'd be using her flame, drawing on her youth and spirit. Maybe it was best he wouldn't be going home. He had a letter for her in his pocket. Should have given it to Rip. Too late to think of that now. She'd mourn him, of course she would, but she'd turn to someone like Marc Revier or John Irwin, a man who could love her with all his soul and heart, worship her with his body, as Shea had done with Socorro.

The soldier was almost deadweight now. Shea tried to talk to him, but his mouth was so dry his tongue seemed to fill it. Thirsty. So thirsty. But not yet like that time in the desert, when he'd torn off his clothes and scratched with broken fingernails at rock shadows, thinking they were water. His spirit had left his tormented body, hovered over the pitiful wreck that kept crawling, though the blood was so thick it didn't even ooze from the gashes and cuts, and the skin was baked to the bones like shrunken rawhide.

Funny. This boy looked a lot like Michael. Michael, his twin, who'd died in the desert. "Come on, lad," Shea urged. "One step at a time. Come on, now."

But the boy wasn't moving his feet at all. Shea got him over his shoulders and staggered onward. The other men were out of sight. Good man, Rip. Keep 'em moving. Get them back to Texas. But I've got to stop a minute. Got to rest.

He was lowering the kid to the ground when fire stabbed through his shoulder. An arrowhead thrust out beneath his collarbone.

Impatient, were they!

Rolling the boy behind a ledge, Shea didn't take time to struggle with the arrow. Sighting at the red of what he thought was a headcloth behind a clump of brush, he fired his revolver. The headcloth seemed to drop. He fired at a moving branch, got off his other shots, loaded the Sharps, and waited.

Nothing. But even if he'd got that one, there were

surely others. He had a little more fight in him than they'd expected. Rather than get hurt, they'd wait him out.

That damned arrow . . . He broke out in sweat, nauseated from the pain. He got out his knife, trying to cut off the head. There was an explosion between his shoulders, tearing through him. Blood bubbled in his throat. In his last conscious motion, he shielded the boy with his body.

The sun fragmented into darkness. Then it was light again, shining and luminous. He heard a voice that for years he'd heard only in dreams and looked up to see Socorro.

Young, beautiful, smiling, she was coming toward him, hands outstretched, holding a flagon. "Redhead burro!" she scolded. "I thought you'd never come!"

She offered the water, cool and crystal. He leaned his head against her breast and drank.

PART III

The Silver Man

1862–1863

VIII

Judah Frost stayed only a few days at Rancho del Socorro. He behaved with circumspection to Talitha in front of others but commanded her to give him pleasure in his bed at night. Since this was Shea's bed, in his room, at first Talitha thought she couldn't bear it; but as she lay waking that first night, shamed and hopeless, she seemed to feel Shea's presence, a strengthening comfort, not a reproach. That sense persisted, gave her endurance. It was as if Shea somehow knew what she was doing for him and was supporting her with his love.

It turned out that Frost didn't need her struggles to arm him to take her. He could become brutally potent by watching her in the lamplight as he caressed her, brushing her nipples to a point with his hands, making her move involuntarily; or he would whisper obscenities, or make her fondle him.

He was a skilled womanizer. After his rape of her over a year ago, Marc's loving had healed that ugliness, taught her delight—and there had been Shea. No matter how she hated Frost, her roused and hungry body began to respond to him in spite of her outraged mind and heart.

"Soon you're going to fly apart," he murmured, stroking her throat, smiling as she quivered when he teased her breasts with teeth and tongue. "I'll feel it when you do, like a fountain of glowing rosy sparks. It's bound to happen, sweet. Why don't you let it?"

She moved her head in angry denial, but as he laughed and took her slowly, sensually, pausing to make her feel to the utmost the pulsing hardness within her, she knew despairingly that it was only a matter of time till that urgency building inside her had to explode.

"I know," he taunted softly. "You'd rather I fell on you with the finesse of a starving wolf on meat. Then you could loathe me with complete integrity, righteously count yourself my victim. But that's not how I want you, Talitha. You're going to belong to me. First your body, then your soul."

She shut her eyes against the shine of him, silver eyes, silver hair, and again she thought him a fallen angel, radiantly evil, a servant of death.

The evening he'd escorted her home, Frost had waited till all the vaqueros were at the supper table. Then he'd told them, in his excellent Spanish, that only his protection could save the ranch from confiscation. "Those of you who bear me a grudge from the past," he said, with a limpid glance at the tight-lipped Belen, "had better put it aside for the sake of your *patrón* and his children. It's true I killed Santiago, but he would have killed me if I hadn't, and there are two sides to what befell him in Sonora. He accompanied me there with the intent of murdering me, and I simply acted before he could."

"Shooting a man is one thing," growled Belen. "But you carried off Señorita Scott." Only Shea and Marc knew Frost had done more than that.

"It saved more killing, didn't it?" returned Frost easily. "The *señorita* was my hostage, but, as I promised, I let her go. Ask her and she'll tell you that only I can keep Don Patricio from losing all he has."

Inquiring eyes swung to Talitha: Belen's angry,

Pedro's troubled, Carmencita's bewildered, the vaqueros' confused. Amazingly, it was James whose gaze locked with Frost's.

"You killed my godfather," he said. "If my sister asks it, I will not kill you now. But I will someday."

Frost only laughed. "You're the Apache cub. Thanks for the warning. But perhaps you'll relent and spare your brother-in-law."

"Brother-in-law?" choked James.

Belen half rose. "What's this, *madama?*"

"It's the bargain." Talitha kept her voice even, but she looked at Carmencita, not her brother or Belen. "Unless I marry Mr. Frost, Shea's name will be given to the Union commander as a Southern sympathizer whose land should be forfeited." She shook her head at a sudden gleam in Chuey's eyes. "No, Chuey. If Frost is killed, he's arranged for someone else to turn Shea in. I'll marry him, and we'll keep the ranch for Shea. I implore you all not to worry about me. I know what I'm doing."

Frost smiled into the hostile heavy silence, the averted faces, James's undisguised hatred, the fascinated stares of the twins and Caterina.

After he had possessed Talitha that night, he lay on his back and said amusedly, "My visits here will be diverting, love. Seldom have I felt such concentrated waves of enmity, especially from your young brother! Most gratifying to know they can't do a thing without ruining my old partner, whom they love as much as they detest me."

"Don't poke fun at James."

"How can I resist? He glares at me with those lapis-lazuli eyes in that Apache face and I want to teach him what he is."

"He's my brother. If you hurt him—"

He closed her mouth with his.

Güero's horse had come in during the night. His brothers, Chuey and Natividad, followed its tracks to where it had been left along the mountain. They hadn't been able to track him over the rocks, but coyotes had been at work, and as they circled the area Chuey found a gnawed arm. They soon discovered what was left of the rest. They brought it home wrapped in a serape and put it in the ground, not allowing their distraught mother to look.

The burial was at El Charco. "When times are better, we'll be going back there to live," said Carmencita. "I want to be able to visit my son's grave. Ay, who did it? Apaches or robbers, may God destroy them!"

Frost accompanied Talitha to the Sanchez home and listened with a smooth face while Pedro said the prayers he could remember and Carmencita sobbed in Talitha's arms. Anita and Juana wept, too, but Talitha suspected it was for their mother's grief more than for their brother.

"You might have had the decency not to come to the burial," Talitha told Frost later. "I'm surprised you weren't struck dead when you held Carmencita's hand and told her all those consoling things about his waiting in heaven!"

"They did console her. And you're a fine hypocrite yourself, Tally, going to the funeral of a man who damn near raped you!"

"I'd be delighted to attend yours."

"Would you, my sweet?" His eyes held hers. It was like gazing into ice frozen deep over dark waters. She went cold to the heart, though his kiss burned as he drew her into his arms.

When he left, saying he'd be back as soon as he'd tended to various pressing business matters, Talitha felt as if she'd been holding her breath and now could breathe again. She slept again in her own bed, and if it hadn't been for Carmencita's woe, she could have believed that everything that had happened from the moment Güero approached her at the hot spring till Frost rode away had been a nightmare.

As soon as she could, she rode to San Manuel,

accompanied by the twins, Cat, and James. Tjúni's husband, a heavy, tall Papago with a broad, kindly face, spoke a little Spanish. An aged female relative was cooking for him and his brood. Cinco scampered about with his half brothers and sister, obviously accepted as one of them; but when he saw Cat, he stopped playing to watch her, then ran inside the mud-daubed house and returned with a willow whistle.

This he handed to Cat, smiling shyly. She jumped down from Mancha and kissed him, looking at Talitha over his head, for she was several inches the taller. "Can't we take him home, Tally? He *is* my brother!"

"That would not be a good thing, Caterina." James spoke sternly. "Cinco may be half your brother in blood, but in soul he is Papago."

Does he think I shouldn't have taken him away from the Apaches? Talitha thought with indignation. *Why, those women of Juh's would have let him starve! And he was fine at the ranch, would have grown up white if only he hadn't felt to blame for Socorro's dying and gone off with that damned old Mangus!*

Because she didn't like what he was saying, Cat stuck out her pointed tongue at James and looked beseechingly at Talitha, who shook her head.

"We can't just whisk him away, dear. But I'll tell his foster father that Cinco has a home with us if he ever wants it. Maybe when he's older he can visit us sometimes."

Or perhaps when Shea came back he could make the acquaintance of this son Tjúni had resentfully kept from him. Not that Talitha blamed the Papago woman much for that. Tjúni must have loved Shea all those years he was married to Socorro. After her death, when he finally took Tjúni to his bed, it was no wonder she'd hoped he'd marry her, though she'd apparently undertaken that there'd be no children. And after Cinco was born, when Shea still refused to make her his wife, no wonder Tjúni had angrily departed with her child to her part of the ranch.

Thwarted, Cat glared for a moment at her brothers, Talitha, and James before her eye lit on Mancha. "James," she said sweetly, "please, will you help Cinco up behind me? I'll take him for a little ride."

James shrugged and did as she asked, glad enough to humor her. By the time they returned, Talitha and Tjúni's husband and his aunt had exhausted all they could say to each other. Saying good-bye with mutual relief, they shook hands gravely all around, and Cat kissed Cinco. As they rode off she kept turning to wave at him. Only when they passed out of view behind a slope did she glance triumphantly at Talitha.

"He loved riding Mancha. All they have in the village are burros."

Talitha frowned. "So?"

"So he'll want to ride horses when he's older. He'll come to us and make *un gran vaquero.*"

"Cat," said Talitha sternly, "you can't mother everyone, and you mustn't play with people as if they were your dolls."

Cat tossed her shimmering black hair. "I haven't played with dolls for years, Tally! *Caray!* I'm almost nine!"

Laughing, she challenged James to a race, and as they dwindled to tiny dots against the mountains Talitha felt a chill. When James went back to the Apaches, it would break Cat's heart—and he would go back.

Apaches or bandits had thinned out the cattle on the eastern and southern ranges, but there was a good calf crop. It was to be hoped that the two thousand California volunteers, in addition to chasing out the Confederates, might bring some order and peace to the Santa Cruz region.

Meanwhile, the vaqueros, with Talitha and the boys, split as they had for the fall cow work, one group working near the ranch buildings in case of alarm, the other combing the remote areas, branding, earmarking, and castrating.

From now on through the hot months they'd have to keep a vigilant eye for screwworm, especially in the scrotums of newly castrated calves. Blowflies would lay their eggs in wounds, and within the day screwworms would be swarming in the injury. If such an infestation wasn't treated within a day or two, screwworms could burrow deeper and deeper into the flesh, feeding on the unlucky animal till it was terribly weakened or even dead.

The juice of black walnut hulls was a good treatment, but more often, when the animal was roped and tied, Talitha or a vaquero pulverized part of a dry cow chip and packed the wound tightly with it. If no air reached the worms, they'd suffocate, and the packing kept the sore protected until it scabbed over.

Talitha could rope and tie a calf, hold it down, or brand, but she left castrating and earmarking to the deft, experienced hands of the vaqueros. Every spring a few cows died in calving, and the orphans had to be brought back to the ranch and fed by hand unless the calf could be matched up with a cow who'd lost her own. Usually it worked to skin the dead calf and tie his hide over the motherless one. If the smell of her own baby convinced the cow that the hungry imposter was indeed hers, she'd let him suck and the problem was solved for both.

Talitha had helped with cattle work for about ten years, and slipping back into its rhythm after Frost's departure increased the feeling of unreality about his return. What was real was that during the summer if the tanks at El Charco went dry they had to be filled from the well, screwworms must be treated, orphaned calves looked after, and the bulls put on the ranges where they were needed.

Fall meant branding late-dropped calves and culling out the cattle that would be driven to market. By then, thank goodness, blowflies were gone.

In the winter, corrals were built or fixed, equipment made or mended, and horses broken, using the slower, gentler techniques that Shea had introduced from what he remembered of his father's rare way with horses. The range had to be ridden over to keep track of the cattle, of course, and then it was spring again, with the new little calves staggering up on their spindly legs and eagerly finding their mothers' warm milk.

Frost came back at the end of May. The familiar pattern snapped when Talitha saw the sheen of his pale golden horse coming along the creek one evening, accompanied by another horseman. He was alive, he was here. Reality was a nightmare again.

In that nightmare, they were married by the Reverend Esau Tranton, who was on his way to California and looked more like a brigand than a minister. He raised his heavy eyebrows when Talitha insisted that she didn't want anyone to witness the marriage, then shrugged and took another pull on his bottle.

"For the handsome consideration Mr. Frost has given me, ma'am, I'd splice you underground or on a mountain, wherever your heart desires." When Frost started for the *sala,* Talitha shook her head. Not in there, where Shea and Socorro had married, not where Guadalupana would look down at the mockery.

"Let's go outside," she said. "I—I'd like to be able to see the mountains."

"Most poetic," Tranton approved.

Frost's down-curved mouth hinted that he guessed her reason, but he gave her his arm with exquisite courtesy. The last of the sunset blazed crimson on them when the final words were said and Frost put on her finger a broad gold band studded with diamonds.

"Beautiful ring, that," said Tranton covetously.

To Talitha, it seemed to sear her flesh. This man, her husband? Truly, according to law? When, after he'd kissed her, he touched her cheek, it was like being caressed by a lion's claw that might at any second rip her bloody.

Tranton went his way next morning, and in a week Frost returned to Tucson, for he estimated his friend Colonel Carleton should arrive about then. Tucson was already in Union hands.

Sam Hughes, the merchant dispossessed by Captain Hunter for his Union sympathies, had returned with the Californians. Hunter, with his rangers and a few Southern sympathizers had left Tucson May 4. Don Esteban Ochoa, also a Union exile, was busily getting ready to freight for the army. Anyone with close ties to the Confederacy had either left with Hunter or refuged in Sonora, just as their Union counterparts had been forced to do that February.

"I've got my freighting company pretty well organized," Frost boasted. "Made a deal with Governor Pesqueira to haul from Guaymas duty free, so I can do it for five cents a pound to Tucson compared to 12½ cents from Yuma plus 3½ for the river steamer and $4 to ferry each wagon at Yuma. Fort Breckinridge has to be supplied, and there's bound to be another post established somewhere along the old Butterfield route toward New Mexico."

"I should think you'd be more inclined to waylay freight than haul it," Talitha said. They were alone and she didn't have to watch her tongue.

He laughed, unruffled. "Freight may not be glamorous, but there's a fortune in supplying troops in this godforsaken, Apache-bedeviled wilderness. After the war, there'll be lots of troops out here trying to tame the Indians, and once the heathens are settled on reservations, they'll have to be fed. More government contracts."

"That's all any of it is to you, isn't it? A chance to make money?"

"What does any man try to do? I'm simply more astute than most. For instance, I've heavily invested in railroads, so I won't be hurt when they supersede mule and ox freight." He smiled lazily. "Would you care to invest some of Shea's money in my freighting company, sweetheart? For old times' sake, I'd give him shares at advantageous terms."

"Shea wouldn't want to be mixed up with you. Besides, what happened to his interest in the freighting company in which he was partners with you?"

Frost shrugged. "The California assets of the Santa Cruz freighting company helped start my new venture, but since Shea, at my presumed death, got the income from the Tecolote mine where we were also partners, I figure we're even. Of course, now that I'm back, I'm reassuming my shares in the mine. I've already hired a superintendent to get it working again. It seems Revier, staunch freedom fighter that he is all these years after he and his idealistic friends defied the Prussian king and fought for general suffrage and liberty, had to throw himself into the battle against slavery."

How strange. Marc had construed the war like that, but to Shea the oppression had been on the part of the North. Shea hated slavery, too, having been close to it in Ireland, but to him the United States was a government that had first invaded Catholic Mexico to wrest away much of its land, and was now trying to bully the Southern states and hold them against their will. The war was many things to many people. For some, like Frost, it was a golden opportunity for fast profits, but men of substantial property on both sides had lost all that they had rather than swear allegiance to the enemy. Southern-born officers of equal conscience and integrity had chosen opposite sides when they'd finally been forced to it. It was an awful war.

"Didn't Revier stop to bid you farewell?" Frost questioned. "He always seemed to have a weakness for you, since the days when he rode over with books to teach you how to read and write."

Weakness? No, Marc had a strength for her. If Shea hadn't been first in her heart, she could have happily loved the young engineer; as it was, she loved him not so happily, knowing she hurt him and hating it.

Turning from Frost, she spoke without expression. "Yes, Mr. Revier stopped to say good-bye on his way to join the Union."

With mock sympathy, Frost probed one of her deepest fears. "What a pity if he and Shea had to fight each other. Much easier to kill men one doesn't know."

"I shouldn't think you'd find anything in that line difficult."

He grasped her hand and noticed for the first time that she wasn't wearing his ring. "Where's your wedding band, my love?"

"It's so broad it makes my finger break out beneath it. Besides, it's not practical to wear when I'm working."

"I judge it highly practical to have you wear a tangible sign that you belong to me."

"But the diamonds will fall out—"

"I'll have them replaced."

"Perhaps you'd like to brand me!"

"I have, where it matters." His eyes went dark. "I had your maidenhead, Talitha. You may have broken down Shea's scruples and dallied with some officer, but that's in the past. I took you first. Now I intend that no one else will ever have you. And you will wear my ring."

As she stared at him he murmured silkily, "Fetch it, darling." There was nothing for it but to get the heavy, glittering ring from a dish on the window ledge.

Taking her to the bed, though it was daylight, he stripped her and had her with brutal swiftness. She set her jaws against the pain, hoping he would finish quickly and leave her.

Instead, he began almost at once to caress and stroke her, fondling her breasts, gently touching the aching place he'd just ravished. "Tender, my sweet?" he murmured. "I'll help you forget that."

In a moment, shocked past belief, she felt his warm,

skillful tongue. Stiffening, gripped with shame at what seemed to her unnatural, she tried to push him away, but he brought her to the edge of the bed, and flame quivered through her as he seemed to feast on the hot, rich honey she felt melting her. Her body arched and she shuddered, then couldn't repress a cry as the flood throbbed through her.

Even as the warm glow ebbed she hated Frost, despised herself. Till now she had managed not to cry in front of him, but he'd smashed her pride. Turning her face into the pillow, she sobbed in guilty humiliation. He took her hand. She felt him slipping the ring on her finger.

"I gave you pleasure today," he said softly, drawing her into his arms and tasting her tears as he kissed her. "But that's not what you'll get if I find you without my ring again. You'll wear it, love, feel it every moment as a mark that you're mine."

He closed his hand around hers, and the diamonds dug into her flesh.

Sewa was two in June, clambering on top of the corrals, tagging after whichever elders took her fancy, though most often at the twins' heels or James's. She was beginning to sort out her languages, though her remarks were frequently a hodgepodge of Yaqui, Apache, English, and Spanish. She shrieked each morning when Cat held her between her knees and combed her straight black hair free of tangles before braiding it into one long plait to be secured with a bit of ribbon. Apart from that ritual protest she seldom cried, and in the bright little dresses Anita and Carmencita made for her she was like a hummingbird, hovering here and there, in constant palpitation. She regarded the laps of all adults as her rightful perches.

One evening she clambered up on Judah Frost's knee and then looked up at his face. He smiled at her. She stared, dark eyes widening, then slipped down and ran to Talitha, who was her favorite refuge in time of trouble. Frost's smile deepened. Everyone watched him in startled silence. Afterward, Sewa kept her distance from him.

As for Frost, it seemed to bother him not a whit that he'd killed the child's father. Why should it? In his days as a scalp hunter he'd probably cut the hair off children her age and blithely pocketed the twenty-five pesos paid by the Sonoran government for scalps of Apaches under fourteen.

James was fifteen in July. He enjoyed the barbecue in his honor, especially since Frost was away on one of his extended Sonoran business trips, and was delighted with his array of gifts: fringed buskins, gauntlets, a new quiver, a wrist protector Cat had painstakingly embroidered. Still, next morning Talitha found him gazing at the mountains with a longing on his face that stabbed her.

"Oh, James," she said, touching his hand. "Can't you be happy here?"

"Happy?" He tilted his head and watched her in some surprise. "I never thought about that, with the People. It was just where I belonged."

The quiet words struck Talitha harder than any excited praises of the Apache way of life could have. She clenched her hands behind her to keep from crying out at him: *Was it for this that I kept you alive, that Shea was branded, that you lived here from before the time you could remember until you were seven? Do you really belong to the Apaches?*

Her brother must have read some of this in her face. "I will stay till Shea comes back or there are so many bluecoats that my people will need protection more than yours," he said. "It's just that I should be going on raids, learning how to do things right. Probably, had I stayed with Mangus, I would have been on four raids by now and could count as a warrior."

"Here you do the full work of a vaquero. Belen says he never saw anyone take to it so quickly."

James moved his broadening shoulders. Already

close to six feet tall, he was packing hard muscle onto his bones. Impossible to believe she'd once carried him around in a cradleboard.

"Belen and Santiago taught me much when I was small. I like vaquero work, though it's funny to doctor screwworms and nurse calves instead of running them off." His smile faded. "Remember what you promised, Talitha? That in the hungry time I may take some of the cattle you say are mine to the Apaches?"

"I remember." She searched his eyes. In their dark blue depths she could read nothing of whether he intended to return. She dared not ask.

Three young hawks fledged by the pair nesting along the creek had left the nest. For the month or so they were learning to feed themselves they pursued their parents, screeching and screaming, catching in midair the snakes, mice, and other food sometimes dropped to them.

When able to fend for themselves, the young vanished, gone to seek ranges of their own, but K'aak'eh still lingered, feeding from what James or the twins put out for him. He could fly, but though he spent the day circling and dropping to earth, it was rarely that he was seen gripping anything in his talons.

His injury must have thrown him off by the split second that made all the difference. He would have perished in the wild, but it scarcely mattered here. He was a beautiful bird, molting into his adult plumage, with his tail now a deep rich rust, his underbody pure white to where the speckling blended into the brown of the shoulders and upper wings.

"I suppose he'll start hunting a mate next spring," Talitha said one day to James as he held the hawk on his padded arm.

A strange look passed over James's face.

Several days later, Talitha, riding back to the ranch from the day's hunt for strays, saw him standing on a hill. He was watching a hawk soar up, up, wheeling toward the sun. Abruptly, it hurtled down. She couldn't see it light, but in a few seconds K'aak'eh was aloft again. There was nothing in his claws.

She was watching the hawk, not James. For a moment she didn't comprehend the shaft that rose like the bird, joined its flight, stopped it. They fell together.

Talitha looked at James then. He had sunk down by a rock, face buried in his arms. She understood with a thrill of pity and horror.

James had loved K'aak'eh. Loved him too much to let him live on as a beggar, crippled subtly, dependent on men.

Talitha wept as she rode home, both for the hawk and for James. She never mentioned what she'd seen. Later, when K'aak'eh was missed and Cat wondered where he was, James went abruptly outside. It was left to Talitha to say that she supposed the young hawk had gone where he belonged, back to wilderness.

IX

Carleton didn't enter Tucson himself until the artillery battery got there and could fire a salute in welcome on June 7, 1862. Next day, he proclaimed martial law, with himself as military governor. No man over twenty-one could remain in the territory unless he took an oath of allegiance to the United States. No disloyal words or actions would be tolerated. Every man must have a lawful way of earning of living.

"Merchants praise Carleton out of one corner of their mouths and curse him from the other." Frost chuckled. "On one hand, he's provided for fair trials, and property and land disputes will be taken before a military commission with the right of appeal to civil courts, once they're established. But while the good citizens are applauding this amazing law and order, the colonel's slapped an occupation tax on all merchants, and each saloon and gambling room has to fork over a hundred dollars every month. This all goes to benefit sick and wounded soldiers. On balance, the people seem glad to have some kind of government again."

Talitha frowned. "If that's how this martial law operates for loyal citizens, I wonder what he'll do to Confederate sympathizers?"

"He's arrested those who didn't have sense enough to leave the country, but Sylvester Mowry's his prime target. There was bad blood between him and Carleton from Mowry's army days, so maybe you think the colonel wasn't pleased to get a letter from the Patagonia mine's metallurgist that accused Mowry of carrying on treasonable correspondence with secessionists, selling Captain Hunter percussion caps, and offering to bet that he'd shortly be governor of the Confederate Territory of Arizona!"

"After the way the Unionists pulled out of here and left us defenseless, I don't think they have any business yelling traitor at anyone!" Talitha said scornfully.

"Careful, love." Frost smiled, sealing her lips with his finger. "Colonel Carleton would judge those words 'calculated to impair that veneration which all good patriots should feel for our country and government.'"

"Patriots!" Talitha laughed bitterly. "My parents were hounded out of the United States because of their religion. Shea was branded and flogged for deserting and fighting against an army he believed was unjustly invading another country to steal its territory. Practically the whole white population here still think of themselves as Mexicans. It's crazy to talk about patriotism!"

"Yet both Shea and Marc Revier, foreigners born, charged off to fight."

"*You* certainly didn't."

Frost shrugged gracefully. "My dear, even Colonel Carleton agrees that my special talents and contacts serve the Union far better in keeping its troops supplied than could my services as a soldier."

He went on to say that Mowry had been arrested, his mine and smelter confiscated, and on June 16, right before Frost left Tucson, a military board had been convened to try the former West Pointer for treason.

"Sylvester manages to be dashing even under arrest," Frost added admiringly. "He brought his mistress, private secretary, and personal servant along to Tucson and paraded through the streets more like a conqueror than an accused felon."

Mowry might better have left his secretary at the

mine. Under oath, the man testified that his employer had not only written to General Sumner and Captain Hunter for protection against Apaches, for which he could scarcely be blamed, but had also written to Jefferson Davis and members of the Confederate cabinet and army. Early in July Mowry was found guilty and sent to Yuma. On July 4 Colonel Eyre with men of the 1st California Cavalry, after losing three men to Apaches, reached the Rio Grande and raised the Union flag amid wild cheers. On July 15 another advance force had a fierce battle at Apache Pass with Indians led by Mangus Coloradas and Cochise. The wounding of Mangus caused the Apaches to drop the fight. Reaching Apache Pass in July, Carleton ordered the establishment of Fort Bowie to protect this hazardous and vital location and proceeded toward the Rio Grande.

Having seen armies and commanders come and go while Apaches and brigands remained, the citizenry yawned and were glad when Carleton marched to Santa Fe, where he became commander of the Department of New Mexico.

"Now that there aren't any Rebs to fight, Carleton'll train all his guns on the Indians," Frost predicted. "I don't envy the Mescaleros and Navajos his attentions."

Talitha scarcely heard. What had happened to Shea? With the Confederate arms utterly defeated in the West, where was he? She had hoped that Revier or Irwin might send word to her through the Tucson garrison, but no private news came, though Frost liked to talk about military affairs and the lobbying of Charles Poston and General Heintzelman to make Arizona a territory separate from New Mexico. Such a bill had narrowly passed the House in May and was awaiting Senate action.

Those favoring creation of Arizona Territory had argued that the region's sixty-five hundred whites deserved more protection than New Mexico could give them against thirty thousand hostile Indians and that the proposed territory's mineral wealth would many times repay the cost of such protection.

Opponents of the bill sneered that all the loyal Unionists had been driven out by the Confederates, that ninety percent of the alleged whites were half-breeds and Mexicans who had no wish to be U.S. citizens, and that the region had better be first rescued from the Confederacy.

"Now that's been done," said Frost complacently, "I expect the Senate will finally pass the bill, but I think I'll go up to Washington when Congress opens in December and pull all the strings I can. Too bad my former father-in-law's in the wrong Congress, the Rebel one."

Leonore, Frost's sweet and beautiful first wife, had been the daughter of an influential congressman. Frost had put it about that she'd been killed in a fall down the stairs, but Talitha would always believe he'd pushed her. When she said nothing, staring out the window toward the mountains, Frost came up behind her. In the possessive gesture she hated, he put his arms around her from behind, cupping her breasts in his long fingers.

"Would you like to go with me, love? We'd travel with one of my supply trains to Camp Bowie, get a military escort to Santa Fe, and join up there with traders heading for St. Louis, where we can get a train the rest of the way."

His hands caressed her, making her hate and despise her body. His desire for it had made her his captive; worse, it responded to his assiduous wooing, constantly betrayed her.

"You promised I could stay here," she reminded him coldly. "It'll soon be time for fall branding, and the children need me."

"Your husband doesn't?" he asked silkily. "What kind of woman are you, Talitha? With the clothes and jewels I'd buy you, you'd be the sensation of Washington society—but you'd rather stuff powdered cow chips into maggoty sores and get black and blue wrestling calves!"

She didn't answer. If she angered him, he might insist she come with him, hampering as her presence would be on the way to St. Louis. "Why are you so eager for Arizona to be separate from New Mexico?" she asked. "You're certainly doing well as it is in hauling military supplies."

"Indeed." He laughed. "But where there's a seat of government, there's rich pickings. I prefer mine closer than Santa Fe." Bending his head, he took her mouth, swept her into his arms. "Well, sweet, if you won't go with me, I must sate myself while I can!"

He left that week. The twins' fourteenth birthday celebration was, for Talitha, also a celebration of being free, at least for a time, of the powerful, handsome, deadly husband Cat used to call the Silver Man.

There had been a good calf crop that year, compensating for stock driven off by thieves and Apaches, so when a young lieutenant from the quartermaster's rode up to the ranch with a squad of men and said he would take all the beef she could sell him, Talitha decided to get rid of barren cows, the scrubbier yearlings, and any beasts that looked as if they might not winter well.

While the lieutenant went to buy ham, bacon, and other supplies from Pete Kitchen, the Rancho del Socorro's herd was culled. The lieutenant gave Talitha vouchers for three hundred head of cattle and twenty mules.

"The paymaster'll be through twice a year to redeem these," he explained as she frowned at the pieces of paper. "But you can use these as you would money."

He gladly accepted an invitation to dinner, sitting with the household while his men lounged on the porch and heartily devoured the food Juana and Anita took them. Sandy-haired, with a fresh, boyish face, the officer freely expressed his disgust at being on garrison duty rather than at the front.

"I'd rather be at Camp Bowie and get a crack at old Mangus or Cochise," he grumbled. "Or over in New Mexico. Going to be lots of action before Col. Kit Carson gets the savages tamed." He went on to say that Carleton, now a general, had issued an order to Carson that all Apache men were to be killed whenever and wherever found and the women and children taken prisoner.

"But what if the Apaches want peace?" Talitha asked. James had muttered something and was staring fixedly at the soldier in a way that brought a scowl of puzzlement to the young man's face.

"General Carleton says if the Indians send a flag of truce or want to make peace, they're to be told they're being punished for their past treachery. As you know, Mrs. Frost, they've frequently attacked after pretending to be friendly."

"I suppose the general figures they certainly won't attack after they're dead," said Talitha dryly.

"That's right." The lieutenant nodded, missing her sarcasm. "Carleton thinks this is the most humane course in the long run—forcing the savages to understand that they'll be left alone only after they give up their depredations."

"Humane?" Talitha burst out. She had no love for Apaches, but she wished they could be persuaded to stay in their mountain fastnesses and live at peace. "Lieutenant, did you know that Jefferson Davis stripped Colonel Baylor of his command exactly because Baylor gave orders to exterminate the Apaches?"

The officer flushed. Talitha reached across Cat to place her hand on James's arm. "My brother's half Apache, sir. Is it your duty to kill him?"

"Mrs. Frost! Of course the general's orders apply only to the hostiles. I do assure you that your—" The lieutenant looked at her and gulped. "Your brother's in no danger as long as he's living with you, or in any civilized fashion."

James said, "Soldiers aren't the only ones who have

to eat, Lieutenant. So do my people. I'll be taking beef to them this winter."

Light blue and dark blue eyes clashed. "Then I'd advise you to keep off the old Butterfield route, where patrols might take you for a thief or a hostile," the officer warned.

Rising, he bowed to Talitha, thanked her for the meal, and soon departed, his men driving the mules and cattle.

Carleton's merciless order put James in a fever to be gone at once, but, yielding to Talitha's pleading, he stayed for the Roof Feast. He couldn't drive forty head by himself, so it was agreed that Talitha and Belen would help him.

Cat and the twins had begged to ride along, but Talitha had refused. The excursion was dangerous. She had no mind to jeopardize Shea's children because her brother wanted to feed Apaches.

On the morning they were to leave, Talitha stared at her brother in shock, hardly knowing him. He wore the buckskin he'd had when he came over a year and a half ago, loose then, now fitting snugly. A leather breech-cloth reached almost to the tops of his high moccasins, which were cuffed just below the knee. The folds of such boots were used, Talitha remembered, to hold extra soles, an awl, a yucca thorn with fiber still attached, perhaps a knife. He carried a knife in his buckskin sash, and cartridge belts crossed over his chest. His long black hair was held out of his face by a red headcloth. Except for the eyes he was pure Apache.

The twins stared, uneasily admiring. Carmencita crossed herself. The vaqueros, except for Belen, watched him with closed faces. But Cat clapped her hands and ran to throw her arms around him.

"James, you look splendid! But you will come back, won't you, as soon as you deliver the cattle?"

On one knee, holding the girl against him, James spoke so softly that Talitha had to strain for the answer to the question she'd been afraid to ask. "I don't know, Caterina."

"But Mangus sent you to us!"

"Yes, but that was before soldiers started hunting Apaches for their lives. My people may need me more than you do now."

Cat's mouth trembled. She scrubbed away tears that sparkled in her eyes. "But—but, James, I love you! I couldn't bear it if you stayed as long as you did before. Please! Come back as soon as you can—"

He sighed. "As soon as I can." He kissed her, held her fiercely, protectively close; and for that moment neither seemed a child.

On the third night they camped in a grassy basin watered by a small creek that meandered down from the northern mountains. "We'll have been seen by now," James said. "Tomorrow you'd better start back."

Out of the shadows a figure materialized. Talitha choked back a scream and reached for her rifle, but James was already on his feet, greeting the giant warrior, who responded briefly, but with affection, before coming to stare down at Talitha.

"So, Shining Girl," he said in Spanish, "you have come to see me?"

"No. My brother brings a present. The vaquero and I have helped him this far, but tomorrow we turn back."

"That is wise. If your brother hadn't been dressed as an Apache, you would all be dead."

He sat then, and as he ate the food they offered he asked about the twins who'd been carried in a double cradleboard that was his gift, and about Caterina. With surprise, Talitha concluded that he really cared. He hadn't forgotten Socorro, who'd saved the lives of some women of his camp.

"And Hair of Flame?" That was his name for Shea.

Talitha explained as best she could about the war.

Mangus sighed heavily. It came to her that he was old, close to seventy, and had been wounded nearly to the death that July at Apache Pass.

"We thought the soldiers were gone for good," he said. "Now they are back. They have made a post at Apache Pass."

"This time they'll stay," warned Talitha. And she told the Apache of Carleton's order. "The only hope for your people is to stop raiding and attacking," she finished. "Otherwise, you'll be tracked and killed like wild beasts."

Mangus laughed. "The whites are poor trackers."

"Then they'll wait and kill you when you come out of hiding."

The huge man got slowly to his feet. "Are we to do as the Mescaleros? Consent to settle on land where there's not enough game to feed our families and where the agent never gets enough food and supplies? I would rather die in the mountains."

He faded into the night as silently as he had come.

"A crippled hawk is fed," James said. "A wild one preys. When it cannot, it is no longer really a hawk."

Next morning two warriors appeared to help James with the cattle. Before them Talitha couldn't kiss James good-bye, but she caught his hand and pleaded, "Come back when you can."

By the time she had stopped weeping, her brother was out of sight.

Christmas was terrible that year for Talitha. James recently returned to the Apaches and certainly in danger from the increased warfare; no word from either Shea or Revier; and always the freezing knowledge that though Judah Frost's mission would take months, he was her husband and he'd come back, just as he'd returned from apparent death.

Ironically, he got letters to her, one from Mesilla, another from Santa Fe, several from St. Louis, passed along by merchant or military trains, brought to her by military patrols, travelers to Sonora, and once by Pete Kitchen.

Pete must have been astonished at her marriage to the man who'd killed Santiago and abducted her, but he never spoke of it directly. He probably took the pragmatic view that she was better protected by a strong ruthless man than a weak good one. It was Pete who brought the news that Sylvester Mowry had been acquitted by the commander of the Department of the Pacific and released from his Yuma arrest in November. He had filed suit in California's Fourth District Court against Carleton and others for more than a million dollars in damages.

"But I reckon he won't be back for a spell," drawled Kitchen. "General Carleton's ordered him arrested if he sets foot in Arizona. 'Course, if we get made a territory, Carleton won't be the boss of us anymore."

Frost's St. Louis letters were jubilant. France and England had been on the verge of recognizing the Confederacy and forcing mediation, but the severe faltering of the South at Antietam had led Britain to reject intervention. The Union victory also set the stage for Lincoln's Emancipation Proclamation, which provided that as of January 1, 1863, all slaves in regions still in rebellion, would be "thenceforward and forever free." The railroad system was breaking down in the South, bringing shortages to both cities and armies.

"It'll take a while," exulted Frost. "But without help from Britain or France, the Rebs are done for."

All more remote and far away to Tally than Shea's stories about Ireland and Revier's about Berlin. Where were they, the men she loved, in that massive struggle convulsing the nation?

It was a cold, drizzly afternoon late in January when Miguel, who was on guard, gave the signal for a single rider. A lone traveler could be a decoy for a whole band of thieves, so everyone got weapons and watched as the scrawniest burro Talitha had ever seen plodded slowly onward.

The rider was scrawny, too, wearing ragged homespun, a villainous serape, and moccasins. He rode head down, as if wounded or exhausted. He halted a little way from the house and took off a tattered hat, revealing lank yellow hair.

"This Cap'n Shea's ranch?" he called.

Forgetting caution, Talitha ran out. "Do you come from him?" she cried. "How is he? Where—"

The young man, scarcely more than a boy, swayed in the saddle, caught himself. "Ma'am, you reckon I could come in before I tell you? I'm plumb tuckered out."

The twins were already taking the burro in charge. Belen put an arm around the stranger and helped him inside. Frost had laid in a stock of coffee, and a pot was kept going most of the time. Talitha poured a cup of it, sweetened it with honey, and gave it to the boy, whose freckles stood out on his weather-burned face.

"Are you hurt?" she asked, battling the urge to seize his slumping shoulders and shake out of him whatever news he had.

"I was, ma'am, but I'm pretty much healed over." He shivered as Carmencita took his soaked blanket and put a dry one around him. "Been a long ride. Ma'am—"

Suddenly, Talitha was afraid. She didn't want to hear what he had to say. "Here, Belen's fetched you some dry clothes. We'll leave you by the fire to put them on. Then you need a big bowl of corn soup and some beef and beans. After that, we'll talk."

A year and nine months had passed with no word from Shea. Twenty minutes more wouldn't matter. And for that twenty minutes she could go on hoping, she could believe—

Patrick burst in, holding a rifle, Miguel at his heels, lugging a bedroll and a canvas bag. "This is Father's Sharps'!" Patrick held it so they could all see the initials carved in the stock, then confronted the stranger. "What're you doing with this stuck in your scabbard?"

"I brought it for you if you're his boys, and you must be." The young man reached under the blanket and produced a revolver, which he tried to hand to Talitha. When she shrank away, he gave it to Miguel. "This is his'n, too." There were tears in his eyes as he turned again to Talitha. "Ma'am, I sure am sorry. I was tryin' to think of some way to tell it right. But I—I guess there ain't no right way, is there?"

She was flying apart, bursting into particles. She was dwindling, melting, vanishing. There'd be nothing left to hear, to feel. Nothing.

Cat gave an odd little moan and buried her face against Talitha. Patrick was shaking. He put down the rifle and stood close to Miguel.

"Ay, *por Dios!*" wailed Carmencita.

Talitha forced her disintegrating self back into her body, took Cat in her arms, and moved close to the twins.

"Tell us," she said.

So Lonnie Chandless, late of the 7th Regiment of Texas Volunteer Cavalry, told how Shea had shielded him with his dying body, and how the Apaches had closed in.

"One of the devils lanced me. I figgered the jig was up, but here comes Lt. Rip Harris with enough men to chase off them slaverin' Apaches. They carried me along with 'em." The husky voice broke completely. "It's on my conscience they left other men who couldn't walk no more, but they took turns and got me out. Not because it was me. Because Cap'n O'Shea died to help me, so they was bound he didn't die for nothin'.

"There's a letter for you, ma'am, if you're named Talitha." Lonnie looked in bafflement from Talitha to the twins, obviously wondering if she could be their mother. He knelt over the canvas bag and rummaged till he extracted an envelope. "See, there's a map drawn, showing how to get here. And I'd of made it months ago, but Apaches jumped me up close to Camp Bowie. Got a hole in my right shoulder to match the one in my left." He chuckled. "Never thought I'd be glad to see Yanks, but that patrol looked like angels, scatterin' them heathens like ducks after June bugs! I reckon those soldiers guessed there was more to my story than just that I was carryin' things to a friend's widow, but they took me to the post and patched me up, fed me till I could ride."

Lonnie looked slowly around him, at the vaqueros, their women, back to Shea's family. His thin shoulders moved in a sigh. "So I've come. You can sure be proud of him, the cap'n. First in a fight, first to help, first to laugh when it weren't easy." He shook his head. "I sure wasn't worth his dyin'! If I can do anything . . . I want to pay back much as I can."

"You'll stay with us awhile," said Talitha. "After you've eaten, Belen will show you where to sleep."

Like one in a dream, she moved into the *sala,* sank numbly down before the madonna, Cat still in her arms. The twins followed. Then the vaqueros and all the women and children except Natividad's Marsát, who was looking after Lonnie.

Dead. Shea was dead last summer.

He might even have been dead when she married Judah Frost to save his ranch for him. What was left now of that strong, beautiful body, of the flaming hair, the doubly branded cheek? How could it be that those blue eyes would never again behold the sun?

Sewa clambered into her lap, stroked at her tears, told her in Spanish, English, and Yaqui not to cry, as if one language might work if another didn't.

"Daddy's not coming back?" Cat sobbed against Talitha's neck. "Never, ever?"

Patrick leaned against the window, clenching his hands. Beside him, Miguel tried to control his heaving shoulders. The women were crying. Vaqueros sat hunched into themselves. If there were someone to say the prayers, lead them in mourning, help them have their grief . . . As Belen came to her Talitha looked up at him, hoping he'd take charge, but the grizzled Yaqui watched her sternly.

"*Madama*, we must have a service, raise a cross for Don Patricio beside Doña Socorro's and Santiago's."

They were all dead. Tjúni, also. The four strangers, of different bloods, who had each died deaths of a sort before joining to build the ranch.

Yes. But Talitha held in her arms the sweet flesh of the children of those on the hill. Patrick must be the image of Shea as a boy. Miguel's eyes were his mother's. And over at San Manuel was a son of Tjúni and Shea.

But I'll never have his baby now, Talitha thought, anguish twisting her inside till she felt she couldn't breathe. *Never hold him again, make him happy after his years of loneliness* . . . That hurt more than anything else, that she could never repay him for saving her and James, for all his kindness, for all his grief.

He's with me now. The voice, Socorro's, was so real that Talitha started and looked around. She saw no one, but in her mind was a flash of Socorro's smile, a strong sense of loving presence, a knowledge that it was well with Shea, very well.

Talitha wept, in cleansing release. Then, still holding Cat and Sewa, she said to the others, "We will miss Don Patricio all our lives, but we must remember he is with Doña Socorro, whom he loved past telling, with Santiago, and his brother who died in the desert and his mother who starved in Ireland and his father who was murdered. We know he gave his life for his friend. There's no greater love than that, no greater honor." Her voice broke. With tremendous effort she steadied it and went on. "Tomorrow we'll place his cross on the hill. But now, let's speak of him and remember."

For an hour, perhaps two, his people made a picture of Shea, each sharing something private, a special thing. When Juana had miscarried, he'd sent her a bolt of red cloth to make a pretty dress; he'd jounced cranky teething children on his big shoulders, always hugged Carmencita and told her she was beautiful, taken the roughest of the riding and cow work, never cursed a man whose rope slipped, though he wouldn't tolerate unnecessary roughness.

"He didn't use our women as most *patrones* would," said Francisco. "And we knew he'd take care of our families if we were killed."

"If there was a question about a calf," said Pedro, "he'd tell us to put on our own brand. He would always ride that last hard mile himself, comb the last thicket."

Patrick took a deep breath. "He always let us try things."

Miguel nodded. "And he sang."

Caterine slipped off Talitha's lap. "I want him back!" she cried, her small face convulsing. "I want him back! And I want James, too! Why does everyone have to go away?" She ran out, into the cold, dark rain.

Talitha found her sobbing in the granary and finally persuaded her to come inside for supper. Several times that night, when Talitha woke from exhausted drowsing to weep into her pillow, she heard strange little whimpers from Cat, but when she went to her, Cat was asleep. Safely nested in the corner of her bed were James's carved hawk and Cinco's little blue bird. Talitha wondered when she'd stopped sleeping with her doll.

The cross was planted in the ground beside Socorro's. It was a bright, chill morning, smelling clean and bracing from last night's rain. Talitha read from a Bible Marc had given her.

" 'Greater love hath no man than this, that a man lay down his life for his friends. . . . There is no fear in love; but perfect love casteth out fear.' "

He'll never come back kept running through Talitha's mind. *Never.* Along with her terrible grief mixed the unspeakably bitter knowledge that she hadn't been able to show her love for him, prove it over long enough time to heal some of his pain and restore at least part of his hope and zest in life.

The two who'd saved Talitha, the two she had worshiped, were gone. Compared to them, she'd always feel like a little girl. Yet she had charge of their children and the ranch they'd built and loved. However inadequate and alone she felt, she must not fail those trusts.

X

Lonnie stayed on. His enlistment was up and his experience with Sibley's drunken blunders didn't inspire him to go halfway across the country to find someplace to fight Yankees. No one would miss him; he was an orphan, taken in by an uncle for the work he could do. When his wound healed he made a willing and eager hand. He didn't want pay, but when Talitha told him roundly that that was ridiculous and that a man who wasn't worth wages wasn't worth his keep, either, he grinned and consented.

"That one," said Belen as they watched the young Texan work with a horse, "he wishes to in some manner make up as much as he can for Don Patricio's death."

Talitha didn't answer. She couldn't blame Lonnie for Shea's death. Rather like the soldiers who'd packed the youngster out so Shea's efforts wouldn't be futile, she wanted Lonnie to have a good life. She would just be glad when the sight of him no longer was like a whiplash on her raw grief.

At least she had Shea's letter. *My love,* he had written. *My dear love.* Telling her to be happy. Telling her to have another love. He had thanked her for that last night, for her comfort and courage through the years after Socorro's death. He had asked that she see to his children, act as their mother. But the last sentences stabbed Talitha to the heart. "You have helped me live, my sweet, but you must realize that part of me died with Socorro. You deserve a whole man, a whole love. Don't mourn me too much. For my sake, be happy." His will, left with a San Francisco lawyer, gave her a quarter interest in his two thirds of the ranch and provided that if any of his beneficiaries wanted to sell, it must be to the co-owners so the place would continue as one large holding, apart from Tjúni's San Manuel.

What would he feel if he knew she'd married Judah Frost? She caught in her breath at a sudden hope.

Could she ask for a divorce? She knew there were such things, though she hadn't the faintest notion how to get one. The ranch belonged to her, the O'Shea children, and Sewa now. Surely not even Yankees would rob orphans for the father's deeds.

She'd never answered Frost's letter, but next day she rode to Tubac and sent a letter to him. She told him that Shea was dead, beyond his power, and that she wanted a divorce. It was her hope that in the whirl and challenge of Washington, with plenty of lovely and sophisticated women available, he'd decide it was scarcely worth the trouble to keep an unwilling wife.

The letter would take weeks to reach him if it did at all, and more weeks would go by before she could expect an answer. Meanwhile, it was unnerving to get letters in that bold slanting script, full of zestful machinations and, always, some phrases recalling past raptures and anticipating others, which, given the circumstances, were more sadistic than anything else he could have written.

He was in high glee over an oyster supper he and Charles Poston had given, inviting congressmen who'd been defeated in their districts and needed a new arena for their talents. These men were plied with oysters, champagne, and the suggestion that if they carried the Arizona Territory bill through the Senate, there would be places for them in the new government.

It was mid-February when a patrol from Tubac

delivered that letter, along with almost unbelievable news.

Mangus Coloradas was dead. The great Mimbreño who for half a century had terrorized New Mexico, Chihuahua, Sonora, Durango, and Arizona had been tricked to his death when he went to parley with white men carrying a white flag.

"Colonel West claims officially that Mangus tried to escape," chuckled the lieutenant who'd brought Frost's letter. "But the word is that he told the guards that Mangus had gotten away from every command that ever tried to get him and left a bloody trail for five hundred miles along the old stage route. West said he wanted the old murderer dead."

The guards had heated bayonets and, as Mangus tried to sleep, burned his feet and legs. When Mangus raised up, they shot him.

So died Mangus on a cold February night, scalped with an Arkansas toothpick. His head was severed and the brain weighed, his skull sent to the Smithsonian Institution.

Taking Talitha's stunned silence as curiosity to know more, the lieutenant assured her that Mangus's head was as big as Daniel Webster's, and the brain of corresponding weight. He added that after Mangus's death the soldiers had attacked and killed a number of waiting Mimbreños.

Could James be one of the dead? The lieutenant shrugged when she pressed for details. "Just a bunch of Apaches. Who cares who they were?"

"One may have been my brother," she told the astonished officer.

She had to get away from his innocently bloodthirsty jubilation. Asking Carmencita to feed him and his men, she almost ran to Shea's room. There, she stared sightlessly at the wall. She knew Mangus's cruelties. As a small captive, she had feared him as she might have a giant monster. But he'd held his hand over the ranch all these years, and he'd been a father to James.

She knew the weighing of the brain wasn't as barbarous as it seemed. Marc had told her how doctors and biologists had been studying and dissecting brains, trying to learn what indicated unusual intellect. Georges Cuvier, the greatest anatomist of his time, had wanted his brain to be analyzed, and Talitha had been so gruesomely fascinated that she'd memorized its weight: 1,830 grams. It was estimated that Cromwell, Jonathan Swift, and Lord Byron had brains of the same magnitude. But whatever white scientists wished to do to their own heads, she wished they had left Mangus's on his body.

What must James be feeling now? If he still lived! She thought for a few desperate minutes of trying to search him out but had to realize the hopelessness of such a quest. He might be in any one of thousands of cañons scattered over half a thousand miles. Then she seized on a slender thread of hope. Perhaps, with Mangus gone, James would come back to the ranch.

That was Cat's immediate hope when Talitha gave a brief version of the lieutenant's account. Only Carmencita had heard him, besides Talitha, and though she may have whispered the grisly details to Pedro, she firmly believed that children, in which category, to their disgust, she included the twins, shouldn't hear more terrible things than they had to.

Weeks passed. James didn't come. Early in March Pete Kitchen stopped by to say that Arizona was a territory, President Lincoln having signed the bill on February 24, 1863.

"So the whole dadburn crew of appointed officials will be swarming our way," grunted Kitchen, rubbing his mustache. "Some mixture! Gurley, an Ohio congressman, is governor. We've got a chief justice of the Arizona Supreme Court from Maine, the secretary of the territory's a New Yorker same as the U.S. marshal, and the rest of the big fish are from New York, Michigan, Connecticut, and Wisconsin." Pete's florid cheeks puffed out with exasperation. "The only ones with any ties to Arizona are Poston and Hiram Read, the postmaster, who used to be a missionary in New Mexico."

Talitha laughed. "Well, no Americans have ties here that go back very long. Will the capital be at Tucson?"

"No." This time Pete really growled. "Those pesky congressmen wouldn't pass the bill till the part calling for Tucson to be the capital was scratched."

"But where else *is* there? Outside of Yuma Crossing?"

"Oh, there've been a power of mines around La Paz, north of Yuma, and they're starting to work back east through the mountains, in spite of the Apaches. Won't be long till there's a fort and town up there somewheres. Reckon that bunch of Yankees might rather start a town of their own than settle in Tucson, which has a name for being on the Southern side."

Pete told her, too, that Carleton was vigorously pushing his commanders to pursue and harass the Indians till they were so thoroughly whipped that the survivors would have to throw themselves on his mercy. Manuelito, the most important Mescalero chief, had been killed while he was trying to surrender, along with a number of prime warriors. Kit Carson protested this to Carleton, and the general allowed him to give back to the band their confiscated horses and mules. Horses and mules in place of husbands and fathers.

Other Mescalero survivors surrendered to Kit Carson, who sent them under escort to Santa Fe to surrender to Carleton himself. Cadete, now the main spokesman, said the Mescaleros were worn out, they were out of powder and provisions, their water holes were guarded by soldiers. They could fight no more, but Carleton should remember that they were men and braves.

Carleton answered that if the Mescaleros wanted peace they must go to the Bosque Redondo on the Pecos. After the war they could have a reservation in their own country.

"So the Mescaleros are pretty much starved down and tamed," Pete said. "But the troopers are finding that the Chiricahuas and Mimbreños are as hard to catch in their mountains as lice in a coyote skin. Killing Mangus has sent Cochise wild. It'll be a long time before Arizona's Apaches come to terms."

And James? Would he stay to the end with the wild Apaches? Would she never know where he was and what was happening?

The spring cow work began. Lonnie made a good hand, but he insisted on always working with Talitha's group. "The cap'n would want me to watch out for you, ma'am," he said doggedly, and that was that. He'd never asked why she'd married another man, and Talitha couldn't bring herself to explain. Perhaps he'd learned the truth from the twins or some of the ranch people. However that was, Lonnie was always near and quick to help.

Before, Talitha had worked for Shea, imagining when he'd return, when he could see how well the ranch had managed to continue. Now she rode and roped and branded because it was what must be done. She felt as charred and dead within as a burned battlefield.

Sometimes on an especially fine morning, distant mountains purple or rosy blue, the near ones green, she remembered Marc Revier's words: "I still have the sun." Her being would affirm wonder and beauty beyond all human woes. But mostly she endured because she had to.

Frost had never answered her on the divorce, though she'd had several letters from him after he should have had her message. It was quite likely her letter had been lost on its tortuous journey. She would write again. But the swing of branding kept her weary, and Frost had been gone so long it was easy to forget for days on end that he was her husband.

Then without warning, except for the lookout's signal, he rode in one evening. Tossing to Chuey the reins of his pale horse, which he'd left with the army in Tucson, he kissed Talitha in a claiming, possessive way that completed her shock, greeted the others pleasantly, but sent his gaze boring into Lonnie.

"You've hired on since I left."

If Frost knew Lonnie's connection with Shea, he might run him off. Talitha hastily explained that Lonnie had ridden in looking for work and had made a good vaquero, especially expert in breaking horses.

Accepting that, Frost washed and sat down, politely inviting the rest to finish their suppers. He knew he was feared and disliked, but that only amused him. Neatly but voraciously, he consumed two plates of beef and beans while he gave an account of what was happening.

Arizona's new officials had been so delayed in starting for the territory because of the illness of Governor Gurley that he, Frost, had decided to come on alone. "I've sacrificed my personal interests far too long to the public weal," he said mockingly, with a look at Talitha that made her feel stripped and vulnerable. "Besides, I have to prepare to supply the needs of a capital. That duty prompted me to decline a post in the government."

"No doubt supplying the government's more profitable than being part of it," Talitha said acidly.

"'Where your treasure is, there will your heart be also,'" Frost quoted piously. He went on to say that though Lee had won a costly Confederate victory at Chancellorsville early in the month, which was May, Grant was advancing on Vicksburg, winning battles on the way. Vicksburg would surely fall, placing the whole Mississippi under Union control and splitting the Confederacy.

"Just a matter of time." Frost smiled. "Of course that idiot Napoleon III is still letting French shipyards build Confederate vessels, and Great Britain plays the same game. Both countries would dearly love to regain some of this hemisphere, and old Nap seems determined to send an army to Mexico."

"Mexico?"

Frost nodded. "Mexico's borrowed heavily abroad, especially from England and France. In order to get back their money both countries have considered taking over the Mexican government, but France now seems the one to actually try it."

Talitha frowned, remembering her lessons with Marc. "Doesn't the Monroe Doctrine warn European powers to keep out of this side of the world?"

Frost spread his long, graceful fingers. "France hopes the South will win. Or, failing that, to have a strong enough foothold in Mexico that the United States won't feel like starting another war the moment this one ends."

Poor Mexico! thought Talitha. So lately losing its war with the United States, never having enough time or resources to give its beleaguered folk any kind of peace, especially on the northern frontiers, where it would be hard to say who most afflicted the people, brigands both Mexican and gringo, or Apaches and Comanches.

"Where's your Apache brother?" Frost asked abruptly.

"I don't know. He went to Mangus before Christmas."

"Maybe he got killed along with a lot of the old devil's family," suggested Frost.

Talitha stared into eyes the color of an ice storm, refusing to flinch. "Who knows?"

Sipping his second cup of coffee, he said lazily, "My dear, I'm sure everyone will excuse us if we retire early. I was so eager to see you that I've traveled without much rest." He smothered a yawn and beamed at the embarrassed or stony faces surrounding him.

Talitha didn't want to argue in front of the others, to

make the twins or the men feel they must protect her. Now the dim nightmare, shoved back and repudiated, was horrifyingly real, as inescapable as the man who rose gracefully to his feet. Talitha felt both frozen and consumed with flame.

"Please," she said. "Could we walk outside for a little?"

His dark eyebrows lifted, but he bowed and offered her his arm. "I'm yours to command. In reason, of course."

They passed through the courtyard where peach blossoms glowed softly in the moonlight, went through the storeroom, and moved past the corrals and along the hillside. With a deep breath, he turned her to face him.

Talitha cried desperately, bracing her hands against him, "Didn't you get my letter?"

"Your letter?" In the silver light his hair was burnished and his eyes like crystal. "What letter, love?"

Whether he had or not scarcely mattered. "Shea is dead. Last summer, during Sibley's retreat from New Mexico. There's nothing you can do to hurt him now. I want a divorce."

"A divorce?" He watched her quizzically. From his coolness, she was sure he'd gotten her message. He sighed in pretended hurt. "It would seem I've failed to win you, sweet, though I know you've many times been raptured in my arms."

"Raped is more the word," she said bitterly. "And I hate you more for that."

"Because I gave you pleasure?" He shook his head chidingly. "However, I've come to expect ingratitude. And I haven't the slightest notion of letting you out of our bargain."

"You want to be a power in the territory. Wouldn't it look better for you to use your influence for a quiet divorce than for me to ask for one and explain publicly how you threatened me into it? And how you began your Arizona career as a scalp hunter?"

He laughed. "My dear, that last would just make me a hero! Except for paying bounty, what's Carleton's Indian policy except extermination? I'm afraid nothing you say can hurt me or help you, because, dear love, you can only be granted a divorce by the territorial legislature when it finally convenes, and you may be sure its members will be slow to anger me."

She believed him. Despairing revulsion made her physically sick. Was there no way, no way at all, to be free of this man who had shadowed her life for the past ten years, returned from the dead to force marriage?

If he were really dead— That answer, the only answer, made her straighten. Frost shook his head, smiling into her eyes. "No, Tally. No. I took the precaution of telling my good friend, the new chief justice of what will be Arizona's Supreme Court, that my wife, though I love her dearly, is erratic to the point of—alas! madness.

"I hope, naturally, to be able to control her, but if I should disappear, he's promised to personally investigate. Would you like the distinction of being the first woman hanged in Arizona?"

Speechless, she stared at him. He smoothed her cheek, then let his hand trail down the pulse of her throat to curve under her breast. "Of course, if the judge decided you were mad, he might put you away for life in some asylum; but I rather imagine, sweetheart, that a person of your spirit would prefer the noose. That's over quickly."

He walked her back to the house. She was glad no one was left in the kitchen or *sala* as he drew her through them, to the room that had been Shea's.

Frost had his freighting business to see to, and that required a trip to Sonora and Governor Pesqueira to insure duty-free transit from Guaymas. On the way back, Frost investigated the placer mines along the Colorado River above Yuma.

"The country around La Paz is swarming with miners, lots of them from California," he told Talitha on his return. "Trouble is, there's not much water for washing out the dirt, and dry-washing's so slow only Mexicans and Indians will do it. No, where the experienced old prospectors like Walker and Wickenberg are heading is into the mountains in about the center of the territory."

"Why don't you try your luck?" Talitha asked.

He laughed, taking her chin in his hands. It was late afternoon, and no one else was in the house. "So eager to be rid of me, darling?" He kissed her till she had no breath and carried her to Shea's room.

Halfway through his lovemaking he paused, gripping her shoulders, shaking her till she opened her eyes. "This must be where Shea took you. Right in this very bed. Do you ever think of that?"

She did. She thought of Shea and tried to armor herself against her husband's ardent, practiced wooing. But when that failed . . . Sometimes when Frost caressed and kissed and teased till the building need within her was savagely released, in that wild-mad moment while that throbbing drummed through her, softening thighs and loins—sometimes in that shamed pleasure she remembered Shea.

Black pupils spread over Frost's cold eyes, leaving only a narrow rim of light gray. "So you do," he whispered. "I don't like other men, even if they're ghosts, in my bed. Keep your eyes open. Call me by name."

"You damned devil!"

He thrust so cruelly that she smothered a scream. He laughed deep in his throat as he battered her, holding her up for his lunging, till she thought she must be riven in half. She was almost senseless when he cried out, pumping into her, then collapsed with his arm across her, pinning her down. When she roused from her painful half stupor, full of revulsion at the smell and stickiness of his juices on her, she tried to slip out of bed.

His arm tightened. "Stay."

"I—I need to wash."

He raised to sniff along her loins like some silvery beast of prey. "Exciting," he murmured. "My odors deep within you, that makes me part of you. You're my proper sheath, Talitha, my soft, warm scabbard." His tongue and hands caressed her.

"Please . . ."

"But I'm being very gentle, love. There, you barely feel that, don't you? Ah, you're quivering. You want more. Like that. And this . . ."

He was gentle, he soothed her as a careful bridegroom might coax a virgin, but he wouldn't let her escape. When the mounting, trembling hunger crested into explosions, he entered her again, piercing into that thick, honeyed sweetness, varying his rhythms, lifting her at last into frenzy.

"Call my name," he commanded softly, pausing as she gasped, involuntarily straining to be quenched.

She looked up at him, becoming aware, bitterly humiliated yet craving the end. "I need encouragement," he murmured. "Tell me you want me. Tell me how it feels. Call me Judah."

The fire in her smoldered down. Sick with frustrated desire, mortified at what he could do with her, she said coldly, "Shall I call you Judas? Shall I tell you how I hate you more all the time and detest myself?"

He slapped her, splitting her lip over her teeth. She arched her neck, burying her teeth in his wrist. He swore and knocked up her head. She felt him rigid as steel within her, fought with maddened ferocity.

Again he rammed and hammered deep within her, stifling her cry of agony with his hard mouth. There was no pleasure for her this time, only savage pain. But when he finished, he did sleep, and she was able to creep away, bruised, aching, but, most unbearable of all, soiled and scented with him.

Supper preparations were beginning. Sewa was rocking on Cat's old hobbyhorse, a work of art lovingly carved by the vaqueros, while Cat, curled up among a number of felines on the blanket-spread *banco,* the adobe bench built into the wall, read aloud from one of Marc Revier's old gifts, a book of Aesop's fables versified by Edmund Waller.

Though she loved to read, she had resolutely ignored the tempting pile of books Frost had brought her from Washington: Kingsley's *The Water Babies,* Christina Rosetti's *Goblin Market,* George Eliot's *Silas Marner,* Tennyson's *Idylls of the King,* and several novels by Dickens.

For Sewa there had been an elegant doll with a china head and real hair, dressed in a richly trimmed taffeta gown with matching pelisse, hat, and parasol. Cat, under cover of proclaiming that Sewa was too little to play with such a doll, arbitrarily put it high up in the niche in their room along with Talitha's Judith doll, named for her mother, brought up by caravan from Chihuahua and given her long ago by Shea.

"Now why do you suppose the willful little creature's so set against me?" Frost had wondered idly after that cavalier disposal of his gifts.

"She has good instincts. And how you have the face to bring Sewa gifts after you killed her father—"

"It would be as well for the future tranquility of our home if you forgot that," Frost interrupted smoothly. He shrugged. "I've never known a female yet who could indefinitely resist presents. Which reminds me. You *will* wear my jewels, love. I had the sapphires made up especially to go with your eyes. And I want to see the diamonds sparkle between your breasts."

Frightened with a sudden obscene dread, Talitha swallowed. "You never bring the twins gifts. Why do you try to win the little girls?"

He shrugged. "Because they're girls. Patrick and Miguel are too old to view me with anything but suspicion. Girl children do intrigue me, though. Didn't I try to buy you from Juh when you were five years old?"

And he'd kissed her when she was thirteen. Cat was ten. Talitha caught his arm. "If you ever try—if you bother either of the girls . . ."

"Jealous, love?"

"If you touch either of them, I'll kill you. I don't care what happens afterward. Do you understand? I'll kill you!"

He'd gazed at her in kindling desire. Taking her hand, he'd urged her toward the bedroom. "So long as you blaze at me like that, my sweetheart, no other woman can do more than tease my fancy." But since that day, Talitha had kept the girls out of his way as much as possible, which wasn't hard, since Cat shunned him and imperiously swept Sewa along with her.

Now, full of brutalized pain, feeling indelibly sullied, Talitha stopped for a moment to look at the two children: Sewa, now three, wirily sturdy with a heart-shaped face, melting eyes, and honey skin; Cat, in a growing spurt that had started the first shy budding of her flat little chest, the faintest rounding of boy-thin hips. Except for Shea's blue eyes and a trace of his determined jaw, she looked as Socorro must have at her age—pointed chin, arched black eyebrows, a lovely mouth curved like a wing.

Pride was in every line of her. When crossed, she reacted with a haughtiness laughable in someone so young and small, but she was also tenderhearted, quick to love, swift to defend the helpless. From adoration for her, the rougher vaqueros eased their methods, at least in her sight.

She had raised and released as many foundling wild creatures and birds as had died in spite of her efforts, and orphaned calves had become hers to feed as soon as she'd grown enough to withstand their lusty tugging on the bottles. These calves, Talitha was sure, would never go to market, but die of old age.

She was finishing the poem in her sweet high child's voice that already had in it the timbre of femininity.

> *"'That eagle's fate and mine are one,*
> *Which on the shaft that made him die*
> *Espied a feather of his own,*
> *Wherewith he wont to soar so high.'"*

Oh, K'aak'eh! James, my brother! Mangus Coloradas! . . .

A great wave of grief swelled up in Talitha, forcing past her usual controls. The maimed hawk was dead, and Mangus the war chief. But where was her brother?

Her heart was wrenched for him as she remembered the little boy shielding his beloved black cat Chacho, insisting he didn't have hydrophobia. And there was his beautiful dappled gray horse Tordillo, killed to feed Apache women and children in a starving time. And K'aak'eh. Then Mangus.

Oh, James, oh, my brother, come back and live with us, love us! Don't stay with those broncos whose time is numbered. Counsel them if you can, convince them they must go to reservations in the end, for the white man's road will blot out their trails. Do what you can to help them, only do not die!

But he might be already rotting in the earth, dead in some skirmish with the soldiers. Frost had passed the word among army officer friends that if they found a blue-eyed Apache, well grown for sixteen years, they should spare him if at all possible, since he was Mrs. Frost's half brother and could be released in her custody. Frost had even offered an unofficial reward if James was turned over to them alive. Talitha didn't think he'd let himself be captured alive, and she doubted that soldiers obeying Carleton's "black flag" tactics, where Apaches weren't allowed to surrender, would take time to check the color of Indian eyes.

James must have had half brothers and sisters among Juh's wives, but he'd never mentioned them, so Talitha had no idea of how close his ties were to the band now that Mangus, his foster father, was dead. All she could do was hope that he would come back, that he wouldn't pick death for himself as he had for K'aak'eh.

She went outside, forcing herself to walk straight while she was in sight of the house, though once in the concealment of the trees she moved slowly, trying to ease the aching soreness between her legs. She felt as if she'd been beaten with a sledge until she was pulpy, swollen.

Undressing, she stepped into the rippling little creek and waded out till it reached her waist. The coolness stung where she was tender, but gradually she seemed less enflamed and congested. There. At least she didn't stink of him. But it would be agony if he tried to have her again before she was over the results of his usage. It was the first time he'd ever really hurt her, and it was the kind of punishment she didn't mean to bring on herself if she could help it.

If only he'd tire of her. . . .

But that conjured up hideous thoughts of Cat, blossoming as she would be in a few years. *If he'll just get himself killed before that; or go off and never come back.*

She laughed aloud in harsh mockery. Those you wanted to return didn't. Those you hated stuck like burs.

It was sundown. Leaving the water reluctantly, she dripped off most of the water, wiped the rest on her skirt, and dressed. She moved through the sycamores and willows and was starting across the small meadow when a voice made her stiffen.

"Ma'am. Can I talk to you a minute?"

XI

She whirled in confusion. "Lonnie!"

"I never spied on you, ma'am. But when I saw you movin' like you was hurt . . ." He flushed till his freckles dimmed. "Well, I figgered I'd just wait and ask you."

"Ask me what?" She eyed Lonnie warily. She was fond of him, felt almost as if he were a younger brother, but her experiences with Güero and Frost had made her quick to distrust men.

His Adam's apple bobbed. "Ma'am . . . Miss Tally . . . I wouldn't overstep for worlds. But the cap'n would want me to look after you. Somethin' don't seem right between you and your husband. When he's here, you never laugh. You have a hard time keepin' aholt of yourself when he touches you."

There could be only one result if this boy tangled with an expert shot like Frost. Talitha managed a smile and shook her head. "Lonnie! What an imagination you've got!"

"Wisht I didn't have none." His tone was somber. "But I'm not imaginin' this, and you know it."

What to tell him? It was useless to deny his perceptions, but she had to keep him from challenging Frost. She put her hand on the young man's arm.

"Lonnie, I—I married Judah Frost for compelling reasons. You're quite right that I don't find it easy. But believe me when I say this: If anything happens to him while he's at the ranch, I'd be blamed by his important friends. It would be disastrous."

The young jaw hardened. "No one could blame you if I killed him and turned myself in."

"You work for me. They'd think I gave the order." She shook him. "Now, listen! I've seen Frost shoot. He's incredibly fast and sure. You wouldn't have a chance. Stay alive, Lonnie. Don't throw away the life Shea saved."

With a crooked grin, Lonnie said, "I didn't exactly aim to fight him a fancy duel, ma'am. You got to remember I kept meat in the pot at home, huntin'. I've sneaked up on many a deer never did me a minute's harm and dropped them. Reckon I can stalk a man."

"Don't, Lonnie. I think he'll get tired of me before too long and stop coming to the ranch. If you really want to help me, don't do anything that would make us lose you."

He scowled, considering, troubled. "I don't rightly know, ma'am. It sure goes against the grain to see you worried. The cap'n—"

"Wanted you to live," cut in Talitha. "Give me your word not to start trouble, Lonnie, or I'll have to send you away."

"Reckon you'd have a time runnin' me off." He laughed, then watched her gravely. "Miss Tally, this place is the most home I've ever had. But even before I laid eyes on it, I'd promised the cap'n, wherever he is now, that I'd see you through to better times."

She was able to smile again, comforted by his concern. Lightly touching his cheek, she said, "Thank you, Lonnie. Just be patient and those better days will come." She hesitated. "I think it'd be wiser if you didn't walk back with me."

He nodded. "If you say so, ma'am. But if things get to where you can't go on, tell me."

As she walked to the house Talitha felt less alone, but

she was also worried that Lonnie, who was very young—well, he seemed so, though in fact he was only three years younger than she—might decide to take Frost out of her life and be killed in the attempt.

She was glad, for more than escaping his arms, when her husband three days later said that he was going to check the operation of the Tecolote mine and come back by way of Tucson, where he also had business.

He returned at the end of August, produced a letter, and handed it to Talitha, who frowned at its neatly slit top. "Of course I read it, my dear," drawled Frost. "It's a husband's duty to protect and guide his wife. But I'd expect you to be pleased to hear from an old friend. Open it, do. I'll excuse you."

She knew that firm, deliberate script. Marc Revier, after all, had taught her to read and write. Her fingers shook. She turned her back to hide them from Frost and drew out the rumpled sheets of paper. Her heart was beating so hard that blood thundered in her ears and head.

Dear Talitha,

I have written to you several times but fear the letters never reached you. In case this one does, I can sum the last two years up by saying briefly that, having no taste for Carleton's mode of Indian fighting, I joined with a Colorado battalion and have seen service with them in Kansas, Missouri, and Arkansas. Though plagued with dysentery and once with pneumonia, I got never a scratch till a battle at Honey Springs close to Fort Gibson in Indian Territory. We fought the Confederates alongside Negro soldiers and "pin" Cherokees, which must have mightily wounded Southern pride, for our mixed-up aggregation won.

However, I took a ball in the knee. It's healing clean, thank the good God, but the surgeon insists

I'll never be fit to soldier again, and my discharge should be through shortly.

I could not have quit while I was able-bodied, Tally, but I tell you freely I'm glad to be out of it. Glad to be coming back to Arizona. I hope Shea is well—that perhaps he, too, has found an honorable way to come home and will be at the ranch when I come by.

How good it will be to see you again. I have dreamed of you amidst the nightmares. My best greeting to all at the ranch and kisses for the little girls.

As ever, yours,
Marc

"Touching, isn't it?" Frost's amused tone knifed into her relief that Marc was alive, her joy that he was coming, that she'd see him again. "A dream among nightmares. Apparently his baptism of fire has moved him to feel magnanimous should Shea have returned to claim you, but will he be so gracious when he knows you've married me?"

Hatred of this pitiless, conscienceless man burned her throat, left a metallic taste in her mouth. She couldn't trust herself to speak but felt as if loathing and contempt blazed from her like heat from a fire.

"Ah," mused Frost. "So you would have taken him since your adored Irisher is dead. Poor Talitha, thwarted twice. Would you rather not see him?"

See him, knowing that they could be nothing to each other? She didn't think she could bear it, after the cruelty of Shea's death, the bitterness of her forced marriage. Yet— She had a flash of his broad, strong face, the frank, kind eyes. She wanted to see him again, hear his voice, reach out to him with her spirit though she couldn't with her hands. How bad was his injury? He would be crippled in some measure, but he must be able to travel.

"I'm surprised you're willing to have him visit," Talitha said to Frost. "He knows all the things you've done—"

"Not all, sweetest. Not even I remember them all."

"He joined Shea and Pete Kitchen's men when they rode after you and you tricked them with that poor prospector's corpse."

"Yes, I suppose it will be a shock to my onetime employee to find me alive. But Marc's seen a lot of blood in the last two years. I doubt he'll want to reopen the past, especially when he sees us so happily married."

"Happily!"

"It had better look that way to him. How sad it would be if the wounded hero came home only to lose his life."

"It could go the other way."

"Marc never saw the day he could shoot with me. And with that game leg, he can't even run away." Frost smiled. "No, Talitha, you'll show Marc how content you are with me. He'll nobly put your welfare above his possessive male instincts."

"You swear you won't hurt him?"

Frost's dark brows drew together. "He's the last man I'd wish to harm. I need him. The superintendent I installed at the Tecolote proved to be a drunken thief. I'm prepared to offer Marc an attractive percentage on top of salary if he'll manage the mine and any others I start in the vicinity."

That relieved Talitha. Frost was capable of great charm and restraint when his self-interest was involved. He needed Marc's skills, so there'd be no sly baiting, no provocations. And even though she might not see him for year upon year, still, if Marc were at the Tecolote, she'd have news of him. There'd be the knowledge that he was a hundred miles away, not thousands. In spite of her shame that he'd think she'd freely married Frost, the thought of seeing him again made her feel alive as she hadn't in months. Blindly, irrepressibly, hope began to grow in her. Marc was alive. She would see him again.

Frost sensed the glow within her. Watching her with narrowed eyes, he said mockingly, "I thought, after Shea, you had nothing left for any other man. Apparently you do. That should make me hate Revier, but I find myself oddly grateful."

"Why?" she asked distrustfully, on guard at once for any threat to Marc.

Frost took her in his arms, kissed the pulse that leaped and hammered in her throat. "Because, though I must have you however I can, I much prefer a live woman to a sleepwalker." He lifted her, bent his shining head to her breast so that his breath was moistly hot on her flesh. "You bloom for another man, my darling, but the perfume entices me."

After that, she tried to be cool and circumspect around her husband, but either his appetite was whetted by knowing that he possessed what Marc could only desire, or he detected the brighter flow of blood in her, her quickened awareness and responses. He never seemed to have enough of her.

And then in October, right after the twins' fifteenth birthday, Marc Revier rode in.

Talitha would have given much if Frost hadn't been at the ranch. As it was, after the alert, as soon as Marc came close enough to be recognized, Frost put aside his rifle and hurried out, drawing Talitha with him.

"Marc!" Frost shouted genially. "It's good to see you, man. Since your letter came, we've been expecting you daily!"

Marc reined his claybank to a halt. Slowly, as if dazed, he took off his hat. Gray showed at his temples. The old scar across his left cheek and eyebrow was a pale seam in his tanned face, and the crow's-feet at the corners of the dark blue eyes were deeper.

"What are you doing here?" he asked bluntly of Frost. "We thought you were dead."

"There was good reason for the mistake," Frost said gaily. He was obviously determined to take no offense. "I was out in California helping Carleton raise troops and came back to Arizona with the California Column in May of '62. Naturally, my first concern was for Talitha, for, as you may know, Apaches and bandits had cleaned out the whole Santa Cruz Valley region except for the Patagonia mine and Pete Kitchen's place." He drew her into the circle of his arm and smiled fondly down at her, but she saw the warning in his eyes. "It was the happiest day of my life to find her alive and well."

And the darkest day of mine—except when I learned Shea was dead.

"What about Shea?" Marc's tone rasped huskily, as if he could scarcely get the words out.

"Heroically dead in Sibley's retreat. The young man he died for brought the news and has stayed on at the ranch. Why don't you ask him for particulars, Marc? It distresses Talitha to dwell on it."

Deliberately, Frost raised Talitha's hand, held it so her wedding ring flashed fire, and kissed her fingers.

Talitha seemed to feel Marc's shock within herself as his breath caught audibly. She couldn't look at him. Why couldn't she at least have seen him alone for a while before he had to know the truth? The truth that was a lie. But which, for his own sake, she must make him believe.

"Are you married?" Marc asked.

"Talitha did me that honor." Frost added with engaging honesty, "I know, of course, that Shea's enshrined in her heart, but I'm grateful for her sweet company." His hand tightened on hers, sending the jewels biting into her flesh. "And I think I may truthfully say, may I not, my love, that I haven't disappointed you?"

Masking the hate that swelled within her, she said quietly, "You've done everything you promised." Turning to Marc, she was stabbed by the pain in his eyes. "But we mustn't keep you waiting there. Give your horse to Patrick and come in."

He looked weary enough to fall out of the saddle. "Thanks, but maybe I'd better push on. I can make Cap Tubac before dark if I hurry."

"Marc!" Talitha came forward and put a hand on his reins. "You can't just go off like that!"

"You come in, Uncle Marc!" commanded Cat. "You look awful tired, and Anita has tamales for supper!"

After a moment's hesitation during which he searched Talitha's eyes, Marc threw back his shoulders. "If you're sure I don't intrude . . ."

"Nonsense!" said Frost heartily. "We're all mightily glad to see you! Of course you'll stay with us while you get your bearings, decide what you're going to do. I've got a bottle of Scotch I've been saving for an occasion, and you're it!"

Marc's face tightened at the extreme friendliness, but he got down. The awkwardness in his right leg turned into a limp when he walked. Not much worse than Santiago's; certainly nothing to keep him from his old business. He grinned at Patrick, who had taken the reins, and glanced from him to Miguel with an astounded whistle as he shook their hands.

"A little over two years and you've grown like this! And Caterina! You're almost a young lady." He bent for her eager hug and kiss and swept Sewa onto his shoulder. "I guess you're the only one I can still carry, Little Flower!" he said.

This was the way Shea should have come home. A pang twisted through Talitha's joy at seeing Marc, but abated in gratitude that at least this beloved man was safe, back from the war.

Supper was festive. Besides flavorsome tamales steaming in their cornhusks, there was wild turkey stewed with spices, beans, squash, panocha, and, as always, quantities of Carmencita's tender, thin tortillas. Though the vaqueros must have been amazed at Frost's cordiality to Marc, they were too courteous to show it. Marc remembered all of them and the women, had a word for each of the children, and remarked how wonderful it was to find the ranch unmolested.

"There's not a mile of the road between Tucson and Calabazas that doesn't have a grave or more," he said, shaking his head. "I'm surprised there are any white people left in the territory."

"Well, there are, with more coming," said Frost. "Tucson's booming because the posts and forts have to be supplied, and miners are thick along the Colorado. It's hard times now, Marc, but those that stick it out will profit when the war's over and the country settles up."

"It won't settle much till Apaches and bandits stop raiding."

"They'll stop. My good friend General Carleton is killing off New Mexican Indians that won't go to the reservation, and the same thing'll be done here when enough troops can be spared."

Marc said slowly, "I suppose it must be. Free Apaches will raid and loot and kill. Yet to cage them is cruel, like caging hawks. It was shameful how Mangus was done to death."

Frost's lip curled. "Tell that to any survivors of the hundreds of people he killed!"

Not replying to that, Marc asked where James was.

Talitha winced. "Last December he took some cattle to the Indians. He hasn't come back."

"We can only hope he wasn't killed with much of Mangus's family right after the chief's murder," Frost said, putting a comforting hand over Talitha's.

Tensing with a hatred turned more bitter and corrosive by her helplessness and his fakery, Talitha kept her eyes down so they wouldn't betray her to Marc. If he suspected how things were, he'd get himself killed, and that would help no one.

He was watching her, his steadiness as calming as the reliability of a massive, ageless rock. "I'm sorry, Talitha," he said at last. "I will hunt your brother if you wish."

"No! You'd be killed or lost. I—I've made up my mind that unless James comes home, I'll probably never see him again—"

"Never?" wailed Cat, putting down her spoon as if her panocha had turned to sawdust. "Oh, Tally, he has to come back! He has to!"

So, though she no longer mourned for him openly, the child still missed him desperately. Jarred, frightened at Cat's intensity, Talitha said, "I hope he will, too, Cat."

"If he knew how much we love him—"

"He has other half brothers and sisters with the Apaches, honey. He lived with them half his life. They must love him, too. Anyway, James has to decide."

Cat pushed away from the table and mumbled an excuse as she fled. Sewa slipped away from the younger children's table and padded after her.

"Poor Katie-Cat!" said Miguel. "It's too bad one of us twins wasn't James. I think she cares more about him than both of us together."

Let her be happier than I have been, Talitha besought the spirits of Socorro and Judith, her own mother. It might be pagan, but she appealed to them as guardians who might have influence with God or whatever powers moved the world. And yet often she had been happy, even before that last rapturous night when Shea finally accepted her love.

No, she'd never complain of loving Shea or think that love wasted. The cruel horror was her marriage to Judah Frost, made infinitely worse now that Marc had returned. She could see in his eyes that he still loved her, that he wouldn't have been too proud to accept what, after Shea, she could give a man, cherish it to fullness.

After supper, Frost, Marc, Belen, the twins, and

Talitha took seats in the *sala.* Frost produced cigars and condescended to offer one to Belen, who politely refused, as did Marc, though they accepted glasses of Scotch and water.

For a time, Frost, like an indulgent stepfather, let the boys ply Marc with questions, puffing reflectively on his fine cigar; but when he rose to pour second drinks, he said amiably, "That's enough, boys. Marc's tired. We must let him turn in before long, but I do have important business to discuss with him first."

Patrick sighed, getting reluctantly to his feet. "Man! Those 'pin' Cherokees can really fight! If the war lasts another year or two, we can go, Miguel."

Miguel stared at him. *"Caray!* On which side do we fight, then? For the South and slavery? For the North, which put a brand on our father?"

Patrick's jaw dropped. With a wave of amused sadness, Talitha was sure that which side to take had never entered his head. Battles were going on, opportunities to prove courage and become a man.

"You look so far ahead you'll never do anything," he grumbled.

"I won't blunder over a cliff, either." Miguel grinned, unruffled. He followed Patrick's impulsive lead when he saw no obstacle. When he had an objection, however, he was immovable, and his twin, fuming, reluctant, would usually give way. "Father's dead, Patrick. We have to act like men and take the load off Tally."

She wrinkled her nose at him. "Don't talk about me as if I were a worn-out mule!"

"No, *madama.*" Miguel bowed with a gallant, if teasing, flourish. "Nevertheless, be assured that I won't leave you to hold off brigands and Apaches by yourself."

"Neither would I," growled Patrick, punching his twin. They went out, scuffling. Belen, too, said his good nights, casting Talitha a questioning look.

She nodded. "Good night."

"Fine lads." Marc smiled. "A shame neither of their parents will see them grown up."

Frost cleared his throat. "I know you're weary, Marc, but this won't take long. You're the best superintendent and geologist I've ever known. The Tecolote needs a strong hand to get it in good running order, and I'm sure I'll find more mines in that region. If you'll work for me, I'll give you ten percent of the profits and two hundred dollars a month."

Marc didn't even consider it. "Thanks, but I have other plans."

"Fifteen percent?"

Marc flushed. "Your offer's very generous. It's just that after two years in the army I want to be my own boss."

"Doing what?" Frost persisted.

"I'm not sure." Talitha, with a flash of insight, knew that he hadn't planned his future too much beyond coming to her. "I might go into ranching. Or try my luck prospecting."

Expelling a ring of smoke, Frost studied his cigar. "There's no way to persuade you?"

"Sorry." Marc grinned, looking younger. "Guess I have the American fever. I want to work for myself."

"But you'd have worked for Talitha. Wouldn't you, Marc?" Frost tossed his cigar in the fireplace, and though his tone stayed soft, it was ugly. "If you'd found her manless, you'd have tried to fill that place. And we all know what your pay would have been."

Marc went rigid. "It's no secret that I'd have married Talitha long ago if she'd have had me. I don't understand you, Judah."

"Well, understand this, you sneaking foreigner! I'll bet you're not crippled in the place that counts, but I'll remedy that pronto if I catch you hanging around my wife!"

Talitha sprang up. "Judah! Are you crazy?"

His arm moved back. He would have struck her except for Marc's grasping his elbow, swinging the arm back till Frost snarled and reached inside his vest. Talitha kicked up, knocking from his fingers the little derringer with which he'd murdered Santiago. At the same moment Marc sent a doubled fist into Frost's jaw with all his weight behind it.

Frost slipped to the floor. Marc rubbed his knuckles and gave Talitha a bewildered glance. "I'm sorry, Tally. But I couldn't let him hit you."

She longed to get her horse and ride off with him, far from this hated man. But there were the children, there was the ranch. And Marc, for his own safety, mustn't guess how it was with her and Frost. Coldly, she said, "I'm sure your intentions were good, but you really mustn't interfere between Judah and me. He was fearfully disappointed when you wouldn't take over the mine. At such times, he's not quite himself."

"Tally!"

"I'm sorry to ask you to ride on, but anything else would be very awkward."

"But you helped me!"

"Certainly. Do you think I wanted to see my husband kill an old friend?"

Marc shook his head in agonized bafflement. "Tally, why are you acting like this? How can I leave, knowing he'll punish you?"

"I can handle Judah," she assured the man she loved. "He doesn't beat me, don't think that. It was just that tonight he was so angry—"

"You want to live with him?" Contempt edged Marc's voice. "I'll leave you in peace, then. Good-bye, Talitha."

With tremendous effort she kept her arms at her sides, bit back the flood of words that wanted to flow from her. "Good-bye, Marc. God go with you."

He stared at her across her husband's body. To kiss him once, rest in his arms—what wouldn't she give for even that much? But she watched him coldly. With a harsh laugh, Marc picked up his hat and limped out through the kitchen.

She heard Belen speak to him in the courtyard. Good. The vaquero would catch his mount, see that he was supplied. But her heart ached that, exhausted and thinking her bought by Frost's wealth and charm, he must journey off alone into the night. It was a wretched homecoming.

Frost stirred and groaned. She went for water, slipping the derringer into her bodice. If Frost tried to go after Marc, she'd shoot him and take the consequences.

He was on his feet when she came back with cloths and a basin of water. He knocked them out of her hands. "I can do without your solicitude, you treacherous bitch! You've only postponed things. I'll settle that crip in good time. Let him get a start, think he's getting somewhere, and then . . ." He laughed ferociously, set his hands at the neck of Talitha's dress, and ripped it to the hem.

The derringer fell to the floor. Talitha reached for it, too furious to care what happened to her if she could just be rid of him. He palmed the gun, then lifted her and carried her to the bedroom.

Anything he'd done to her before was nothing to what she endured that night. And all the time, Marc was riding away, thinking she preferred this devil to him!

XII

Belen's explanation that Marc had been too restless to sleep and had decided to push on made the vaqueros' eyes go politely blank. Nor did anyone mention the bruised swelling on Frost's jaw. No one could see Talitha's bruises, the marks of his teeth and fingers on her body. She ached when she walked or sat or rode, constantly reminded of the savage uses he'd put her to.

This couldn't go on. She'd rather die than live like this. It would be a good bargain, if she could first kill Judah Frost. But if she were gone, what would happen to the children? Who'd hold the ranch together till the boys could take over?

A few more years, she concluded dully. Somehow, some way, she must manage that long.

That week, the culls went to market at Tubac. Lonnie, who was helping herd the cattle, asked if, after they were disposed of, he might take a week or so off.

"Saw some of Pete Kitchen's Opatas last week on the southwest range," he said with a mysterious grin. "They tell some interestin' stories. Since the cow work'll be slack for a while, ma'am, I'd purely like to mosey over to those mountains south of Yuma and have a look."

"Gold?" asked Frost with carelessness that was a little too elaborate.

Lonnie shrugged. "That's what the Opatas say."

"Whereabouts?"

Lonnie looked uncomfortable. "Oh, somewheres along the Devil's Road."

"That's a long road, son." Frost's smile didn't reach his eyes. "Dangerous to travel alone."

"Reckon I can take care of myself," Lonnie replied. As if enthusiasm overwhelmed caution, he added, "There's an old mission in the dunes. Most of the time it's covered with sand."

"The Mission of the Four Evangelists?" Frost asked.

"That's it."

Regretfully, Frost shook his head. "I fear Kitchen's Opatas were just spinning you a tale, lad."

"Sounded real to me," maintained Lonnie. "You follow the wash from Tinajas Altas, west, to a cone-shaped mountain with a dry riverbed running past. Down the river and west, is the mission—when it's not blown over with sand."

"No place to go alone," Frost said positively. "If thirst doesn't get you, Areneños will. Listen, I have to go to Yuma Crossing and don't mind detouring a bit. If there *is,* as rumors go, a store of gold and silver, I'll detail some trusted men from my freight company to pack it out, and we'll split. Isn't that better than getting killed trying to get it out by yourself?"

Lonnie considered. "Reckon so," he said finally. "The Opatas didn't want the gold themselves because they think the dead guard it, but I'm less scared of the dead than of them Areneños, which are supposed to be poison mean!"

Frost put out a long, slim hand, with beautifully kept nails a trifle long for a man. "Then we're partners! I'll meet you in Tubac day after tomorrow and it'll be Ho! for the Four Evangelists!"

Under pretext of last-minute instructions, Talitha got Lonnie aside by the corral. "Be careful," she warned him. "Even if you find the gold, Mr. Frost might decide not to share it."

Pushing back his yellow hair, Lonnie grinned boyishly. "Shucks, Miss Talitha, I know a trick or two myself. Don't you worry."

He swung into his saddle, pulled down his hat, and moved after the ambling cattle. Talitha wasn't aware of Frost's cat-footed approach till he spoke in her ear.

"Fond of him, aren't you?"

"He's a nice boy."

"Boy?" Frost's lips quirked down. "More of a man, Tally, especially in the way he looks at you. He's muscled out a lot from the stray who wandered in here last winter."

"He's still only a boy. If he's devoted to me, it's because Shea saved his life."

"Talitha!"

Argument would only make him suspicious. Shrugging, she stared at her husband. "You're very rich, Judah. You don't need more gold. If Lonnie doesn't come back, you'll answer for it."

"My love! So many fatal things happen in the desert."

"They'd better not happen to him. If they do, I'll see that charges are filed against you in the military court in Tucson."

He laughed. "And I'll tell my sad story of disaster and hint that, alas, my wife had too much tenderness for the young man—an ex-Rebel she'd harbored—and sought revenge where none was merited." Chuckling at her astounded anger, he put an arm around her. "Why must you always suspect me of villainy, sweetheart? As you say, I can give the lad his share and never miss it. That's what I intend to do."

"You promise?"

"Of course! This may well only be a wild story anyhow." He sighed ruefully, caressing her throat. "I assure you, Tally, when you learn that I don't like threats, our marriage will run much smoother."

She couldn't trust him, but apparently Lonnie was on guard. There was nothing more that she could do.

Without Frost, the whole atmosphere of the ranch was freer and happier and the work went smoothly. As the week passed after the vaqueros returned from Tubac, Talitha hoped Lonnie would return soon, and as fervently hoped Frost would be a long time about his business in Yuma Crossing. He'd never been at the ranch for the Roof Feast, and she hoped he wouldn't be this year. It would be hard enough to celebrate the founding of the ranch now that all four of its original owners were dead, but Frost's presence would be a blight.

Another week passed. Mesquite beans that had been drying on the roofs were stored in the round granary bins, and Talitha, with the twins and Cat, went up the mountain after piñon nuts and were back in four days with a good store of the thin-shelled, small, but delicious nuts. Belen took advantage of Cat's absence to slaughter a hog. She'd refused to eat pork since she saw a pig killed when she was about three, nor would she eat wild game.

"I would if I were hungry enough," she said in response to the twins' teasing. "But I'm not that hungry."

She ate beef only in stews, and less and less of that. Talitha had worried at first that such a diet would make Cat weak, but when it hadn't, she stopped trying to cajole her. It was part of Cat, her quick, passionate sympathy, incongruous as it was on a cattle ranch in a violent country where even human life was cheap.

Two days after they returned from the piñon excursion, the lookout struck the signal for one rider. As the household took their positions, Talitha gasped.

It looked like Marc's claybank, and she thought he was the broad-shouldered horseman. But wasn't that Lonnie's spotted horse he was leading? What was that serape-wrapped bundle draped across the pinto's saddle?

It *was* Marc.

Telling Carmencita to get some food ready, Talitha ran out, followed by the twins and Cat. She'd never hoped to see Marc again. What had brought him? She was terribly afraid that the answer swayed across the saddle of the other horse.

"Cat," she panted, "you go back and keep Sewa inside."

"But I want to see Marc!"

"You will. But right now, do what I say."

Cat went reluctantly. Patrick called to Marc, "Where's Lonnie?"

Marc didn't answer till he was close enough to speak in a normal voice, jerking his head toward the shapeless huddle in the blanket. "I brought him home to bury."

Talitha's hand flew to her throat. Lonnie? Dead, after Shea and others had saved him? Dead, so young? When, as he often said, he felt for the first time he belonged someplace, that he had a home?

"How—" she began, but could get no further.

Marc watched her a moment, the harsh set of his face softening. "Here, boys, if you please." The frontier hadn't taken away his European courtesy. Handing each of them the reins of a horse, he dismounted, wincing as the weight came down on his bad leg.

Coming to Talitha, he took her hands and held them strongly. "Talitha, your husband is dead. Does that grieve you?"

She stared at him, fierce, unholy joy flaming through her, momentarily overwhelming her desolation over Lonnie. "Grieved? I'm glad—so glad! Oh, Marc, I've wanted to die! But are you *sure?* He came back once—"

"Not this time, he won't. I found him sprawled below the third tank at Tinajas Altas. The first two were dried up." Marc shook his head. "There was plenty of water in the third one, but he didn't make it. He was weak from a bullet in the shoulder. I buried him there on the little slope above the wash, where so many others lie beneath crosses. His horse was dead, too. It's terrible that so many manage to reach the tanks, but if the first one's empty, and it often is in dry times, dozens lack the strength to scale the steep, smooth stone."

"An awful way to die." Much as she hated Frost, she wouldn't have wished that death for him. "But he deserved it, if anyone ever did. What about Lonnie?"

"I wondered what Frost had been up to, so I followed his tracks down the wash. A few hours from the tanks I found Lonnie, what was left of him. He and Frost had tangled. You have a notion why?"

Talitha nodded. When she could speak, she said, "Lonnie . . . guessed how it was with Judah and me, even before you came. After that, I think he knew how I . . . feel about you." For a moment their eyes met, and she could see his passion in his eyes.

Briefly she explained Frost's threats, the way he'd made it impossible for her to defy him. "Lonnie knew there'd be trouble for me if Judah was killed where I could be blamed for it. That's why he made up the story about knowing where that lost mission is." She trembled with anguish. "And Judah killed him! It's my fault."

"Your fault? You gave the boy a way to pay back his captain. In the little time I was here, I could see that Lonnie was happy at the ranch, but it must have troubled him to know that Shea could have been there, but for him."

She shook her head, blinded by tears.

With a gruff sound of pity, Marc drew her into his arms. "Oh, my stubborn darling! If you'd only told me how it really was. . . ."

"You'd have tried to kill him and he might have killed you!" She sobbed against the deep, regular pounding of his heart. "I couldn't have borne that, Marc! But Lonnie . . ."

"Until he did something big for Shea's loved ones, I don't think he'd ever have felt he'd a right to be breathing. Let him go in peace, Tally. Look at what he did as Shea's love reaching from beyond death. Now, let's go and give his poor bones an honorable burial."

But first Marc drew her close, gently tilted up her face, kissed her tears, then found her lips. What started as a tender kiss turned suddenly to long-denied hunger. Talitha welcomed him with her arms, her mouth, the whole length of her body, but mostly with her heart which could finally be his.

Lonnie was buried beside Shea's cross, his remains still wrapped in the serape. Marc read some words for Talitha could not.

"'Amen, amen, I say unto you, Except a grain of wheat fall into the ground and die, it abideth alone: but if it die, it bringeth forth much fruit.'

"'I have fought a good fight, I have finished my course, I have kept the faith.'" Marc paused. "Our young brother did all these things. Let us pray for him, then, and honor his courage."

The ranch people knelt. Amid the murmur of prayers and soft weeping, Cat sobbed against Talitha. "Wh-why does everyone die, Tally? Die or go away?"

"They don't, honey. Sometimes they come back or live happier than ever."

But there were too many crosses on the hill. Though Frost's death had lifted a crushing weight from her—though she was grateful to the depths of her being that she and Marc now could make a life together—when Talitha looked at the rough cross that spelled out Lonnie's name and his twenty short years, she felt that parts of herself lay buried in each grave: her childhood with Socorro; the girl who'd ridden with the vaqueros, petted and spoiled, with Santiago; and with Shea, the child, girl, and woman who had loved him all those ways and all those years.

But with Lonnie, the nightmare of Judah Frost was

gone. Marc raised her to her feet. With Sewa in his arms and Cat clinging to Talitha's hand, they walked down the hill together, Marc's limp reminding Talitha that he, too, had endured his private hells, yet had the will to love her.

"I have a lot to make up to you," she said, touching his scarred cheek.

He smiled. "Don't be humble, Tally. It's not your nature."

"I'm a better judge of that than you are!" she began, then caught herself at the wicked twinkle in his eyes. "Oh, Marc, you're—"

"I look forward to hearing all about myself," he assured her. "But there are many things I've been saving up to tell you."

His voice was stern. Was she now to get a recitation of all her follies and shortcomings? They had reached the house. Leaving the little girls in the courtyard, Talitha marched into the *sala* and turned on him with her chin raised high.

"Well? Tell me!"

He touched her hair with his big hand. "I love you." He kissed her forehead and then her eyes. "I love you," he said, claiming her mouth. "That's what I want to tell you. Over and over, in every way there is."

All the grief, all the despair, all the bitter waiting melted into a foundation for this joy, this peace, this rightness. "Oh, my love," she said, laughing through her tears. "Welcome home! Welcome to me."

She was his woman, not second best as she would always have been to Shea. If it hadn't been for Socorro's death, she'd never have thought of Shea as a lover at all but would have loved Marc with no reservations, no mixed and tortured loyalties.

But she had protected the children, she had kept the ranch, she had honored the debt she owed her foster parents. At last Marc was here and she was free to love him.

As he swept her close, she caught a flash of Socorro's smile and seemed to hear Shea laughing. Then all she could heed were Marc's kisses, his strong, enfolding arms.

PART IV

Caterina

1869–1871

XIII

Cat woke to *Las Mañanitas,* yawned, smiled, and stretched. The vaqueros had started singing it by her window on her eighth birthday, the year her father had gone away, and had done it ever since. Though it seemed a bit ridiculous for Chuey and Rodolfo, who must be at least forty, and Belen, turned sixty, to be serenading a girl on her sixteenth birthday. Not knowing how to gracefully drop the custom, they'd probably keep it up till she married, bless them. She lay there, loving them, the ranch, her life, then slipped out of bed and ran to the window.

"Thousand thanks, *caballeros,*" she laughed. "You give my birthday a beautiful beginning."

Rodolfo's elegant mustache was sprinkled with gray, and Chuey's smallpox-pitted face was beginning to have creases reminiscent of Pedro's, his father's. Belen, though much the oldest, had almost unlined skin and his hair was still black. They bowed, these rawhide men who'd taught her to ride and use the *reata,* wished her felicitations, and left the courtyard with the awkward, bowlegged gait of men who never walked if they could ride.

On her birthday mornings, before she did anything else, she went up the hill to her parents' graves. Father wasn't there, of course, but his memory was.

She'd started doing that as soon as she began to

understand that her mother had died giving birth to her, but it wasn't a pilgrimage of grief or guilt. She hadn't really missed a mother. Talitha had been that, and there was Anita, her milk-mother, and dear Carmencita for a grandmother.

Father was different. She remembered him well, his red, waving hair, the blue-gray eyes, the cheek branded for James's sake. James! Was he never coming back? She wouldn't let herself even think that he might not be alive. It was almost seven years now that he'd been away, but she still ached when she let herself remember. She forced her thoughts away from him.

She'd mourned her father more than anyone had known, for Talitha had been in such distress that she'd moved about like a sleepwalker. Thank goodness that wretched Judah Frost was gone and Talitha was happy with Marc. They had been married in the *sala* during the Roof Feast in December of 1863, the *sala* where Cat's parents had made their vows, though no priest could be had.

I shall marry there, too, Cat thought. Making her bed and dressing quickly, she wondered if she'd already met her husband. Many girls were mothers at her age.

Paulita, her companion from babyhood, had last month married a miner from the San Patricio, which Marc had returned to operation after the war. Anselmo Lopez had become a vaquero at the ranch so Paulita wouldn't have to leave her family, but he was the only new hand at the main ranch, though at El Charco, where Pedro and his family had returned, two brothers of Natividad's Papago wife, Mársat, had started work. Ramón, Chuey's son, at thirteen rode with the vaqueros, and at both El Charco and the Socorro sons were growing up to fill their fathers' boots, daughters to maintain the households.

Some would leave, probably, but others would make up for that by marrying new people. Cat wondered again whom she herself would marry.

Lt. Claybourne Frazier was certainly handsome and

gallant. Assigned to Camp Crittenden, founded in 1867 close to where old Fort Buchanan had been, the young cavalry officer stopped at the ranch more often than could possibly be necessary. Several times, off duty, he'd gone riding with Cat, her brothers, and Miguel's wife, Juriana.

Now there was a proper romance! The French had invaded Mexico beginning in the winter of 1861–62, took Mexico City in June 1863, forced President Benito Juárez to flee, and installed Maximilian, Archduke of Austria, as emperor in 1864. Fierce fighting continued, however, and when the French landed troops at Guaymas in 1865 and began overrunning Sonora, Governor Pesqueira refuged at Calabazas, where he was shown every courtesy by the commander of Fort Mason, the new post above Pete Kitchen's ranch that had replaced the makeshift one at Tubac.

After listening to stories of French atrocities in what had, after all, been his mother's homeland, seventeen-year-old Patrick, who was spoiling for a fight anyway, declared that he was going south to help the loyal Sonorans battle the invaders and conservatives who'd joined with the Imperialists. Miguel thought he was quite mad but, when all arguments failed, fatalistically went with his twin. Belen had asked them, if they were near Alamos, to ask at the nearby Tres Lobos mine for his brother, Juan Leyva.

The twins, with a few of Pesqueira's more militant followers, got to Alamos, their mother's old home, in time to fight in Gen. Antonio Rosales's desperate attempt to retake the old city against tremendous odds. The general and a third of his men were killed.

The survivors retreated, but they were back in a few months with Gen. Angel Martinez. His cavalry and machete-wielding soldiers took the city and pressed on. By mid-September of 1866, the French garrison at Guaymas had sailed off, leaving the Mexican Imperialists to die or make peace. Though it would be February of 1867 before, under extreme U.S. pressure, all

French troops left the country, and June when poor, proud, foolish Maximilian died before a firing squad, fighting ended in Sonora that bloody September of 1866.

Even Patrick had had more than his fill of fighting. The twins started home but stopped at the Tres Lobos mine to inquire for Belen's brother.

Juan Leyva had died in a mine accident several years before, but his daughter Juriana was constantly harassed by the mineowner's son, who thought any pretty Yaqui girl should be honored by his attentions.

Miguel, usually so calm, had come upon the young dandy trying to force the girl. Without even knowing who she was, Miguel had, with furious, quiet efficiency, beaten her attacker senseless. They knew there would be trouble when he crawled home, so the twins decided to leave at once, asking Juriana to give Juan Leyva a message. That was when they learned that he was dead and that they'd saved his daughter.

Then Miguel, usually so cautious and controlled, had asked her to come with them and marry him as soon as they were past the vengeance of the mineowner. Juriana looked at the stranger, took a long, deep breath, and put her life and happiness in his hands. She stopped only long enough to say good-bye to her dead mother's *comadre,* with whom she lived, and tell her where she was going. They'd been married in Hermosillo. Juriana would have to stop riding before much longer. She was expecting their first child.

It was probably a good thing they'd married in Mexico, for Arizona law forbade marriage with an Indian, Negro, or Oriental. Marc, a delegate to the first territorial legislature, thought it a bad law and had opposed it then as well as trying to get it repealed last time he served, the year before.

The kindest view of most of his fellow legislators was that a foreigner didn't understand the dangers of miscegenation. When Marc pointed out that alliances took place anyway and the children were entitled to protection, he was hooted down and asked if he had his eye on some squaw. He trounced the questioner after adjournment, but the law remained.

Miguel and Juriana would probably stay at the ranch, where they occupied Shea's old room, but Patrick was getting restless. Marc had taught him a lot about geology and mining, and he was talking of prospecting that fall in the mountains east of the San Patricio mine, shrugging at reminders that the Apaches in those parts were as predatory as ever.

"If Tom Jeffords could make friends with Cochise, maybe I can, too," he grinned irrepressibly.

Jeffords was superintendent of the stage line that carried military mail between Fort Bowie and Tucson. After repeated attacks on his men and himself, he'd decided to seek Cochise out and ask if he'd let the mail service operate in peace. Cochise must have been astounded at the bravery of Jeffords in coming alone. After deliberating a day, he'd told Jeffords his men would be allowed to pass unharmed; and, almost incredibly, his word had been kept.

"Besides, wasn't I carried in Mangus's cradleboard?" Patrick demanded, eyes dancing.

"So was I," retorted Miguel. "But it didn't turn me loco!"

"You're just jealous because Juri won't let you come," Patrick taunted. "Never mind. I'll take Cinco and we'll find our fortune while you're cutting calves and fighting screwworms."

Cinco, fourteen now, had worked at the spring branding and was due again that fall. Since their return from Sonora, he'd become good friends with both his half brothers, often went hunting with them, and silently worshiped Cat in a way she found disconcerting.

He *was* her brother, as much as James was Talitha's, but she'd only seen him a few times before that spring. The shy little boy she remembered who'd given her his blue bird and whistle seemed entirely different from the tall boy who had Tjúni's coloring but his father's cast of feature and slim, muscular build.

I've changed, too, thought Cat, peering into the mirror as she brushed her hair. Tally said her hair was as black and soft as Socorro's, her eyes as blue-gray as Shea's. The hair dipped in a widow's peak which, with her delicately pointed chin, gave her a heart-shaped face. A rather short nose and prominent cheekbones made her, she thought, somewhat resemble a cat. Maybe it wasn't a pretty face, but she comforted herself that it was at least unusual and she had nice teeth and skin.

She smiled slowly, trying to guess what the effect would be on Lieutenant Frazier. That made her wonder what Jordan, Talitha's young uncle, would think if he could see her primping, and *that* made her stick out her tongue, then whirl from the mirror at Sewa's giggle.

"So you're awake!" Swooping down on the nine-year-old, Cat hugged and shook her. "Are you going up the hill with me?"

Sewa nodded, slipping her narrow feet out of bed, taking off her nightgown, and wriggling into a cotten dress. Her father, Santiago, lay beside Cat's parents, and for several years now the younger girl had made the early-morning journey with Cat. Poor Lonnie, beneath the fourth cross, had no children, but perhaps he knew that Talitha had planted wild roses on his grave.

And Santiago. From things Talitha had said, Cat was positive that he'd loved Socorro. Did he know that his daughter, with eyes as golden as his own, knelt at his resting place and prayed for his peace?

Cat sat between her mother's grave and her father's cross. Silently, she remembered all she knew about them, things she would pass on to her children and their children of this man and woman who had loved each other so much that the tall, red-haired Irishman's heart had gone into the grave with his wife.

You're together now, Cat thought. *Please help me to*

be kind and brave and loving as you both were. Then she didn't think anymore but was simply with them as the early sun warmed the hill.

Sixteen was grown up and she hadn't expected big presents, or many of them, but when breakfast passed and dinner with only smiled "Happy birthdays," Cat began to feel a bit subdued. It wasn't that a present had to be expensive, imported from San Francisco or the East. But not to get anything . . .

Chiding her disappointment, she spent the afternoon gathering hackberries and squawberries with Sewa, Talitha, and Paulita. She was washing the stickiness of squawberries off her hands when Sewa called. "Come out to the corral, Cati! Jordan has something to show you."

Jordan? This younger half brother of Talitha's father was twenty-five but he seemed much older. Coming out from Iowa three years ago, he'd first worked on his brother's ranch on the Verde River in central Arizona, had decided he'd like to see more of the territory before he settled, and had come to work at the Socorro a little over a year ago.

Beyond the fact that he wasn't a Mormon like Jared Scott, Cat knew little about him. He spoke even less than Miguel, though he took in everything that was said. More than once Cat had broken off in confusion when, in the midst of some rash or joking declaration, she'd found his contemplative hazel eyes watching her, his mouth curved in faint amusement.

At such times she felt younger than Sewa and smarted at what she took for patronizing indulgence. He wasn't *that* much older! Now, surrounded by the vaqueros, their families, the twins, and Marc and Talitha, Jordan held the reins of a glorious blood-bay gelding, smoothing his neck, talking to him gently. It was a marvel to the ranch folk that an Iowa farm boy was so skillful with horses. He must have bartered with someone, perhaps one of the officers at the camp, for

Cat had never seen this horse, or one of his exact coloring, a rich brown-red so dark it was almost black, on the ranch.

"What a beauty!" She spoke softly to the gelding. Only when he seemed to accept her did she smooth his muzzle, pat his strong-muscled neck. "Where'd you get him, Jordan?"

"Bought him from a Kentuckian who needed a stake for prospecting. How do you like him?"

"He's marvelous!" She flushed, then glanced quickly from beneath her lashes to see if Jordan had that odious smile. He didn't; he was truly laughing and for once looked as young as he was, sun turning his brown hair almost red. "What are you going to call him?"

"Sangre might be good. It means fire and spirit as well as blood."

Her eyes widened as she noticed the saddle. The horn was inlaid with silver, and so were the rigging buttons and rings. The bullnose tapaderos fastened to the stirrups were tooled in a rose design to match the work on the skirts. The headstall of the bridle was silver-mounted, and silver conchos flashed as Jordan put the reins in Cat's hands.

"He's from all of us. The saddle and bridle are from Marc, Talitha, and your brothers. Happy sixteenth birthday, Caterina."

"Happy birthday!" the others chorused.

Cat's chest tightened. And she'd thought they'd overlooked her birthday! "He's too beautiful!" Tears stung the corners of her eyes. "And the saddle! It's too much!"

"I thought so." Patrick grinned, tweaking a lock of her hair. "But then Miguel pointed out that you've never had a new saddle and your present hand-me-down's close to falling apart."

Miguel nodded. "It's time you turned Mancha out to grass. She's as old as you are!"

Cat ignored their teasing. "Sangre!" she whispered, caressing him. "Beautiful blood-bay *caballo!*"

"Get your guitar, Chuey!" called Patrick. "She's going to make up a song to him!"

"I've worked him with a blanket," Jordan said. "He won't shy at your skirts. And he handles light, seems to read your mind. Of course, he's used to English words. Cluck and he starts. Whoa and he stops."

Cat glanced at Talitha and Anita. "May I? Just a short ride?"

Anita chuckled. "Didn't I know you'd have to have your gallop? Supper will wait—but not too long."

Besides her beloved Mancha, Cat had ridden dozens of horses, but she was awed by Sangre. "Please love me," she murmured in his ear. "You deserve the best rider in the world, *un vaquero muy grande,* but I'll be very good to you!"

Kilting her skirts, she mounted as decorously as possible. He turned at the shift of her weight and the pressure of her legs, appearing not to need even a touch of the rein on his neck, and paced springingly along the trail down to the creek, one ear and eye watching ahead, the others directed toward her to pick up her intentions. Because of the way a horse's eyes set, he can see in all directions and each eye works independently. Belen said it was nature's way of protecting him from enemies coming up from behind.

When they were a little used to each other, she rose slightly, leaning a bit forward. He skimmed into a smooth lope that ate the distance. Oh, to ride like this, on such a horse, wind stinging his mane against her face! There was no finer, better way to be sixteen.

"Ah, *mi caballo!*" she called to him, laughing joyously. "We'll travel many miles together, many years!" She thought to herself that she must have been crazy that morning to wonder whom she was going to marry. Who wanted to trade such freedom for keeping house for a man?

Reluctantly turning home, Cat insisted on rubbing Sangre down herself and giving him grain in a nosebag.

Sighing happily, she watched him lie down in the dust and roll vigorously before he rose and trotted off.

Jordan and Belen, who'd apparently waited for her, smiled at her praises for Sangre and walked with her to the house, where they all washed at the bench outside before entering the big kitchen.

"I'm glad you like the horse," Jordan said, handing her a clean corner of the coarse towel. "He's been well trained but has all his spirit."

Cat nodded somewhat ruefully. "He's much too wonderful for me."

"What do you mean?" Jordan frowned.

She had to think a moment. "I won't need all the things he can do—won't use him till he really has to try, the way a vaquero would."

Jordan regarded her quizzically. "You think horses—and people—should be pushed to their limits?"

She hadn't thought of it that way and floundered a bit. "It makes them stronger if they are. And it seems a shame to do only part of what's possible."

The young man's frown vanished. His hazel eyes laughed down at her. "Don't feel sorry for Sangre yet, Caterina! I've got a notion you'll drive man or horse either one to the end of his tether!"

That was the sort of remark that would have made her angry if he hadn't just joined in giving her the most splendid horse in all Arizona and Sonora. Now she only laughed and hurried into the house. She was disheveled from the ride, but she couldn't keep the others any longer from their meal.

Horrors! There was Lieutenant Frazier lounging in the front door, talking with Marc and the twins. Too late to retreat. Gray eyes lighting, he came forward, bowed gallantly, and wished her happy birthday.

"I brought you a small gift." He presented a tissue-wrapped object. Was it accident that his fingers brushed hers? "I hope it's not presumptuous of me to stop by at such a family occasion."

Talitha would already have invited him to supper. Annoyed though she was at being caught with windblown hair and a dress the worse for berry picking and her ride, Cat could scarcely do otherwise than say, "We're always glad to have guests, Lieutenant."

He obviously expected her to open his gift. Unwrapping it, she found a book by an author who was new to her, Mark Twain. "This *Innocents Abroad* is his first book," the lieutenant said. "But his story 'The Celebrated Jumping Frog of Calaveras County' made him famous two years ago. I had asked my sister to procure a copy of Miss Louisa May Alcott's *Little Women,* but the bookseller was out of that and recommended this. I hope you won't find the way Twain pokes fun at Europe's treasures and traditions too offensive."

"It sounds like tremendous fun," Cat assured him. *How could such a dashing-looking cavalry officer sound such a prig?* "Thank you, and please thank your sister."

He managed to sit next to her, but if he'd had any hope of semiprivate conversation, it had to vanish when Jordan took the seat directly opposite.

"Well, Lieutenant," he said amiably, "have you chased any Apaches lately?"

"We're always scouting," Frazier replied somewhat defensively. "But we never seem to encounter the devils. They fade into the ground. Tom Gardner, who sells the camp produce, has been attacked so often that soldiers are detailed to guard his place, but we can't station men everywhere. By the time we get word of a raid, the redskins are gone."

Talitha shook her bright head. At twenty-nine, quietly glowing with the love she and Marc had for each other, she was in the full bloom of strong, proud beauty. The birth of blond little Shea three years ago had made her figure richer, softening a slight angularity, just as Marc's cherishing had eased the sternness brought by too heavy and too early burdens. Dear

Tally, she deserved her joys. If only James would come back. . . .

That thought hurt so much that Cat refused to dwell on it and concentrated on what Talitha was saying. "Poor Larcena! Her brother, Jim, was ambushed and killed last year. Now it's her father and favorite brother. Shea and I went to see her after she survived that lancing the Apaches gave her in 1860."

When the lieutenant raised his eyebrows, Talitha explained how newly wed Larcena, one of the Pennington daughters, had been abducted along with a little Mexican girl, lanced eleven times, shoved down a ravine, and stoned. Left for dead in the snow, she at last roused enough to drag homeward. After sixteen days with only a little grass to eat and some spilled flour she found at a lumber camp, she crawled to a lumbering road and was rescued.

With a certain shock, Cat realized that nearly everyone at the table had survived disasters that might boggle this young officer's mind, though they all accepted them matter-of-factly. Marc, Belen, and the twins had fought through wars; Talitha had seen her relatives killed and burned by Apaches, watched her captive mother die, been forced to fill Socorro's place, to lose Santiago and Shea.

And James? Cat flinched from the memory. Every vaquero had lost kin to Apaches or bandits. Sewa was orphaned. So, for that matter, were Cat and her brothers, but the love of Talitha and the ranch folk had kept them from feeling alone.

Marc turned the subject to the new governor, Anson P. K. Safford, of whom he thought highly. "He served two terms in the California legislature and was chairman of the committee on education. He's proved himself a public-spirited man who intends to stay in the West, unlike our first two governors, Goodwin and McCormick, who came and went, using their appointments as steppingstones."

"He sounds rash." Jordan grinned. "Didn't he just marry, in July, a girl he met in April in San Francisco?"

Talitha smiled at this uncle who was several years her junior. "He waited till he was thirty-nine, which isn't very impulsive. Maybe he makes up his mind quickly when he sees what he wants."

"Maybe." Jordan's hazel eyes touched Cat. This time he had that curious little half-smile on his lips. She immediately turned to the lieutenant and asked if he wanted more tamales.

He took one, thanked her, and said respectfully to Marc, "I'm glad you have a good opinion of Governor Safford, sir. Your experience in the legislature must have given you insight into the kind of administrator the territory needs."

"Safford wants to start educating Arizona's children, all of them. He knows well enough that something has to be done about the Apaches, but he's shocked that there's only one public school in the state, at Prescott."

"But, dear," frowned Talitha, "in that very first legislature didn't you set aside money for public schools?"

"Indeed we did." Marc chuckled. There was considerable gray in his brown hair, but his frank blue eyes were young. "There we sat in a two-room cabin made of pine logs so new they still wept pitch. There hadn't been time to chink the walls and the wind kept us well ventilated even with all the hot air we filled the place with. An early storm drove us out completely and we adjourned to the governor's mansion to do our law-making. A far cry from the last political body I attended, the 1848 Prussian constituent assembly in Berlin."

He went on to tell how the nine-member Council and eighteen-member House of Representatives had fittingly enough elected Charles Poston as their first delegate to the United States Congress, for without his tireless endeavors there still might not be any Arizona Territory. They'd instructed Poston to besiege Congress for mail service and money to pay and equip volunteer Indian fighters, and then they got around to education.

"In the end," Marc concluded, "we elected a Board of Regents for the university we hope to have someday, gave two hundred and fifty dollars to the mission school at San Xavier, and granted two hundred and fifty dollars each to the county-seat towns of Prescott, La Paz, and Mohave for schools, provided the towns raised matching amounts. Tucson could have had five hundred dollars by making instruction in the English language part of the curriculum. Only Prescott matched the money."

Cat sniffed. "Why, that means Talitha's given more money for schools than the legislature!"

As Judah Frost's widow and only traceable beneficiary, Talitha had inherited his businesses. She had cleared his considerable debts by selling his shares in several freighting companies. Not wanting to profit from the estate of the man she'd hated, she turned some of the proceeds from the Tecolote mine, which Marc administered, over to San Xavier's school and used the rest for a school and infirmary at Tecolote as well as pensions for aged or disabled miners and their families. Part of the profit from the San Patricio was spent in similar ways.

Suddenly, Jordan, though pleasant in manner, seemed bound to harass Lieutenant Frazier. "I can't understand, sir, why the Apaches are worse than ever when there are so many forts and camps. You'll have to forgive me if I can't see that the army does much but escort government officials and their own supplies."

Frazier colored to the roots of his fair hair. "To control over thirty thousand Indians there are fewer than three thousand troops in Arizona, Scott. They're scattered among nine posts so separated by distance and rough country that it's almost impossible for one post to come to the aid of another. Sickness has been a problem, too. Camp Crittenden seems to be healthier than most, but often there are more men sick with intermittent fever at Camp Wallen than are fit for duty."

Marc interposed mildly, "There may have been some failures of common sense over at Camp Wallen. I understand that the men and officers complained constantly of sleeping in their 'A' tents till General McDowell reminded them of General Order 80 which instructs men to make their own shelters out of what's at hand. That was when the commanding officers got a Mexican herder to show them how to make adobes. Is it true, Lieutenant, that Wallen's being abandoned?"

Frazier nodded. "Next month." He brooded a moment, then swung on Jordan and counterattacked. "There'd be long faces among the civilians, sir, if we didn't escort the paymasters! Why, the territory lives by supplying the army! If it weren't for government contracts and sales, where would your freighters and merchants and farmers be?"

It was a fair thrust. Jordan chuckled. "It's like my father used to say. We worked all summer to grow enough grain to feed the horses through the winter so they could plow for the grain next summer."

Frazier was not to be mollified. "We get infantry when what we need is cavalry. And though we're better off directed by the Department of California than that of New Mexico, what we really need is a Department of Arizona."

"It'll come," Marc said. "Safford's traveling to Washington at his own expense to plead the special problems of our territory. I think he'll get at least part of what we need." He smiled down the table at Cat. "This is no way to celebrate a sixteenth birthday, is it, *chiquita?* Chuey, Rodolfo, get your guitars and let's have a *baile!*"

XIV

In spite of his limp, Marc danced with Talitha, and also with Cat, murmuring teasingly in her ear, "One thing that's quite nice for a birthday is to have two handsome young men paying court."

"Two?" she puzzled.

He glanced at Jordan, who was whirling a gasping, laughing Anita. "You mean you've never guessed?"

Unaccountably distressed, Cat shook her head. "Not Jordan. He thinks I'm a child."

"Does he?" Marc smiled and surrendered her to the lieutenant.

He danced as well as Marc, who'd learned in Berlin and taught the vaqueros how to play a waltz, but Claybourne Frazier's strong hand on her back, his fingers holding hers, gave her a strange, breathless feeling, as if something she both feared and desired were about to happen.

"Your uncle gibes me about Indians," the lieutenant said with a harsh laugh. "But if he thinks anything he can say will stop me from coming to see you—" He broke off in confusion. "Forgive me, Miss O'Shea. That sounds presumptuous of me. But you can't know how eagerly I've waited for your birthday. With your consent, I want to ask your stepfather if I may call on you."

Cat gulped, stared, and swallowed again. Her confusion seemed to restore Frazier's usual confidence. He drew her a little closer, laughing. "Is it such a shock? I'll be bound everyone else guesses, including your vigilant uncle."

"He's not my uncle," said Cat, recovering her breath. "And Marc isn't my stepfather." She explained the relationships of the household, to the lieutenant's mounting astonishment.

"It's all so . . . irregular! Mrs. Revier no blood relative of you and your brothers; Mr. Scott her uncle instead of her brother, no kin of yours in either case; and that pretty little Indian girl no kin to any of you!"

"She's Santiago's child. We couldn't love her more."

Frazier glanced with awed admiration at Talitha. "A remarkable lady! So, when your mother died, she raised you, though she was only a girl herself?"

"She's been my mother and sister both. When she was only six and captive in an Apache camp, she mothered her baby half brother, fed him on piñon-honey gruel when Juh's wives would have let him starve."

"Half brother?" The lieutenant's eyes narrowed.

"Her mother became Juh's wife. She died in childbirth."

The lieutenant made a small whistling sound between his teeth. "Where is this half-breed brother?"

Cat stopped dancing. "Don't call him that!"

"I'm sorry." The lieutenant passed his hand across his eyes. "It's just such a shock." He smiled cajolingly and moved back into the lilting dance. "Where is Mrs. Revier's brother?"

"We don't know." Cat bit her lips to stop their trembling and her eyes stung. If only James were here! She would give anything, yes, even Sangre, if James would come back. "He took some cattle to Mangus Coloradas, his foster father, a month or two before the chief was treacherously killed by soldiers early in 1863."

Now it was the lieutenant's turn to stop in his tracks. "*Treacherously?* That old scoundrel!"

"The white men pretended to talk peace, but when they tricked Mangus into their camp, his guards tormented and killed him." Cat wrested free of the officer, glaring at him with clenched fists. "Mangus was my parents' friend! My brothers slept in the cradleboard he gave them! And he took good care of James when he . . . went away for the first time."

"Mangus was a bloodthirsty, murdering heathen!"

"You can't call him that under this roof!"

Frazier's jaw dropped. "Are you telling me to go?"

"Yes, if you're going to talk like that!"

"But it doesn't make sense! One minute you're all talking about Larcena Pennington and how dangerous the Apaches are, and the next you're furious with me for telling the truth."

"What truth is that, Lieutenant?" asked Jordan. Slipping an arm around Cat, he drew her away. "In any case, you've monopolized our birthday lady much too long. I haven't even had a dance."

Frazier bowed. "Good night, Miss O'Shea." His voice was tightly furious. "May I wish that this next year will bring you happiness—and, I trust, more . . . maturity?"

Swinging away, he sought out Talitha and Marc to take his leave. Jordan smiled down at Cat.

"Want to tell me what that was all about?"

"He—he called Mangus a murdering heathen!"

"Well, so he was," said Jordan calmly.

Cat made a sound of outrage and tried to pull free, but Jordan held her inexorably, then dipped her so low she went off balance and only his arm and hands kept her on her feet.

"Listen, Katie," Jordan began quietly. It was the first time he'd called her that, though it had been Shea's name for her. A wave of longing for her father welled up so powerfully in Cat that tears sprang to her eyes and she averted her face. Jordan's arm tightened. "Honey, why are you crying?"

"I—I—you called me Katie."

"Is that so awful?"

"N-no. It's just what Daddy called me."

"It seems right for you. But if you'd rather I didn't . . ."

"No," she said hastily, freeing her hand to dash away her tears before she smiled at him. "It's nice to hear it again. Caterina's so long and Cat's so short. Katie's in between."

"So it is," he agreed seriously. "So, Katie, allow me to say that though I don't especially like the lieutenant, you can scarcely blame him for saying of Mangus what, in fact, is true. It'd count more if you told your family's experience of Mangus, which is equally right."

She knew he was saying what was reasonable and wise, but she was still angry. Lifting her chin, she stared vindictively after the vanishing lieutenant and blurted, "He called James a half-breed!"

Jordan was still for a moment. "Ah," he murmured. "So that's what it was. You think a lot of James, don't you, Katie?"

"I guess I love him more than anyone in the world."

Jordan missed a measure, recovered, and said, "Why's that, honey? I know you love your brothers and Talitha and Sewa. You seem to love all the ranch people. Yet James comes first?"

She nodded, remembering James with the aching sadness that overwhelmed her when she let herself think of him. "James doesn't have anyone really his own. Talitha wanted him to grow up white. She loved him but hated the Apaches for what happened to her mother and uncles."

"And James is part Apache."

"Yes, and he's proud of it. His father was a renowned warrior. Mangus was his foster father."

Reflectively, Jordan said, "Sounds to me, Katie, as if you're mixing sympathy with love."

"I'm not *sorry* for James. He'd never allow that. But he's . . . alone."

"Maybe not."

She frowned, glancing up. "What do you mean?"

"How old is James?"

"Twenty-two in July," she said immediately.

"Haven't you thought he might be married? He could even have a child or two."

Such a thought had never entered her mind. Angrily, she rejected it. "I don't believe it! He wouldn't—"

"What better way to make himself all one thing?"

There was frightening reason in that. The idea of James having a wife, any wife, filled her with desolation. She didn't understand why, except that he was hers in a private way she couldn't explain.

"He'll come back," she said resolutely. "And he won't be married, either."

Jordan sighed. "Why do you feel this way about him? As far as I can tell, Cinco, your half brother, is in the same fix of being betwixt and between white and Indian."

"Cinco was raised pure Papago. He and his Indian brothers and sister own Tjúni's land. He's never had a second's worry about where he belonged. Besides, no one wants to kill or drive out the Papagos."

They danced in silence, Cat tense and on edge, Jordan preoccupied. At last he said, "What if he never comes back, Katie?"

Her heart contracted. "Don't say that! I couldn't bear it."

He lifted her easily from the doorsill, danced her down the porch. "Seven years. You were only nine. Can't you be longing after someone you've dreamed over and imagined till you've created a James that doesn't exist?"

"James is real. I haven't made him up." To convince Jordan, Cat pulled out a secret memory that she kept buried deep. "An outcast Apache caught me on the way into the mountains not long after James came back to us and was taking me away to sell. James followed and killed him. It hurt James a lot that the first man he killed was an Apache."

"It would've been fine if it'd been a white?"

She twisted away. "You're as bad as the lieutenant!"

"Am I?" Jordan caught her close. In the light from the window his face was grim, a stranger's. "Has Frazier done this, then?"

Lifting her face, he kissed her, stopping her outraged protest with his hard lips, which burned punishingly at first as she struggled in shocked fury, then grew softer, caressing, beseeching as they demanded, draining her of strength.

Quiet in his arms a moment after he raised his head, she found his strength oddly comforting and felt an irrational desire to stay close to him, hearing that deep, steady pounding of his heart. It was Jordan who stepped back and held her at arm's length.

"Well?" he said. "Has Frazier done that?"

Angry again, the curious truce of their bodies snapped by his scornful words, Cat flamed at him. "It's none of your business!"

"It's very much my business." He held her firmly. Short of kicking or biting, she couldn't escape. She *wouldn't* let him drive her to such childish resorts.

Gritting her teeth, she stood as tall as she could, which wasn't very. "Please enlighten me, Mr. Scott. When did whom I do or don't kiss become your concern?"

"When I decided to marry you."

Her heart stopped, then began to thunder in her ears. "You! Marry me?"

"That's what I said."

Curiosity overcame her half-flattered, half-outraged surprise. "When did you start thinking anything like that?"

He laughed dryly. "I started thinking exactly that about the minute I laid eyes on you June 18, year of our Lord 1868." When she looked up at him in astonishment, he added softly, as if recalling a dream he didn't want to lose, "When I rode in, you were in the corral, feeding an orphan foal, a black one. The wind blew your hair into its mane. I thought you were like a colt yourself—long-legged, wild, with a glossy new sheen on you."

"Like a colt!" She choked with laughter. "My goodness, Jordan, what a compliment!"

"It's not a compliment. It's how I saw you." His tone roughened. Letting go of her wrists, he put his hands on her shoulders. "I loved you then but knew I had to wait. It wasn't hard for a while—as long as you still looked like that knobby-kneed colt. You don't anymore."

"Are you sure?" She tried to lighten the taut awareness building between them.

It wasn't unpleasant, but it was strong and potent. She sensed its danger and wanted to control it till she understood it better, as one is wary on a strange, powerful horse while exhilarated by that leashed force. A tremor shook him.

"How can you understand?" His breath caught raggedly. "You're still so young! It's different anyway for women, I guess. I ache when I see you and hurt worse when I don't, as if a grizzly had torn off part of me and the rest was raw and bleeding."

The pain in his voice quenched her excitement, leaving her sorry and full of guilt. "Jordan—"

"Don't!" he said between his teeth.

"What?"

"Don't pity me. I'm not a starving foal or calf or raccoon or bird, like those you're always taking care of. I'm a man. I'm going to take care of you."

"But—"

"You hadn't a notion, had you?"

Mournfully, she shook her head. He laughed in a veering of mood that again sent her off balance. "It's all right, honey! I won't die while I wait for you to grow up. You may even flirt with your captains and lieutenants, try your fancy paces." He grinned and held her face between his long, hard palms. "Just remember I saw you first."

He lifted her over the threshold, surrendering her to Patrick while he danced off with Juri.

No more than a few minutes had passed, yet Jordan's kiss had swept Cat past a threshold as real as the one he'd physically danced her over, one she could never recross. Her mouth would never be the same again; nor her body, nor her heart. Was this how it was to be a woman? Would she love him? Was that what he'd made her feel, that tremulous, stormy, turbulent force? Whatever it was, she was glad to escape it now, in the refuge in her brother's arms.

"Cat!" He was giving her a little shake. "What's the matter with you? Why did Jordan take you outside?"

She made a face, hoping her tone was natural. "He gave me a scold for telling Lieutenant Frazier he couldn't call Mangus a murdering heathen and James a half-breed under this roof."

Patrick's red-gold eyebrows arched up. "So that's why Frazier stalked out as stiff as if he'd swallowed a bayonet! You may have lost your chance to marry a future general, Katie-Cat."

"Why does everybody all of a sudden start to talk about my getting married?" She grimaced. "You're a lot older than I am, five years! And Miguel's almost a father. Why don't *you* get married?"

He whistled. "Out of sorts, aren't you? Truce, little sister! Marry when you will, and so shall I, but not for a long time! There's lots I want to do without worrying about leaving a widow."

"Like hunting for gold?"

"Silver will do. Copper, even."

"When you go, Patrick, watch for James."

"I will. But he taught me to track. He'll see me first."

"You—you wouldn't kill him?"

"No!" The first shocked protest was followed by a

wry qualification. "Not unless I had to. But if he comes at me with a lance or a club, Cat, would you rather have me die?"

"He won't do that! Don't you remember?"

"What?"

"Tally says he promised our mother, before she rode off for the last time, that he'd take care of you twins, that he'd never let anything hurt you."

"Quite some promise for a seven-year-old," teased Patrick. "We're big boys now, Cat. Somehow we got through a war without James's help." He hushed her with a finger on her lips. "Don't fret. Next to you, Miguel, and Tally, I love James. I'd sure never hurt him if there were any choice."

It was time to dance with Miguel, then the vaqueros. Though she couldn't keep from watching Jordan when she saw his reddish-brown head higher than that of the other men, he never asked for another dance. She didn't know whether she was glad or sorry.

Patrick stayed at the Socorro for the fall branding and the *baille* given to celebrate the twenty-first birthday of himself and his twin.

The whole population of the Santa Cruz Valley from Magdalena to Tucson seemed to have turned out, including officers from Camp Crittenden and Camp Wallen, and of course all the El Charco folk were there.

Every person at the party lived under constant threat from Apaches and brigands, but for tonight they made merry and came together, neighbors in spite of the distances that separated most of them. Those who lived too far to go home would sleep wherever room could be found.

Two whole beeves roasted over fiery coals between the *ramada* and corrals. Iron and copper kettles of rice, beans and tamales simmered over smaller fires and tortillas, coffee and mescal were served from a wagon bed. Benches had been made for the comparatively few women, but they were so much in demand for dancing that none, from Sewa to an aged aunt of Doña Rosa's, got to rest for long.

Claybourne Frazier was back for the first time since Cat's birthday. If he'd watch his tongue, Cat could hold hers, so when he bowed and asked her to dance, she accepted.

"Amazing celebration!" He laughed. "I must write my mother all about it."

"Where is she?"

"St. Paul, Minnesota. My father's in command of the Department of Dakota, which was created in 1866 out of the departments of the Platte and the Missouri. Poor mother! She loathes cold weather, not to mention Yankees."

"She's from the South?"

"Both my parents are. South Carolina." Almost truculently he added, "My father, who's now a brevet major general, was an early West Point graduate. Unlike many of his Southern-born classmates, he thought his first loyalty was to the Union. Mother didn't agree. They fought a highly uncivil war of their own all through the big one. Thank heaven, I was at the Point most of the time." With a shrug, he dismissed the awkward subject. "How do you like being sixteen?"

Cat laughed. "It's much like being fifteen."

Not really true. But after kissing her that night, making his astounding declaration of intent, Jordan had practically ignored her. Of course, he'd been out branding most of the time, but what had he done tonight? Thus far he had danced with all the women but herself and—

Incredible! There he went with Sewa, dwarfing the dainty little girl. Cat smiled brilliantly up at the lieutenant, who stifled an exclamation and drew her closer to him.

"Miss O'Shea! With your permission, I'd like to ask your guardian's consent to call on you."

"Call on me?" she echoed, wondering for a moment what he meant. Then she realized that he was again asking to visit her, not simply stop by the ranch. "Why, I—that's kind of you, lieutenant, but—"

"Are you keeping other company?"

"No."

Jordan's one-sided proclamation and subsequent aloofness was scarcely courtship. Besides, he hadn't asked her what she thought about it, just stated his claims like some *conquistador* saying a place belonged to some distant king no matter what the natives wanted!

"Do you find me distasteful?" persisted Frazier.

"You can be very nice," Cat tried to think of a tactful way to say it, could come up with none, and simply blurted, "I don't want to get married for a long time, Lieutenant Frazier."

He laughed in a way that removed any sting from his words. "Bless you, neither do I! But I'd like to take you riding, escort you to the occasional festivity that's fit for ladies. I promise not to importune or woo you fervently till I'm at least a captain—unless you want me to."

Put that way, it didn't sound alarming. Her eye caught Jordan swinging winsome Doña Gertrude in the firelight. Going to marry her, was he, after he'd exhausted himself with everyone else? Cat glanced at Frazier from beneath her eyelashes.

"Well?" he urged, gray eyes eager.

She nodded. "All right, Lieutenant. You may speak to Talitha. She's my guardian."

"But surely Marc Revier—"

"Father left Talitha in charge of us." A new thought struck her. "Of course, the twins are twenty-one today! I suppose they might be my guardians, in a way. But it's Tally you must ask."

Frazier gave a bewildered chuckle. "It's a complicated household. Do you and your brothers own the ranch and that mine I've heard mentioned?"

"Just shares. Father's will left Tally a quarter, which isn't really enough. Without her, the ranch and mine would have been lost during the war. Then, Sewa has her father's shares." At the officer's baffled look, Cat tried to make it simple. "Our parents owned two thirds of the properties they shared with Santiago. That two thirds is quartered to my brothers, Tally, and me. Santiago's third is Sewa's, undivided."

"Then she ought to be quite an heiress."

Cat had never thought of it that way but had to nod slowly. "I suppose."

It followed that the O'Sheas were a little bit rich, though wealth was only of relative importance in this region. It couldn't buy your life from Apaches or bring rain when the fields were dry and cattle were thirsty. People were what mattered here, their courage, strength, and judgment.

A captain from Camp Wallen was approaching. Frazier pressed Cat's hand. "I'll speak to Mrs. Revier," he promised, and, surrendering her to the other officer, went off to do just that.

Why was it that birthday dances had suddenly become so hazardous? Cat was far from sure that she really liked Claybourne Frazier and wanted more of his company than she already had. But, since he agreed with her that marriage was out of the question for years, it might be a good way to learn something of men, rather than wait till Jordan decided she was old enough to court seriously.

If he still cared about her at all, the way he was acting tonight! He hadn't even been friendly. She craned her neck and soon located him, dancing with one of Doña Rosa's pretty nieces and obviously enjoying it. If he was going to act like that, why had he spoken to her at all, given her that kiss that she sometimes felt in her dreams? He was horrid and exasperating. Even if he asked her to dance now, she wouldn't.

She had been making appropriate murmurs at the captain's complaints about Camp Wallen and was jarred to full attention only when he asked where she was from.

"Why, I was born here," she said. "Not at the ranch, but between here and Sonora. Of course, this was all still Sonora in 1853; it wasn't till the next year the Gadsden Treaty was ratified and this became part of the United States. But," she added proudly, thinking about it for the first time, "I'm of the country, though my father came from Ireland and my mother from Alamos."

The captain, middle-aged, with graying sideburns, shook his head. "You poor child! To spring from this barbarous land and know nothing else!"

"I don't want anything else. Marc's been to lots of places. He says we have the most beautiful mountains and skies anywhere."

"Mountains! Skies!" The captain eyed her pityingly. "You speak like a savage, my dear young lady. But perhaps it's as well. How could you be content here if once you enjoyed the advantages of a city? Shopping, theater, museums, conveniences, and, most of all, no fear of being killed by Apaches!"

"Cities are smoky, filthy, and full of disease," she retorted. She'd never been in a city, not even little Tucson, but Marc had talked about the squalor as well as the wonders of New York, Berlin, London, St. Louis, and San Francisco. "I'll take my chances with the Indians any time."

"Really, Miss O'Shea—"

"Forgive me, sir, but I haven't had my dance with this young lady."

Smoothly, firmly, Jordan took her out of the captain's arms and swept her into comparative shadow. "How you do get into disputes with these officers!" he teased. "What would you do without me to rescue you?"

"I'd do very well. If you'd rather dance with everyone else, please don't sacrifice yourself."

"Katie!" He twinkled. "Can I hope you're jealous?"

Insufferable! "Why should I be jealous?" she sniffed. "I've just told Lieutenant Frazier he could ask Talitha for permission to call on me."

Did Jordan's arm tighten? She couldn't see his face in the shadows. Oddly enough, she felt in the wrong, as if he hadn't provoked her sharpness, but when he spoke, his careless tone removed that edge of guilt.

"You're bound to be wooed by the officers, honey. We might as well get it over with."

"We?"

He nodded, giving her a whirl so sudden she had to cling to him to keep her balance. "Yes, my sweetheart. Because after your dances and rides and flirtings, I'm going to marry you. When you grow up." His voice roughened. He held her close for a moment. Sweet pleasure-fear shot through her and her knees felt heavy. "I won't rush you, Katie. And the only way I can keep from that is to hold back. I can't court you just a little."

So that was why he'd been aloof. Regretting her commitment to Claybourne Frazier, she gazed up into Jordan's steady hazel eyes. "Jordan, maybe—"

She wasn't sure what she wanted. It didn't matter. He cut in almost harshly. "No, Katie. I could besiege you, drug your senses, make you think it was love, but that's not what I want. Give us time, darling. But during that time, remember I'm your friend. You can come to me for anything."

His mouth just brushed her forehead before he gave her into Miguel's arms.

A few days later Patrick and Cinco headed east. Belen rode with them to help drive the cattle Talitha sent to James each fall. She always had them left in the basin where she'd parted with her brother late in 1862, and though the herders had never seen anyone, neither had they been molested.

The vaqueros couldn't have liked this feeding of their enemies, but they remembered James and respected

Talitha's love for him. No one knew, of course, whether he got the cattle, but at least Talitha could hope she'd helped prevent his having to sacrifice another horse to feed hungry women and children.

"Be careful," Cat whispered to Patrick when it was her turn to kiss him good-bye. "If you see James, tell him to come home."

Patrick gave her a chiding squeeze. "Katie-Cat, maybe he *is* at home. And," he added, laughing, "it may be a lot healthier for me if I don't see him!"

Cinco, grown so tall at fourteen that her head reached only to his shoulder, stood before Cat, waiting till she looked at him. Though his face wasn't as angular as Patrick's, its brown leanness showed the heritage of their common father. It came to her, with a bit of shock as it always did, though she knew it perfectly well, that he was her brother, too.

Rising on tiptoe, she kissed his cheek. "Take care of yourself, *hermano mío*. Find your gold and come back quickly."

"I'd rather find turquoise," he said in his soft voice. "The color of the little bird I gave you. The color of your eyes."

Troubled by his manner, she didn't know how to answer him till she remembered that he was only a boy, scarcely more than a child. By then he was on his horse.

His shadow, against the sun, was that of a warrior.

XV

Sangre was pure delight, spirited but responsive, one ear and eye bent always toward her, the others alert for what was before them. She loved to brush him till he gleamed a rich red brown so dark it was almost black and to comb out his thick sable mane. She still rode Mancha and was pleased that her two loved horses had become best friends, keeping company in the field or corral, resting their heads on each other's withers and rubbing tenderly.

The way that horses formed special attachments had always beguiled Cat. Geldings often had special mare friends, treating them almost after the manner of possessive stallions, but many had an amazing love for colts. Sangre had never exhibited that till a foal of Ceniza's began to approach him and Mancha, thrusting out its head and opening and closing its mouth in a way that clearly indicated its youth. Like most grown horses, Sangre wouldn't fight a colt, and he somewhat dourly ignored the filly's overtures till Mancha accepted her. After that, the three were inseparable.

"Like a family," Cat said with a laugh to Belen, then sobered. "In a way, it's sad that Sangre can't sire a foal of his own."

Belen snorted. "He'd only run it off, once it was a yearling or coming two-year-old."

"Well," floundered Cat, "I guess I wish he could be a

stallion—have his own herd, be sort of a splendid tyrant."

Belen shook his head, smiling. "You astonish me, small one. When a band of horses travel, who leads them?"

Cat frowned. "A mare."

"What mare?"

Cat thought of the lead mares of various *manadas*, traits they had in common. "She's strong and well grown, though not old. She seems to know where the best grass and water are, and where to find the best protection in a storm. And with all that—well, the others just naturally follow her. The stallion's behind to keep the herd together and protect it, but surely he's the real boss!"

"The leader is the leader." Belen chuckled. "For sure, the stallion has his uses, but any stronger one can take his place. The lead mare must be much more than strong. She knows how to keep the band alive."

"Like Talitha!"

After a startled glance, Belen laughed from deep in his barrel chest. "True, *chiquita. La madama* has the qualities of the finest lead mares." He watched Cat searchingly. "So will you when you're older—if you learn not to be betrayed by pity. This land requires a tougher skin."

She looked ruefully down at her wrists, gnawed by a teething kitten. "I can't help it, Belen. If something's hurt, I feel sorry for it."

He glanced toward Jordan, who was working with a fractious mare everyone else had given up on. Jordan spoke to her with firm gentleness, smoothing her trembling flanks, accustoming her to his hands.

"*Bueno,* Caterina. Be as tenderhearted as you please as long as we find you a kind, brave man. *La madama* will lead our band a long while yet."

"She'd better. I could never take her place."

Belen looked toward the crosses on the hill. Sadness made him look his age. "That's what my *doncellita* thought when Doña Socorro died. But she raised you and your brothers. She held the ranch through the war, through Don Patricio's death. Thank the good God she now has a strong man to cherish her."

Cat nodded, unable to speak for the sudden welling of grief for her father, for the mother she'd never known. Why did people who'd loved each other as they had have to die so young?

Though they went riding on most days the lieutenant was off duty, he also spent many evenings at the ranch, sitting as close as possible to Cat while nutmeats were picked out, clothes mended, and ropes and hackamores made. On such occasions Jordan usually seemed to find some pressing duty away from the house, but, somewhat to Cat's chagrin, he stuck by his resolve to delay his own courtship.

As well as singing songs and *corridos,* they discussed everything imaginable from John Wesley Powell's navigation of a thousand miles of the Colorado River's torrents and rapids through the Grand Canyon in the northern part of the territory to Wyoming Territory's granting women suffrage for the first time in the United States. When Talitha applauded the admittance of Arabella Mansfield to the Iowa bar as the first case of a woman lawyer in the States, Marc pointed out with a smile that Mistress Margaret Brent had been attorney for Cecilius Calvert, Lord Proprietor of Maryland, in the 1640s.

"Georgia, Mississippi, Texas, and Virginia won't be readmitted to the Union till they ratify the Fifteenth Amendment," Marc added. "It's sure to be adopted next spring, made a part of the Constitution. It says no citizen shall be denied the vote because of race, color, or previous condition of servitude."

"But women are classed with lunatics, felons, and children!" Talitha grimaced. "If we lived back in the States, Marc, I warn you that I'd join Susan Anthony's Woman Suffrage Association!"

"I should hope so," Marc said. "And when I run for the legislature again, woman suffrage is going to be part of my program." He grinned at Frazier. "Will you vote for me, Clay?"

"In spite of, not because of, your views on women voting," the lieutenant said a bit stiffly. "To my mind, voting, like warfare, is debasing to female sensibilities."

"I can shoot as well as you can," Cat thrust.

"But you never kill anything," he retorted, coloring to the edges of his fair hair. "So where's the use of it?"

"So I can kill if I have to."

Pacifically, Marc interposed. "I hear there's about to be an official inspection of the arms at Camp Crittenden, Clay. What's your opinion of them?"

"The fifty-caliber Spencer repeating carbines and rifles are fine, but there are still quite a few single-shot Springfield rifles. The switch from caplock guns to metallic cartridges is just about complete. And of course, we have forty-four cap-and-ball six-shooters, mostly Remington Model 1858, the better to shoot each other with in the brawls that form the greater part of our recreation."

"Life at the post is that dreary?" Marc asked.

Frazier shrugged. "There's baseball, and the athletically inclined can work out on the horizontal and parallel bars, but for officers and men alike the main pastime is drinking. Surgeon Semig claims all the liquor sold near the post is below proof, but it's enough to cause murders and suicides."

Little Shea had climbed into Sewa's arms and fallen asleep, his pale blond head against the long black plaits that fell over her thin chest. Putting down a shirt she was mending, Talitha took her little son but paused on her way to the bedroom.

"Marc, why don't we send the men at the post a Christmas dinner? Beeves to barbecue, lots of good food, and our best guitar players?"

"Would your commander object?" Marc inquired.

"He'd bless you forever," said Frazier.

So the men at the camp had a brighter holiday than they would have otherwise, but the ranch festivities were slightly shadowed by Patrick's continued absence. True enough, as they all reminded each other from the time of the Roof Feast through the Day of the Three Kings when the vaqueros' children expected gifts from the wise men, Patrick and Cinco had set no particular time to return, but they'd have been at the ranch for the feast days had it been manageable.

The lieutenant's official gift to Cat was an exciting new historical novel, Blackmore's *Lorna Doone*. When they took his suggested stroll along the creek, he took her hand and slipped a ring on it.

"Not a betrothal token," he said hastily, anticipating her protest. "It's a signet ring some Frazier had cut down for his lady. When I wrote Mother about you, she sent it to me."

"I can't wear it, Clay." They had been on a first-name basis for some weeks; when everyone else in the family called him Clay, it sounded foolish for her to persist in Lieutenant Frazier. "It's a special ring."

She took it off, but when she tried to press it into his hand, he captured hers. "You're a special girl, Caterina. It would please me if you wore the old Frazier signet."

She laughed, trying to lighten the moment between them. "It's too much like a brand. I don't belong to anyone."

A pulse throbbed in his temple. His gaze burned her. As she tried vainly to withdraw her hand, he forced the ring on her finger. "I've been too patient," he said thickly. "Well, my dear, if you want frontier wooing, that's what you'll get!"

Crushed against him, his mouth avid on hers, she could scarcely breathe. He was strong, but she was furiously shocked at being handled that way by him and, impeded though she was by her skirts, she brought up her knee with enough force to send him doubling backward. She stripped off the ring and threw it down.

"I—I'm going to walk awhile alone, Lieutenant! You'd better use the time to say your farewells and get your horse."

His face was clammy. He straightened with difficulty, staring at her with a tormented mixture of hatred and thwarted desire. "If you think a kiss is worth getting your brother or Revier shot, I'll tell them myself."

"I don't want anyone shot. I—I'll just say we no longer agree."

He looked past her at the winter-naked cottonwoods any sycamores. "I think we never did." His mouth twisted. "I still want you, Caterina O'Shea. But you won't get another chance to refuse a Frazier ring." He picked up the signet and started up the slope.

No one asked questions when she came home a little after she saw his horse take the way to Camp Crittenden. After supper and an evening of songs, stories, and munching piñon nuts by the fire, Cat started to follow Sewa to bed. Jordan overtook her in the courtyard.

"Did you just weary of the lieutenant, Katie, or did he offend you?"

Annoyed at his acting like a guardian, she said coldly, "If he had, I'd tell Marc or my brother."

"He won't be calling anymore?"

"No."

"Who's next? The captain from Wallen? That other lieutenant from Crittenden who keeps finding excuses to drop by?"

"Right now I don't want anyone dropping by." She remembered, with indignation, that she wouldn't have let Frazier call if Jordan's attentions to every other female hadn't made her want to give him a lesson. "Men are tiresome creatures. I'd rather they all left me alone!"

"A butterfly can't creep back into its safe, cozy

cocoon. And those who see its loveliness can't be blamed too much for reaching for it." He placed his long, hard fingers on her cheek and let them lie quiet, warming her. "When strong winds buffet, Katie, you can always perch by me. I won't break your wings."

Bewildered, almost sad, she tried to make out his expression in the dim light from the window. "Yet you push me into the winds."

His voice, too, held a note of sadness. "You're as lovely as a butterfly, but your spirit is an eagle's. It must have freedom. The eagle who stops flying to peck in a barnyard is as silly as the hen who tries to fly toward the sun."

She thought of James and K'aak'eh. And in the moment of that thought, Jordan left her.

It was a relief to be quit of Claybourne Frazier's attentions, with which she'd never really been comfortable. When officers from Crittenden and Wallen, apparently learning that Frazier no longer paid suit, found excuses to stop at the ranch and chat with her, Cat was so distant that none of them summoned the courage to ask if they might call formally.

"Poor man," said Marc as the captain from Wallen rode off dejectedly one evening. "I believe he's decided you nourish an unrequited penchant for Clay Frazier."

It was the first time anyone but Jordan had even indirectly asked what had happened between her and the lieutenant. Cat shrugged. "I suppose it's easier to think that than that I just don't care to spend time with him."

"La belle dame sans merci," teased Marc. He smiled at Talitha, still proudly, clearly, her lover. "But most women worth having can be like that."

Wonderful to see them so richly happy, yet it made Cat feel woefully alone. Miguel and Juriana were absorbed in each other and their coming baby. Patrick was still gone. Sewa was a child. *I'm not anymore,* thought Cat. But she didn't feel grown up, either. All she was sure of was that the longing for James grew worse, not better, and that it was more than time to hear from Patrick and Cinco.

With that everyone agreed. Cat overheard Miguel telling Marc that if his twin hadn't come by the time Juriana's baby was born, he was going to look for him.

"Leave it till after the branding and I'll go with you," Marc said. Seeing Cat, he warned her. "Don't mention this to Tally. Just pray we get news of your scampish brother soon."

In March, Juriana and Miguel's baby was born, a delicate little girl with thick black hair, dark brows that slanted upward, and a soft cry, "H'lah!" that began like a sigh of wind and increased to a roar that was astonishing coming from such a tiny being. She was named Vicenta Socorro Elena María, for her grandmothers, but young Shea called her Vi, pronounced Vee, and her other names were forgotten.

New calves dropped. Cat got her usual orphans and was glad for Sewa's help in feeding the lustily tugging, leggy creatures. Watching the calves, it was hard to believe that in twelve years their teeth would be wearing down to stubs and long curved horns would be marked with growth rings, the first representing three years, the others a year each. Animals lived such short lives compared to people. Thank goodness, Sangre was only three. She'd have him for a long time yet.

Wild flowers spangled the hillsides amid freshening grass. Earth and air vibrated with new life. Mares went off a distance from their bands to foal, nuzzling the newborn, nickering. After a few minutes a colt would struggle to its thin legs and find the warm udder. Within an hour it could travel a bit.

For a few days, even gentle mares would be nervous at the approach of humans and move their colts away as quickly as possible. Most foals were born at night. Belen said that gave extra protection from predators.

That spring, one young mare fought a wildcat off her colt but was so mangled that she died, though Chuey heard the uproar in time to rescue the foal and add him to Cat's charges. She was feeding him one morning, facing eastward, when she saw three figures on the horizon.

Since the establishment of Camp Crittenden, the ranch no longer kept a lookout posted days and moonlit nights. Leaving Sewa to feed the colt, Cat ran to alert the men. By the corral, Belen was peering into the sparkling distance. The horsemen acquired form. Belen's frowning squint broke into a joyous smile.

"Patrick! Cinco, to the left, I'm almost sure!"

Cat's heart pounded. "Can you make out the third?"

Belen shook his head. But it was possible now to make out the set of the horsemen's heads and shoulders. Suddenly, Cat *knew*.

"James!"

She caught the reins of Chuey's saddled horse. Miguel was already mounting. Together, they raced toward the three, who had topped the last hill and were riding down the broad valley.

When they met, she and Patrick flung themselves from their horses to embrace. Cinco glowed as she pressed his hands. But James waited, aloof, his face unreadable. As she turned joyfully to him the words of delighted welcome stuck in her throat.

This was a man. Not the boy of fifteen she remembered, but an Apache warrior, long black hair held out of his face with a red headcloth, high moccasins reaching to the knee, thighs iron-hard where the breechclout fell away. He wore a cartridge belt and his bowstring crossed his muscular brown chest.

Only his eyes, the color of a blue storm, were the same, but they watched her in such a different way, guarded, almost hostile, that after a hastily murmured greeting she turned away.

At the ranch all was happy confusion as Patrick examined his new niece and told what had happened. Yes, he and Cinco had found a rich vein of silver four days east of the San Patricio and had begun working it with a half dozen miners recruited from Mexico. They had amassed a considerable amount of ore and were planning to engage a pack train to take it to a smelter when James rode into camp.

He was one of a war party bound for Mexico. Fortunately, he'd recognized Patrick's hair and explained to his companions that this white-eyes was like a brother and he was sworn to defend him. After considerable argument, it was agreed that the miners wouldn't be harmed if James could persuade them to abandon what would surely become a settlement in Chiricahua country. James's half brothers, Juh's full-blood sons, had supported him, but they had also told James that a warrior with divided loyalties was no good. Let him stay with the white "brother" he valued.

"So the miners went back to Mexico, the Apaches took our mules and supplies, and the ore will sit there till calmer days," Patrick finished, slipping a careless arm around Sewa, who had come close to gaze solemnly at him. "We fought off bandits, had a cave-in, and barely saved one man from being mauled to death by a grizzly. I'm ready to stay home awhile."

"Good!" said Miguel. "We're just half through the branding." He looked at James. "Can you still use a rope?"

The corner of James's mouth twitched. He spoke slowly, giving some words inflections that made them sound foreign, hesitating over others that he must have nearly forgotten. "In these years I have driven more cows and mules and horses, I think, than any vaquero."

No one cared to pursue that. Talitha brought little Shea to him. "Here's your nephew, James."

The fair-haired four-year-old stared up at the splendid barbarian. Awed, he whispered, "You—you're my uncle James?"

Regarding him quizzically, James nodded, as if pleased that the child was curious but not frightened. "I am your *shidá á,* your mother's brother."

Shea gave a soft, delighted laugh, as if he'd just befriended some fabulous creature of his dreams. He threw his small arms as far as they'd go around his big uncle. "I'm glad you're home," he said.

James didn't answer. His brown hand rested on Shea's blond curls, but his eyes were fixed on the mountains.

James's return in the midst of the branding season helped him slip back into the ways he'd known seven years ago. Everyone was too busy to watch him for Apache manifestations. He shared Patrick's quarters, and he'd put away his headcloth and breechclout, asked Talitha to trim his hair, and now looked like an especially tall vaquero with blue *norteño* eyes.

James was old enough now to accept Talitha's sisterly spoiling and was on good terms with the twins, who were inclined to treat him with the respect they'd had from babyhood for one eighteen months their elder—the seven-year-old who'd gone off with the giant Mangus, the fourteen-year-old who'd returned during the war and taught them to track and use bows and arrows. The men accepted him as Talitha's brother and a good hand with stock, however he'd acquired the skills. Only Cinco watched him with distrust. He went home as soon as the branding was done, instead of lingering through the summer as had been his custom.

Seeking out Cat to tell her good-bye, Cinco handed her a little packet. Opening it, she gasped at the painstakingly carved turquoise bird, its spread wings detailed with feathers, its eyes flecks of obsidian. "I found the stone in a cañon near the mine," Cinco told her, scuffing his boot in the dust. "I carved it for you winter nights."

"It's beautiful!" she praised. "Why, Cinco, you're an artist!"

He shook his head, the ruddy glints and thickness of his black hair a heritage from Shea like his straight nose and lean features. "I'm not an artist, Caterina. I only wish to make pretty things for you. Blue things, like your eyes."

"I still have the bird you gave me long ago when we were children. The whistle, too."

He pulled a small crucifix out of his shirt. "And I still have this you gave me. I think it protected us against the Apaches."

"James did that."

Cinco's face hardened. "It's not good for him to be here. One cannot trust Apaches."

"You can say that when he saved you!"

"It wasn't the miners or me he cared about. Only Patrick."

"You still owe him your life."

"Yes, and I hope I may pay him back. A Papago shouldn't owe an Apache anything but an arrow or a smashed skull."

"If you ever hurt James, I'd hate you! We all would."

"First, I must save his life." Cinco climbed on his horse.

Cat sucked in her breath, tried to push the turquoise bird into his hand. "If—if you feel that way about James, I don't want this!"

"It's yours anyway," he said. "If you throw it in the marsh or down a mine, it will still be yours." As she stared up at him, he said slowly, in the courteous phrase picked up from the vaqueros, "I am your servant in all things, Caterina, but I cannot trust an Apache."

She watched him go. Clenching her hand on the bird till its wings hurt her, she started to throw it away. But Cinco was her brother. So she trudged up the hill and put the blue amulet on the stones that covered Shea's grave.

"From your son," she said.

On April 15 of that year, 1870, Arizona had been separated from the Department of California and made a separate military district. Gen. George Stoneman took command in May. A former lieutenant with the Mormon Battalion when it passed through Tucson in 1846, Stoneman was under orders to implement President Grant's peace policy and feed Indians who seemed inclined to leave off warring and settle on reservations.

For this he was roundly abused by the territorial papers and citizens, especially when it was learned that he intended to inspect Arizona's posts and close down those he judged unnecessary. Supplying the posts was a huge business, and though the argument raged again over whether it was cheaper to import government stores through Guaymas or get them from San Diego via Yuma, neither way was cheap.

"Soldiers are here to protect the civilians," said Marc, "and civilians come to supply the soldiers. No wonder Sherman thought the best thing to do was pull out the settlers and let the Indians have the place."

They all knew that wouldn't be done. Even though Indian raids were as bad as ever, since the war miners, ranchers, settlers, and merchants had come in increasing numbers. In addition to Arizona City near Fort Yuma and the settlements north along the Colorado like La Paz and Ehrenberg, Prescott thrived as a mining and military center in spite of losing the capital.

The first U.S. Land Office had been opened in Prescott in 1868, but many early settlers were "preemptioneers," claiming their lands before the federal surveyors came. The Homestead Act of 1862 had entitled any citizen or intending one twenty-one years of age or older and the head of a family to own 160 acres of public land by settling on it for five years and paying $1.25 an acre. Its rugged mountains, desert stretches, and raiding Indians had kept Arizona from filling up like more hospitable regions, but it still had almost doubled its population, not counting the military, since it had become a territory.

Contrasting with Apache raids were the Tucson Glee Club and the bathhouse and barbering establishment opened by a Negro, Samuel Bostick. Seven nuns arrived late in May, greeted with fireworks and ringing bells. A few weeks later, Sisters Emerentia, Euphrasia, Monica, Martha, Maxine, and Hyacinth had opened a school where girls could study twenty-nine subjects, including sacred and modern history, chemistry, bookkeeping, French, and the making of artificial fruits and flowers. Board and tuition for a five-month session was $125. Governor Safford commended the academy, but he was still determined to establish free public schools throughout the state and had urged Marc to help by running for the legislature again that fall.

"I guess I will," said Marc without enthusiasm when the subject came up one night at supper. "At least, located as we are in an old freight warehouse with the quartermaster's yard behind us, the honest braying of real mules often blots out that of imitations."

Miguel groaned. "I'm glad we'll be busy with branding when the electioneering gets frenzied along about October. Two years ago there were soldiers at Camp Crittenden who voted there and then went to other precincts to vote again. The *Arizona Miner* claimed that hundreds of Mexicans voted for McCormick two or three times in Tubac and Tucson."

That Prescott paper had said quite a few other things about the federally appointed Easterners who were, of course, Republican, though they called themselves Union or Independent. From Goodwin on, they had tried to make peace with the Democrats, holding that the territory was so beleaguered that all white men should make common cause. Goodwin had even appointed fiery secessionist William Oury first mayor of territorial Tucson.

"I'm not going to buy any votes," Marc said mildly. "It'd suit me fine to stay right here. But I'd like to help Safford get his schools, even if most people think it's crazy to worry about that when bandits or Apaches may finish them off any time."

Cat glanced nervously at James. There was no way for him to avoid hearing his people spoken of often in tones of hate or fear. How did he feel about it? His face was a mask.

In the weeks since his return she'd managed to come no closer to him. There seemed no connection with the boy she'd adored, who'd saved her from the outcast Apache and taught her to shoot a bow. This tall, dark man with the broad shoulders and lean flanks made her aware of herself in a strange, prickly, uncomfortable way, so that she began to suspect that perhaps the awkwardness came from changes in herself.

She wasn't the eight-year-old who'd flung her arms around Talitha's lost brother to welcome him home, nor was she the ten-year-old who'd mourned when he went back to his father's people. She was almost seventeen; she had been proposed to, if Jordan's aggravating declaration counted, and she had been courted by a handsome if not very satisfactory lieutenant.

Surely she should have known how to act with this savage stranger. But his eyes, the only thing familiar about him at all, seemed to draw her strength right out of her. When he looked quickly away, as he invariably did, she felt plunged in shadow; lonely and deserted, no matter how many people were around.

Sometimes she wished he had never come back. But if he left now, it would be like losing the sun.

About mid-June Lieutenant Claybourne Frazier rode up with a dozen troopers. While the men were watering their horses and being fed on the porch by Anita, Frazier ate with the family and poured out an angry story.

Tom Gardner's ranch had been raided on the eighth. Apaches killed one man and carried off a Mexican boy as well as driving off a herd of cattle.

"By the time Gardner got word to us, we couldn't catch up with them," smoldered the young officer. His gray eyes seemed drawn to Cat, but his face tightened and he looked swiftly away. "We found where they'd camped and made moccasins for the boy. At least it seems they don't intend to kill him. That ought to be some comfort to his mother, though she seems absolutely out of her mind with grief."

"Poor woman," said Talitha, instinctively putting an arm around Shea. "I'll go to see her, make her understand that the Apaches are good to the boys they decide to adopt."

Frazier's mouth curled. He stared at James. "Yes. They want to turn them into traitors, don't they?"

Talitha stiffened. Marc said firmly, "You forget yourself, Lieutenant."

"Do I?" Frazier gave an unpleasant laugh. "If Mrs. Revier's half brother deserves your trust, surely he'll help us track hostiles when they've committed an outrage like this. He knows their hideouts and habits. When all we see is barren rock, he could find a trail."

It was fatally true. James was being forced to choose again, as when his Apache kinsmen and companions had repudiated him for protecting Patrick and Cinco.

"It's not fair!" Cat protested fiercely. "Whatever James does, either whites or Apaches will blame him."

"He's got to decide," said Frazier. "He's living with whites. He owes them something." He looked at Talitha. "What if you were the mother of that boy they carried off? Or the wife of the man they killed?"

White to the lips, Talitha said in a clear, taut voice, "I still wouldn't ask my brother to betray his other people."

The lieutenant smothered an execration. Marc started to rise but was checked by Talitha, who caught his arm.

James got to his feet. "You are right, *nantan*," he said to Frazier. "I should not be among the whites." He strode out.

"James!" Talitha sprang up to follow him, but Marc held her back. "Let me talk to him, dear."

Cat scarcely heard. The only reality was James's resolute back turned on them. *"I should not be among the whites."* He'd go away again, and this time, she knew, he'd never come back. Running after him, she burst into the room he shared with Patrick.

"James! Don't! Please don't!"

He seemed not to hear as he opened a chest and began to stuff his belongings into a rawhide bag. She caught his arm, planting herself between him and the chest. "Don't pay any mind to that stupid soldier! This is your home, James!"

He shook his head. "No, Caterina."

"You—you won't go back to *them*?"

He smiled slightly at her tone. "They don't want me, either. But the mines need men and don't worry about bloodlines. I can work and live like that, maybe, without betraying anyone."

It was better than his returning to the Indians, but she felt she couldn't stand losing him before they'd made friends again.

"Let me go with you," she said, tears stinging her eyes, salty on her lips.

His body went rigid. She heard his breath catch before he slowly released it in a sigh that was like a moan. "Caterina, small one, you don't know what you say."

She did. She suddenly understood why she hadn't been able to treat him like a brother.

He was her man, though she still loved the boy in him, ached for the youngster trying to find a place between two worlds. Bowing her head against him so that she heard the speeding pound of his heart, she said, "Let me come."

His arms closed around her. Only for a moment. He put her from him. "What sort of life could you have with me?"

"That it is with you is what matters."

"It's easy for you to say that now—you, whom everybody has loved, standing in your home. But would you think it among strangers where you'd be just another miner's woman?"

"Yes, if you wanted me."

Violently, he turned from her and gathered the rest of his possessions into the bag. "Marry Jordan, Caterina. He's a good man who will take care of you."

"James—"

She broke off at the sound of approaching steps. Patrick and Miguel crowded into the room, while Marc stood in the door with an arm around Talitha.

"You're not leaving because of what that weakling lieutenant said?" burst out Patrick.

Talitha was very pale. She watched her brother beseechingly as Marc spoke firmly. "We let Frazier know he was way out of line. You can't pay attention to every coyote that yips, James. We don't expect you to turn on your Apache kin."

"I thank you for that. But the soldiers and your neighbors will expect it." James gave a somber smile. "When I do not, in a while they may decide I am organizing or helping the raiders. Then all of you might be in danger. I am going."

Patrick scowled. "Where?"

James grinned. "I think I will become Santiago Montaña and look for a job in the mines. Maybe there I won't be expected to track Apaches or slaughter white-eyes."

Color came back to Talitha's face. Slowly, Marc nodded. "Not a bad idea, till the Indian troubles quiet down, at least. If you worked at the San Patricio, you could visit us when you had a mind to. I expect they're hiring, but let me write a note to the manager, Don Buenaventura, just to be sure."

Stiffly, James said, "If they don't need me, I'll find work at another place."

"Don't be a mule!" said Patrick forthrightly. "The way the turnover is, if they don't need you this week, they will next. Anyhow, this way Miguel and I can ride over and we can all go hunting."

Hesitating, James looked at Talitha, who watched him with her heart in her eyes. "All right," he assented.

He rode away within the hour, but at least he wasn't going back to the Apaches. He'd be little more than a day's ride away. Now that she knew the truth of her feeling for him, Cat was determined to make him acknowledge it, too. When he was making his farewells and would have shaken her hand, she defiantly raised on tiptoe to kiss him. On the mouth. Feeling a wave of triumph as a tremor went through him, she smiled and said, "Come back for St. John's Day."

That was only ten days. She could wait that long. Maybe by then he'd see how stupid it was for them to be apart. He hadn't said he loved her in words, but his arms had, and his startled mouth.

It would all work out. They'd marry in the *sala,* where her parents had pledged themselves before Guadalupana, where Marc and Talitha had spoken their vows. Then they'd live at the mine till it was all right for them to come back to the ranch. Her mind veered away from exactly what that meant. Surely it wouldn't be long before the Apaches had to see that their only chance of surviving was to settle on reservations. Once they stopped raiding, James wouldn't be under pressure to help hunt them down.

Patrick should be married by then, too, and they'd all have quarters added on, maybe forming a second courtyard, and their children would grow up together, no one caring that some of the cousins would be one-quarter Apache. Handsome children they should be, with blue eyes and dark hair, though she hoped at least one would carry her father's red hair.

While she fed orphan calves and colts, helped spoil little Vi, and fought the summer battle with screwworms, Cat beguiled the time with such dreams. But James didn't come the Day of San Juan, not for the feats of riding, the roping contests, the feasting and dancing.

As the evening wore on and she had to accept that he wouldn't be there, Cat's smile grew fixed. She longed to escape the merriment and sob out her disappointment and wrath against her pillow.

Telling Miguel, who'd asked her to dance, that she had a headache, she slipped away from the flaring light and shadows near the corral and was crossing the courtyard to her room when Jordan came up beside her.

"It's not midnight, Cinderella! Anyway, you can't run off till we've had a dance."

"I don't feel like dancing."

He took her hand, moving toward a bench among the trees surrounding the well. "Then let's talk a bit."

"What about?" she asked guardedly.

"You."

"I'd rather not. My head—"

"Your head might clear if you talked about whatever's making you so strange. You're always changeable, Katie, but of late you're smiling to yourself one minute and looking ready to cry the next. What's it all about?"

Since his announcement at her birthday almost a year ago that he was going to marry her, Jordan's behavior had baffled and piqued Cat. He seemed to bide his time, tolerantly waiting for her to—what? Grow up? Well, whatever his plans were, she'd better put him straight on hers. She didn't want to hurt him, but it would be worse to let him go on thinking that someday, when he judged her ready, he could claim her.

"I'm going to marry James," she blurted.

His fingers bit into her wrist. "You're *what?*"

"I will marry James."

She couldn't see his face, but she felt his distress in the shock of his fingers, the tension of his body. Sorry for it, but now certain that she must convince him that he must put her out of his heart, she added almost pleadingly, "I've always loved James."

"Like a brother."

"Not anymore."

Jordan released her as if her flesh burned him. "What does Tally say about it?"

"I—I haven't talked to her yet."

He turned swiftly, taking her shoulders, giving her a little shake. "And James? I'll bet you haven't talked to him, either! Have you?"

"I have so! At least—anyway—" She floundered. "He knows!"

"Knows?" echoed Jordan grimly. "He may know what you want, but has he had a chance to say what he thinks?"

"He's worried about being caught between Apaches and whites, but I can help him. Except for when he was little and Talitha fought to keep him alive, he's never had anyone to put him first."

"God!" said Jordan. "I don't know whether to be jealous of the poor devil or feel sorry for him!"

"You needn't do either," she said frostily, trying to rise.

Jordan held her still. "I don't take James for a weakling you can badger into doing something he figures is a bad idea, Katie. I like him; he's a man. If you do marry, I'll have to make myself big enough to wish you happy, and I will. But till the day you're really married to someone else, there's nothing you can do to keep me from believing you're going to be mine."

She thought he'd kiss her then and braced to deny him, but he only caressed her cheek and kissed her lightly on the forehead as he drew her to her feet.

At her door, he said, "Katie, I'll always help you. Any way I can. Don't be too proud to ask." He touched her cheek again and turned into the darkness.

August was a terrible month along the Overland Road. Apaches killed two stage drivers, captured one stage and killed everyone on it, captured a pack train and killed all the men, and overran a stage station only twenty-two miles east of Tucson and killed all but one of the attendants.

The citizens of Tucson, alarmed and angry, raised enough money to send out a small company of militia, unmounted, to join with regular army troops in pursuing the marauders.

"Safford's in command," said Marc. "Spunky thing for him to do. And it certainly ought to help his Independents get votes away from the Democrats in the elections."

Patrick said with scorn, "Foot soldiers after Apaches? I bet they never lay eyes on one—though you can bet the Apaches will see them!"

"All the same," said Talitha, "I'm grateful that James is at the mine."

Silently, Cat echoed that. It must have taken him a while to get used to the work. Perhaps the manager wouldn't let him off till he'd been employed for a time. Surely he'd come for her birthday."

He didn't.

Racked alternately by anger, hurt, and alarm, she scarcely slept that night. Next morning she went to Talitha and said that she wanted to ride to the San Patricio to make sure James was there.

Talitha frowned. "I'll send the twins, or a couple of vaqueros. They can take some message to Don Buenaventura so that James won't get his hackles up. I'd like to know myself that he's settled in at the mine."

"I want to go, too."

Talitha's face, the one Cat had known as a mother's since infancy, was sad now and the blue eyes looked deep into her. "My dear, my dear, he can't be tamed. I love him, he's my brother, but until he has some peace in himself, he can only cause you grief."

Though she wanted to throw herself into Talitha's arms, pour out her hurt and bewilderment and hope, Cat made herself stand straight and proud.

"Maybe I can cause him happiness. Maybe that will

give him peace." The concern in Talitha's clear gaze was hard to endure. Desperately, Cat invoked what everyone on the ranch knew but never talked about. "You loved my father, Tally. The boys say he drank too much and was lots older. He might have caused you sadness if he'd come back, but you'd have gone on caring, wouldn't you?"

Talitha got to her feet and stared out at the brilliant autumn sky. "I still care. All my life I will love him, and all my death, though I love Marc, too." Tears glistened in her eyes.

Tally never cried. Cat took her in her arms. They wept together, for Shea, for James, men they both loved; wept also for each other as women fated to joy and pain. Then Talitha said, "I'll talk to Miguel and Patrick. If you're going, better it be with them."

Belen came, too, for he'd made the trip a number of times and knew his way through the passes. Unencumbered by pack mules, they could make good time till they got into the tortuous mountain trails, so, rather than spend the night along the way, they left before dawn and carried grain to fortify their mounts since they'd have little chance to graze.

At the San Pedro they watered the horses, loosened their cinches for an hour's rest, and gave them the grain. When they resumed their journey, the mountains grew more jagged and the trails, when visible, were often rock stripped of softening earth or grass by the wearing of wind and rain. Cat had never been this far west. Belen shook his head as they passed through several valleys where cattle had thinned the grass till none was left to anchor the soil and torrential desert rains had washed away much of the earth.

"Grass won't grow on rock," Belen said. "Once, in these valleys, the grama was waist-high. Along roads where freighters travel, it's even worse. Oxen can't find enough to eat so the freighters are using mules. When they can find nothing—" He spread his hands expressively.

Rancho del Socorro cattle were kept to a number that didn't overgraze the pastures and were shifted from time to time to give the grass time to recover. When heavy rains came, the grasses and other plants kept it from cutting channels. Instead, it spread out over the valleys like a shallow lake and soaked in.

"More cattle are bound to come into the territory," mused Patrick. "Right now, most of the beef for the army is driven in from Texas. That seems pretty foolish."

"We can't stock more heavily without hurting our grass," Miguel pointed out. He shrugged unhappily. "But there'll be cattlemen come in who won't know or care about that. They'll see the tall good grass and won't realize how little rain we get and how hard it is to bring back a range once it's destroyed."

And as domestic animals used the graze there'd be less for wild things, deer, antelope. Less game for Indians, who'd have to steal more of their meat or go on reservations to be fed. Cat suddenly thought of K'aak'eh, and how the maimed hawk had never been able to catch its prey. The hawk had disappeared; for some reason, Cat had never wanted to ask James what had happened to him.

There were a lot of things she'd never ask James. Nevertheless, she loved him. Or perhaps because of them, wounds where his softer nature had eroded down to hardness like soil from a trampled slope.

The sun was dropping behind the western mountains as they descended the trail clinging precariously to the cliffside. Part of the way, they dismounted and led their horses.

A bugle sounded faintly. Belen grinned. "Good to know the guard's awake even if it does seem to be payday!"

Indeed, the little plaza formed by the miners'

quarters, company store, headquarters, school, infirmary, and chapel was swarming with people. Belen explained that on paydays mescal peddlers, cardsharps, and anyone with something to sell flocked up from the nearest little Mexican town and helped the miners get rid of their wages.

They were met halfway to the camp by five armed miners and Don Buenaventura himself, a slender, sad-eyed man of middle years who waxed his mustache to points. He prickled Cat's hand with them as he bowed low, seemingly overwhelmed at the unexpected pleasure of meeting one of his *patronas.*

After inquiring after the health of Talitha and Marc, he begged to escort them to the village and offer them his quarters. He would move in with the bookkeeper. Of course the young *patrones* and *patronita* mustn't judge the camp by its payday aspect. The men worked hard at dangerous tasks. It was understandable that they were somewhat rough in their diversions.

He kept talking as they rode into the camp. In spite of the manager's offering to help with their horses, they preferred to take care of them themselves, though Cat kept scanning the crowds around the monte dealers or mescal sellers.

"Is Santiago Montaña here?" Patrick asked Don Buenaventura as they started for the manager's quarters.

"Oh, the man recommended by Don Marcos! To be sure. One of the best workers. But when not working he spends little time in camp. I saw him go up the cañon with his rifle this morning."

"We want to see him," said Patrick. "He taught us a lot about hunting when he worked at the Socorro, and was our friend."

"Bueno." The manager smiled. "He prefers to live alone, so he made himself that small house at the end across from the headquarters. He may spend the night out—often he does—but he'll faithfully report for work

in the morning—and not *muy crudo* like everyone else."

Don Buenaventura's spacious quarters were in one end of the headquarters, furnished with crude furniture bedecked with the best serapes and such touches of elegance as could be brought in by pack train: gilt mirrors, silver candelabra, lamps, pewter and copper-ware.

An old woman with an alert squirrel face and twitching nose hurried to make fresh tortillas and reheat sauced turkey and rice. Then, with the help of a young girl, she made pallets in the main room for the twins, and Belen, and fetched hot water to the bed-room so Cat could wash.

The window faced James's small adobe, but there was no sign of him. Cat burned with impatience to see him, but at the same time she began to grow nervous. Would he be angry that she'd come? What would she say to him? How could she make him know that wherever he was, she wanted to be, too?

Don Buenaventura sipped coffee with them as they ate, obviously surprised that Belen sat at table with the O'Sheas. Patrick explained that Marc had wanted to be sure all went well at the San Patricio but was too busy with the coming election to come himself. The twins had volunteered, wanting to see their old friend Santiago, and their sister had come along for the outing.

Don Buenaventura frowned. "Such outings can come to tragic ends in this wild country. God guard you safely home, *patronita*."

After the meal, Patrick wanted to play monte and Miguel went along to keep him out of trouble. Don Buenaventura took himself off to the bookkeeper's, the girl and old woman were busy in the kitchen, and Cat was left to her own devices.

It was dark now. Outside, merrymaking continued by several fires, and a dance was getting underway to the strumming of guitars. During supper Cat had kept an eye on James's house, but no one had entered and it remained dark.

In sudden determination, she went back to arrange the pillows and coverlets in Don Buenaventura's big bed so that a hasty glance in candlelight would show what seemed to be a sleeping form. Her brothers *might* decide to look in on her. She brushed out her hair, took a clean chemise from her saddlebag, blew out the candles in the big room, and stole carefully across the clearing to the house her love had made for himself.

She couldn't see in the darkness, but her hands found a shirt of his hanging on a peg. She pressed it to her face and drew deeply into her lungs the scent of him, mixed with that of woodsmoke. A table. A bench. His bed was straw matting covered with serapes.

As she touched where his body had lain, Cat's blood seemed to slow, run heavily molten. Her breath came jerkily. Standing to undress, she touched her breasts, wishing her hands were his. She put on the chemise and lay down, sinking luxuriantly into blankets that had held him.

Even if he didn't come home before she'd have to get back to the manager's bed, it was balm to lie in his bed, in his house. She wouldn't sleep. Just rest here and think of him, his eyes and hands and mouth.

Querido. My love. James. . . .

XVI

She woke to violent hands, a hoarse, enraged voice that panted in Spanish as a hard knee parted her legs, "Have it, then, whore! I need a woman, even you!"

Something rammed painfully at that secret place which had occasionally, when she was riding, brought her an urgent pleasure she hadn't known how to bring to a finish, which had one time throbbed to delight in a half-waking dream of James. But this was a nightmare. She cried out, writhing: "James!"

The cruel rigidity thrust convulsively deep, then seemed to melt, no longer hurting, laving her torn entrance with a slow, warm seep of juices. Shuddering, he wrenched himself from her, setting his hands on either side of her face as if that would help him see her in the darkness.

"Caterina! Not you—"

"I—I wanted to see you."

She heard his teeth grit together. "So you lay in my bed and I took you for that town *puta* who's been after me every payday!"

She put her arms around him, forgetting her shock and hurt in the joy of touching him, holding him like this. After all, if that was what happened with men and women, it's what she would have wanted after they were married. She was sure it would be a lot different when he was loving her, kissing and caressing her. But even if it always hurt like that, she could stand it if he'd do the nice things first.

"It wasn't your fault," she said. "What could you think, when you found a woman in your bed?"

He sat up, not touching her. "You are a child."

She sat up, too, stung by his tone. "I'm seventeen. From what you've told us of Apaches, I'd probably be a mother now if I were one of them."

"If you were an Apache girl, you wouldn't be a child."

"Ohhh!" She searched her fund of vaqueros' words for something bad enough to hurl at him. *"Cabroncito! Sangrón!* Man because the midwife said so—"

Startled laughter burst from him. She hit him as hard as she could. It was like striking rock. Wrist and knuckles smarting, she realized her behavior had confirmed his slighting remark. She wanted to cry, but that would only make things worse. Pride warred with her love for him. Who was he, a half-breed, to attack and mock her? She should get up and walk away now, put him out of her heart. Smile at Jordan or some young officer.

But that would be a lie. Lifting her head, she tried to keep her voice steady. "Maybe I do seem a child to you. But I can learn. I love you, James. Let me be your woman."

He was silent.

What could she say now? What could she do? A withering thought pierced her. All the time, she'd been sure he loved her. What if he didn't? What if he cared for her only as an older brother?

She took a long, slow breath. If that were so, she had to leave him in peace, of course, without any more begging. She put her hand out to find his face.

It was wet with tears.

"Oh, James!" She closed her arms around him. "I'm sorry I've made you feel bad. Please . . ." She began to cry herself, miserable at this ending to what she'd dreamed would be a happy meeting.

He took her in his arms then, cradled her against his bare chest. "What can I do, my soft wild kitten, little *gídí?*" He rocked her back and forth. "I'm a warrior with power from the Sacred Mountain, but I cannot fight you."

They lay down together, her head on his shoulder. He covered her against the cold. Though she felt his hardness against her thigh, he didn't try to have her again; he only touched her face, throat, and breasts as if they were wonders, smoothed her shoulders, the arch of her back, and her lean rider's hips with warm, gently fingers. Honey-fire sweetened her veins. She felt like a flower, unfolding at his touch, opening, inviting. When she tried to kiss him, he laughed softly.

"Apaches don't do that."

"Well, you can! Let me show you."

It was made difficult by his embarrassed chuckles. Losing patience, she bit him lightly. He turned her over on her back and closed her mouth with his.

"Is this how? Is this how you like it, *gídí?*"

That bewildering part of him, swollen so that it was hard to believe it could be soft and vulnerable, pressed against her side. She'd seen enough horses and cattle mate to understand his need, and her own body craved him in spite of the ache between her legs.

Trying to ease herself beneath him, she whispered, "Please, James. Please—"

"No. You are sore where I broke your seal. I'm sorry I hurt you, *gídí.*"

"James . . ."

He lay back again, holding her so tenderly that her flaring rebellion ebbed. She found it unspeakable comfort to know the strong smoothness of his body, the deep, regular pounding of his heart against her cheek.

"Let me tell you how it would be if you were an Apache girl," he said, and she suspected he found it necessary to force his attention from that curious, independent part of his body.

"When your *ch'ich'ilwod* came upon you, your first woman flow, a special lodge would be made for you. Inside this universe, during four days, you'd be made a woman by rites taking you through the mysteries of White Painted Woman. At night the Gahan, good spirits who live in mountain caves and in the four great directions, would come as masked, painted dancers. They'd come from east, north, west, and south and dance around a great fire, waving their painted wands, wearing headdresses plumed and ornamented with a black cloth to cover their faces expect for little eye-holes. They'd dance while a shaman celebrated rites in the lodge, with women attending you. On the fourth night you'd dance, too, and at sunrise run around a basket of ceremonial things, and back to the deerskins in front of the lodge, four times, while the shaman would sing. The last time you'd take a feather from the basket. Then the lodge would be taken down. Your parents would give the people gifts. And everyone would know you were a woman."

"I should hope so, after all that!" Snuggling her head deeper into the curve of his arm, she tried to imagine the flickering fire, the towering masked dancers. "Do boys have anything like that?"

"No. We go to the Sacred Mountain for power and act as servants on four raids, but there's nothing like the maiden's ceremony. That celebrates the holiness of being able to give birth." He twined a lock of her hair around his finger. "Apaches are sad if they have no daughters. It's through them descent is traced."

"I thought Apache women were drudges and were always getting their noses cut off!"

"Only for adultery. Our women are chaste. Of course, they work hard; there's much to do. But they can have power from the spirits, too. Some are shamans. Some go into battle with their husbands. Of the Mexican women captured and taken to wife, I've never heard of one who'd go back to her people even when given the chance."

She didn't remind him that his own mother hadn't been reconciled to her captivity, nor had Talitha. "How do Apaches marry?"

"After a man proves he can support a family by taking part in a number of raids, his parents may choose a girl for him, or he may have his eye on one he's seen at ceremonials or about her errands. His father or uncle goes to talk to her parents, and if agreement's reached, he leaves a gift of horses, blankets, or guns. The horses, usually between two and six, are tied near the girl's lodge during the night. After a decent wait, if she takes them to water it means she's consented. It's thought bad of a girl to leave horses waiting a long time without water if she intends to have the man. If she won't take care of the animals, the man finally gives up and takes them away."

"It seems hard on the horses."

"It seldom is, *gídí.* Since the families have talked, it's pretty certain the girl will accept the gifts before they're made."

"Then what happens?"

"Often the man has made a lodge in some pleasant place a distance from the camp. He may take his bride there for a week or so. Sometimes, they just build a lodge close to the girl's parents and live there from the start. In that case, the bride's mother cooks for them for the first few months."

Cat frowned. "But I've heard Talitha say a man's mother-in-law can't speak to him, look at him, or even be in the same house at the same time! That seems strange if the young couple's expected to live close to her parents."

"It's how mothers-in-law and sons-in-law show their respect for each other." James laughed. "Anyway, the lodge entrances are usually out of sight of each other. If a woman meets her son-in-law, she just throws her blanket over her face."

For the first time Cat was thinking of Apaches as they lived together, not as fearsome plunderers. They had as many rules and customs as any people. She began to understand, a little, why James had stayed with them.

Caressing his face, she said dreamily, "I want you to make up a lodge like that, maybe by the hot springs, where we could be alone awhile. But I want to be married in the *sala,* like my parents and Marc and Talitha."

James stiffened. "Married, Caterina? It cannot be."

"But you love me!"

"Too much to let you make such a mistake. It's not good to hang between two worlds. Your fingers grow numb at last. You drop into the chasm."

"We could live here at the mine," she ventured. "Or build a house somewhere on the ranch."

"You've always been surrounded by people who love you, *gídí.* You'd miss that, as flowers miss the sun. I can't take everything you have and give you only me."

"You're all I want!"

"It's as I've said," he replied grimly. "You're a child. A spoiled one."

Storming at him would only harden that conviction. With tremendous effort she restrained an outburst and waited till she could speak in an even, though rather sarcastic tone.

"When will you consider me a woman?"

He didn't answer for a moment, as if stunned. Then he began to laugh, hugging her to him in spite of her outraged resistance. "I remember your mother used to call your father a redhead burro for his stubbornness. What would she have called you?"

"She'd have had a large choice, since I was given all my great-aunts' names," said Cat haughtily. "She was my age when she met my father and no one ever said she wasn't a woman!"

"She was a lady of valor and compassion."

"And you think I can't be?"

He sighed. "I'd call some of your bravery ignorance. Of compassion, you have too much. Always sorry for the sick or hurt or orphaned. I think that's why you've thought you love me."

"Yes, you look a lot like those little calves I feed! Stop dodging, James. When will you believe that I know what I'm choosing? One year? Two? Five?"

He was silent for a long time. At last, reluctantly, he said, "Let's talk about it in a year. But you're not bound to me, *gídí.* If you decide to marry Jordan, or if you meet some other man, my heart will be glad for you, though heavy."

Only then did she realize she was holding her breath. Slowly she released it. A year seemed forever, but it *would* pass.

"Will you come for the Roof Feast?" she asked.

"I'll try." He sat up, bringing her with him. "Are you staying at Don Buenaventura's? You'd best get back. It'll be dawn soon. The card players and revelers were sleeping where they fell when I came home, and that's been some hours ago."

A time that had begun as nightmare ended with hope. He loved her. Knowing that, she could wait. He held her and they kissed. "You're learning to do that very well," she teased.

"I suppose I'll get used to it, though it seems a dirty habit. I'd never do it with anyone but you."

"Good!"

She clung to him. He kissed her again and told her to dress. Hurrying into her clothes, she stood with him at the door. "Remember the Roof Feast," she said, then touched his cheek and hurried across the way to the headquarters. Belen might be sleeping in front of her door. She went around to the bedroom window, blessed the fact that it was low enough to clamber through, washed herself and threw the water, which must be somewhat bloodied, out the window, and fell into bed. The way James had taken her hadn't been anything like her vague dreamings. But if it hadn't happened he'd probably never have admitted he loved her.

Since few miners were fit for work next morning, it was an unofficial holiday. The twins invited James over for a big breakfast. Fortunately, Patrick talked enough for everybody.

For a while, Cat could no more have looked directly at James than she could have stared straight at the sun. She felt as if her body must glow for all to see from his caresses. That other dull pain was all but forgotten. She longed to tell her brothers, Belen, and even Don Buenaventura that in a year she and James would marry, but she knew he wouldn't like that, would think it a mark of her alleged childishness.

After breakfast, the twins and James went hunting. Cat complimented the old woman on breakfast and, though her help was refused in the kitchen, she tidied the bedroom and then, heart thudding, walked over to James's little house.

His home consisted of a single room with a window facing the western mountains. There was a stone fireplace built into the adobe with adobe *bancos* on either side of niches for cooking needs: a cast-iron skillet and several clay cookpots, one half full of dried-up stew which Cat, wrinkling her nose, carried to the edge of camp and scraped out for the dogs.

She put the pot to soak and then finished looking around James's home. A table of rough wood, a washtable with a basin, garments on pegs, riding gear in a corner. And the bed where they'd been together and talked, the sweetness of that blotting out those frightful moments when James had thought she was that persistent whore.

Doubtless lucky it had happened that way, breaking down his reserve, forcing him to be honest. Cat smiled as she carried the serapes outside and hung them across some manzanita bushes to air. She scrubbed out the stewpot, cleaned the rancid skillet, and went across to the company store, where she bought several strings of red chilis which would be decoration as well as seasoning, a chicken ready for the pot, apples, rice, cinnamon, cones of raw sugar, tortillas and sweet breads just made by the storekeeper's wife, and other things to make the house more homelike: several bright cushions, colorful mats, handblown glasses and a jug, candles and pottery candleholders, several woven baskets, a mirror, and a blue-robed Guadalupana standing on a crescent moon. She charged these to her percentage of the mine's revenue, telling the storekeeper to take his bill to the bookkeeper.

Returning to the house with her booty, she arranged her purchases for utility and ornament: the mirror above the washtable where it reflected the smiling Guadalupana fitted in a niche above the bed; the chilis beside the fireplace; cushions and mats on the *bancos;* one candlestick in a niche near the bed, the others on the table.

In the meadows beyond the camp, where children were having a hilarious game of seeing how many could pile on a gentle burro before the last was pushed off, Cat watched and hoped she and James would have, oh, at least four children, two boys and two girls, with one to carry her father's flaming hair. She gathered goldenrod and asters, then wandered to the trees along the stream, collecting yellow aspen and flaming maple leaves to complete the bouquet she arranged in one of the clay pots.

At Don Buenaventura's for a light noon meal, she explained her morning's labors to the old woman by saying that James was her foster mother's brother and she'd promised to do what she could to make him comfortable. At this, the woman's nose-twitching, disapproving manner vanished. She said that in the future she'd see that the young man, who was decent and civil though he kept to himself, was eating properly. There was always food left from Don Buenaventura's table, so it would be no trouble.

Cat thanked her warmly and went back to the store, where she bought the finest rebozo and gifted the housekeeper with it before she went to the little house she loved to be in where she could think of James.

Someday his bed would be hers, too, for all the rest of their lives. *Till then, when you lie here, remember me,* querido, *the way we were last night.*

Everything was done. She added wood to the fire to keep the chicken cooking, stirred the rice for the stew she was making him, and felt like a woman able to manage a house and care for her man.

She'd hoped to be at the house when he saw all she'd done, but she also wanted to look fresh and comb her hair, and so she didn't see him till supper.

"The Three Kings must have gotten mixed up and visited me today," he said when he joined them for supper. "I thought I'd gone into the wrong house or was dreaming; but when I rubbed my eyes and looked again, it was all still there."

Cat flushed as her brothers looked at her in surprise. Miguel laughed. "You're the one who worked the miracle, James, if our wild one set your house to rights. Talitha says Cat never threw out anything in her life—or put it up, either."

Cat kicked him under the table and said sweetly, "That's what Juri says about you."

Belen said, "Young birds don't furbish their parents' nests, but when the time comes they know how to make their own."

Patrick plunged through the banter to ask Don Buenaventura if it were true that rich copper ores had been spotted in the Mule Mountains to the south.

The manager shrugged. "Much copper. I've seen it myself. But only silver or gold is worth the risk of Apaches and bandits, Don Patricio."

"That'll change. Marc says more and more inventions will need copper parts."

Miguel sighed. "You'll never be happy, will you, as long as you have your skin in one piece?"

"I just like hunting for hidden things," retorted Patrick. "Branding calves and fighting screwworms isn't how I want to spend my life!"

"Get married," advised his twin. "That'll keep ranch life exciting enough even for you."

Patrick snorted. "I'd have married Juri, but you beat me to her, and I haven't met another girl I'd want to settle with. Reckon after Christmas I'll just have to go see what I can find. Like to throw in with me, James?"

For a moment James hesitated. Then the interest in his eyes vanished as wind might snuff out flame. Cat knew he was remembering that, traveling with a white, he'd be expected to side against his people in case of any conflicts. "I'll stay here," he said.

Cat was sorry he felt trapped but relieved that she'd at least know where he was. Once they married, she was sure, she could make him feel that with her he had a place, a home where he belonged.

Everyone was tired. James went to his house shortly after supper, and the twins began to make down their bedrolls. Cat went to the bedroom. After she'd brushed her hair and washed, she blew out the candle and leaned against the window, waiting till her eyes could make out the vague outlines of James's house.

No light. He must already be stretched to his tall length on the bed they'd shared last night. Did he remember? Did he wish she was with him now?

She longed to steal across the clearing, enter his house, slip into his arms. For a moment she closed her eyes and imagined it before she made herself get into Don Buenaventura's big bed.

There was always the chance of being discovered; but, more imperatively, instinct warned her not to crowd her lover. He needed time to get used to the truth bared between them.

Smiling in the dark, she skipped over that terrible beginning to remember everything he'd said, his caresses, the way he'd begun to like to kiss.

She was his. He was hers. One day the whole world would know it.

James had gone to work before they were ready to leave next morning, but Cat hurried into his house long enough to smooth his bed and look about, assuring herself that he couldn't forget her with all the signs of herself she'd left him.

It was less than three months till the Roof Feast. Then it was nine months till her birthday, but surely she'd see him in between. And perhaps he'd change his mind if she could convince him she was really grown up before that.

She scarcely heard anything the twins or Belen said as they traveled the long miles home, arriving after dark. Hugging Talitha, Cat answered her unspoken question.

"James is fine. And, Tally, he says he'll try to come for the Roof Feast!"

Talitha relaxed visibly. With quick sympathy Cat understood something of how Talitha had worried over her brother all these years. "He's going to be all right," she said softly, squeezing the older woman's hand. "It's going to be fine."

But when she glanced up to find Jordan's hazel eyes on her, hurt naked in them for an instant, she realized guiltily that for him it wouldn't be happy.

From the first, territorial Democrats had believed the federal appointees were black Republican carpetbaggers out of political favor in their home states sent to Arizona to "fatten at the public crib." The big issue that fall of 1870 was who should serve as territorial delegate to Congress, Richard McCormick, a former governor, or Peter Brady, a respected Tucsonan who'd been active in business and politics since coming to the region in 1853. Talitha remembered that he'd passed through the ranch with Gray's surveying party and had been at the defeat of a large Apache raid on Calabazas. Selected by the Democratic convention that had met in Tucson September 17, Brady was certainly much more a man of the territory than McCormick, a New Yorker appointed to the governorship in 1866.

Two of the three territorial papers hurled nasty epithets at McCormick and his supporters, but he won the November election—through fraud, the papers accused. In Arizona City, four hundred ineligible Indians, men and women, had voted.

"We believe in the right of women to vote," wrote the editor of the *Weekly Arizonan,* and went on to say that he thought it would have been more gallant of the merchandise company that had arranged the fraud to have "first extended this right to the white ladies of Arizona City and compelled the squaws to remain for next season."

The paper gave McCormick a withering send-off to Washington, naming him a Republican "of the blackest dye," a carpetbagger clothed in "apostasy and degradation" and "mired down in filth and debris of bartered principle."

"Thank goodness that circus is over," said Marc, who'd run as an unopposed Independent and been overwhelmingly elected in spite of having fought for the Union. He smiled grimly. "I see the way voting works here, the way the press and speakers try to stir people up rather than touch their reason, and I wonder if this is what I fought for so long ago in Berlin."

"You were elected," reminded Talitha. "So were lots of good men. Even with fraud and abuses, surely it's better for people to decide who'll make their laws rather than have them decreed by a king. And it's something, after all these years of chaos, to finally have a government of our own rather than being an afterthought of Santa Fe or Mesilla."

"You're right." Cheered, Marc nodded. "I think

Safford will be a fine governor. I want to help him get those schools started."

The ranch sold most of its beef that fall to Camp Crittenden and Camp Lowell in Tucson. The flare of autumn leaves along the creek and mountainsides faded, harvest was over, and snow crowned the Santa Ritas. It was time for the Feast of the Roof.

Cat helped eagerly with the preparations, helping Anita wrap tamales in cornshucks by the dozen, cracking thin-shelled piñon nuts for use in candy and cakes, grinding acorns for stew, spreading squash seeds to dry for use in *pipian,* the spicy sauce used on turkey and vegetables.

Cat had hoped James would come the night before, and as the day wore on she began to imagine all sorts of horrible things. Perhaps he'd been waylaid by bandits or Indians. Maybe he was sick. He could have been hurt or killed in a mine accident. He could have gone back to the Apaches. . . . One disastrous possibility after another chased through her mind. Of course, the feast wasn't held till evening. It was a long day's ride. If he hadn't left till that morning, he could still be on his way.

It was almost sunset when she saw a rider coming from the east and ran out to watch him approach. Soon, from the way he sat his horse, she was sure it wasn't James. Drooping, she was turning to the door when Jordan spoke, shielding his eyes.

"Wrong man, Katie? Looks like Lieutenant Frazier to me."

Mouth sour with disappointment, she went to help Anita, leaving Frazier's welcome to Talitha and Marc. They invited him to stay for the festive meal, of course, and he behaved as if he'd never stopped calling, though he hadn't been at the ranch since the day he'd challenged James to help track Apache raiders. She heard him say that he'd been out with Governor Safford's volunteers.

"We covered six hundred miles and stayed out

twenty-seven days, but we never caught a single Apache," he growled to Marc. "Most discouraging duty on the face of the earth."

Helping serve the food, Cat managed to avoid him till after the meal; but when she sat down to listen to the singing, he found a place beside her, so close that she was flinchingly aware of his hard-muscled arm pressing against hers, of the taut, hungry eagerness of his young body.

"I've missed you, Caterina."

She had no answer for that. He turned to her, his face only inches from hers. She smelled mingled male odors: tobacco, leather, sweat, and soap. In spite of his youth, sun and weather had formed lines at the corners of his gray eyes. He looked older, leaner, tougher, till a winning smile softened the lines in his face.

"There's going to be a Christmas dance at Calabazas. Would you let me take you?"

"Thank you, Lieutenant, but . . ." She had no desire to hurt him, cast around for an excuse, and realized she did indeed have an unarguable one. "I'm engaged."

His jaw dropped. "Engaged?" he echoed blankly. Glancing around, his gaze fell on Jordan, who was, undeniably, watching them. "To him?"

"No."

Their eyes locked. The edges of his nostrils showed white and his lips thinned over his teeth. "I can deal with a refusal, Miss O'Shea. No need to invent an engagement."

"I'm not inventing."

A slim ash-colored eyebrow lifted. "If you're going to marry the man, it's strange that you seem ashamed to name him. Or is this . . . engagement a secret from your guardians?"

There was no way out, though Cat wished she'd simply refused the lieutenant's invitation. Was it tempting fate to pretend that what she prayed for, what James had promised to consider after her birthday, was accomplished fact?

She was engaged; James wasn't. But there was nothing for it but to face the young officer haughtily. "I'm going to marry James Scott, Lieutenant."

"James Scott?" It actually wasn't his name but was all that Cat could think of. Frazier's eyes flicked to Talitha, then swept back to Cat with sudden shocked comprehension. "The half-breed? That Apache?"

She brought back her arm and slapped him as hard as she could. His head snapped back. The white prints of her fingers showed in the redness staining his tanned cheek.

The music drowned out the sound. No one had noticed except Jordan, who was making his way toward them. Frazier's breath came in a hiss.

"So you want to be a squaw?" he said in a murderous voice, beneath his breath. "I would have married you, made you a lady. Maybe, when he's tired of you, I'll buy the use of you for a bottle of mescal."

Rising as Jordan loomed above them, Frazier bowed low and said very softly, "I hope I have the privilege of shooting your buck and bringing you his body."

"Be sure I'll kill you if you do," Cat said just as quietly beneath the strum of guitars. "I'd rather have James dead than you alive, or twenty like you."

His eyes blazed down at her before he straightened.

"Need help getting your horse?" Jordan asked.

"I can manage, Scott." Swinging brusquely away, Frazier made brief good nights to Marc and Talitha and was gone.

Jordan gazed down at Cat. "Want to tell me what that was all about?"

Tears choked her. She stumbled to her feet and started blindly for the door, needing to escape the crowded noisy room, to go where she could vent her frustration and anger—her fear, too. For Frazier was an officer in an army committed to hunting down Apaches.

Jordan put a hand beneath her arm and guided her out on the long front veranda where he'd kissed her that night of her sixteenth birthday which seemed so long ago. "What's the matter, Katie? Should I go after Frazier and give him a trouncing?"

She shook her head. "I'm afraid I've done enough to stir him up. He called James a half-breed again."

"Now why would he do that, knowing what hot water it got him into last time? I'd have sworn he came in tonight bent on behaving mild as a lamb."

"He probably did," Cat said dolefully. "But when he asked me to a dance, I said I was engaged and then—*Caray!* What a mess I made of it!"

"And lied, too, Katie. You're not engaged."

"I am!"

He watched her steadily in the light splashed golden from the window. "I think you mean you coaxed, bedeviled, and beguiled poor James into agreeing that at some distant date you'd seriously talk about getting married."

Exactly right. How could he know? She glared at him, spun away, and burst into tears.

"Here." He brought her against his shoulder. "I'm better to cry against than that adobe."

He let her sob till the storm was over, then got out one of the handkerchiefs Talitha kept the men supplied with and mopped her face, made her blow her stopped-up nose. "Want to tell me about it?"

Haltingly, she told him everything except how James had taken her that night by mistake. "And he promised to try to come for the Roof Feast," she finished. "Maybe something's happened to him. Maybe—"

Jordan said roughly, "Lord's sake, Katie! He's hoping you'll get enough sense to see it wouldn't work."

She jerked away with an outraged cry, but he caught her wrists and held her inexorably. "He hasn't said he'll marry you. You badgered him into agreeing to *talk* about it after your birthday."

"You—you don't want me to marry him!"

"You bet I don't. I want you myself." He brought her

hard against him. She heard the heavy pound of his heart, was overpowered by the male longing that radiated from him, barely under control. "Katie, Katie! I'm sure James loves you. But he's man enough to want to save you from the troubles he's pretty sure to have. By himself he can manage, move on when a place gets impossible. But with a wife, maybe children? Let him go, honey, for both your sakes."

She said as if it were a vow, "I'll marry him."

Jordan sighed. "I want you to be happy. Whatever that takes. If you ever need me, Katie, don't be too proud to ask."

Her heart swelled with feeling for him. If it hadn't been for James, she could have loved this man with the honest hazel eyes and kind, strong hands. He loved her with his body and with his heart, and both were sound and good.

Humbled, saddened, she lifted his hands to her lips and kissed them. "Thank you, Jordan. You'll find a girl who's lots nicer than I am—"

As if something had snapped in him, he turned up her face and stared at it as if he'd fix her forever in his mind. She closed her eyes to escape that desperate searching. His mouth took hers, achingly, savagely, before he turned away violently, striding off into the darkness.

Jordan was strong. He'd do very well without her. But James—James had no one of his own. She faced the bitter wind and fought back her tears.

Since he hadn't come to her, she'd go to him. In any case, he needed to be warned that Frazier might make trouble for him if he found out where he was. Cat didn't want to spoil tonight's celebration, but tomorrow she'd talk to Talitha.

XVII

Once again Cat rode down the cañon trail into the mining camp. Marc had come to inspect the mine and Belen was along for protection. Patrick was preparing to leave on a prospecting trip to the north, so he'd stayed at the ranch. Don Buenaventura once again yielded his house to his visitors, and while he and Marc talked Cat hurried across the clearing in the twilight to invite James to eat with them.

Had he seen them ride in? Would he be glad to see her? Heart thudding till she felt choked, short of breath, she paused in the doorway and softly called his name.

No answer. He wasn't there. And as she peered into the almost dark room, she saw that the madonna no longer hung above his bed. The cushions were gone from the *bancos;* gone, too, the mats, glass jug, baskets, and mirror she'd chosen so happily and arranged while pretending this was their house, hers and James's.

She shrank against the wall. Why had he put her gifts away? Didn't he want to be reminded of her?

Did he still live here? Kneeling, she touched the serapes on the pallet bed, recognizing the broad black and brown stripes. They were his, the blankets they'd slept beneath. She pressed her face to their roughness, trying to find some sense and smell of him.

What did it mean? Perhaps he *had* seen them coming and slipped away. That thought jerked her erect. A rush of angry hurt brought her to her feet. After he'd taken her as he had, called her *gídí*, and talked all night long, he hadn't come to the Roof Feast. He'd even put the things she'd placed around his house out of sight. She'd go home tomorrow and forget all about him!

Yet, as she crossed to Don Buenaventura's house, she remembered the renegade Apache who'd kidnaped her collapsing with James's arrow through him, and how James had been shaking when she threw herself into his arms. She remembered how tenderly he'd nursed K'aak'eh, how he'd defied his Apache kin to save Patrick. And that night when, at last, he'd loved her with his strong, hard body, admitted that he cared for her.

Forget him? As well forget the blood in her veins, the air she breathed.

After the old woman and the girl had cleared the table, Belen went to visit friends, while Marc and the manager lingered over brandy and *cigarros*. Cat retired to the manager's bedroom and looked across to James's house.

No light showed. Maybe he'd gone to bed while she was at supper, or maybe he was staying out till he thought she'd abandon hope of seeing him that evening. Either way, he'd learn that when she came to see him, she was going to.

Determinedly advancing on the bed, she arranged the coverings and pillows to look like a reclining form in case Marc glanced in, took the packet of candies and little cakes Talitha had sent, and scrambled out the low, wide window.

James hadn't come home. After putting Tally's gift on the table, Cat paused by the bed. Should she wait for him there as she had before?

No. The way he'd used her as an importunate whore wasn't a thing to bring to his mind. Besides, if he guessed who she was, he might go away and leave her sleeping.

Shivering, Cat took a serape, wrapped in it, and settled on a *banco* to wait, leaning against the molded adobe of the fireplace. There were no embers. Either James hadn't eaten at home or his meal had been cold. When they were married, she'd see he had a hot supper every night, all the things he liked.

Smiling, Cat pictured straight-backed little boys with James's startling eyes, at least one with her father's flaming hair; and a girl who'd look like Socorro, the mother she'd never known. Tired from the long day's journey, she began to drowse and had to keep waking herself when her head drooped.

Late. So late. Why didn't he come?

She roused to sounds of undressing. In the dim light from the door she saw a tall dark figure bend to lie down on the pallet. A heavy odor of mescal filled the place.

Cat had often seen vaqueros, even her brothers, drink themselves senseless at fiestas. She remembered her father's methodical, steady drinking. Drunken men didn't shock her, though they caused a certain disgust. She was realistic enough to know that the mescal might be her ally this night; it might loosen James's iron control.

When he'd been breathing heavily for a time, she stood up and came to the bed. Putting the extra serape at his feet, she undressed, prickling from chill, and lay down with him, trying to escape the sour taint of mescal.

His body was strange at first, but, emboldened by his heavy slumber, she pressed closer to him, let her breasts touch his warm chest. That strangely frightening yet vulnerable part of him began to stiffen. She touched it wonderingly, and it throbbed beneath her fingers, a delicate velvet pulsing constrained and restricted by his flesh.

He groaned. Murmuring what sounded like her

name, he raised himself to enter her, lunged deeply, quivered, buried himself within her, and was emptied.

His fluid laved the parts hurt by the violence of his possessing. Cat held him, head on her breast, oddly touched with pity. So much of a man went into that act, his whole force and energy, leaving him spent. But James was straightening now, shifting his weight from her.

"Gídí! It's you, not a dream!"

She laughed softly, caressing his lips, his eyes, the strong high bones of his cheeks. "If that's how you behave with dreams, I hope I'm in all of yours."

He didn't answer. She said reproachfully, "I hope you haven't become a drunkard. Do you have mescal every night?"

"No. But I saw you riding into camp when I came off work. I was afraid to face you, *gídí.* So I went to a friend's and didn't come home till I was sure you were long asleep."

A lump swelled in her throat. "That's not nice of you, James. And it wasn't nice not to come to the Roof Feast."

He sat up heavily. "Caterina, I'm trying to let you forget me."

"You promised—"

He placed his fingers on her lips. "I know. You make everything seem possible. You dazzle me, like sun in the eyes. I think it might work. But when you go and the world turns dark, I see clear again."

"Is that why you hid the madonna? Put away the things I got for the house?"

"How could I bear to see them, *gídí,* when I was telling myself I must let you go?"

The pain in his voice took away her old anger, but a new kind was growing, along with a fierce determination. She sat up and flung her arms around him. "You might as well stop thinking like that, James! I'm not going to let you go! You say it's dark without me. How do you think I feel? Now, are you going to keep your promise to marry me my next birthday, or shall I just make you do it now?"

"I said we'd *talk* on your birthday, not *marry,*" he protested, then chuckled. "And how would you make me?"

"Like this."

She touched that amazing independent part of him. He caught in his breath. *"Gídí, gídí,"* he said against her throat. "You make me drunker than mescal."

They sat down. He loved her sweetly, and they slept, waking, rested, to love again. Then she told him of the grudge Claybourne Frazier bore him and warned him to keep out of the way in case soldiers came scouting near the mine.

"Poor *nantan.*" James shrugged. "It must be hard on his pride to know you prefer an Apache to him."

"You're as much white as Apache."

"Not in my heart. That's why you shouldn't marry me."

"You've promised!"

He kissed her. "On your birthday we'll decide. But you must promise, too, not to come again. That'll give you time to think."

She nestled against his shoulder, wishing she never had to leave. "But, James, what if I have a baby from tonight?"

She felt his heart stop before it leaped and started to pound. He placed his spread hand upon her belly, covering it. "If that happens, send word. We'll marry at once."

With that and a long embrace she had to be content and go back in the faint graying to Don Buenaventura's bed.

Cat's monthly flow had always been irregular. She scarcely noticed its absence in January, but as Feburary ended her breasts were painfully tender and all she felt like eating for breakfast was a little hard bread, much as Talitha had been doing. Talitha, whose graceful figure was just beginning to round with her second child.

Holy mother! Was she herself with child? The thought struck Cat with blinding force one morning as she saw Talitha outlined against the window. Involuntarily her hand slipped to her own stomach and rested there as James's long fingers had that night, as if promising to protect anything he might have started there.

He had said to send for him, had promised to marry her. That was what she wanted, wasn't it? Then why didn't she feel triumphant?

She knew well enough. James hadn't taken her of his own will. She'd seduced a drink-befuddled man still half dreaming. He loved her, yes, but, in a way, she'd tricked him. It was a long time till her September birthday, but Cat wished passionately that she could have waited till then, or till he'd felt it was all right.

Calculations told her the baby would come in September. Her brothers would most certainly not be calm about her having a child out of wedlock, and she flinched from how Jordan would feel. It was all she could do, now, to bear the way he sometimes looked at her. As for Claybourne Frazier . . .

She bit her lip. Nothing for it. James would have to know. Should she tell Tally yet?

She shrank from doing anything. Belen, any of the vaqueros, would carry a message for her. Then James would come. They would stand before the madonna in the *sala*, just as she'd always planned, and be married the right way.

But it wouldn't be the right way. James would come to her chained, not free. The days passed. Her breasts ached. She ate dry bread and did not send for him.

News had leaked out that General Stoneman was recommending that the half posts in Arizona be abandoned, including Camp Crittenden. Governor Safford went to Stoneman's headquarters at Sacaton to urge an all-out war on the Apaches. Stoneman said his soldiers were doing all they could and that he was under pressure from advocates of Grant's peace policy to try to induce the Indians, by peaceful means, to leave off their raiding. Completely disgusted with Stoneman, Safford went on to Washington early in March to plead for a stronger commander and more protection.

Raids and killings seemed to increase. For the first time cattle were run off from Rancho del Socorro. Mangus's long shadow was starting to dwindle. On March 18 the Hughes ranch near Crittenden was attacked, one man killed and much property destroyed.

Tom Gardner, whose ranch had been raided innumerable times and who kept sentinels on guard after the style of Pete Kitchen, stopped by the Socorro at suppertime and laughed heartily when Talitha remonstrated with him for being out alone in such dangerous times.

"Lord love you, ma'am, didn't I carry an Apache bullet under my heart for a couple of years till the Crittenden sawbones dug it out? I'm not marked to die by the heathen—just to be stolen blind."

"They like your beef and horses," Marc agreed, pouring his neighbor a stiff drink.

"They sure do." Gardner took a deep swallow, sighed, and chuckled grimly. "I'd gladly make a treaty with 'em; if they'd leave my place alone, I'd give them a quarter of all I raise and a quarter of my livestock increase. But they've outsmarted themselves. They've taken my work teams and I can't raise as much for them as I could have otherwise."

As in the war days, a watch was posted during the daylight hours and weapons kept close at hand. After some consultation the El Charco people decided to stay at the south ranch but hired several more vaqueros, as did the home ranch.

Cinco was among these. He hadn't gone prospecting with Patrick this time, preferring to work with cattle when he wasn't hunting mountain lions. He was already so well known for his skill in killing those elusive big cats that ranchers in northern Sonora as well as southern Arizona who were losing foals or calves to a lion who'd developed a taste for them called on Cinco and his dogs.

At sixteen Cinco had a man's height, but his face retained its childish roundness and slightly snubbed nose. He had a shy, sweet smile. The muscles of his strong young neck swelled against the gold chain of the small crucifix Cat had given him many years before.

"I still wear your present," he told her, dark eyes luminous as he gazed down at her. "Do you have my blue bird and whistle?"

"I gave the whistle to little Shea," she said somewhat guiltily. "But I keep the blue bird in my window." She didn't tell him she'd put the turquoise bird up by his father's cross.

She hadn't seen Cinco in almost a year and felt awkward with him. He was half her brother, yet that was not what caused the deepened timbre of his voice when he spoke to her. When he learned she was pregnant, what would happen to the adoration in his look? She *must* send for James; there was no other way.

Covering her desperation with a light laugh, she said, "I must get you a new chain. That one is too tight."

He said, "I would change it only for another one from you."

James came that night after supper, ate hungrily of the jerked meat stew and tamales Cat and Talitha put before him, and asked for a fresh horse. He needed to be on his way that night and by dawn be as far from Camp Crittenden as possible.

Lt. Claybourne Frazier, on the trail of stolen mules and horses, had stopped to rest his command at the mine and had recognized James. He'd demanded that James help track the marauders, and when he'd refused, the officer put him under arrest.

"I think he'd have found an excuse to shoot me before we got back to Crittenden," James said wryly. "Anyway, last night I got away on one of his horses. I can't go back to the mine. Even if he didn't look for me there every time he had a chance, he made me sound to the miners like a traitorous half-breed who might betray them any time it was to my benefit."

"You can stay here," said Talitha. "Marc can take it all the way up to General Stoneman and the governor if Frazier tries to bother you."

James shrugged. "There's not much they can do if he's already shot me as an escaped prisoner and horse thief. With all the raiding going on around here, I don't want to give your neighbors any reason for hard feelings. I'm going up to Camp Grant."

"That's where the Aravaipa Apaches have been coming in," said Marc. "Apparently they want peace if the government will feed them and guarantee them a safe place to live."

James nodded. "I think I could do some good there as an interpreter. But from what the soldiers said, people are starting to blame them for raids by other Indians, mostly Chiricahuas. If any Aravaipa are sneaking off to join such groups, maybe I can convince them they must stop before they endanger the whole nation."

"Sounds worth trying," Marc approved. "But when you've done what you can, come back to us, James. This is your home. Frazier's going to get a sharp lesson if he keeps trying to commandeer you."

James said nothing, but the stubborn set of his head and shoulders told Cat more plainly than words that he was determined not to cause his white family trouble. It was a poor time to give him her news, even if it hadn't looked as though she weren't going to have a moment alone with him. In a few months he could see with his eyes, but by then so could everyone. What should she do?

Talitha persuaded him to lie down and sleep an hour, promising to wake him. During that hour she and Cat packed saddlebags with clothing and food, Belen selected the best of the young horses, and Marc readied a bedroll, wrote a letter to the Camp Grant commander, Lt. Royal Whitman, and got out a Spencer carbine, a Remington .55 cap-and-ball six-shooter, and plenty of ammunition.

In spite of the busy preparations, the hour was an interminable torture to Cat. As they finished filling the second bag with *pinole,* jerky, dried fruit, and nuts, Talitha's clear eyes looked into Cat's with understanding much deeper than pity.

"Would you like to tell James it's time to go?"

Nodding, Cat hurried through the *sala* to the bedroom that had been her parents' and now was Marc's and Talitha's. James lay face down on the serape rug, not the bed. Cat leaned over him, stroking his black hair.

"James," she murmured. "James, *querido.*"

He stirred, long eyelashes lifting from his cheek. She felt she would drown in the blueness of his eyes, shocking in that brown Indian face. *"Gídí."* He smiled, and laid his hand on the side of her neck where she felt her pulse leaping as if to escape her veins and run in his.

"Oh, James," she whispered, fighting tears. "Let me go with you!"

"To Camp Grant?" Astounded, he sat up and took her in his arms. "Caterina, you know it would never do. You don't belong in an Indian camp."

"But—" *I'm going to have your baby,* she wailed silently.

He rocked her gently against him. "Let me help the Aravaipa settle, *gídí.* Maybe I can persuade some of the wild bands to come in if they see it's safe."

When she would have protested, he kissed her till they both were trembling. Drawing back, he said huskily, "Prove to me that you're a woman, Caterina. Let me do this thing for my people."

She felt as if she were strangling. "How—how long?"

"Two, three months, maybe a little more. Be patient in this, *gídí,* and I'll believe you're a woman. We'll marry; even if, being a half-breed, I have to take you to Mexico to do it, and then we'll build a *jacal* in some cañon and raise horses, mules, and children just as stubborn."

How could she try to keep him from doing what he could to end the slaughter between his people and hers? A few months— She could wear loose clothes. And he'd be marrying her gladly, not because he had to.

Taking his strong-boned face between her hands, she kissed him. "Hurry up with whatever you have to do at Camp Grant and come back to me! I begin to understand why Mother called Father a burro! Are all men so stubborn?"

"They are if they're men." He rose, pulling her with him, and held her in a last long embrace that almost made her cling to him, whisper the truth. As he straightened, he watched her proudly. "I love you, *gídí*. You are my woman."

She put her hands behind her so he couldn't see her drive her fingernails into her palms. "It's time you rode," she said.

A few days later Cinco burst in with frightful news told him by troopers who'd stopped to water their mounts. A party of Mexicans returning to Sonora after a celebration in Tucson had been wiped out near the border, and Leslie Wooster, a young farmer-rancher living near Tubac, had been killed, along with his beautiful common-law wife, Trinidad Aguirre.

"I've worked in harvest for Don Leslie," choked Cinco. "He was very good, very kind. And Doña Trinidad—always bright and laughing. They were beautiful together." He passed his hand over his eyes. "How can this be, Don Marcos? Why does your government not protect your people?"

"The soldiers try, Cinco. But who can find Apaches in their own mountains?"

"The ones who did this may not be so far away," returned Cinco darkly. "My people think the whites are big fools to feed those Apaches at Camp Grant. When the men say they're going on a hunt, does anyone think they might be hunting people and plunder?"

Cinco lived in the vaqueros' quarters, so Cat didn't think he knew about James's visit. Marc had thought it best to keep that as quiet as possible to lessen the chances of James's whereabouts leaking out to Frazier.

Looking up at the tall Papago youth, Marc spoke sternly. "You don't want to spread that kind of talk unless you know what you're talking about, son. If those Apaches stay put and prosper it could decide the others to come in for peace."

"Peace!" Cinco's lips curled back from his teeth, stripping the hint of boyish softness from his face. "For three hundred years Apaches have lived by raiding my people, and the Pimas, and the Mexicans. You can't think, Don Marcos, that they'll stop now!"

"The government will feed them, teach them how to grow their food."

Cinco laughed harshly. "Will you teach the hawk to plow with his talons, to sow grain and eat it?"

"The Aravaipa are cutting hay for the soldiers and are glad of the work and pay," countered Marc. "You know well, Cinco, that many bands already plant and harvest crops. If the government will set aside lands where they won't be pushed out by settlers and give them a start in raising livestock, they could soon be living like anyone else."

Cinco regarded him in alarmed pity. "Apaches don't like to raise stock. They steal and eat other people's."

"That's not a law of nature, lad."

Cinco shook his head. "Doña Trinidad . . ." His eyes

blazed with hatred. "The only peaceful Apache is a dead one! With permission, Don Marcos, I will go hunting. I am angry. I must kill something."

Scarcely waiting for Marc's reluctant nod, he strode out. In a moment they heard him whistling for his dogs. Cat started to go after him, but Talitha caught her arm.

"No use, dear. He's been raised pure Papago, to hate Apaches. And there certainly is reason."

Cinco was Cat's brother; he had been a brown little boy with soft eyes. Now he was warrior age, a cunning killer of lions, and he hated Apaches. She prayed that he and James would never meet.

XVIII

The March 25 *Arizona Citizen* listed Apache depredations for that month. Between the eighth and the twentieth there had been four separate attacks in southern Arizona, animals run off, property destroyed, and eight people killed, including Don Leslie and Doña Trinidad. Apaches had also attacked the mail rider between Tucson and Tubac, though they hadn't killed him. Charging that post commanders were dispensing rations to the murderers, editor John Wasson demanded, "Will the Department Commander longer permit the murderers to be fed by supplies furnished by the people's money?"

Leslie Wooster had had many friends in Tucson. His killing and that of his young, beautiful wife led to a public meeting. Some were in favor of waiting to see what help might come from Washington. Others wanted a citizens' militia to take the field as quickly as it could be organized. After argument that lasted far into the night, it was agreed to send a committee of five, headed by William Oury, to urge General Stoneman to do something about the increasing violence.

They found him on the Gila River a little way from the new town of Florence. Stoneman told them he had only enough horses to mount one cavalryman in five. He couldn't send more troops south, but he did promise constant patrols in the Santa Cruz Valley and along Sonoita Creek, and that Camp Crittenden wouldn't be closed down till at least after the harvest was in. Further, Stoneman thought there were enough men in Tucson and along the Santa Cruz and Sonoita to look after themselves.

Marc, who'd been in Tucson when the committee returned, ran a hand through his graying hair as he told the family about it. "There's talk of forming a volunteer force to go on a three-month campaign," he said. "I've promised to go if it's organized."

Both Cat and Talitha stared at him. "Marc," whispered Talitha. "What if James—"

He put a protective arm around her. "James isn't raiding. He'll be doing his best to bring peace. But we won't have it, Tally, till the Apaches learn they won't go unpunished after one of their sprees of looting and killing."

Shea ran off for the bow and quiver and arrows James had made for him before he left for the mine. He said importantly to Sewa, who was rubbing little Vi's gums to ease her teething, "Don't be afraid, Sewa! I'll shoot any Apaches who try to get you!"

"Your uncle James is part Apache," Talitha rebuked him sharply. With the unborn child pressed between them, she buried her face on her husband's shoulder and wept.

Cat had no one to lean on. Feeling cold and sick, she prayed for James and the tiny beginning life he didn't know about. Let there be peace. Let there be no more killing. . . .

She started as something warm and soft covered her shoulders.

"You look chilled, Katie," said Jordan. His hazel eyes watched her in concerned puzzlement as he stepped back from draping the shawl around her. "Are you feeling all right? You haven't been yourself lately."

I'll never be myself again; I'll always have a child, someone I must look after. How joyful that would be if James were with her. If he weren't—

She shut that thought away. It was too terrible. He'd promised. He'd be back. She forced a smile at Jordan.

"I'm fine. I just wish there weren't all these troubles."

He said quietly so that only she could hear, "You must worry about James. I'm sorry, Katie." And she was sorry for Jordan, who was so kind, whom she almost loved. She was glad when Sewa brought the baby to her so that she could look down at her and hide the tears that blurred her eyes.

There was a short lull in the raiding. Then, early in April, seven men working on a road between Phoenix and Bradshaw were attacked; four were killed and horribly mutilated. Wagon trains were ambushed near Date Creek and Agua Fria, leaving two men dead and three wounded. In mid-April Cinco and Rodolfo, who'd ridden in to Tucson for supplies returned with news that Apaches had driven off cattle and horses from San Xavier, about eight miles south of Tucson, making for Cebedilla Pass in the mountains to the north. When a Papago brought the word to town, some fourteen men saddled and rode in pursuit, joining a party of Papagos who were hot after the raiders.

"Rodolfo and I rode, too." Cinco's tone was a mixture of boastfulness and chagrin. "We chased them fifty miles, crisscrossing through the Santa Catalinas, before we caught up with the man they'd left to guard the stock and bring it in if we gave up the chase. We killed him and brought back the animals, except for four the Apaches had killed." Cinco paused, looked around, and added triumphantly, "Those raiders were headed for Camp Grant!"

"Just because they cut through Cebedilla Pass?" scoffed Marc. "From there they could have headed for the White Mountains or the Verde, almost anywhere. Probably a gang of roving Tontos."

"These weren't Tontos!" flamed Cinco. "Some of my cousins were among the Papagos. They recognized the Apache we killed from a missing tooth he had in front.

They had seen him at Camp Grant; he was for sure a Camp Grant Indian!"

Talitha was pale. "Be careful what you say, Cinco. We've heard there are close to five hundred Apaches at Camp Grant now, mostly women and children. They came in because they were almost starving; in fact, that must be a large part of the reason the Apaches are taking such risks now in their raiding—they need those horses and mules and cattle to eat. At Camp Grant they're working for farmers and cutting hay for the army, planting their crops in safety, drawing rations. Would they endanger that to steal a few mules?"

"That dead Apache was from Camp Grant," retorted Cinco.

"Out of hundreds of Indians, one or two young bloods might join a raiding party," reasoned Marc. "Lieutenant Whitman claims that his Aravaipa stay near their camp, and they're counted every third day when he issues rations."

"The Apaches have moved five miles upcañon from the soldiers," Cinco parried. "Don Marcos, you know well that three days is long enough for them to take part in a raid and be back to draw their rations and fool the lieutenant into thinking they've been there all the time, nice and tame." Cinco swallowed hard. "I know that Mangus was the friend of those who started this ranch and that Doña Talitha's brother is half Apache, but such things shouldn't blind you to the truth."

"Nor should hatred blind you," Marc said gently.

Clenching his hands, Cinco looked from one of them to the other. For a few seconds his dark eyes probed Cat's. "Cinco—" she began, starting to plead.

He left them.

Three days later Apaches struck a settlement on the San Pedro, killed four men, and ran off a yoke of oxen and several horses. The *Arizona Citizen* for April 15 said there could be little doubt that the raiders were the same ones chased toward Camp Grant a few days earlier; they must have rested there and then swooped down on the San Pedro.

The same issue published General Stoneman's report on the military posts. He wanted to abandon seven posts, including Camp Lowell at Tucson and Crittenden, claiming they served little purpose but to provide a market for the hay and grain of people living nearby. He went on to accuse merchants of fleecing the army by charging high prices for shoddy goods, such as warped glass, condemned paper, paper water buckets that were supposed to be made of rubbery gutta percha, and "wool" blankets of buffalo hair. That did nothing to improve feelings between the military and civilians.

Marc rode to Tucson to attend one of the citizens' meetings and returned full of disgust. "They persist in blaming the troubles on the Indians at Camp Grant—as if the territory weren't full of Indians starved enough to take almost any chance for food! But nothing's going to happen. They bicker and argue about who'll be officers, but only fifty dollars has been raised for an expedition, and until they get Camp Grant out of their heads I won't contribute a cent."

Cat paced nervously to the door and gazed at the mountains that separated her from her love. "Does the commander at Camp Grant know his Apaches are being accused?"

"Of course he knows. He flatly denies the charges."

"Do you think we ought to warn James?"

"He'll be in Lieutenant Whitman's confidence. He'll know what's been said."

That was bound to be true, but Cat felt on edge and could tell that Talitha did, too. The very air seemed dense and heavy, as it might be before a thunderstorm, packed with force that must explode though it was quiet for the time. The vaqueros started their spring cow work heavily armed, and though Cat was soon busy feeding orphans, this season wasn't like any other she remembered.

It wasn't the threat of Apaches or bandits. She'd

grown up thinking of them as just part of life, like drought, death, and the occasional severe winter snow. Some of it must be anxiety for the new little life growing inside her, but mostly there was a sense of brooding, a strained waiting.

This was one of the year's busiest times, so Marc frowned when Cinco asked a few days off to attend a fiesta his Papago relations were holding at San Xavier. It was, however, the only favor Cinco had ever asked, so, after a moment, Marc nodded.

"Have a good time, lad, and get back as fast as you can. You're one of our best with the branding iron."

Cinco turned to look at Cat. He unclasped the slender gold chain from his muscular brown neck. "Keep this for me, Caterina. The fiesta may be rowdy, and I don't want to lose it."

She smiled and took it, still warm from his flesh, and put it around her own throat. Some merrymaking was what he needed to get his mind off the Indians at Camp Grant. "Go with God, Cinco. *Buen fiesta!*"

He stared at her for a long moment. Her brother, son of Shea and the desert woman, Tjúni. Why was it she could never feel with him as she did with the twins? She loved him, but it was constantly brought home to her that they could never understand each other. He was as Papago as if his stepfather had been his true one.

Her smile died under the intensity of his eyes. "Caterina—"

He broke off and was quickly gone. Half an hour later she saw him riding west, armed with rifle, bow and arrows, and, she was sure, at least one six-shooter.

Sighing, she turned from the door. Would there ever be a time in Arizona when a man could ride weaponless to a fiesta?

April ended and the first days of May passed, and Cinco hadn't returned. "It's a long fiesta," Cat worried.

Late in the afternoon of May 3 Cat, on watch, saw a rider, but he was mounted on a dark horse, not Cinco's dun. She rang the signal for one visitor and hurried down to get her rifle and watch out the window. Tally, Anita, Juri, Társat, and Paulita put the children under Sewa's charge in the *sala* while they took their agreed-upon positions. The men were all out branding.

As the horseman neared, Társat, Natividad's Papago wife, cried out in surprise. "It's my brother, Francisco!"

The women put down their weapons and welcomed the young man, who almost fell out of the saddle. Társat led the horse to the corral to be watered and rested while Francisco was brought inside and given coffee and food.

"Cinco's all right," he assured them in Spanish as they questioned him. "He's at the foot of the Black Mountain southwest of San Xavier with the other enemy killers. Sixteen days he must stay there to be purified and undergo the rituals that make him a 'ripe' man. I've come to tell you he'll be home after the victory celebration."

Enemy killers? Victory?

Cat tried to speak, but her voice rustled weakly, trapped in her throat. It was Talitha who said sharply, "What are you talking about? What has Cinco done?"

Proudly, Francisco told them. He himself had been one of ninety-two Papagos who had joined with forty-eight Mexicans and six Anglos to show the Camp Grant Apaches that they couldn't kill and raid and then run back to the army for protection and rations. Meeting at the head of the Rillito eight miles northeast of Tucson on April 28, they started out that evening and traveled by moonlight till they were far from Tucson, rested, traveled on next day, camped again, and then traveled all the next night.

Jesus Maria Elias had been elected leader, somewhat to the chagrin of white-bearded Bill Oury who had to stand some joking about how few of the eighty-two Anglos who'd promised to undertake a volunteer expedition had actually come. Elias knew the country better. Besides, back in 1863, he'd been with Captain Tidball and some California troops and Papagos who'd raided an Apache camp on the Aravaipa. Since the Papagos were Christians, they dipped the babies in water to baptize them before they knocked out their brains.

This time there'd been no baptizing.

Mexicans and Anglos, armed with carbines, waited along the bluff above the camp to kill any Apaches who tried to escape that way. The Papagos, led by Oury and their chief, surrounded the wickiups on the other three sides. Dawn was nearing.

Few Papagos had firearms, but they had bows, arrows, sharp knives, and mesquite clubs. Stealing into the huts, the Papagos cut throats and crushed skulls, shot arrows into bodies. There were few men in camp, but children grow up to be Apaches and women produce more of them, so it was useful killing. All over in half an hour.

"Since he'd never killed before, Cinco had to drop out of the attack as soon as he got his trophy," Francisco explained. "He smeared his face with charcoal and waited with the other enemy killers. Lots of Apaches fled across the Aravaipa and hid in the hills, but we killed enough to teach them a lesson. We burned the *ranchería* and took about twenty-eight children captive."

Numb with disbelief and horror, Cat stared at the triumphant warrior. "James!" she cried. "Was James there?"

Francisco looked puzzled. "James? Who is James?"

"My brother." Talitha steadied her unwieldy body by leaning on the table. "He's young and strong, about twenty-four. He has blue eyes. . . ."

"Most heads were so smashed that no one could guess about eye color," the Papago said. "But there were no young men in camp. They were probably off thieving and murdering."

Talitha looked suddenly old. "And when the warriors

return and see what's happened to their families, what do you think they'll do?"

"No more than they already have," muttered the Papago. This was clearly not the welcome he'd expected. Defensively, he peered at Talitha. "With permission, *señora,* what was your brother doing there?"

"He's half Apache," Talitha said. "He hoped to get more of his father's people to come in for peace."

Francisco's face twisted. "Peace? For whom? The Apaches are glad to be coddled by the soldiers, and perhaps they don't raid close to the camp, but the lion will eat grass before Apaches stop their plundering!" He got to his feet. "I've brought Cinco's message. Now I will go to San Xavier for the dancing."

As he passed her Cat noticed dark brown-red splotches on his white cotton garments. Did blood splatter when a head was crushed?

James. Where was James?

Cat saddled Sangre and went hunting for Marc. Talitha wanted him to go to Tucson or even Camp Grant to look for James and also to buy any Apache children that could be located.

"Any that have no family left can live with us," Talitha had said, her voice controlled, though she was white to the lips. "Oh, my God, how can such things happen?"

The same question burned through Cat as she glanced up at her parents' crosses on the hill. The only bit of hope she had was that, according to the Papago, James hadn't been in the village. But even if he lived, what would this do to him?

Cat crouched low against Sangre's mane and wept. For women and children who had waked to die, and for James, and even for Cinco, though she hated him now.

She found Marc branding while Belen roped calves and Natividad and Rodolfo flipped and held them. His smile died as he watched her.

"What is it, Cat?"

"Talitha's all right." That fear quieted, Cat couldn't go on for a moment. Then, shutting her eyes against the sun, she choked out the story.

Belen crossed himself, grimly sad as he bowed his head, but the other vaqueros nodded approval and fierce gratification.

"My brothers-in-law went on that raid," said Natividad proudly. "It was the first time of one of them to kill an enemy, so he'll be undergoing the purification, too, like Cinco. Ay, Don Patricio would be proud of his son!"

"He wouldn't!" Cat shut her eyes and gripped the saddle horn to keep from falling. "My father would never kill women and children!"

No one answered, but pleased satisfaction showed so plainly on Rodolfo's and Tivi's faces that Cat felt she'd go mad with the horror of it—that these kindly men, who'd sung for her birthday ever since she could remember, thought such a slaughter necessary and good.

"Take charge, Belen," ordered Marc. "I don't know when I'll be back." Limping heavily, he went to saddle his hobbled horse. Within minutes he and Cat were riding toward home.

"I want to go with you," she said. "I have to go with you."

He sighed and shook his head, but after a long look at her he didn't argue.

They left before dawn the next morning, heavily armed. They found Tubac exulting at the news, glad that Leslie Wooster and Doña Trinidad had been avenged as well as the many others slaughtered by Apaches up and down the Santa Cruz.

"Let's not stop here," Cat said in a strangling voice.

Marc nodded. They rode swiftly through the little town with its crumbling presidio and rested and watered their horses a few miles north.

Cat refused to stop at any ranches for the night. "They'll all be happy, talking about what a brave attack it was and how it'll teach the Apaches," she said bitterly. "I can't bear it, Marc."

They spent the night in an abandoned adobe, which, as Marc pointed out with quiet force, had at least three times been raided by Apaches and the settlers living there wiped out.

"What happened at Camp Grant is terrible," he said, "but where were all the men? Cat, I have to tell you I think it's quite likely some of them have been on raids. Eskiminzin, who seems to lead the Aravaipa though he himself is a Pinal Apache, is blamed for dozens of murders and raids from the San Pedro to the Santa Cruz, burying men to the neck in anthills, roasting their brains over small fires. You've heard some of this."

"Yes. But when there's a name, many things are tacked to it."

They hadn't made a fire for fear of attracting Indians or bandits, but there was enough light left for Cat to see Marc's frown. "You've heard Tally speak of Larcena Page and how she's lost her father, brothers, and husband to the Apaches. Well, you'll also remember that Larcena herself was taken captive, lanced sixteen times, tossed over a cliff into a snowdrift, and left to die. Eskiminzin was one of the five Apaches who did that."

Cat shrank. Brokenly, she said, "But it's not Eskiminzin who was killed! Or the warriors who go on raids! It was women—babies—"

Marc took her in his arms and held her while she sobbed. "We'll try to get James home," he said. "And we'll do what we can for the captive children."

Next day they passed in sight of Black Mountain, where Cinco was being instructed in the rituals of war, bathing in cold water, blackening his face, cleansing his weapons of enemy blood. San Xavier was quiet now, but there'd be dancing and singing tonight, as every night throught the sixteenth when the enemy killers would return for their final rites of cleansing and the great victory fiesta.

Painfully, as if tearing flesh, Cat wrenched her thoughts from Cinco. Never again would she think of him as her brother. When she got home, she'd throw his blue bird into the fire.

Whom had he killed? An old woman? A girl her age? A boy the age of Shea? A baby like Vi?

Images tormented her; she saw him bringing down his club, ripping with his knife. Justice whispered to her that James had surely killed, too, but she was certain he wouldn't have hurt women or children.

Cat had never been to Tucson, and except for the company store at the San Patricio, the only store she'd been in was the one at Camp Crittenden. Ordinarily she'd have longed to go into Zeckendorf's or Lord & Williams or one of the other merchandise dealers who freighted in their goods. It would have been fun to eat in the Shoo Fly, which Marc had so often mentioned, though she couldn't go in the saloons. The Territorial Capitol looked like the old warehouse it was, and the urgings of the bullwhackers in the quartermaster's corral behind it made vaqueros' language pale. Camp Lowell on Military Plaza had two adobe mess halls, but the men lived in two long lines of tents. As well as an arsenal, corral and hay yard, there was a post pigpen.

Wagons drawn by oxen or by four or even five teams of mules creaked past the Pima County Courthouse, and next to San Augustin Church was St. Joseph's Academy for Young Ladies.

The noise and confusion—the barking dogs, the playing children, the bustle of freighters—would ordinarily have enthralled her. Marc said there were over three thousand people in town, an unbelievable number. There were also great heaps of smelly rubbish and manure, and a burro rotting where it had apparently died. The town of dusty, narrow streets and mud houses seemed pestilential to her, a place that bred murder as its garbage hatched flies. She looked at every man they passed and wondered if he had been at the butchering.

"I must ask some questions," Marc told her. "Would you like to look in the stores, or shall I get a room for you at Neugass' Hotel?"

It was late afternoon and Cat was weary, but she didn't want to spend the night in that town. "I'll wait in the church," she said, and that was what she did, praying for those killed and their families, praying for James, till Marc touched her shoulder.

They camped north of town on the Rillito that night, sharing tamales Marc had bought, while he told her what he'd learned. Sam Hughes, adjutant general of the territory, had supplied the wagon of Sharps, Spencers, ammunition, and food that had outfitted the expedition. The commander of Camp Lowell had heard rumors and sent messengers to warn Lieutenant Whitman at Camp Grant, but the news had come too late.

Over a hundred Aravaipa were dead, all but eight of them women and children. Others were missing. Whitman was doing what he could to convince the survivors that his government and the army had had nothing to do with the outrage and was trying to recover the stolen children.

"Most of the fighting men are alive, and jumping the two of us would be a tempting vengeance," Marc said. "Let me go to Camp Grant, Cat, and you wait for me in Tucson."

She shook her head, tears coursing down her cheeks. Marc sighed but didn't argue. Perhaps he knew she was so full of shame and pity that she felt revulsion at living in a world where such things could happen. If it was so for her, what would it be for James?

They didn't take the Apache trail through Cebedilla Pass but traveled the easier, longer wagon road skirting the Catalinas, going through Cañada del Oro. After spending the night under a giant mesquite growing beside a wash, they reached Camp Grant that afternoon.

Some of its adobe buildings must have been left from old Fort Breckinridge, abandoned at the start of the Civil War. The dilapidated tents looked almost as old, and the mud-chinked log buildings looked as if their branch-and-mud roofs would leak in any rain. Facing the parade ground were the bakery, guardhouse, commissary, hospital, officers' quarters, and sutler's store. The forge, stables, and butcher's corral were beyond the quartermaster's storehouses.

A guard asked their business and called another soldier to escort them across the parade ground. The door of the adjutant's office stood open. A worn-looking officer in rumpled blue rose from a table to greet them and told the soldier to take care of their horses.

Marc introduced himself and Cat. The officer said he was Royal Whitman, in charge while Captain Stanwood was away on a scout. When Marc explained their business, the lieutenant shook his head.

"I knew James. Even if his face had been unrecognizable, there were no strong young men among the slaughtered. I took about thirty soldiers to the *ranchería* May first to bury the dead. Survivors came while we were doing that, men who'd lost their whole families, women with missing children." He paused, running a trembling hand through his hair as his bloodshot eyes seemed to stare blindly at a horror he would never escape. "I fed them and talked with them, promised to do what I can about the captive children. Eskiminzin was there with his little daughter, the only one of his family he was able to save. He believed me when I said the army had had no part in the killing, nor the farmers living nearby. He knew that men from Tucson had stirred up the Papagos."

"The talk in Tucson is that animals stolen from San

Xavier were found at the *ranchería,*" said Marc. "Worse, so were a brooch of Doña Trinidad's and one of her dresses."

Whitman shrugged. "They'll say anything to justify what they did." He sent for coffee and patiently answered their questions about James.

Yes, the young man had talked to the officer about trying to persuade more Apaches to come in; in fact, Whitman thought he'd been away on such a mission when the massacre occurred. No, James hadn't been seen. Some of the Aravaipa were settling near Camp Grant again, trusting in the army for protection. If Marc and Cat wanted to ask the survivors about James, the interpreter Merejildo Grijalva would go with them.

It was a useless expedition. In the makeshift village that had sprung up near the camp, even the children were hushed. Men and women, some wounded, gazed into space or moved numbly about. All Grijalva could learn was that James, who'd been well liked though he was Mimbres, had gone out a few days before the attack to persuade more Apaches to settle at the post.

One young woman came up to Cat and pleaded with her, tears glistening in her eyes. "She asks if you can get her child back," Grijalva explained. "A little girl, about four years old. Very afraid of the dark."

"Tell her we'll do what we can," Cat said and pressed the woman's hand.

After spending the night in the absent commander's quarters, Marc and Cat left early next morning. "At least it seems likely that James is alive," Marc comforted.

Cat nodded, but her heart ached, both for the misery she'd seen and for James. She was terribly afraid. What would he do now? It didn't bear thinking of, yet she could think of nothing else.

Riding south, Cat and Marc were in sight of Black Mountain when a Papago crawled toward them, calling feebly. Getting down, they ran to him. An arrow protruded from his shoulders, and he was coughing bubbles of frothy blood.

"Blue-eyed devil," he gasped in Spanish. "Apaches! Cut throats of enemy killers!"

Blue-eyed? Cat's heart beat faster.

Marc cut off the arrowhead thrusting from the man's chest. When he tried to pull out the shaft, the man gave a great cry. Blood poured from his mouth. He died while they held him.

Lowering the body, Cat and Marc looked at each other. Without a word, they sprang on their horses and made for Black Mountain.

All the enemy killers were young men. All of them were dead, crumpled near the bodies of their guardians who'd been instructing them. Cat recognized one of Mársat's brothers. Cinco's eyes stared up at the sky, unseeing, from his blackened face. His head was almost severed.

Kneeling, dazed, Cat whispered his name. *Blue-eyed devil . . .* Had James done this, killed her brother? Who had, in his turn, killed a child, an old man, a woman?

She closed Cinco's eyes and put the crucifix from her neck in his lifeless hand. Then she began to scream.

Cat couldn't remember the ride to the ranch, though she dimly heard the shots Marc fired to signal the Papagos, dimly remembered the wailing of the women as their rejoicing turned to furious grief. When she really knew what was going on again, Marc had gone to collect the ransomed children and restore them to the Aravaipas, along with any he could buy in Tucson.

Rousing to find Talitha trying to feed her gruel, Cat sat up in bed. Her throat was sore and an echo of mad cries lingered in her ears, but her mind was clear. Too clear.

She caught Talitha's hands. "Tally! James—it must be James who killed Cinco!"

Talitha's fair head drooped for a moment before she straightened her shoulders. "It seems likely. There aren't many blue-eyed Apaches. And James is all Apache now, Cat. We have to face that."

And my baby?

Refusing the food Talitha offered, Cat said, "I don't want any. Please Tally! I—I'll be all right. Just leave me alone."

But when Talitha was gone, Cat got up and dressed shakily. She took the little blue bird Cinco had given her, got her knife, and started up the hill to her mother's grave and her father's cross.

She put the bird by Shea's marker, above the turquoise carving, protecting it with rocks. "I hope you and Cinco are friends now," she said.

She made a prayer for Santiago, and poor Lonnie, too, then sat beside her mother's grave. *I've always wondered what you were like. I've always missed you. Please, my mother, be with me now.*

Taking the knife from its sheath, she was wondering how to best use it when a shadow fell across her. Swooping down, swift for all her bulk, Talitha snatched away the knife, then gave Cat a resounding slap that made her ears ring.

"What do you think you're doing?"

"I—I—" Impossible to meet the blue blaze of Talitha's eyes. "James. Cinco."

"Cinco's dead. James is Apache." Talitha's words stung like whips. "What are you? A coward?"

Mutely, Cat hugged her knees. "It's too much for you?" Talitha flamed on. "You can't stand it? Then you've a lot of gall to kill yourself on your mother's grave. She was brave."

"I'm not brave." Cat's voice frayed. She had to battle for control before she could go on. "I just love James. Now he's killed Cinco and he'll kill lots more and I—I'm going to have his baby."

"A baby?"

Cat nodded.

"Does he know?"

With a shake of her head Cat said, "I was going to tell him when he stopped on his way to Camp Grant. I wanted to go with him. But he needed to try to get more Apaches to come in. He—he said when he'd done what he could, he'd come to me and we'd get married."

Talitha, heavy with child, sank down by Cat, and at that moment something stirred deep inside Cat, a movement in her vitals.

Her baby? Almost half its time in the blind womb gone. A girl or a boy? With the look of James?

"Oh, my God," Talitha breathed. She was trembling and tears ran down her face. "James! James!"

Aghast, for she'd never seen Talitha so close to losing control, Cat put her arms around the older woman. "Tally! Please Tally!"

With great effort Talitha steadied, but the pain in her eyes was like a piercing cry. "I've always known he might turn wholly Apache. After what he's seen, I can't bear to think what he'll do now. He won't care whether he lives or dies. Sooner or later, Cat, he *will* die."

"No!" Cat wailed, covering her ears.

Inexorably, Talitha caught her hands, made her listen. "If you love James, Cat, have his baby. Our James, my brother, your lover, is dead, but you can see to it that something of him lives on."

"Yes. I can do that." Desolated, Cat saw the years stretch before her, years when James, if he lived, would kill her people and be hunted in turn; but though she sickened and trembled, she made a vowing. "I *will* do that."

Talitha put her arms around her, and they wept.

Marc was gone for several weeks, restoring the children ransomed at San Xavier to their people, bargaining for others in Tucson, though few of those were given up since the families who'd taken them in felt it a duty to rear them as Christians and redeem them from savagery.

The territorial papers, as well as the Western press in general, strongly supported the massacre as self-defense, insisting that Camp Grant Indians had been guilty of raids and murders the army would do nothing to avenge. The Eastern press published a letter Lieutenant Whitman had written to another officer which gave details of the bloody attack. Horrified Easterners demanded that something be done. President Grant called it "pure murder" and promised a thorough investigation. More to the point of settling Arizona's problems, at Governor Safford's urging Grant had arranged for Gen. Stoneman's transfer and replaced him with Gen. George Crook in June.

Crook had a reputation as a firm, just soldier who believed the Indians had to be subdued before they'd live in peace. Arizonans looked forward to his coming even as they mourned the death of courageous young Lt. Howard Cushing, killed along with four of his command in a fight with Cochise and a large band of Chiricahuas near Bear Spring in the Whetstone Mountains to the east.

Reluctantly, Marc added that Eskiminzin and his surviving people had tried to rebuild their *ranchería* near Camp Grant, but a patrol of soldiers from Fort Apache had ridden into the cañon and blundered into the Apaches. Panicked, the cavalrymen opened fire, and though none of his band was killed, Eskiminzin had told Whitman that the whites had twice broken the peace and that he was taking his people into the mountains.

Just before Marc left Tucson, he'd heard that Eskiminzin had eaten supper with a white friend, Charles McKinney, who had a farm on the San Pedro. They talked, drank coffee and smoked. Then Eskiminzin thanked his friend, drew a pistol and shot McKinney through the head.

"Why?" shuddered Talitha. "Why his friend?"

Somberly, Marc said, "To show that between white and Apache there can now be no peace or trust."

In the first week of June, Lt. Claybourne Frazier stopped at the Socorro about nooning. Stiffly refusing to eat with the family, he officially informed Talitha that her half brother James was reputed to be the raider known as Fierro who was swiftly making his name one of terror, blazoned by burning homes and wagons, red with the blood of his victims.

"If he stops here, Mrs. Revier, it is your duty to hold him and send for the military. Any other course will make you a traitor to your race."

Talitha flushed angrily, but before she could reply Marc closed his hand protectively over hers and said coolly to the officer, "I think we know our duty, sir. It is presumptuous of you to take that tone with my wife."

Frazier glanced at Cat. Tight-lipped, he said roughly, "The warning is for everyone, Mr. Revier." Then, eyes dilating, he sucked in his breath and turned crimson to the roots of his pale blond hair. "Miss O'Shea, I didn't know that you had married."

No one spoke for a startled moment. Cat felt as if everyone were staring at the slight rounding of her belly beneath the cotton dress. Except for Talitha no one knew, though it could only be a matter of weeks before her condition was obvious. Frazier must have noticed because he hadn't seen her for a long time and the thickening of her waist was immediately evident.

In the awkward silence Jordan said easily, "Miss O'Shea has been betrothed to me since her sixteenth birthday. We decided we'd waited long enough."

"It only remains for me to wish you happy," Frazier said. Bowing, he turned abruptly and strode out into the sun.

Jordan got up from his seat at the end of the bench, came to Cat, and dropped on one knee beside her, taking her hands, pressing them to his face.

"Katie," he said huskily, "I've been waiting. I've always loved you. This may not be the right time, but still it is the time."

PART V

The Maimed Hawk

1881

XIX

In Scott Valley, lush with grama grass, watered by the oak- and sycamore-shaded East Verde River, corn stood high and tasseling in the fields that late summer of 1881. Cucumbers, pumpkins, squash, and melons ripened on trailing vines; there were rows of cabbage; peas and beans were hulled and drying; and potato plants were starting to wither as a sign that it was almost time to dig. Apple trees were weighted with fruit that grew rosier each day, and there were apricots, plums, pears, and cherries in the orchards cared for and shared by the Scott clan.

Shut out of fields and gardens by rock walls and post fences—for Jared would have none of the barbed wire coming into use—sheep, cattle, and horses grazed in bountiful pastures. There were stout pigpens and chicken coops, and Jared's pride, a pack of greyhounds, to keep off preying coyotes, raccoons, and foxes. They coursed down jackrabbits, too, a frequent food in Scott Valley, along with venison, wild turkey, and quail.

The houses and outbuildings were sheltered by great pines and immense spreading oaks. Each dwelling had a wellhouse where butter, milk, and cream kept cool in the hottest weather, immersed in rock water troughs. A few miles east, where the valley widened even more, Thomas Scott had a sawmill, and a grist mill below Jared's house served people for miles around. A mail rider traveled past on one of the good roads General Crook had made, and Mormon neighbors came to worship in the little steepled church Jared had built in the broadest part of the valley.

They also sent their children to the school Cat taught during the winter months. She still smiled to remember how Governor Safford, who had persuaded Jordan to start the school, had visited several times, mounted on one of his handsome mules, and ridden off after quizzing the pupils, his satisfaction evidenced by the lusty way he was singing "There's a Land That Is Fairer Than Day," his favorite hymn. In a territory bedeviled by Apache and bandit raids, where most people were occupied with mere survival, Safford had stubbornly insisted that all children must be educated, and by the time he left office in 1877 Arizona was studded with schools he'd prodded and persuaded people into starting.

Cat enjoyed teaching. Ten of her fifteen scholars were Jordan's nephews and nieces, but they took no liberties because of the kinship. Michael, her son, found it a bit galling to be the schoolmarm's child, but hints that his love of reading made him a sissy brought such swift chastisement from his fists that few boys even much larger than he dared his wrath more than once.

Students at Scott Valley learned some things that were probably not taught in any other school in all Arizona. Besides the standard spelling, arithmetic, grammar, geography, and reading, Cat taught how Papagos lived in the desert, harvesting mesquite beans and saguaro fruits; of the Yaquis' holy pueblos and valiant fighters; of Mexico's struggle for independence from Spain and its later war with the United States when her father, an Irishman, had changed sides to fight for Mexico. And she told them all she knew of the Apaches.

Of Ussen, the supreme god, who, as a rain shower, had given White Painted Woman a child, Born of Waters, who had grown up to kill terrible monsters and teach his people the right way to live; of the way a boy sought power on the mountain and became a warrior by serving humbly on four raids; of how girls were initiated into womanhood with rites binding them to White Painted Woman and celebrating the awesome ability to bring forth new life.

She told how Mangus Coloradas had given her brothers a twin cradleboard and how that great chief had died by treachery. One gangling fourteen-year-old had sniffed at that and raised his chapped red paw.

"Miz Cat, my daddy says we'd ought to kill every savage in the territory. Says crooked contractors make fortunes feeding them and the army and the reservation just gives 'em a place to rest and draw rations till they're ready to break away again."

Cat decided that if the students could hear that sort of talk, they could hear about the Camp Grant massacre, and she told them. That night, several outraged parents descended on Jared and her. As head of the school board, he calmly told them he agreed with everything his sister-in-law was doing, and anyone who didn't like it could try whipping him. No one felt that lucky, and Cat continued with her unorthodox curriculum.

Jared, still vigorous and hearty at sixty, red hair faintly seasoned with gray, was Talitha's father, an officer in the Mormon Battalion who'd settled on the Verde twenty years ago and taken a second wife who'd given him three sons before dying of ague. Besides Jordan, two of Jared's other half brothers had built homes along the Verde and had growing families. All the clan except for Jordan were Mormons, and life in the little settlement had a strong dedication to work, sobriety, and high morals.

Jared could shoe a horse, build a house, dig a well, plow the straightest furrow beneath the Mogollon Rim; and on winter evenings while the women sewed, knitted and, mended, he told stories about the white temple at Nauvoo, the forced search for lands to the west, how he'd marched with the Mormon Battalion through Arizona while it was still part of Mexico, his adventures in the California gold fields.

And there had been plenty of excitement since then, here on the Verde. A wrestle with a bear whose claws had indelibly scarred his back and sides; the epic of Mormon settlements spreading down from Utah to cluster in the Arizona Strip and thrust down the valley of the Little Colorado, renowned as being "too thin to plow but too thick to drink." In the past few years settlements had been started on the San Pedro, the Gila, and the Salt. Mesa, laid out in 1878 on the same plan as Salt Lake City, would someday have a temple, but till then couples who wanted the solemn rites that bound them through eternity traveled to the nearest temple at St. George, Utah, armed with "recommends" from the local bishop that they had been living according to the laws of the church.

Benjamin, Jared's eldest son, had just returned with his dainty little bride, Ruth, from such a wedding trip, which had taken a month each way. They spoke with awe of Grand Falls, higher than Niagara, spilling down lava flows, primeval ancient eruptions from the San Francisco Peaks; looming walls of ancient Indian fortresses, friendly Hopi and Navajo farmers tilling their fields, deserts where water had to be doled carefully from barrels and the few springs were bitter; the harrowing ascent and descent of Lee's Backbone, horses straining to keep from plunging into the cañon; towering cliffs and the high, pine-scented Kaibab forest, until at last, glimpsed across fertile fields and the surrounding settlement, gleamed the spired white temple.

Twenty-year-old Benjamin was like a younger brother to Cat, who'd kept house for Jared's womanless family since Jordan had brought her to the Verde ten years ago. She was also fond of fair-haired little Ruth, who, for all her butterfly looks, could milk and churn, make cheese and soap, bake crusty bread, and sew much finer and neater stitches than Cat's. Still, when they glowingly talked about their honeymoon trip, Cat, with a pang, would avoid Jordan's eyes.

She had tried to be a good wife to him. She had been, in all the things that could be willed, in outward behavior. But she couldn't pretend passion in his arms, response to his loving, be it tender or desperate.

"Can't you forget him?" he had breathed one time.

When she couldn't answer, he'd dressed and gone out, not returning till morning. He had never again reproached her even that much. She'd tried to make up in other ways for what she couldn't give him, but she was glad they lived with a large household where it was easy to avoid private conversations and even much private life.

As time dulled her grief over James and Cinco, as the busy life in a new place among new people dimmed memories, and as Michael Patrick, her son, born on her own September birthday in 1871, grew from baby perfection into a wiry little boy who was now, at ten, almost as tall as she and proudly carried her father's flaming hair, Cat was often content, sometimes happy.

She missed Talitha, her brothers, and all the Socorro people, of course. Cat had refused to leave the ranch till after Talitha's baby girl, Judith, was born that July of 1871, and she often wondered what the little girl was like. Patrick had visited several times, for he had mining interests now at Prescott, Wickenburg, and Bisbee. On his latest journey he'd brought his bride, a radiant Sewa, just turned seventeen.

"Guess without knowing it I was just waiting for her to grow up," he'd said, and the way they looked at each other brought a lump to Cat's throat. He looked so much as she remembered their father, except for that branded cheek. And Sewa? In her dark beauty, those black-lashed golden eyes, something of Santiago lived, mingled at last with the flesh of the woman he'd loved and the man who'd been his comrade. They had a daughter, born in 1876, named after Cat, who had never seen her. And Vi had a brother.

Sometimes Cat yearned for her loved ones and the ranch till she felt almost sick and would have given anything for a long, comforting talk with Talitha. Then she'd remind herself sternly of how good Jordan was to her, and how glad she was to have her son, something of James to love and to nurture to what James might have been if life hadn't tragically shaped him into Fierro.

Michael always had an orphan animal or bird to raise, or a hurt one to cure. Young as he was, he was called to help with his small, sensitive hands when a mare or a ewe or a cow was having a hard time giving birth. Apart from the skill he was acquiring, there seemed to be an actual quality in him that helped animals or people get well.

Jared had accepted her with great kindness, lavishing on her some of the love and care he hadn't been able to show Talitha. To this day he didn't know that his lost wife Judith had borne a son to Juh, not the Nedhni chief presently the terror of northern Mexico, but a Mimbreño, dead for years. Still less did he dream that his supposed nephew, Michael Patrick, known as Mike, soon to be ten years old, was the grandson of Juh and the son of the raider Fierro, whose name brought terror from the Mogollon Rim to the Sierra Madres, from Apache Pass to Fort Grant.

Mangus had killed his scores, Cochise his hundreds, and Victorio and Geronimo were at large, but Fierro was more feared. His lightning strikes, first along the San Pedro, next on the Gila or Salt, then on roads leading to the booming mining towns of Bisbee, Wickenburg, and Tombstone, brought back the terrors Apache raids had caused when Gen. George Crook took command in 1871, when the Camp Grant massacre had shocked the government into paying some attention to Arizona.

Congress had already appropriated some money for setting up reservations, and in August of 1871 President Grant's peace commissioner, Vincent Colyer, an idealistic Quaker, arrived in Arizona to talk with the Indians, hear their grievances, and select temporary reservations for them. He was convinced that the whites were completely to blame for all the troubles, and General Crook's plan for an all-out campaign to kill or bring in the hostiles had to be delayed till Colyer left in October.

It was a good thing he'd traveled under military escort. The outrage of the citizenry was summed up in the *Arizona Miner,* which said the people "ought in justice to our murdered dead, to dump the old devil into the shaft of some mine, and pile rocks upon him until he is dead. A rascal who comes here to thwart the efforts of military and citizens to conquer a peace from our savage foe, deserves to be stoned to death, like the treacherous black-hearted dog that he is."

President Grant had threatened to put Arizona under martial law if the men who'd carried out the Camp Grant massacre were not brought to trial. A military court would have surely found them guilty, so, with reluctance, the grand jury indicted more than a hundred men, who were tried in the person of Sidney DeLong in December 1871. The others would be found guilty or innocent along with him. After a five-day trial, when Lieutenant Whitman seemed more the defendant than the accuser, the jury spent only nineteen minutes in finding DeLong not guilty.

Crook hadn't been idle during Colyer's visit. He had organized five companies of the 3rd Cavalry under the ablest officers in Arizona and tempered them with a grueling seven-hundred-mile expedition from Fort Bowie near the New Mexican border north to Camp Apache and over the Mogollon Rim to Camp Verde and Fort Whipple, the departmental headquarters near Prescott. Along the way he recruited Apache scouts. To supply his men Crook turned painstaking attention to his pack train. Each mule was of the best, with a packsaddle specially fitted to it, well shod, fed and groomed. Packers who drank and ill-used their animals were dismissed and good men hired. As a result, Crook's mules carried an average of more than three hundred pounds compared to the Army's usual one hundred and seventy-five. The Apaches respected Crook who was just and fair and kept his word, a quality highly valued by them. They called him *Nantan Lupan,* or Chief Gray Fox. An expert hunter, inured to hardship, preferring a mule to a horse and comfortable old clothes to a uniform, Crook didn't swear, smoke or drink. This astounded the citizens though they were impressed by his erect, muscular height, stern face and keen stare. The Apaches, though, knew him at once for a warrior and a friend.

Coyoteros came in to Camp Apache, Aravaipas and Pinals to Camp Grant, the Tontos to Camp McDowell, Mohaves to Camp Verde and Date Creek, and the Hualapais to Beale's Springs. An Army officer was in charge at each place. Food and clothing were to be issued and the Indians encouraged to farm, cut and sell hay and wood, and become self-supporting.

Before Crook could go after the Apache holdouts, though, in March of 1872 President Grant sent another peace commissioner, a one-armed Civil War hero, the so-called Christian General, O. O. Howard. Unlike Colyer, Howard listened to both sides. Though he told Crook to pursue hostiles who absolutely refused to settle on reservations, he tried to deal with Indian wrongs. Among other things, he compelled the Mexican families who'd adopted six of the little Camp Grant captives to return them to their relatives. He also persuaded seven leaders from the Papagos, Pimas, and Apaches to come with him to Washington to meet "the Great White Father." He hoped to impress them with white civilization and show the Apaches that resistance would only bring their destruction. These leaders returned with Bibles, medals, and new blue suits, while

Howard penetrated into the Chiricahuas to talk with Cochise.

Escorted by Tom Jeffords, Cochise's blood brother, who had years before won protection for his stagecoaches, Howard parleyed for eleven days, hearing all of Cochise's quarrels with the whites, going back to when soldiers had hanged his kinsmen at Apache Pass in 1861. In the end, the Chiricahua chief agreed to peace, provided his people's reservation was in their home country, and that was promised.

As soon as Howard had departed for Washington in November of 1872, Crook ordered commands from seven posts to converge on the Tonto Basin, pursuing hostiles wherever found. Jordan served as a civilian scout under famed Al Sieber. As often as possible, women and children were to be protected and prisoner warriors well treated and enlisted as scouts. But at the end of December, at Skull Cave, cornered Yavapai refused to send out their women and children and defiantly sang death songs, battling till seventy-five were killed. Only eighteen women and children lived to be taken captive.

A January campaign in the Superstitions was followed by the murder of three settlers near Wickenburg. The killers refuged in Turret Mountain, a columnlike butte west of the Verde, and thought no one could follow, but soldiers crawled on their bellies, by night, up the steep, loose-rocked incline and charged at sunrise, killing most of the men.

The Indians had thought Skull Cave and Turret Mountain unconquerable strongholds. Defeated at both places immediately after they had raided white settlers, they had to realize there was no eluding the Gray Fox's troopers, now led by scouts who knew every trail and retreat. Most warriors came in for peace.

Crook's efforts to make the Indians self-supporting, able to raise most of their food and sell hay and corn to the posts, were unpopular with contractors and settlers who wanted to supply both posts and reservations.

Civilian agents had replaced military supervisors in December of 1872. Dishonest ones paid for inferior food or supplies the Indians never even got. Crook angrily condemned such corruption, but he was transferred out of the territory in 1875.

That year the Bureau of Indian Affairs moved the Tontos and Yavapai from Camp Verde, where they were irrigating and growing their own food in familiar country, down to San Carlos, which they detested. Coyoteros from Camp Apache were also sent there, much against their will.

This cramping of feuding bands together in country most of them didn't like was bound to lead to outbreaks. When some Chiricahuas began raiding in Sonora and the San Pedro Valley, this band was ordered to also go to San Carlos. The peaceful ones, including sons of the now dead Cochise, unhappily obeyed, while the wilder ones stayed out, raiding on both sides of the border.

Jared said that none of it would have happened if the Mimbreños and Chiricahuas had been left on their familiar reservations. He shook his graying head over the Mormon settlements on the Gila that were diverting so much water that some downstream Apache crops had failed.

"I never thought to feel sorry for Apaches," he mused. "Not after what they did to my wife and her brothers and father, or the way they raided and killed in the sixties. But now they know they're whipped. They're trying their best, the most of 'em, to live on a little scrap of land when they've had the run of all of what the Mexicans called El Gran Chichimeca, the northern wilderness."

Jordan nodded broodingly. As a civilian scout for Crook, living closely with the Apache ones, he had much respect for them. "They're cheated and starved and lied to till it's no wonder they break away." He looked at Cat, and she knew he was thinking of James. "If I were one of them, I reckon I'd rather take Nana's or Victorio's or Fierro's way. Die free in the mountains rather than cooped up for whites to make a profit off me."

Young Benjamin, whose red hair was more carrot-hued than that of his father and uncle, cast a keen blue glance at Jordan. "Didn't you know that Nocadelklinny who's holding dances around the Cibecue on the San Carlos reservation?"

"He was one of our best Coyotero scouts," said Jordan. "He was sent to Washington and met President Grant—got a peace medal that he wears around his neck."

Jared frowned. "After all that, seems funny he'd stir his people up. Agent Tiffany gave him permission to dance at first, but now he's getting nervous and wants the army to stop it."

Jordan shrugged. "I don't think Bobby, as we used to call him, meant to stir up anyone. I hear he went to an Indian school at Santa Fe for a while and learned a little about Christianity. What must have really stuck with him was the resurrection. You can't blame him for wanting to bring dead chiefs back to help their people."

A chill shot down Cat's spine. "That's what he's doing?"

"That's how it started." He was dancing near the graves of Eskiole and Diablo. That gives a notion of how desperate the Apaches are because they're scared of the dead. More Coyoteros started coming to the dances and now I hear the Fort Apache scouts are attending."

Jared said dryly, "The mail carrier was telling folks at the mill that when Nocadelklinny didn't resurrect anyone, some warriors threatened to kill him. That's when he said the leaders wouldn't return till the whites were driven out."

"I expect what Bobby said and what others say he said have gotten pretty well mixed," Jordan replied slowly.

Benjamin put his hand over Ruth's as if to protect her. "Whatever started it, that kind of thing's bound to pull in some hostiles. They say Tiffany's scared because bands that have usually been feuding are getting together for the dancing. There are even rumors that Fierro's been drawn in."

Cat stiffened at the name. Jordan's gaze was like a steadying touch, but no one else noticed.

"Fierro!" whispered Michael, James's secret son, whose dark blue eyes, shockingly like his father's, shone with eagerness. "I'd like to see him someday!"

"You'd change your mind in a hurry!" scoffed fifteen-year-old Dick, Jared's youngest son. "He'd cut off your eyelids and—"

"That's enough, Dick," rebuked Jared.

Beneath the checked tablecloth Cat's fingers twisted and locked. James on the Cibecue, a few days' ride away? She would give anything, all the rest of her life, if she could see him one more time as the man she had loved, James, before he became Fierro.

Looking at their son, the childish moldings of his face just starting to become firm, Cat's heart swelled with pride and grief. If only James could know his son! If Michael could know his father!

But James was irrevocably Fierro now. If they met, Fierro would kill their son. He had a peculiarity. Instead of capturing likely young Mexican or Anglo boys to keep and train as warriors, he killed them all, saying he spared them torment.

James! Oh, James!

Talk turned to whether Tiffany was guilty of graft, adding to the Apache unrest. Jared, who had met the agent, thought him personally honest, though surrounded by grafting contractors and officials.

"Tiffany started a school for the Apaches," Jared pointed out. "And he's tried to keep miners off the reservation or at least make them pay royalties to the Indians for what they take out. I'd guess it's exactly because Tiffany is honest that he's being accused by those whose little games he's spoiling and they won't stop till they bring him down."

Cat scarcely heard. She was remembering a boy with a hawk on his wrist; one teaching her and her brothers to track, to shoot with bow and arrows. Remembering the rough serapes and the hard strength, changing to gentleness, of this man she'd loved. He'd promised to talk of marriage on her eighteenth birthday, the very time she labored and panted to bring forth his son in a strange place among people who, though kind, except for Jordan were strangers.

Years, her hard-earned peace, shredded like a rotten veil. Unable to sit still another moment, she rose and swiftly began to clean the table. She couldn't meet Jordan's troubled eyes.

The men of Scott Valley were cutting wood on the slopes above the valley. Women and older children were stripping husks from ears of corn, leaving stalks to hold the naked ears while the kernels hardened.

It was hot. Cat kept rubbing blinding sweat from her forehead, but there was nothing to do about the way chaff itched between her breasts and along her neck and arms. It would be a good harvest, though, enough for all the families and with some left to sell. With a wave of homesickness she remembered the cornfields along the Sonoita, the mill her father and Santiago had made. How wonderful it would be to see Marc and Talitha again, the children, her brothers, Belen—all the ranch folk.

Perhaps when harvest was over, before school started, she'd ask Jordan to take her and Michael for a visit. In a few years Michael should really start spending some time at the Socorro, for he'd inherit Cat's share. She was glad he had a legacy. Jordan had freely given Michael his name, but Cat shrank from her son's taking up Scott property. For Jordan's sake she was sorry they'd been unable to have children, but the deepest part of her was fiercely glad she had borne her only child to her only love.

Young Dick, a bit sulky at being left to work with the women and children, shaded his eyes, gazed toward the east, and gave a shout. "Soldiers!"

Peering from beneath her palm, Cat made out blue-clad riders coming up the valley. When the other women all looked frightened, for they'd been brought up on stories of how the U.S. Army had occupied Salt Lake City and more than once been the arm of Gentile persecution, Cat said, "I'll see what they want. We don't want them riding over our fields."

Rolling down her sleeves, she pinned up her hair as best she could, hurrying toward the wagon road that ran between the houses and the fields, eyeing the visitors as she went. Apache scouts were with the troopers, dressed in a mixture of white and Indian clothes. And that captain on the fine black horse—something about him, the set of head and shoulders . . .

Approaching, he dismounted, sweeping off his broad-brimmed hat. Pale yellow hair, trim mustache, face weathered by years of Arizona sun. Cat knew Claybourne Frazier before he knew her and stepped back in surprise.

"Caterina! I mean—Mrs. Scott! I should have guessed from the name of the settlement, but I've been away so long, serving in Dakota, that I'd—"

"Forgotten?" His confusion put her more at ease, and she laughed. "Why should you remember people from so long ago?"

He was in control now and gave her a grim little smile of his own. "It wasn't you I forgot, dear lady, only your husband's name."

Gray eyes scanned her. She flushed, aware of the odor of her body, the way sweat made her dress cling. Frazier had always made her feel as if her femaleness were somewhat gross, repelling but at the same time attracting him. His gaze sent perverse awareness shooting through her. He said huskily, "When I've allowed myself to think of you at all, I've pictured you plump and bewattled, flocked about with children. But you—you're what my dreams kept saying."

"That's not why you're here, Captain. What do you want?"

He straightened, his tone formally chill, though not loud enough now for his nearest men to hear. "There's been an uprising near Cibecue Creek. Four soldiers were killed, and Nocadelklinny. The Apache scouts mutinied for the first time. Colonel Carr was warned we shouldn't use them since they were related to Nocadelklinny's followers and some had joined his dances. Carr should have sent to Fort McDowell for their Yavapai, Hualapais, and Chiricahua scouts. But Tiffany wanted Nocadelklinny dead or alive, before the next dance. General Willcox telegraphed that he must be arrested, and though he surrendered peacefully, some Apaches opened fire. Soldiers fired back, and Nocadelklinny, who was calling on his followers to fight, telling them that he'd come to life again if killed, was shot by his guard. His wife grabbed a pistol, but she was killed before she could pull the trigger, and his son charged us and was shot. The command was lucky to get back to Fort Apache."

As Cat stared in shock at such disastrous news, Frazier went on to say that a general uprising was feared. Fort Apache had been attacked, though the warriors soon went off in search of easier pickings. Troops were being brought in from New Mexico and even California. A number of settlers had been killed, and it was rumored that Geronimo had broken out again, along with Juh and Cochise's son Nachez.

"I'm ordered to warn civilians to congregate for safety and form militia to protect themselves," Frazier concluded. "I seem now to remember hearing that your husband was a scout." Eyes narrowing, the officer pondered a moment. "I have orders to rendezvous in this valley with other patrols before moving toward Fort Apache, but there's a chance some renegades are gathering at Turret Mountain to sweep along the Verde. If Scott Valley militia would make a short expedition in that direction, it could head off the trouble before it develops."

Cat frowned. "Surely that's what you soldiers are supposed to do."

"We can't be everywhere. My orders are to move for Fort Apache as soon as the patrols gather. We've been pushing, and the men and animals need a rest."

They did look bone-weary, even the scouts. "Why don't you make camp up near the mill?" suggested Cat. "I'll send for the men, and you can talk to them about forming militia. We have plenty of milk, butter, eggs, and fresh vegetables if your troops would relish them. Since we've been working in the fields, we don't have much baked goods to spare, but you're welcome to what we have."

Frazier laughed. "Anything would taste wonderful after bacon and hard bread. After we go into camp, I'll send some men for whatever you can spare. Don't worry; I'll pay for it. My troops need some encouragement!"

"I'm sure no one would want pay," Cat assured him, but she didn't ask him for supper. In spite of his courtesy, he made her uneasy. "We'll get the food together and send some of the children over with it."

He bowed, a seasoned, experienced man now, not the impulsive young lieutenant who'd courted her more than ten years ago. Another time, another place, in what seemed a past life.

She didn't like him, never would, and repudiated the physical response she felt to him. For all Jordan's tenderness, all the loving of his strong, clean body, she'd never felt a hint of that drowning, almost unbearable joy she'd had with James. Her matured woman's instinct told her this soldier's lean brown hands and hard mouth could rouse the fires she'd thought forever quenched. The faint smile edging his lips said he sensed this.

"Thanks for all your kindness, madam. I look forward to enjoying as much of it as possible during our bivouac here." Before she could answer, he swung on his horse and signaled his troops back up the valley.

XX

Fetched down from their woodcutting by young Dick, the Scott Valley men conferred with Frazier, counseled together briefly, and decided that by patrolling now they could prevent serious depredations later. Jared invited Frazier to supper, and details were worked out afterward with all the Scott Valley men and those living near enough to be called in for the planning.

At least twenty well-armed men could be gathered quickly and others picked up on the march. At sixty, Jared was the oldest, fifteen-year-old Dick the youngest. Frazier would leave a trusted scout, who had been at the storming of Turret Mountain in 1873, to assist Jordan, who would lead the force.

"I doubt there'll be even a skirmish," the captain said, clearly relieved and well satisfied. "It's only if the wild ones in this region can get together that they'll be a threat to more than isolated farms or travelers. They'll see you even if you don't spot them. When they know they'll get a hot reception here, chances are they'll make for the White Mountains and try to follow Geronimo and Juh."

"What if we take prisoners?" Jordan asked. He and Frazier had treated each other with remote courtesy, making no reference to the past.

"I wouldn't." At Jordan's shocked glance and Jared's angry rumble, the officer shrugged. "Take them to Fort

Verde, or hold them here till a patrol can take them in charge."

Jordan nodded. "And you won't leave our families unprotected?"

"My word of honor," Frazier replied easily. No one cared to bring up the possibility that some of Jordan's force might not come back. Cat's torment over James was compounded by anxiety for her husband and the other men.

After Frazier was gone, she and Ruth packed jerky, dried fruit, and wheat crackers in their men's saddlebags, put in extra socks, and made up bedrolls. Jared, Benjamin, Jordan, and Dick cleaned their weapons and filled their cartridge belts.

A knife seemed to turn in Cat when Michael begged to go along. James had been that young once, with no blood on his hands.

It was late by the time they blew out the lamps and went to bed, but Cat couldn't sleep. Would there be a general war? Where was James? Would Jordan return safely? Claybourne Frazier's eyes mocked her till she moved closer to Jordan, seeking comfort.

Rousing, he took her in his arms. This night she loved him back with desperation powered by fear, a realization of how the steadfast way he had cherished her had given her refuge and let her rear James's son.

That all seemed threatened now; they were caught in a rising wind that would leave nothing the same. So she gave herself fully, with urgency, answering her husband's kisses and caresses as she never had before. In spite of their weariness, they loved and slept and loved again.

The second time, he laughed softly, in the tender pride of a male desired by his woman. "If taking a scout brings this on, Katie, I'll go every week."

"No, you won't!" she said and seized him tightly, almost as if he were her child she would protect. She said then what she had never said during all these years, and she knew that it was true, though it didn't change how she felt about James. "I love you, Jordan. I really love you."

His breath caught. Her hand on his cheek encountered tears.

"Oh, Katie! I've hoped! How I've hoped— You were always sweet, you've done all you could, but I've wanted more than that."

At last she understood how Talitha, still loving the dead Shea, had been able to make a good, sound life with Marc Revier. James was the same as dead to her; she must accept that. It was Jordan with whom she must make her life and her son's.

Kissing him, she gave a choking little laugh. "When you come back, it'll be different, Jordan. I'll make up to you—"

He hushed her with his fervent, joyful kiss.

They lay together so sweetly that they seemed to flow together, joining, and at last they slept.

The men were on their way by daybreak, and the women and children had all the chores to do before going to the fields to strip corn. They could see the soldiers at the head of the valley, some lounging, others shoeing horses and mules or refurbishing gear. They were apparently under orders not to drift around the settlement, though the scouts and a few of the troopers went hunting and returned with a deer and several rabbits.

Cat hadn't invited Frazier to supper, but when he stopped by while they were at table, there was nothing she could do but invite him to join them.

It was a simple meal of side meat with gravy, biscuits, string beans, squash, potatoes, and blackberry pie, but Frazier praised it and ate with such unfeigned appreciation that Cat relaxed a bit.

Military men probably acquired a certain gallantry, and she valued his because of her placid life among men who scorned flirting or thought it downright sinful. From the way he refilled his plate, he'd been drawn here for a change from camp cooking; and if he wanted admiration, little Ruth was giving him plenty of that, russet eyes wide in her heart-shaped face, as he talked of Dakota and a recent assignment in Washington.

When he said good night after enthralling Michael with the story of Custer's defeat at the Little Big Horn, he smiled equally at Ruth and Cat, again complimenting them on their cookery. Cat retired, chiding herself, even the slightest bit piqued. She didn't want to be pursued by Frazier, but it was deflating to think his compliments were common coin, carelessly tossed to any woman. Though how she could give him a thought, with Jordan out discouraging renegades, the reservation about to burst wide open, and James somewhere out there . . .

Unable to sleep, she went to the room Michael shared with Dick. Enough moonlight came through the one window for her to make out her son's face, the mouth curved down, dark eyebrows winging upward. If only James could see him. If only he could know . . .

Blinded with tears, she fleetingly smoothed the thickly curling red hair. He thought Jordan was his father. It almost had to be that way. How could you tell a boy he was the son of Fierro, the hated and ferocious raider? Michael's skin was slightly darker than the Scotts', but that was attributed to Cat's Spanish heritage, though she herself was fair.

Maybe, when she was very old and Michael himself had children and grandchildren, when the names of Fierro, Mangus, and Cochise might have the ring of legend, then she might tell Michael.

Michael stirred and muttered, as if her distress pierced his sleep. Leaving him, she lay in the bed where she and Jordan had been last night and wept till exhaustion sent her restless dreams.

Late the next afternoon the corn stripping was finished. The boys went swimming, and though Cat couldn't join them, she resolved that after chores were done she was having a swim herself, in a deep pool sheltered by high rocks that lay below the orchards. She would also wash her hair and luxuriate in being clean all over.

Telling Ruth and Michael that she'd be back before it was really dark but to go ahead with supper without her, she collected clean clothes, soap, and a towel and started across the orchards for the river and her private place.

The sun was just sinking below the mountains and the air was immediately cooler, though these early September days were still hot when the sun beat down. Clambering over boulders along the bank, she climbed down to the little semi-dam, hung her fresh clothes and her towel on a sycamore stump, and hurried out of her sweaty, soiled garments.

Sure enough, the water was warm and the heat of the rocks, punishing in the day but pleasant now, kept the chill off. She lathered her hair and body, rinsed in a higher level, and lay there in a shallow pool, tired muscles relaxed and grateful.

A pebble skittered. Jerking erect, heart in her mouth, she looked for a rock or natural club in the same instant that, with relief and shocked embarrassment, she saw Frazier on the outcropping above, outlined against the blue twilight, much closer to her clothes than she was.

He showed not the slightest inclination of apologizing or turning away. Smiling down at her, he said genially, "Though you fled me, Caterina, I had hopes of seeing you this evening. Though not in my fondest dreams dared I hope to see so much!"

She had instinctively crossed her arms across her breasts, but there was nothing more she could do to shield herself from his raking gray eyes.

"This does no credit to your uniform, Captain."

He strode lightly down to her, pausing a few yards away. "I don't intend to make love to you in my uniform, my elusive, long-desired one!"

He began to unbutton his coat. Unbelieving, Cat choked, "You—you can't mean to—"

With a grim laugh, tossing down his coat and unbuckling his belt, he began to swear at her, soft obscenities, words she'd never heard before. "You want me as much as I do you. I saw it in the way you looked at me last night. That husband of yours is strong as an ox, but I doubt he knows how to pleasure a woman."

Springing up, she retreated, desperately watching for some weapon, some means of defense. "Is—is this why you sent Jordan away?"

He chuckled. "The renegades are real enough. While taking care of that threat, I saw no reason not to follow King David's example. Unfortunately, I doubt that your husband, like Uriah of old, will fall in any battle."

"I—I wouldn't marry *you!*"

"I don't especially wish to *marry* you." He shrugged. "I'm going to rise higher than my father, the brigadier, and your predispositions would hamper that. But no woman has calmed the fever you gave me. It's raged intermittently, like malaria. Now I intend to be cured."

Catching her arms, he brought her against him, laughing as she struggled, claiming her mouth.

"Jordan will kill you!"

"Will he?" Forcing her down in the grass, he roughly caressed her, tasting her breasts, savoring her throat. "You won't tell him. Because, my proud, lovely Caterina, you're going to like this so much you'll meet me every chance we have."

"You—you coward!"

"No, love. Arms are my profession. Should you make the mistake of telling your husband, I can kill him very easily in a way that'll look like self-defense. I'd like to take off these boots, but, damn you, if you won't hold still—"

She arched upward with frantic strength, sending him off balance, though one leg and arm still clamped her.

Her fingers closed on a rock. She crashed it with all her might against his head and was astonished when, convulsing with a guttural cry, he suddenly collapsed. She hadn't hoped the blow could be that disabling. Then she saw the figure above them, breechclout over trousers, high Apache moccasins rolled at the knee.

One hand held the war club that had crushed Frazier's skull. Brains and blood oozed over her breast. Paralyzed, she waited for the blow that would kill her. But the tall Apache dropped his club, kicked Frazier off her, and knelt down.

"Gídí!"

James's eyes, the thunderstorm blue of their son's, watched her from the face of a savage with a red stripe painted beneath the eyes and across the nose. Flesh taut over cheekbones honed to sharpness, he had the arrogant, harsh beauty of a hawk.

She scarcely knew him; and yet she did.

Heedless of the dead man beside her, his blood streaking her body, she reached up and was in James's arms, weeping with joy, alive again after all these years, a quietly shriveling tree revived by blessed rain. For an unreckonable time they held each other. She felt complete, as if a severed part of her had magically returned, healing a subtle wound that must eventually prove fatal.

"Gídí," he said at last. "How did you come here?"

She told him.

"We have a son?" he asked, amazed, the English words slow. He tilted her face back as if to read it, though now the light was dim. It would be some hours till the moon rose. "A son, *gídí?* And you never told me?"

"I was going to, before you went to Camp Grant." She laughed shakily. "Remember, when I asked to go with you, you said the people wouldn't trust you if you came with a white woman? After that . . ."

They were both silent. After that he'd killed Cinco—

and since, so many more. What his thoughts were she'd never know. The night wind pierced her and she began to shiver uncontrollably.

"We must make you clean," he said.

Carrying her to the pool, he washed away the blood, then dried her carefully, as if she might break. She clung to him, wordlessly pleading, feeling the violent response of his manhood. But he pushed her away and thrust her dress into her hands.

"Jordan has raised my son. I will not betray him."

Shamed but still consumed with longing, she whispered, "Just this once, James! Once to remember—"

"No!"

Turning his back while she dressed, he seemed to be thinking aloud. "I have eight warriors. They're waiting for me to decide if we should attack that camp of soldiers at the head of your valley. We could hit them by night, when they're not expecting Apaches, then sweep the settlement. But I cannot do that to Jordan's people, those who have sheltered you and my son. I will tell my warriors that. I can't compel them, but I believe they'll listen to me."

Cat shuddered. "If they don't?"

"They'll have to kill me." James laughed. "I don't think any of them will want to try that. We can push on toward the reservation and find plenty of soldiers to fight there."

Cat shut her jaws against an outcry. What could she expect? His sparing the camp and valley was more than she could have dared hope from Fierro.

What *had* she hoped? That their reunion, so deep, so absolute, should end abruptly seemed too cruel, unbearable. But what could there be for Jordan's wife and Fierro?

They must separate again, like a river sundered by a volcanic upsurge of primeval rock. But it would be as if he took with him her blood and breath and left only a flesh-covered skeleton.

All the passion of her being rebelled. Wildly, she

thought of begging to go with him; but even if he allowed it, and she knew he wouldn't, Jordan would try to track them and might be killed.

There was nothing for them. But even in her agony she was grateful to have seen him and been in his arms again. And at least he knew they had a child. Michael, born of their loving, would live and act, be some part of them in the world long after they were dead.

That must have been in James's mind. Near Cat but not touching her as she dressed, he said, "Our son. What is he like?"

"Oh, James!" That they would never see each other, never share pride and joy, never have even the simple, everyday father-son things . . . Swallowing, Cat brought herself under control and tried to give her love at least a picture of his boy.

"His eyes and the bones of his face are just like yours. His skin is in between yours and mine, though the sun keeps it more like yours. He has curly red-gold hair like my father's and Patrick's, and I think he'll be tall."

"But what is he like?"

"He's good at all the things boys do and already can work hard. He loves to read. I've taught him to shoot a bow and arrow, and he knows about White Painted Woman and Born of the Waters." Cat struggled, trying to make some coherent linkage of all the things that were a normally intent, inquisitive ten-year-old who was yet altogether different from his friends. "He's always taken care of hurt animals and birds. He's cured quite a few of them, and he's better at treating bad cuts and burns than even Jared, who's taught him all he knows. It seems to hurt him when someone else is hurt. Maybe he'll be a doctor."

James lightly smoothed her face. "That would be good. I have killed men. He may heal them."

"Is it true that you were at Nocadelklinny's dancing?"

"Yes. I came because all the clans were gathering,

dropping their selfish feuds, drawing together. It was a hope. There is none now."

"You could go to Mexico." Cat caught her breath in sudden hope. "James, you could drop all this warring! Go home to the Socorro, live far up some cañon as we used to think we'd do!"

He shook his head. "I cannot abandon my people. I hope our son will help them someday. You must go to your house now. I'll blot the sign of what happened and dump the officer closer to his camp so they'll find him in the morning."

She longed to throw herself into his arms, but his manner forbade it. She raised her fingers to his face and touched the beloved features, trying to brand them on her senses.

"Good-bye, James. I love you. I always have. I always will."

"Good-bye, *gídí*. Take care of our son."

Her legs seemed to have no strength, yet somehow, commanded, they carried her away.

Frazier's body was found next morning, only a short distance from the sentry. The scouts identified the moccasin tracks as Mimbreño. It appeared that the captain had gone for a walk and been killed by a single renegade who, inexplicably, hadn't ambushed the sentry or tried to run off any animals.

The other patrols came in that day and next. The captain leading one of them assumed command of the joined forces. They buried Frazier on a gentle slope, blowing Taps, at the time that Jordan and his men rode in, and early next morning the troops set out for the embattled reservation.

Keeping their weapons handy, the Scott Valley men went back to their woodcutting, but they worked where they could watch their homes and come at once if needed. They had found plenty of signs on their expedition and exchanged shots with two Apaches who got away, but their presence seemed to have discouraged any gathering at Turret Mountain.

"The tracks of one group seemed headed for the Mogollon Rim," said Jordan. "Others went off in the direction of San Carlos. The army's in for hot times there, and we'd all better keep an eye peeled."

"Especially after the way they murdered Captain Frazier right at the camp," said young Dick excitedly. "It's funny they killed him instead of making off with the mules and horses or stealing our women and children."

Ruth's lips quivered as she looked at Benjamin. "Poor Captain Frazier! He'd had supper with us the night before and seemed such a pleasant, entertaining gentleman."

Cat said nothing. She didn't want anyone dead, but she couldn't pretend sadness at Frazier's killing. In fact, she was so numbed at meeting and losing James that she did her work mechanically, unable to take her thoughts from him. Terrible to realize that unless his head was brought in for a price, she'd probably never know what had happened to him. There would be word of a raid here, an attack there, and finally no more rumors.

The day after the troops moved out, a young lieutenant came riding hard, accompanied by a single scout. To the men who came down from their felling and riving and the women who came from their work he gasped out his story.

The patrols had fanned out on the way to San Carlos, hoping to meet any hostiles in their way. His group had been ambushed by eight or nine warriors, who killed a dozen troopers before another patrol swarmed after the fire and joined the remnants of the first, driving the Apaches into the rocks above the river and killing most of them. But the leader was still alive, refuged in a cave. The scouts had recognized him. He was Fierro!

Cat smothered a cry. Jordan put his arm around her. "What do you want us to do?" he asked the lieutenant.

"We don't want Fierro to get away," the young man said, thankfully draining the buttermilk one of the women had gone to bring him and the scout. "But we need to be on the march for Fort Apache. If we storm him, he can kill maybe half a dozen before we get him, and we don't have time to starve him out. But if a few of your militia would take over—"

"We could take Fierro!" Dick shouted, eyes shining. "Dad! Jordan! We could catch or kill the biggest of them all!"

"Will you do it?" the lieutenant asked. "I don't have to remind you that you're protecting your own lives and your families."

"You don't have to remind us," Jared agreed dryly. As he glanced around at his kinsmen and neighbors there was a chorus of assent.

"Rest while we bring our teams down and get ready," Jared advised the weary young officer. "Where is Fierro?"

"About twenty miles up the Verde, in a cave beneath that big cliff that's shaped like an eagle with its wings spread," said the soldier, sliding off his sweating mount and thanking Michael, who led the horses off for watering and graze. "If we can leave within two hours, we'll be there by night. That's when we have to watch closest, in case he tries to slip away."

"Well, I guess we can take over that chore for you," said Jared. Turning to the valley men, he asked for a dozen volunteers. The others would stay to guard the settlement. In a few minutes the selection was made. Once again Jordan was the leader.

Cat heard it all through a burning haze. James trapped, perhaps wounded, maybe even dead by now? And if he lived, Jordan constrained to be in charge of the force that would kill or starve him out.

The men were already hurrying, some to bring tools

and teams from the forest, others to see to their rifles and other preparations. Jared came to Cat.

"I'm sorry, Katie. If there's a way to save him alive, I will. If he'll surrender—"

"He won't."

Jordan gave her a long look of pain and love and pity. Then he strode off toward the mountain for his team.

Cat didn't follow. An hour or two till the group started? If she left right now, she could get there before Jordan's men did. Perhaps she could persuade James to give up. Probably she couldn't; but she could help him if he was hurt, take him food. Be with him at the end, whatever it was.

Sangre, seldom ridden now, pastured across the river, not on this side with the commonly used stock. She couldn't carry a saddle to him, but she could take a bridle, a blanket, and one of the leather surcingles the children sometimes used to hold a blanket on when they didn't have a saddle. She hated to leave without a word to Jordan or the others, but they mustn't guess what she was doing. She felt no disloyalty to them. She wasn't going to help Fierro fight; only to live if that might be, or, failing that, to die. At the house she hastily got jerky, nuts, and dried fruit, then started for the stable.

Not to see Michael— Her heart leaped as she met him coming out of the shed where he'd been rubbing down the horses, giving them some grain.

She gave him a quick hug, which he squirmingly resisted, and a quicker kiss on his brown cheek. "Michael, I just have to go for a ride, and I'm taking Sangre. I don't want anyone stopping me with Indian scares, so, unless you're asked, don't say anything about it till suppertime."

His brows rushed together. "Won't you be back by then?"

Her heart wrenched. But he was surrounded by love, by good people who cared for him. He didn't need her the way James did.

"I don't know when I'll be back," she said, pretending to be cross. "Goodness, Michael, don't be so grouchy! Have you got any food down your sick fawn today?"

"Guess I'd better try again," he said, and, his mind turned to one of his "patients," he hurried away, bright hair brushed by her fingers. She looked after him for just a second, then moved into the stable.

Sangre came at her whistle, lipped the handful of grain she'd brought him. He was sixteen now, but in excellent condition. Cat didn't have time to ride as often as she'd have liked, but when she did, he gave her all she asked.

The blanket was far less comfortable than a saddle, but at least the surcingle kept it from slipping. They were shielded from the settlement by the thick growth of trees along the river, and Cat, while they were on level land, nudged the bay into a lope. When the valley narrowed again, she had to keep close to the river, where trees and rocks made progress slow.

As she rode, speaking now and then to Sangre, who kept one ear pricked back to her as he always had, she remembered James as a boy of fourteen when he first came back from the Apaches, how she'd missed him when he returned to them, how strange he'd seemed when he came back, and how her love had grown. She remembered his little house and smiled to recall her happiness in buying things for it, pretending it was theirs. . . . They'd never had a place together, only two nights on serapes spread on straw matting.

Still, they had a son, straight and quick and kind, with healing in his hands.

She thought of her brothers then, and wished she could see their children, and Marc and Talitha's Judith, and Shea, who must be fifteen now, and the children of her old ranch playmates. Faces of those she'd loved passed before her. Anita, her milk-mother; Carmencita; the vaqueros, especially dear, barrel-chested Belen; Talitha, who'd been both sister and mother.

And she remembered her tall, flame-haired father, with the brands marking his cheek, one given in hate, one accepted out of love.

Her mother she could not remember, but she felt oddly close to her now.

She let Sangre drink when he was thirsty but didn't stop till, in late afternoon, she was challenged by a scout, who brought her to the commanding captain. The scout said Fierro was still in the cave across the river. She told the captain she'd known Fierro as a boy, that he'd been her foster brother.

"If I can talk to him, perhaps he'll surrender," she said.

The captain, a brawny, sandy-haired man, stared at her curiously. "And what does your husband think of this, Mrs. Scott?"

"He doesn't know I came. Naturally, I'm very anxious that he and my foster brother don't fight each other."

"I don't know . . ." The captain deliberated, rubbing his mustache. "Truth to tell, Mrs. Scott, I don't want Fierro to surrender. We've just buried thirteen good men he and his renegades killed."

"But you don't have time to wait him out," Cat reminded. "You want my husband to do that—and I have to keep them from hurting each other."

A lieutenant cleared his throat. "Why don't you let her try, sir? We have to get to Fort Apache, but it still doesn't look good for the army to leave civilians to smoke out a savage they couldn't kill or capture."

Abruptly deciding, the captain frowned at Cat. "You're not taking him ammunition?"

"No," she said truthfully. Before she'd gotten close to where she expected soldiers, she'd fastened the packets of jerky, nuts, and dried fruit around her waist beneath her skirts.

He shrugged. "All right. Guess it can't hurt to try, though why you'd own up to having a foster brother like that beats me! Sure he won't fire on you?"

"I'll call to him." She stroked Sangre, held his muzzle close to her a moment. "Will someone look after my horse?"

A trooper took the reins. Dryly, the captain said, "You'll excuse me if I don't escort you to the river?"

Cat laughed. "By all means, Captain."

"Good luck," he said.

As she approached the bank, she shouted. "James! It's Cat! I'm coming across!"

"Caterina?"

"Yes."

"Don't! Stay where you are."

"I have to talk to you."

"Talk's no use."

"I'm coming."

"Stay there or I'll shoot!"

She didn't believe him; and if he would shoot, nothing mattered any longer anyhow. Her love was in danger. Kilting up her skirts, she threaded a way over boulders and drifted logs, wading shallows till at last she climbed up a spill of great rocks on the opposite side. The cave was above and beyond it, the top of the jagged hole visible.

As she made her way up the rocks, she saw several bodies—Apaches, sprawled where they had fallen. Animals had been at them and they were beginning to smell.

The cave had been used as a shelter, for the natural boulders fallen in front of it had been filled in with more rocks so that a breastwork about four feet high shielded almost the whole mouth. One man could hold off attackers for a long time here, since they'd have to scramble, exposed, up the rocks from the river.

As she approached the opening James raised up and drew her behind the rough wall. "*Gídí!* Are you crazy?"

He had a scalp wound and a grazed shoulder, but no hurts that looked serious. Unfastening the food, she handed it to him. "James, isn't there some way you can slip out of here? The soldiers have to leave, but they've got Jordan to bring Scott Valley men to wait you out."

"Jordan?"

"Yes. He—he has to, James."

"I know, *gídí.*" He took her in his arms. After a moment he said slowly, "There's no way out. They have sentries posted on the cliff above and men along the river. There's a drip from the rocks so I have water; but the captain's right—they can starve me out."

"You—you could surrender." Gripping his arms, she pleaded, "James, after a while you could slip off the reservation, go live somewhere on the Socorro—"

"No, *gídí.* I've been Fierro too long." He sighed. "But I won't try to kill the man who raised my son, who's taken care of you. Go back to camp. Then I'll make a break for it, before your husband comes."

"But they'll kill you!"

"Unless they're very bad shots, which soldiers often are. I'm done in any case, little one. It's only a matter of how long and who kills me."

"I won't leave you."

He kissed her. She pressed against him as if to be part of his flesh, lost in him. Flame coursed between them, wild, consuming, the defiance of love facing death.

"You have come to me," he said. His voice was very deep in his throat. "Ussen has granted this last time. It can be no hurt to Jordan that a dead man loved his wife."

"I was your woman first," she whispered. "I have always been your woman."

They lay in the soft dust of the cave, pouring into each their love and life and strength, and lay quietly awhile. Then James got to his feet.

"If Jordan will grant the favor, don't let them take my head into San Carlos. Stay in the cave till it's finished, *gídí.*"

"You may get to the top."

He flashed a grin. "If I do, then I may live to be an old man down in Mexico." He kissed her. "A strange custom, but I like it!"

Taking his rifle, he dodged out of the cave and started running. There was a shout from above.

James was firing. Bullets sang.

As James went down, Cat ran after him. *Jordan, forgive me!* she prayed. *Take care of Michael.* A great inpact spun her around, but she made a lunge. With her last strength she threw herself across his body.

PART VI

The Flames of Tomochic

1906–1917

XXI

It was early May of 1906, as Christina Revier Riordan walked along a sandy arroyo in the hills near Cananaea Mexico. She felt a wave of homesickness for Rancho del Socorro. In her heart it was still home, where she belonged. After two months of marriage to Fayte Riordan, she still felt a visitor in his home, a pampered mistress, not a wife. The house still ran exactly as it had before she came, which, she had to admit wryly, was perfectly well.

What was it her grandmother Talitha had murmured to her after the wedding in the *sala,* where four generations, beginning with Chris's great-grandparents, Shea and Socorro, had pledged themselves before the smiling dark little Guadalupana?

"We marry strangers, dear, but grow into each other. Be patient and bright and loving, a lamp for your home, Christina."

Good advice. Chris had tried to follow it, but her throat swelled with longing as she remembered Talitha and her other grandparents, Patrick and Sewa. Marc had died a few years ago. Since then, her great-uncle Miguel had managed the family's mining and railroad interests. Patrick was in charge of the ranch, helped at the Socorro by Diego, one of Natividad's grandsons, who had married Aunt Vi, Miguel and Juriana's daughter. El Charco, the southern part of the place, was run by Juan Vasquez, Pedro Sanchez's grandson.

Fascinating how it grew, the interwoven web of families and alliances. Aunt Judith, Marc and Talitha's daughter, had married a nephew of Jordan and Jared Scott and lived in a pleasant valley beneath the Mogollon Rim. Aunt Vi's brothers were both geologists, Marc operating out of Prescott, Christopher from Yuma. Chris's mother's brother, Sean, had married one of Tjúni's granddaughters and become a mining engineer in Mexico. It was while Chris had been left with them that—

The bright day went dark. Blackness shot with flames. Taking a deep breath, Chris invoked the sweet face of Teresita till the nightmare faded, till she could see again. Her heart stopped slamming and she drew in the sight of mountains in all directions, purple, blue and pink according to the light, with the Huachucas rising on the north side of the border.

That Austrian physician Sigmund Freud, whose works on dreams and nervous ills she had read, would have said her blindness after Tomochic was hysterical, that Teresita's curing had been hypnotic.

Perhaps. But both had been real.

Chris pushed the memory from her, concentrating on finishing her mental roll call of mingled Reviers, O'Sheas, and Scotts, and then smiled as she thought of Sant. Santiago Scott was some kind of cousin, the grandson of her great-aunt Caterina. The family all knew that Aunt Caterina's son, Michael, though reared as his own by Jordan Scott, was truly the child of Talitha's Apache half brother, James or Fierro, with whom Caterina had died.

Michael had studied medicine, married the daughter of an army officer, and in 1894 gone to serve the exiled Chiricahuas who had been moved that year to Fort Sill, Oklahoma, after a wretched sojourn in Florida and Alabama.

Back in May of 1885, some Chiricahuas, never reconciled to leaving their old ranges, had broken out of the San Carlos reservation. Led by Nana, Geronimo, Nachez, Chihuahua, and Mangus, the son of the great Mangus, they swept through southwestern New Mexico into Sonora, burning ranches and murdering.

General Crook made two campaigns into Mexico after them, for an agreement had been made between that country and the United States to allow each other's forces to cross the border when in hot pursuit of desperadoes or hostiles. On the second campaign Crook worked out a surrender which Geronimo accepted; but before they could leave for Fort Bowie, a trader sold the Indians some mescal and scared them with stories that they would be killed once they reached the Fort. Geronimo and some twenty warriors with about that many women and children fled back to the Sierra Madres. The other prisoners, after reaching Fort Bowie, were sent to Fort Marion, Florida.

Crook felt he had followed the best course with the Apaches. Further, he'd promised those who surrendered that they'd be kept only two years in the East before they could come back to Arizona. Now Sheridan and most Arizonans and New Mexicans wanted them kept East permanently.

Unhappy with his superiors' decisions, Crook resigned his command and was succeeded by Gen. Nelson Miles, who was given a total of five thousand men, a quarter of the whole U.S. Army, to put an end to Apache troubles. He set up twenty-seven heliograph stations to keep track of hostiles; a message could flash over eight hundred miles across mountain peaks in under four hours.

At last, on September 4, 1886, Geronimo surrendered in Skeleton Cañon, near the border. With soldiers everywhere, the old raiding days were done. Besides, most of his warriors wanted to join their families who had been treacherously sent to Florida, though they'd been living peacefully at San Carlos.

In August all Chiricahuas at the reservation had been put under guard and taken to Holbrook, where they were put on a train to Florida. Their number included many scouts who had served Crook faithfully. General Crook was outraged, but his protests were ignored along with those of Capt. John Bourke. They were sure mountain Apaches would sicken in the flat, low, humid place they'd been sent, and especially denounced the imprisonment of the scouts. Moreover, instead of being united with their families, as Miles had promised, the men had been sent to Fort Pickens, while their women and children were crowded miserably at Fort Marion. Children over twelve were sent off to the Indian school at Carlisle in Pennsylvania and the younger taught by nuns, to the fury of San Augustine's Protestant clergy.

It was an awful winter for the half-naked, crowded Apaches, separated from husbands or from wives and children.

At last, General Crook's bitter protests and the work of Captain Bourke with Herbert Welsh of the Indian Rights Association convinced President Cleveland that something should be done to remedy the situation. Most of the Apaches were sent to Mount Vernon Barracks in Alabama and the families of men at Fort Pickens were allowed to join them there.

But the sandy earth wasn't good for farming, and rations were insufficient. By the fall of 1887 disease had broken out, especially tuberculosis. Lozen, Victorio's famed warrior sister, was one of the many who sickened and died. Seven children dying of tuberculosis were sent back to Mount Vernon from the school for Indians at Carlisle, Pennsylvania, to which children over twelve had been assigned. Their deaths were soon followed by a dozen more.

Crook visited the imprisoned Apaches in January of 1890 and promised to plead their cause again in Washington. He did that, but died of a heart attack in March, still fighting for his former enemies and the scouts who'd been his friends. When the Indians heard of his death, his former scouts sat down in a great circle, let down their hair, bowed their heads, and wept.

The argument over where to send the Chiricahuas raged on. When Congress appropriated money in 1894 to scatter them on military reservations throughout the country, even General Miles, who'd shipped the innocent three quarters of them to Florida along with the guilty, thought it was cruel and unfair. He suggested the Indian Territory again, and in September the War Department ordered them to be moved there and settled on lands of the Comanches and Kiowas who twenty years earlier had been compelled to give up their wanderings and raids that had ranged from Kansas into Mexico.

It was to Fort Sill that young Dr. Michael Scott with his wife, Rosemary, and their small son, Santiago, went to treat the Chiricahuas, who were divided into village groups, with each family having ten acres on which to grow food. In this land of rich pasture and water, the Indians were proving as good at raising cattle as they had previously been at stealing them. They liked the young doctor, who seemed almost an Apache in spite of his red hair, and came to him for advice.

In his second winter at Fort Sill, while coming home from attending a sick old woman, Michael's horse snapped a leg in a gopher hole and fell on him, breaking his neck. Sick with grief, never very strong, Rosemary developed pneumonia and died within the month. Since her parents lived the nomadic life of the military, it was decided that little Sant, as he was called, would be better off with his father's relatives at Rancho del Socorro.

Patrick had gone to fetch him. Chris, at five, was a whole year older and had no intention of letting him forget it, but when Patrick got out of the buckboard, lifting down a tired little boy who held tightly to him and hid his face from all the strangers rushing to greet him, Chris, remembering in a vivid rush how it was to suddenly look into a sea of strange faces, however kind, tugged at her grandfather's arm.

"Let him come with me, Grande." That was the name she'd struck on for calling all her grandparents and great-aunts and uncles. "You grown-ups scare him. He can have my bed tonight. I'll tell him stories till he goes to sleep."

"That might be best tonight," Talitha agreed. "Take him to Chris's room, Patrick, and I'll bring him something to eat."

Chris had the room that had once been shared by Caterina and Sewa. Since there was plenty of room, the hobbyhorse that Caterina, Sewa, Vi, Shea, and the other children had used, with its real horsehair mane and tail, stood by the fireplace. On the niche above was the carved wooden hawk James had given Caterina, and in a larger niche sat the Judith doll Shea had given Talitha when she wasn't much older than Chris was now, though Chris found it hard to imagine her grandmother being a child instead of the one who saw to everything and looked after everyone.

The twin cradleboard with its turquoise and charms, given by Mangus Coloradas to Chris's grandfather Patrick and Uncle Miguel, hung on the wall. It had been Talitha's idea to put all these treasured family things in Chris's room and tell her the stories that went with them.

When her grandfather put Sant down and two vaqueros brought his trunk, Chris took him over to the horse. "Azul was your grandmother's. I'm too big to ride him, so he's been lonely. He's glad you're here."

The little boy carefully touched the mane. "I can ride him?"

"He'll be sad if you don't." Chris turned to the trunk, which Patrick had opened before he left. "What do you sleep in?"

He came over and burrowed around till he found a

white nightshirt. "You go 'way," he blurted, clutching it to him. "It's not nice to undress with girls, Mama says. . . ." His face crumpled as he remembered.

Chris put her arms around him and let him cry, though she'd started to snap his head off for telling her to leave her own room. "Let me help you get your shoes off," she suggested when his sobs were less convulsive. "Then I'll wait outside while you get into your nightshirt. Grande Talitha will bring you something good to eat—"

"Not hungry."

Chris got off one shoe and looked up at him grimly. "You have to eat, or you'll get sick, and then you can't go riding on a real horse or learn to rope or do anything. And I won't tell you stories."

"What kind of stories?"

"Good ones."

"You'll tell them till I go to sleep?" He looked around the room, and she read his thoughts. Who, more than she, knew about fear of the dark? "I'll ask Grande Talitha if we can have another bed. Then I'd be right here if you wanted a drink or something." She gave him an encouraging smile and stepped into the courtyard.

He needed to be taken care of. Listening to the splash of the fountain among the pomegranate trees, she felt a rush of gratefulness that her own parents were alive, though her father's serving in the legislature, now moved back to Prescott, and going into business there kept him and Mother away most of the time. Here at the ranch with all of the Grandes, she didn't miss them much. They'd never been part of her daily life. Daddy's work as a geologist had kept him on the move and his Katie had followed, leaving Chris with what she thought of as her Big Family. The one time Chris had been taken along, when she was about two years old, she'd been left at Tomochic with her nurse and Cruz while her parents went on a hazardous mule journey into the Sierra to get ore samples from an old mine.

She couldn't remember any of that. The first memory of her life, burned forever in her consciousness, was a blazing church, women and children running out, crumpling and screaming as they were blasted down by bullets. Chris saw that from the house where Cruz, the giant Tarahumare, guarded her and her nurse. Then she saw nothing, only blackness shot with flame.

Later, she'd know why every male of Tomochic over thirteen had died fighting or been killed when they ran out of water and ammunition. The fiercely independent Tarahumare-Spanish mixed people of the little mountain village had in their church two paintings reputedly by the great artist Murillo. If copies, they were good ones. The governor of Chihuahua thought they would make an excellent gift for President Porfirio Díaz' wife, thus ensuring his own "reelection" to office. The henchman sent to steal them was stopped by the men of the town, whose leader, Cruz Chavez, pointed out that the governor should buy his gifts and not rob a poor village. Tomochic kept its pictures, but its people were reported as being dangerous rebels. Part of this was because they believed in the young faith healer, Santa Teresa de Cabora, who was being denounced by many priests as a heretic and was feared by the Díaz government as an incendiary revolutionist because rebelling Yaquis, Mayos, and people like those of Tomochic revered her, came in thousands to be healed, and made her their patroness.

An English mine manager telegraphed the Díaz government, protesting the "lawlessness" around Tomochic and asking for protection. In vain, Chavez pointed out to the manager that in two hundred years his villagers had never waylaid a pack train and that if the manager was afraid, the Tomochitecos would themselves escort the silver to Guerrero.

Knowing they were considered rebels, though not really understanding why, Cruz Chavez and his men went to Cabora to seek counsel from the girl they venerated as a saint. Meanwhile, learning that her arrest had been ordered, Teresa Urrea and her father went to Cocorit and surrendered. The Tomochitecos, fighting off an army ambush, reached her home to find her gone. They prayed in her chapel, however, and started back to Tomochic, pursued by soldiers and skirmishing. Some of them may have gone to Arizona to buy guns, because by the time they returned to their village in February of 1892, they had repeating Winchesters, vastly superior to the smoothbore single-shot Mausers of the Federals.

Cruz Chavez prayed daily at the altar. If his people submitted, he and a few others would be shot and the rest of the men conscripted into the army or sent as slave laborers to the henequen hells of Yucatán, but it might touch off a blaze among the smoldering Yaquis, Mayos, and Tarahumares that would force the government to respect their rights.

The Mayos did rebel in May, and Díaz ordered Teresa Urrea to be deported. Her father went with her. She was his illegitimate daughter by a vaquero's daughter, and though he was a wealthy *hacendado* with many children, legitimate and otherwise, it was this girl with the wavy dark red hair and lovely brown eyes that he loved to the extent of going into exile with her for the rest of his life. He never believed her to be a saint; indeed, she herself said she wasn't and only used the healing power God had given her. Before the cataleptic trance that lasted for over three months in 1889 when she was sixteen, she was a merry, mischievous girl who played the guitar and sang *corridos,* though she'd always been able to do things that seemed uncanny. Her strongest playmates couldn't lift her unless she allowed it, and she had flashes of seeing things happening far away. After the long trance, she had the gift of healing. Soon thousands of maimed, crippled, diseased folk made their way to her father's ranch.

"You can see." Twelve years later, Chris would still hear that softly thrilling sweet voice. *"Christina, small one, you can see."*

Cool hands had touched her eyelids. A surge of delicious sparkling coursed through Chris, centering in her eyes. "God's world is beautiful," went on the musical voice. A sweet smell, like flowers, came from those hands. "Look at me, Christina."

And she did. The first face she saw since those terror-stricken ones in Tomochic was that of Teresita. Glowing, luminous eyes enveloped Chris before, smiling, Teresita kissed her. She refused pay from the astounded Reviers and O'Sheas who'd driven to Bosque, the ranch where the Urreas lived that year of 1894, only three miles from Tumacácori. Chris's Grandes left money, though, for feeding the poor who came for healing, and this was accepted.

Chris never saw her again, but she never forgot that voice or that lovely face and those wonderful eyes. The Urreas had moved to El Paso, and after a time to Clifton, Arizona, where Teresita had died only this January, in her thirty-third year.

Five-year-old Chris had been remembering all of this, waiting in the courtyard for her some-kind-of-cousin to get ready for bed. When at last he called her, she hurried inside as Grande Talitha arrived with rich, cheesy corn soup, flan, and a big glass of milk.

"Feed myself," he told his great-aunt, who smiled and put the food tray on the table by the bed.

"You do that," she said. In his white nightshirt he looked like a wingless angel. Raven hair, skin a trifle darker than Chris's, startling blue-gray eyes. Gravely, Talitha shook his hand. "We want you very much, Sant. We feel very sad about your mama and daddy, but we'll try to do for you what they would have. We'll love you as they did. Tomorrow you can start knowing us, but for now I'll leave you with Chris." At Chris's whisper, she said of course a bed could be moved in, the men would do it now.

Then she was gone with an efficient whisk of skirts. Chris perched on the edge of the bed. "Start your soup while it's hot," she admonished. "And now I'll tell you about that cradleboard. Mangus Coloradas was a great chief . . ."

So Chris and Sant had grown up together, playing with the ranch children, sliding on and off burros, learning to use small *reatas,* reenacting the Earp-Clanton shoot-out at the O.K. Corral in Tombstone, or playing soldiers after Geronimo.

By the time Sant was six, he decided that he was too old to sleep in a girl's room and asked if he could live in Cruz's small adobe. Cruz, though he remained Chris's particular and watchful guardian, was glad to have Sant, though a somewhat jealous Chris remarked that they reminded her of Jack and the giant in the beanstalk story, for Cruz was some inches over six feet tall, and his broad chest was like a drum. He was a blacksmith and presided over the ranch smithy, hammering out everything from horseshoes to wheel rims and plows.

Chris and Sant had ridden together, helped work cattle, gentle horses. Sant could do all those things, but it was at setting bones, curing infected wounds, rubbing away headaches, and tending orphaned wild birds and animals as well as the ranch ones that Sant excelled.

Those who had known his father said Michael had been the same. Talitha taught him the Papago cures she'd learned from Tjúni, and what James had told her of Apache medicine. Cruz remembered some of his grandfather Nōnó's cures. The other ranch people were eager to share their favored *remedios* with young Santiago, named both for his grandfather, James, and the vaquero who had loved Socorro and who slept on the hill beside her. Talitha said his golden eyes looked out of Sewa's face.

Chris was glad to carry his blood in her, united at last with that of Socorro and Shea. She was proud, in fact, of all her blood: that of Talitha and Marc; Judith and Jared Scott; the Irish Don Patricio who must have been a gay and gallant man; Socorro's Spanish strain;

Santiago's mingled Apache, Opata, and Spanish. All had played their parts in this land of mountains and deserts, of high grass and luxuriant giant trees growing in watered cañons and along creeks and rivers.

After years of darkness, she could never see enough of trees, flowers, birds, people, horses and cattle of all colors, the graceful cats descended from Talitha's Chusma, brought by Santiago in Gold Rush days, or of changing light on mountains, near and distant, the far ones looking pink or pale blue or purple, soft, enchanted colors, though you knew that in reality they were harsh rock, here and there covered with a little earth and determined plants and trees that could dig in tightly to defy the wind and torrential rains, which after long droughts came down in fury that sluiced away the earth.

Even though Rancho del Socorro had been careful to shift its cattle from range to range, giving the grass time to reseed, it was no longer the deep, luxuriant growth older folk remembered. Cattle trails made channels for the heavy rains to erode. These grew into gullies, chisled deeper by each thunderstorm, down which the waters poured, carrying off good soil.

The San Pedro Valley to the west, once high with sacaton grass and pleasant groves of trees, was now a criss-cross of arroyos and mesquite thickets. This had happened in the lovely Verde Valley in the north. Droughts of the early '80s continuing into the '90s had caused cattle to eat the grass right down to the ground. With no rain and no time free of grazing, the range was devastated.

Then the rains came—in floods, torrents. But there was nothing to hold them, no small plants and grasses to suck them into the depleted earth. Instead, rivers, creeks, and gullies stripped the earth to its rock skeleton. The once rich, life-sustaining topsoil of grazing lands roiled down the Verde to the Salt and Gila, into the Colorado, and dumped into the Gulf of California.

Eighteen ninety-one saw the peak of the cattle industry in Arizona. The next year saw its disaster. An unusually severe drought and lack of water forced the sale of thousands of head and by summer of 1893, when a great panic in the east caused a punishing drop in beef prices, Arizona ranches lost half to 70% of their stock.

The Socorro lost less than most, having steadily reduced herds to fit the graze. Red and white Herefords grazed now where only only the tough little Mexican cattle, with a mix of curly-haired Texas *chinos,* had ranged. But the horses were still mostly descendants of those early ones Talitha had told Chris about—Shea's blue-gray stallion, Azul, Socorro's pretty chestnut, Castaña, Santiago's Noche, Talitha's beloved Ladorada—and some of the many burros had the doughty blood of Viejo, who'd survived the clawing of a mountain lion and killed it with his hoofs.

Chris smiled now, even as she sighed. Remembering her home, the family, ranch people and animals, the place of her grandparents and great grandparents, Chris felt a wave of desolation even as her eyes delighted in the play of the hawks. She belonged at Rancho del Socorro; at Los Robledos, she was one of El Senor's luxuries, not a necessary part of the place's functioning.

This gnawed at her as she walked slowly toward the big house, walled like a fortification on top of a small hill. If only Sant were here!

Suddenly, she could no longer deny how much she missed him. He'd been like a brother till that spring when Fayte stopped by the ranch on business and began coming as often as he could. He'd been there for her sixteenth birthday, celebrated by a barbecue and baile, attended by friends and neighbors from all over southern Arizona.

From first sight, she thought Fayte the most excitingly attractive man she'd ever met. When, accidentally, their hands brushed, sweet fire hummed through her. His gray gold eyes, unexpectedly encountered, made her stiffen with shock. She liked the ironic quirk of his mouth, the way his broad shoulders tapered to lean belly and flank. But he seemed quite old to her. The notion that he might watch her with the same interest she surreptitiously fixed on him had never entered her mind till he danced her away from the lights of the fires and lanterns.

"Mr. Riordan—"

"I want to talk to you without shouting."

Pausing by the ramada, he held both her hands. As her sight grew accustomed to the dimmer light, his eyes seemed to glow, filling her with tremulous delicious fear.

"Christina," he said softly, "I want to marry you."

XXII

She gasped. It was the first time he'd called her by her first name, even! "Why, I . . . I . . ."

He took her face between his long hands, laughing tenderly. "You haven't guessed? Come now, sweetheart, you can't think I've had that much business with your grandfathers!"

"I . . . I didn't think."

He made an impatient sound. His mouth found hers. He kissed her like that, hands still tilting up her head. She could feel him trembling, leashed male force fighting his control. This weakened her till she would have fallen if his arms hadn't closed tight around her, bringing her against the strange, lean hardness of his body, which turned her soft, made her melt. His kiss was no longer light, tentative, but hungry, pleading and, urgent.

He didn't touch her breasts with his hands, but they crushed against him as he pressed her so close that her nipples ached. Wild longing for relief made her cling to him, blinded, receiving him, craving more, all, of this new, delightful wonder.

At last, with a strangled breath, he lifted his head and stepped back, though he still supported her. "Oh, Lord, honey! I knew you'd be sweet, but—" Staring at her, his eyes darkened. "Would I be first?"

"First?"

His hands tightened impatiently. "Oh, not to kiss you. Any man would try for that and you couldn't stop him. But are you—has anyone—"

Flustered, he broke off as Chris angrily jerked free. "You mean, am I virgin? Are you?"

Dull red mounted to his tawny hair. "What the hell kind of a question is that?"

"You asked me."

"Damn it, girl, that's different! What kind of man could be twenty-six years old and never have had a woman?"

"I don't know," she said frostily. "But your question is insulting. If you want someone who'll certify her virginity to merit your proposal, you can look elsewhere."

His eyes narrowed. The curve of his nostrils whitened and the pulses hammered in his temples. "Looks to me like a girl would be proud to say she was pure."

She laughed cuttingly. "I don't see why she should say anything. Good night, Mr. Riordan."

She whirled and left him. The rest of the evening she flirted and laughed and danced, sparkling with vivacity powered by outrage.

Pure? Virgin? She was. She had never been kissed before, but she'd die before she'd tell him so. The important things about a man were bravery, good humor, the will to work for what was important, loyalty, tenderness, the ability to love and share and comfort. Surely these were what counted in a woman, too?

Talitha and Sewa had them in abundance; from what Chris had heard, so had Socorro and Caterina, So much proving hadn't been demanded of Aunt Vi or her own mother, Katie, but Chris was sure they possessed the strength of those other shining women, whose faith and courage glowed like lighted candles in her mind.

Virgin, indeed! Socorro and Talitha went ravished to

their marriage beds; Caterina was with child by James-Fierro when she married Jordan Scott. Their men had prized *them,* not a piece of membrane.

Sant didn't dance, but he sensed that she was exhausted, as he always seemed to know things about her. Bringing her lemonade, he made her sit down with him on one of the benches at the rim of the firelight.

"What's wrong, Chris?"

"Wrong?" She laughed brightly, though she couldn't meet his gaze. "Why, nothing! I'm having a lovely time!"

"You're angry. You've been that way ever since Fayte Riordan took you to the ramada."

Blood heated her face. "Sant! I never thought you'd spy on me?"

'I watch you." His voice was calm, as if he spoke to a petulant child, though he was a year the younger and for a very long time she had watched after him.

That had changed, she realized suddenly. When? Somehow, imperceptibly, in the past year or two, he'd begun to look after her—and she hadn't even noticed!

"I watch you," he said again. "Only in case you need me. Only in case you might get hurt. I don't spy."

She chuckled. Impossible to be out of the sorts with him. Touching his hand, she laughed and felt herself relaxing. "You're right, Sant. I was angry. But it just seems ridiculous now."

'What?"

"That Mr. Riordan asked what he did and that it made me so furious."

Sant's face went bleak, skin tightening over bone so that he looked suddenly all Apache. "Riordan . . . what did he ask?"

Close as she was to Sant, she was embarrassed to tell him. Besides, he looked in the mood to pick a fight. Well grown though he was, he was no match for a man in his early prime who'd grown up in mining camps.

"He asked me to marry him," she evaded.

Starting, Sant looked as if he'd been stabbed before

he controlled his face and looked at her intently. "That made you angry? I thought girls liked proposals even if they didn't want the man."

Chris sipped busily on her lemonade, then attempted to banter. "Now what would you know about girls, Sant?"

"Not much. But I know a lot about you."

"Well, there's nothing for you to look ireful about," she assured him. "I can handle Fayte Riordan."

"Are you going to? Marry him, I mean?"

"No!" Then she remembered that kiss, the ecstatic, tempting promise of Fayte's embrace, and felt her first tinge of regret for dismissing him so peremptorily. "That is," she finished lamely, "I . . . I don't think so."

"Chris, don't do it."

"Why?"

"He has a room of trophies. Grizzly, elk, bighorn, jaguar."

She closed her mind to that. Predators who took too many calves or colts had to be killed sometimes, but she always hated it. "What's that to do with me?" she asked.

Sant said grimly, "You'd be a trophy, too. In his bedroom."

She sprang to her feet. "I don't know why everyone's being horrid tonight!"

She'd seen no more of Fayte that night of her *baile*, but a week later he was back, leading a beautiful buckskin mare whose silver-mounted saddle glinted in the sunlight.

Chris had been watching Sant gentle a colt and turned from the corral at the sound of hoofs. Fayte Riordan swept off his soft gray hat and looked at her.

"Will you marry me, Christina Revier? Will you ride home with me on this mare I've brought for you?"

She stared up at him, trembling inwardly, feeling his gaze caress her as they both remembered. "Do you have any other questions?" she asked clearly.

"No."

She moved forward to stroke the mare's smooth withers. "Then I will marry you. If my parents agree."

"I've already talked to them. They said it was your decision." He laughed delightedly. "They'll be down from Phoenix for the wedding in a day or so. Preacher's coming, too."

"You were mightily sure of yourself!"

He grinned and swung down from his big black horse, giving the reins to a vaquero as he took her in his arms. "I've always been lucky."

When they moved apart, Sant was watching her with such stricken pain that she suddenly ached. She could understand that. If he were the one leaving, it would rend the fabric of her life. But they were growing up—she *was* grown up, almost married! She hated to leave the ranch, but women went with their husbands. In spite of this knowledge, in spite of her marriage, she was finding it hard, very hard, to make Fayte's home hers too. She sighed, diverting herself with stories in the sand: dainty leaflike tracks of a lizard, the tail mark of a kangaroo rat hopping along in its search for seeds, myriad quail prints. The angle and depth of the larger tracks cutting across the wash said a deer had run this way. On the slope a black-tailed jackrabbit froze, morning sun showing through his black-tipped long ears, blending perfectly with the sandy bank. Reassured by Chris's lack of menace, he bounded off through the grass. She knelt to examine some coyote droppings, crumbling them in her fingers.

Wild greens mixed with rabbit fur, the vertebrae of a snake, a few ventral scales, the fur of some kind of mouse or rat which might have, of course, been in the snake. Later in the summer coyotes could feast on mesquite beans and watermelons, special favorites, though they'd eat almost anything. Chris loved to hear them at night, shrill yip-yipping that often swelled from a lonely voice into a chorus. She was afraid that Fayte shot them any chance he got.

He was sure they killed newborn calves. Chris argued that most such victims were probably already dead or so weak they were dying. Her grandfather, Patrick, was certain eight rabbits ate as much as a cow and thus were really more of a threat to livestock than predators that kept them in check even if these occasionally did take a calf or kid.

Fayte dismissed her arguments, laughing indulgently as he drew her into his arms and kissed her. "I'm glad you have a tender heart, but suppose you just worry about me?" For a time, fresh-married, intoxicated with each other, such embraces had swept differences out of their minds.

Resting in their big bed, head burrowed into Fayte's shoulder, Chris would trace the lean planes of her husband's face, the joining of strong neck to collarbone, feast her eyes on the wonder of him, feeling blessed that she could see the long mouth, the smoky gold eyes beneath dark gold eyebrows. His skin was brown where sun touched it, his hair the golden dun of winter grama grass.

Tan and gold and brown he was, and she thrilled with joy and pride that he was hers; that she could touch him everywhere, make him gasp with delight, give him peace that drained hardness from his face and left him smiling as he slept, so that she could picture him as a little boy, the way he'd been before his parents died.

At eight Fayte had been shuffled from one set of reluctant, overcrowded relatives to another in various Colorado mining towns where the immigrant Riordans had found work. He ran off when he was eleven, not that anyone cared, and worked in liveries, mercantiles, restaurants, hotels, wherever he could find a place to sleep and earn enough to eat. In spite of his half-starved boyhood, he grew tall early, went to work in the mines when he was fifteen, saved his wages, and went prospecting with an old man who claimed he knew where there was silver.

The vein played out in a few years, but it gave Fayte

money to invest, and he bought into flamboyant Col. W. C. Greene's Cananea mining properties in northern Sonora. He was a working partner, though he spent most of his time on the huge ranch acquired from the heirs of Gen. Ignacio Pesqueira, who had been governor of Sonora most of the twenty years before he was forced from power in 1876.

Los Robledos, The Oak Grove, was a dream come true for the orphaned son of immigrants, a small kingdom where his word was law, altogether different from Rancho del Socorro where vaqueros ate with the family, where children of the workers and owners played and went to school together, addressed each other as familiars.

There was none of that at Los Robledos. The women who worked in the big house seemed to hurry to be through with their duties and return to their quarters. The kitchen was presided over by Lee Sung, who worked with his queue tied up around his head to keep it out of the food. He was devoted to Fayte, who'd rescued him from some rough handling back in Denver, but seemed merely to tolerate Chris. She felt excluded from her own kitchen.

Now, approaching her husband's house, she felt a great wave of longing for her family, especially for Sant. His words about her being Fayte's trophy came back with searing force.

Paralyzed by the intensity of her sense of uselessness, she stood still for a moment, gazing at the hills. Then she collected herself and breathed deep as if taking in courage from the sparkling air.

The house wouldn't be hers till she made it so. She was Fayte's wife, not his mistress. High time she acted like it instead of feeling sorry for herself!

Marching into the entry hall, she confronted the bighorn ram's head which was the first thing she'd seen when Fayte carried her proudly into his home. The great horns spiraled back, then curved around toward the front like an almost closed crescent moon. The glass eyes stared at her as she reached up to lift it from its iron peg.

What with the mounting slab, it was heavy. She stood there a moment, wondering what to do with it, then moved down the corridor to Fayte's study. A conquistador's helmet, picked up somewhere in New Mexico, hung between two windows. Setting it carefully on a couch, she put the bighorn in its place, stood back, and thought it fitted the space quite well. She hung the helmet in the entry, nodded with satisfaction, and went back to the kitchen.

"I want to make some panocha," she told Lee Sung, who was deftly chopping vegetables with a long knife. "The wheat has to be sprouted first, of course, so I'll just put it to soak."

His voice frowned, though his face was expressionless. "Missy say what she want, I fix."

"Thanks, Lee Sung, but I like to cook sometimes." She smiled, trying to soften him. "I won't get in your way."

"Better one person cook, missy."

"Please show me where the wheat is."

Chris thanked him for his help when he was done and went to Fayte's big bedroom—she still couldn't think of it as hers, too—feeling exhilarated. How silly she'd been, waiting and hoping to feel at home here without doing things to make it so!

Tomorrow she'd go about setting up a little school for the ranch children where she could teach a few hours a day. Fayte had discouraged it when she had wanted to try it earlier. He thought education only made workers discontented and ready to quarrel with their employers. His life had, understandably, hardened him. It was up to her to make him kinder, more trusting. Anyway, how could she expect him to treat her like a woman when she let him dominate her as if she were a not particularly bright child?

She rang the bell four times, the signal that bath water should be brought to the chamber attached to

Fayte's room. It opened on the inner patio and could be serviced from the kitchen.

It was the one thing at Los Robledos of which Chris thoroughly approved. An immense copper tub sat on a tiled dais near a long tiled shelf holding French soaps, lotions, brushes, thick towels, and washcloths. One whole side was mostly window, looking into a small garden separated from the main patio by a wall so that it was utterly private except for the birds that came to drink at the fountain where a nymph perpetually eluded a sea god though he had one hand on her shoulder. A pomegranate grew in this protected space, its trumpetlike brilliant red flowers changing almost perceptibly into fruit, and passionflowers and jasmine covered the walls.

Stripping off her dusty walking skirt and high-necked blouse, she tossed them in the hamper with her daintily embroidered camisole and drawers, slipped on a robe, and entered the bathroom. As if by magic, the tub was nearly filled with warm water and a clean mat was placed beside the tub. Tossing the robe to a wicker chair, Chris tied her hair up and stepped into the water, lowering herself with a sigh of contentment, adding a splash of the scented bath oil Fayte himself enjoyed.

He liked her to wear pretty, comfortable clothes for dinner, which they ate in the big dining room with Lee Sung serving. The wine was served in crystal goblets and the serving pieces were of heavy beaten silver.

She was rinsing soap from herself when Fayte came through the door, closed it, and lounged back, arms crossed. Though he was her husband, loved to see her naked, and had made her proud of her body, under his smoky golden stare she suddenly wanted to hide herself. She felt a chill go up her spine.

"I take it you decided to do some rearranging, my love. I should have told you I like things where I have them."

Stung by her fear as much as by the lazy admonishment, she cradled her knees to her breasts. "Then perhaps you shouldn't have married me! I can't stand looking at that ram every time I come inside. I don't feel at home here at all; it's your house, not mine!" She paused for breath. 'I'm making panocha tomorrow, and I'm going to start a school and—and if that damned bighorn can't hang someplace but the entry, I'm going home!"

His eyes narrowed. He came a step closer. "That's rather mixed, Christina. But one thing's certain. You are home."

"I don't feel like it. I don't *do* anything, I'm just here!"

Unable to bear the way his gaze traveled over her, she stood up, in the same motion covering herself with a towel. "If you want everything to stay where it was before I came, if what I want doesn't matter to you, then I'd better go away!"

In one long stride he was beside her. "You're my wife. You're not going anywhere."

He ripped the towel from her, flung it down, and lifted her out of the tub. Standing her on the mat, he dried her roughly; then, catching her up in his arms, he carried her in to their bed and almost threw her across it.

He kicked off his boots, undid his belt. Chris sprang off the bed on the opposite side and ran for the door, but he caught her and held her with one hand while he finished shucking off his clothes. When he put her on the bed again, he pinioned her hands above her head, lifted her hips with his free hand, and plunged into her.

It was the first time he'd taken her without wooing, caressing, kissing, nipping and fondling and teasing till she could scarcely wait for him. It hurt. He seemed to batter at her. She writhed and fought, afraid of being broken, afraid of this stranger.

Then that crescendo. For a second he seemed to hang frozen above her as she felt that violent pulsing of his seed. A shudder racked him. Usually the force and passion of his loving awed her, made her feel tender, almost pitying, as it drained to leave him quiet, peaceful in her arms. This time, frightened and aching from his assault, she tried to get up when he collapsed beside her, but he pinned her with his knee and long arm, pulled her head to his shoulder.

"My dear little wife, if you don't know where you belong, I'm certainly going to teach you!"

She lay stiff, frightened and angry, aching where he'd rammed her, though the worst pain and confusion was in her mind. How could he love her and treat her like that?

Shocked, humiliated, she wanted to get away where she could weep out her hurt and disillusionment, but he began to stroke her with his long, skillful hands, fondling, kneading the places where her muscles tensed against him. He nuzzled her breasts in that way that reminded her of a deer feeding sweetly in a grassy meadow, worshiped her so ardently with his lean, strong man's body that she soon wanted him in spite of everything, opened to him with a cry of supplication.

He took her in a way that soothed the earlier hurt, lifting her with him to a wild turbulence that swirled them into an ecstacy so powerful it left them drained, light, tender in each other's arms.

"I love you," he murmured against her throat. "Little witch, if it disturbs you so, the mount can hang in my study. You're my real prize."

He rang for more water, bathed her himself this time, rubbed lotions into her flesh with loving possessiveness. Happy at their renewed closeness, she told herself she should have asked to move the bighorn, should have handled the whole thing better.

She had learned; so had he. Now she must learn to be the mistress of Los Robledos, just as she must become Fayte's wife as well as his sweetheart.

He was quick with his bath and was dressed by the time she had brushed her hair. "Don't pin it up," he said, coming up behind her, his smile reflected in the huge plate-glass mirror, fingers lifting the thick waves of burnished auburn. "Tie it back with that dark green velvet ribbon that matches your eyes." He laughed, trailing his hand along her shoulder. "Skin of gold, emerald eyes, bronze hair—you're most unusual, my love."

She shrugged as she tied back the unruly mass. "There's red hair in my family, and yellow, brown, and black. Mix Yaqui, Irish, Scots, Apache, Spanish, German, and Mexican, and I suppose you could get all kinds of results."

"I like your result!" he said. They smiled at their handsome reflections in the mirror, kissed, and went hand in hand down the corridor.

If Chris put her mind to it, she could explain when copper had become a giant force in industry and finance. Edison had invented his electric lamp in 1879 and the use of copper power lines had greatly increased the need for the ore. Engines, automobiles, farm machinery, pipe, engraving plates, telephones, and telegraphs raised world production of copper from 4,000 metric tons in the 1830s to 240,000 in the '80s.

Chris could remember when electric lights and a telephone were installed at the Socorro and when, last year, her father and mother had driven home from Phoenix in the first automobile to park near the corral and alarm the horses. In spite of all her son's urging, Talitha had refused to set foot in the shiny Packard.

"Yes, I know they're making flying machines, and I suppose these wretched snorting monsters will clutter up the roads till a horse can't travel," she said. "But thank heaven I'm old enough not to have to learn to live with such 'progress.' I'd rather remember Mangus and old Fort Buchanan and how it was to ride to Tubac for Colonel Poston's parties."

Poston had died in 1902, living his last months on a small pension voted him by the Arizona legislature. So many were gone. Pete Kitchen, his ranch sold after the coming of the railroad, his fortune melted, had died in

1895; William Oury died in 1886, less than a year after defending the Camp Grant Massacre before the Society of Arizona Pioneers.

It was a new century, a new world, and copper was needed to build its machines and conduct its electricity. Fayte's partner, Colonel Greene, paid the highest wages in Sonora at his mines, but lately there'd been rumors of discontent, and as Lee Sung served dinner Fayte did what he seldom would; he aired his worries.

"Our Mexicans have always been happy with their wages till some of the Western Federation of Miners men came in and started stirring them up. Hell, they get three pesos a day—several times what they can get for ranch or other work!"

"But don't *norteamericanos* get five dollars a day, U.S. money?" asked Chris. "With a peso worth fifty cents, that means the Mexicans get less than a third of Yankee pay."

"It's what they're worth."

"Oh? Then how come Cruz made a coil spiral spring that kept the self-feeders behind the batteries going when your expensive American mechanic who gets paid five times as much could only turn out springs that broke in half an hour?"

"Somehow Cruz figured out that by hammering the drill steel and tempering it with fish oil, he could make forged steel, which is what springs are made of," said Fayte. "No one gave him more credit for that than McAllen, our American mechanic."

"But McAllen still draws his big salary, while Cruz gets four pesos a day."

Fayte made an exasperated sound. "For top production we need Americans in key places. We can't get them without paying premium wages. Governor Izabal flatly told us early in May, with backing from Díaz, that we must lower wages by fifty centavos a day because our scale was throwing the economy out of balance and the ranchers and farmers were screaming."

"A bad time to cut wages, just before Cinco de

Mayo." That was the great patriotic festival which celebrated the Mexican victory over the French at Puebla that had brought the collapse of Maximilian's puppet regime.

"The radicals played on it. They made a lot of inflammatory speeches and that new Marxist rag, *El Centenario,* reported them."

"I read the text of some of the speeches. They didn't say anything that wasn't true. It's not right for foreigners to make huge profits here and pay workers next to nothing."

Fayte's eyes narrowed. "We pay the highest wages in Mexico. We'd pay a bit more, probably, if the government permitted."

"It's a bad government!" Trembling, Chris remembered the burning church at Tomochic, the faces of the women and children glimpsed before her world went dark.

"Díaz has got factories and railroads by encouraging foreign investments. He knows that's the only way to bring Mexico out of the dark ages."

"It's still the dark ages for workers. They can be virtually enslaved for debt and their children inherit the burden. As for what's been done to the Yaquis, no words can describe it. Mexicans and gringos want their fertile bottomlands, so they're being killed or shipped off to slave labor in Yucatan."

During the government's efforts to subdue the fiercely independent Yaquis, a number of Grande Sewa's and Grande Tía Juri's relatives had refuged on the Socorro or found work at the San Patricio. Others had taken rifles and gone back to hide out in the Sierra Bacatete and harass the soldiers.

Fayte shrugged. "God knows how much drill steel they've pilfered to make into machetes, knives and arrow points for war. Savages can't be allowed to raid and plunder at will."

"The Yaquis only want to be left in peace to farm the lands their prophets and angels sang for them."

"Your Yaqui blood is showing," Fayte teased. Rising, he came around the big table and caressed her shoulders as he kissed her. "Come, love, let's have an early night. Colonel Greene wants me down at the Oversight mine early in the morning."

Alarm shot through her. "Why?"

"Oh, there's talk of a strike. But the mayor's on our side, and the judge and justice of the peace. I think they'll talk sense into the men. All the same, stay out of Cananea tomorrow."

"Can't something be done about the workers' grievances? Even if wages can't be raised, the company store could sell things cheaper, and the houses could be improved. Or—"

"The prices at the company store are lower than at any mine in Mexico," Fayte said, jaw thrust forward. Drawing her to her feet, he put his arm about her, and as soon as they were out of Lee Sung's sight he swept her off her feet.

"I can't get enough of you," he said huskily, burying his face in her hair as he kicked open their door and strode to the bed. "My wild little sweet one, I'll never get enough of you!"

He loved her hungrily, as if it were the first time. When by the time they lay deliciously spent and drowsy, she decided it would be best not to irritate him by bringing up the rumored strike again that night. She fell asleep in her husband's arms, feeling safe, cherished, protected.

When she woke in the morning, he was gone.

XXIII

Chris spent an uneasy morning, though she made panocha and began an herb garden in the courtyard. Usually she was glad Los Robledos was cut off from a view of Cananea by the mountains but today she wished she could see what was going on. The skies above the mines were clear, not hazed and plumed with the usual smoke from the smelter. No distant sound of trains or mule packers drifted through the quiet hot morning of the first day of June, 1906.

Fayte didn't come home at noon. When Lee Sung asked if Chris would have her meal alone, she couldn't bear it anymore, not knowing what was happening.

"Thank you, Lee Sung," she said. "I think I'll walk toward town to meet my husband. He should be along any minute."

Lee Sung scowled. "Mister Fayte tell missy stay here."

"I'm just going to meet him."

"Mister Fayte say—"

"I know what he said."

Turning sharply from the disapproving cook, she took her straw hat from a rack behind the door. On impulse, she collected some of Sant's old clothes she sometimes rode in, and went out into the dazzling light, taking a cow trail around the mountain to save time.

She walked briskly in spite of the heat. Within twenty minutes, the tall smokestacks came in view, and the two-story house of Colonel Greene, clapboard with wide porches. Chris scarcely glanced toward it.

A group of flag-carrying workers was moving toward the lumberyard. She was too far away to be certain, but the man standing in front of the closed gate gripping a big fire hose looked like George Metcalf, manager of the lumber works, and that was surely his brother beside him.

Chris couldn't hear what was said as she hurried forward, but she saw a blast of water hit the workers. They rushed the men at the gate. Rifles barked. Three workers went down, the rest surged forward. The Metcalfs lay still when the men stabbing them finally rose from their bodies.

Frozen, Chris stood on the slope while the fire and blood of Tomochic clouded her vision. Where was Fayte? Had the workers already killed him? Had he killed some of them?

Some of the workers gathered up their dead, while others set fire to the lumberyard. The sight of real flames cleared the blinding haze from Chris's eyes. The workers, carrying their dead, were moving toward the town hall. Chris kept north of them, desperately watching Greene's house. She couldn't guess at the number of strikers, but it must have been several thousand.

Greene's two autos tore through the thick crowds at unbelievable speed, scattering people in every direction, and stopped at his house. The portly, mustached colonel ran up the veranda and emerged with a rifle and several armed men at the same time that about forty company employees from the bank and store, heavily armed, made their way to the mansion, along with the water-hose cart.

Fayte was beside Greene and got into one of the autos with him while several other company men got in the other. Apparently Greene hoped to check the mob at the bridge, but by the time the vehicles got there, the crowd had already passed.

The autos spun about, careened up the street, stopped in the vacant lots in front of the Greene house. Fayte, the colonel, and the others jumped out, ranging themselves with the other company men to confront the strikers, who were now past the jail and surging up the principal street, led by a man carrying a red flag.

A company man grappled with the leader. A striker fired, Greene shot one of the leaders, and Fayte and the others opened fire. Three more strikers fell.

The mob scattered, some making for the jail. Greene signaled his men to the house.

Fayte saw Chris then. Shifting his rifle, he ran toward her, caught her wrist, and hustled her into the house, where Mary Greene, the colonel's lovely young wife, was trying to calm several hysterical American women.

Eyes a tawny blaze, Fayte rasped, "What are you doing here?"

"I—I was worried when you didn't come home."

"So now you're where I have to worry about you on top of those damned red-flaggers!" Fayte's grasp pained her arm. "Stay inside, hear? And don't come out unless the house starts to burn. If those strikers get hold of some dynamite they could wreck the whole town."

Greene called for volunteers to go guard the jail so the police could try to control the strikers. Fayte went with this detachment. Greene's men were well armed because the night before, warned of the strike, he'd ordered a passenger car and engine to take him to Bisbee, where he collected all the guns at the Copper Queen store—ninety-eight rifles and twenty pistols—and ammunition. Getting back to Cananea about four in the morning, he'd passed out the weapons to his most trusted employees. He'd also sent a messenger to Hermosillo, the Sonoran capital, to urge Governor Izábal to send troops.

Telegraph wires hummed messages to President

Roosevelt, the Secretary of State, and the commander at Fort Huachuca. If help came, it would have to be from across the border in the United States. Mexican troops were stationed at Magdalena, as were Emilio Kosterlitzky's feared and famed *rurales,* but it would take them several days to reach Cananea. Colonel Greene phoned Walter Douglas, manager of the Copper Queen mine at Bisbee who got the Bisbee marshal to ask for volunteers.

While news of various appeals for help buzzed through the Greene mansion, shooting echoed in the streets. The strikers had broken into pawnshops and taken guns and ammunition. Some drunken American cowboys got on the roof of the hotel and fired at anything that moved, from chickens to their own countrymen.

Late that afternoon Fayte came wearily in. "Twenty more of the bastards dead and dozens in jail," he said, gulping the coffee Chris brought him. "A train's taking the women and kids to Bisbee tonight. You'd better go."

She stared at his haggard face, stepped to one side so that she could hold his head against her without anyone noticing. "I won't leave you."

Stiffening, he drew away from her. "You'll do as you're told." He wolfed down some bread and meat before he went down to the streets.

Mary Greene touched Chris's arm. "I can lend you some clothes and a suitcase, dear. It'll only be for a few days."

"Thank you," said Chris, choosing to avoid argument. As soon as the colonel's gentle wife moved off to comfort a sobbing young bride, Chris quietly made her way to the back of the big house and slipped out. If she were at Robledos when the refugee train left for Arizona, Fayte would probably let her stay.

Her thoughts were a welter as she made her way down the hill to the valley that led home. The smoke from the lumberyard lingered in her nostrils as the sight of men dying haunted her inner vision. The Metcalfs had been stabbed to death with the sharp, pointed ends of miners' candlesticks.

The strikers, by force of numbers, might kill all the Americans, but when the troops and *rurales* arrived, there'd be such bloody vengeance that Chris shuddered from the thought.

Cruz had miner friends, even some relations. She'd tell him what was going on, ask if he'd try to reason with the men. She found the giant Tarahumare in the smithy, hammering out a prospector's pick. Fayte swore the ones Cruz made from ⅞-inch bars of drill steel were the best to be had and would outlast any number of commercially manufactured ones.

Face broadening in a smile, the barrel-chested Indian put down his hammer, then sobered as he read her distress. "Doña Christina, what is wrong?"

She told him quickly. Before she had finished, he reached for his shirt. "I'll talk to my cousins and friends. Maybe the fighting can be stopped before anything worse happens."

"Don't you need your rifle?"

"I'm not going to shoot anyone."

That simplicity made the giant seem dangerously vulnerable. "Let me go with you," Chris said.

"Doña Christina! It is not possible."

"Not for Señora Riordan, perhaps, but—one moment, Cruz!"

It took her only a few minutes to shake out Sant's old trousers and shirt, pull them on, stuff her hair up into her hat. The clothes were baggy enough to disguise betraying curves. Cruz gave her a look of dismay when she rejoined him, but she tugged at his arm.

"Let's go!"

They went the other way around the mountain. The lumberyard was still burning. A group of armed men, still in their Sunday suits, begrimed now, some of them bloody, were making for the smelter.

"There's Jorge," breathed Cruz. "Stay here,

señora!" Striding forward, he called out, "Cousin!" just as one of Greene's autos plummeted in front of the men, blocking their way.

It all must have happened in seconds, though to Chris, watching as the setting sun glanced off rifle barrels, it seemed to happen in eternity, in a timeless moment when she tried to scream and nothing would come from her throat.

Fayte was one of the men taking aim. His rifle pointed at Cruz, and his eyes must have been as they were when he killed an animal. A fusillade rang out. Bullets spun men around, sent them staggering. Cruz flung up his great arms as he pitched backward. As the unhurt strikers fled Chris ran toward him and fell on her knees.

Blood pumped from a great hole in Cruz's back. She tore off her shirt, trying to stuff it into the wound, even as he whispered her name.

Then his blood was the blood of Tomochic, the lumberyard blaze the burning church, before both swirled into blackness.

She couldn't see, but she could hear. From the whispers of the servants, she learned that over two hundred Bisbee volunteers had crossed the border Saturday morning and offered their services to Governor Izábal, who waited on the other side, having made an all-night trip from Hermosillo. General Torres swore the men into the Mexican forces, and they were soon on their way to Cananea.

When the train pulled in, Greene raised a cheer for the governor, though none of the townsfolk joined in. Apart from their dead and imprisoned men, it was a blow to their pride to see the Sonoran governor jump at Greene's whistle. The volunteers marched to the smelter, and Greene and the governor made an inspection by auto.

By noon, the crowd had swelled. Izábal tried to speak, but the crowd shouted him down with their grievances. Greene spoke next, telling the men he was their friend and had always tried to treat them fairly, paying them as much as he could.

He had no answer, though, to satisfy the repeated question of the murmuring crowd: Why didn't he pay Mexicans the same wages as Americans?

The Bisbee volunteers got back on the train and stayed there till Colonel Kosterlitzky rode in at sunset with his *rurales*. He sent word to all parts of town that anyone, Mexican or American, found on foot in the streets after dark would be shot. He also told the Bisbee men he could handle things, and by ten that night the volunteers had left for Arizona without having fired a shot.

On Sunday Colonel Greene went around the camps, urging the men to go back to work. He also let it be known that he knew who the Western Federation of Miners organizers were, and that they would be arrested. About three hundred union members left town. Meanwhile, Kosterlitzky searched out a score of the *huelguista* leaders and jailed them. He also reinforced Greene's invitation to the men to go to work by saying that those who didn't would be drafted into the army and sent to fight Yaquis. Next morning, all the men who were not dead, jailed, or union organizers were back at work.

But Chris still could not see. She lay in the big bed and drank thirstily, though she refused food. When Fayte forced some broth between her clenched teeth, she vomited it.

"I want to go home," she said, speaking for the first time. She had heard Fayte, the doctor, the Greenes, talking to her before but had not been able to make the effort to answer.

Fayte wiped her face with a cold cloth. "You are home." He sat down, drew her into his arms. "You're not really blind, sweetheart. You can see again when you make up your mind to."

"I never want to see your face again."

His body went rigid. "Cruz had no business down there."

"He went to try to persuade the strikers to stop fighting."

"How in hell could we know that?" Fayte's hands tightened. He gave her a shake. "Damn it, you could have been killed! If you hadn't pulled off your shirt—"

"I want to go home."

His breath sucked in. His weight lifted from the bed; she heard the door closing. Then he stripped away the sheet and roughly pulled off her gown. He took her like a storm, willing her to respond to him, kissing, caressing, handling her first roughly, then with patience, but she endured his passion and gentleness alike.

When he was through, when he lay spent, head on her breast, she felt a certain grief for him, but it couldn't erase the way he'd looked as he fired into the men. He'd recognized Cruz. But he hadn't given him a chance to say why he was there.

Teresita! she thought, and tried to call up the *santa*'s face. But there was only darkness.

When the doctor came again, and told her she must eat and build up her strength, she said she wished to go back to the Socorro.

After the doctor left, she heard him arguing with Fayte, giving his opinion that she would recover much better in her childhood home. "She's young and delicate, Mr. Riordan," said the physician. "I understand your reluctance to send her away, but I believe the sooner you do, the sooner she'll be restored. She's not maliciously refusing to eat. Her body is rejecting nourishment because, temporarily, she has no will to live."

"That's crazy!"

"It's my best advice, Mr. Riordan."

"I won't let her go! Damn it, she's my wife!"

Chris felt separated from it, as if they were talking

about a stranger. Still, tears squeezed through her eyelids before she drifted into the sleep that seemed always to be waiting.

Sant was there. She knew his hands closing warm and strong over hers before his voice touched her like balm. "Chris. Are you all right?"

She couldn't answer, but she gripped his hands more tightly. If only she could see him. . . . Why had she ever married Fayte, why had she left Socorro? Cruz would still be alive if he hadn't followed her.

Fayte's tone was harsh. "You're upsetting her, boy. The doctor says there's nothing the matter but female hysterics."

Chris clung desperately to Sant and was grateful when he made no move to withdraw. "Maybe she should come home for a while. Grande Talitha's worried about her."

"My wife is staying where she belongs, in my house."

Chris struggled up, so weak she fell back immediately. "I want to go home! I want Talitha!" *I want Sant.*

"I'll get better doctors," Fayte said stubbornly. "I'll do anything to cure you, but you're not leaving."

"I won't be married to you anymore, Fayte. If you keep me here, I won't eat."

"You don't know what you're saying!"

"I do. Whatever the law says, I haven't been your wife since you fired at Cruz."

"Christina!"

She turned her face from the sound of his voice. "Get yourself another trophy. Someone to decorate your house and be an admirable Señora Riordan."

His tone thickened with outrage. "You can't forget your damned family, can you? Revier y O'Shea! You've always belonged more to them than to me!"

"Their blood is mine. I'm proud of it."

"Prouder than of being my wife?"

"I'm not your wife anymore."

Fayte drew in a shuddering breath. "No use talking to you now; you're not responsible. Go home with your cousin. In a few weeks, I'll come to see you."

Drained, she didn't argue further. He was holding himself on a tight rein and might release his anger on Sant. He rang for the women to help her dress and pack.

"The *señora* requires only enough for a few weeks," Fayte told them, and again she didn't protest. To be free of him, free of this house, that was what mattered.

Sant had brought Miguel's Packard. Fayte carried her to it, crushed her against him for a long moment. His mouth bruised hers. "Get well, my love. I'll see you soon."

But I will not see you.

"Good-bye, Fayte."

With all her will, she fought back tears till Sant had turned the auto and they were a distance down the road. Then she wept.

Back at the Socorro, her sight returned slowly as she talked with Talitha and her family and went around the place with Sant patiently guiding her. First she saw dim shapes, then the light behind them; then distinctness increased till she saw as well as ever.

When she remembered Cruz falling, the bleeding wound she couldn't staunch, blackness welled up again, but Sant helped her through those times, holding her, touching her eyes with his hands.

So she could see her husband when he came early in July, a month after the strike, driving one of Colonel Greene's autos. He was lean, somehow ragged-looking in spite of his expertly tailored clothes.

"Christina!" His eyes glowed as he sprang up on the veranda and took her in his arms. "You're all right! You can see!"

"Yes." She pitied him, couldn't believe she'd ever loved him, ever hungered for his touch.

"Wonderful! We can go home tomorrow." He smiled

at Talitha, Miguel, Juri, Patrick, and Sewa, who had all been enjoying the evening view of the mountains. "You've been good medicine for my wife. I can't thank you enough."

Patrick, Chris's grandfather, got to his feet, his thick mass of red hair only lightly veined with gray. "Sorry, Fayte, but—we thought you understood. Our lawyer's started divorce proceedings."

Fayte's arms tightened convulsively around Chris before he pushed her away, eyes blazing like a cornered mountain lion's. "The O'Shea lawyer will get the divorce because there's a Revier in the state legislature and your family's been here forever and owns half of southern Arizona! Isn't that right? A latecomer from Colorado who lives in Mexico might as well keep his mouth shut!"

The earlier trace of embarrassed apology left Patrick's voice. "A big public show isn't to anyone's interest, Fayte, but if you want to try to keep a woman who doesn't want you, go ahead. Just let me say that whatever the court decides, Chris stays where she wants to be."

For a terrible moment Chris thought Fayte would draw the revolver he wore buckled to his waist. His hand paused above it, then dropped heavily. Ignoring the others, he looked at Chris. Her heart wailed for the pain in his face, but there was no way back to him.

Between them lay Cruz, dead men who'd wanted only to be paid as much as Americans, and, in an obscure but intensely felt way for Chris, the murdered of Tomochic who'd died for their rights.

Not fair, perhaps, or rational. Fayte wasn't an evil man. But he craved riches, and to gain them he was willing to see other human beings simply as machinery, to be maintained as cheaply as possible, and scrapped when they were worn out or broken down.

"This is what you want?" His voice was a whisper.

Tears brimmed to her eyes. She nodded silently.

He turned without a word. When he was gone, she

went into Talitha's arms and cried till she was empty, light as a dead leaf.

She hadn't seen him again. Cananea had been one of the sparks that blazed into the still raging conflagration of the Mexican revolution.

Eleven years later, Chris still felt as if there were a small empty hollow in her heart, though she was usually too busy to notice it. Not only did she teach the Bisbee miners' children through the week, but on Saturdays, and several days a week through the summer, she took them walking, trying to show them what wonderful plants and creatures lived in the desert and how they managed to survive.

On this day in early June, up Tombstone Canyon, she had shown them how cacti grew under nurse plants which protected them while they were small, though the cacti might later grow up through the tree's limbs and even flourish after it was dead. There'd been a pack rat's nest under a vast clump of prickly pear, and Chris had told the wide-eyed youngsters how he was an ornery old bachelor who lived alone except when mating. Females were solitary also, except when rearing young.

"You're sol'tary, too, Miss Revier," blurted Sulev, one of the Slovak children. "You ever goin' to rear any young?"

She laughed in spite of a pang and tousled his yellow hair. "You take all my energy! And I guess I am about as cantankerous as the grouchiest old pack rat."

He squeezed her hand shyly, letting it go before any of the other children could notice. "You're not *real* grouchy, Miss Revier. And on Saturdays you're not like a grown up at all."

Most of the foreign-born miners were Mexican or Slav, but Chris taught Cornish, Irish, Swedish, Austrian, and Italian youngsters, too. The mixture made for colorful holidays. Last month the Cinco de Mayo dance had been held in the Pythian Castle just two days after the Day of the Holy Cross when Mexicans marched up Brewery Gulch to a cross on the hill. Serb and Polish members of the Greek Orthodox Church celebrated January 7 as Christmas and St. Savo's birthday on January 27. In spite of this mingled population, no Chinese were allowed in town. The local laundries wanted no competition and that was the business Chinese often went into. Chris had spoken against this to the mayor and various other leading citizens, who either looked blank or reminded her that such emotionalism was the reason why women had still not been given the vote.

Near Castle Rock they stopped to watch leaf-cutter ants stripping a small tree and carrying the severed bits to their hill where the stored leaves would mold and provide food. Thousands of workers streamed in and out of the hill that might be sixteen to eighteen feet deep. Chris found their industry depressing, though marvelous. No time for play or meandering or friendship, just a round of mechanical labor to ensure the continuance of the colony.

"Remind you of something, lady?"

Startled, for she'd heard no steps, she looked up into a face paler than most one saw in this sunny region. Rebellious chestnut hair curled close to the young man's skull, looking as if it had been hewed off with a knife. His mouth turned down like a wing, bittersweet, and deep gray eyes watched her as a wild thing peers out from its stronghold. He wore work shoes, faded Levi's, and a blue shirt, and his flesh hadn't caught up to his height yet, so that his bony wrists and frame gave an impression of immaturity belied by mouth and eyes. He had a guitar slung over his shoulder.

"I—I was wondering if that's how people look to God."

His mouth quirked. "I'm not God, but that's how the main lot of people look to me. Except they don't always even get their food and a place to shelter. They store up riches for their bosses while they get just enough to keep them going. When they can't go anymore, they're kicked out."

Was he one of the IWW organizers who'd brought on the strike at Jerome late in May? The United Verde workers had been granted the Miami scale of wages, $5.25 a day for underground work, and had voted to go back to work, though the closed shop still demanded by the Industrial Workers of the World and the Western Federation of Miners had been denied. Several men had been killed, but the violence at Jerome seemed mostly over. Was it moving here?

"Phelps-Dodge pays good wages," she told the young man.

He laughed sardonically. "Is that what you teach these kids?"

"Of course not! I teach them arithmetic, grammar, spelling, science, history—"

"Ah, history!" Rocking back on his heels, he eyed her mockingly. "What do you give the poor little devils? Magna Carta and George Washington? That Arizona became a state in 1912 on Valentine's Day? I bet you don't say what happened to the Indians!"

"You'd bet wrong!" Turning to Sulev, Chris said, "Please tell this man about Cochise and Mangus Coloradas."

Sulev did, adding that Geronimo, of coyote power, who could make the dark last while he stole upon his enemies, had died in Oklahoma, but that in 1913 the Chiricahua prisoners of war were allowed to either take up land in Oklahoma or move to the Mescalero reservation in New Mexico. "They could have had their old lands around Warm Springs," the boy added, "but when the leaders traveled back to look at them, the grass was gone and it wasn't the good place they remembered."

Chris glanced challengingly at the stranger, who had stopped grinning and was watching her with surprise.

"How can you get away with that in this part of the country?"

"It's history." Chris knew that her family's prestige tempered the criticism she got. "Some of these children's parents went to the first school in a miner's shack above Castle Rock. When the whistle blew for a possible Indian attack, they followed their teacher into the mine tunnel to hide. My students hear plenty of that."

He watched her, still with that disbelief that somehow pleaded to be convinced. Half under his breath, he said, "Have they heard about Joe Hill?"

She shrank from the name. Who hadn't heard of Joe Hill, Joel Hagglund, and four bullets fired into his heart by the State of Utah, in November 1915? He had been executed over the pleas of President Woodrow Wilson, the Swedish minister, Helen Keller, and many who felt he was being killed for his ardent support of the Wobblies, the IWW, rather than for a double murder of a shopkeeper and his son for which there was only the flimsiest circumstantial evidence.

Too cruel, too close, too bloody. She couldn't teach it yet, though she could now tell the older students about Cananea and weep only in her heart.

The stranger shook his head. "You haven't told them." He unslung his guitar, leaned up against a rock, tuned the instrument, and began to sing, smiling at the children in a way that drew them close, as if he were about to share a secret.

"'The copper bosses killed you, Joe,
They shot you, Joe,' says I.
'Takes more than guns to kill a man,'
Says Joe, 'I didn't die.'
Says Joe, 'I didn't die.'

"And standing there as big as life
And smiling with his eyes,
Joe says, 'What they forgot to kill

Went on to organize,
Went on to organize.'"

He finished the song in a clear, haunting voice that brought tears prickling back of Chris's eyes, threw back his head, pulled a mock long face, and began a song she knew, a parody written by Hill.

"Long-haired preachers come out every night,
Try to tell you what's wrong and what's right;
But when asked how 'bout something to eat
They will answer with voices so sweet:

You will eat, bye and bye,
In that glorious land above the sky;
Work and pray, live on hay,
You'll get pie in the sky when you die."

By the time he finished that song, the children were singing the chorus with him. Then he glanced at Chris for just a second before he half closed his eyes, lashes fringing his cheeks in a way that gave him a boyish, vulnerable look.

"Who's goin' to be your man tonight,
Who's goin' to be your man?
You walk the streets in a yaller gown,
Sayin', 'Who's goin' to be my man?'"

Chris wore a yellow dress. She couldn't take her eyes from his fingers, long, skillful, bringing such music. A slow, warm trembling ran through her.

Play me—touch me, oh, tune me, the way you do the strings. It was years since she'd wanted a man. The sudden violence of her desire terrified her.

"We have to go, children," she said. "Good day to you, sir. You play very well."

He rose with a last caress of his guitar and bowed. "May I see you home?"

"There's no need."

"My need." His look was disarming, and his tone laughingly burlesqued. "I'm hungry, pretty lady. Won't you give a poor wanderer something to eat?"

Her heart seemed to stop. She was feverish and icy at once. "I'll find something for you."

By ones and twos, the children left them. They passed the Warner Hotel, the YMCA, and moved up Opera Drive past the school to the small house where Chris lived alone, except for Nicodemus, her handsome, green-eyed black cat.

At the door, she turned in sudden fear. What was she doing? She knew nothing about this man, except that he was surely IWW, a man of trouble. His eyes met hers steadily. The slight smile vanished, replaced by a bleak hunger, a loneliness and desolation so strong she experienced it physically.

"Pretty lady."

"What's your name?" she asked desperately. As if it might be a magic, a means to conjure him away, break free of this . . .

"Johnny Chance."

He was younger than she, but taller. His thin body blocked the sun. She opened the door. He stepped in behind her and took her in his arms.

XXIV

She did give him food, but much later. He helped set the table and slice the bread while she scrambled eggs with green chilies and cheese.

"You're a good cook, too," he said, filling her coffee cup as naturally as if they'd been sitting in her small kitchen like this for years.

She flushed. "Did you—did you think—?"

He shrugged and grinned, eating with gusto. "I certainly hoped!"

Should she stammer and blush and say she'd never done such a thing before? Explain she had been taken by his boy's face, his voice, his hands on the guitar? It had probably been true of other women before her. Yet the way he'd loved her, bringing her to joy, using his lean, finely jointed, body for her pleasure before he had his own—surely that had been different with her?

"Are you staying in town?" she asked.

"Start work tonight." At her surprised look he added mischievously, "Yes, I get meals at my boardinghouse, but I figured I'd much rather have whatever you'd give me."

So he hadn't been starving, though he'd looked that way. Was the other hunger also pretense? She straightened and gave him a level look. Whatever his appetite, hers had been real. And he had fulfilled her as Fayte had never done. What was it with the boy? A fragility, something that completely disarmed her?

"Johnny Chance," she said slowly. "Is that a real name?"

"Joe Hill gave it to me. Before that, on the San Pedro waterfront where he found me, they just called me 'Kid' or 'Hey, you!' or whatever they could twist their tongues to. I was lucky to get work. After the big business panic in 1908, a third of all workers were out of jobs."

"But you must have had a name."

"I never knew it. Or my folks. The orphanage called me Henry. Ran off as much because of that as the grub and beatings."

So that was it. The lonely, unwanted child still looked out of his eyes, shaped that wistful, cynical smile. "So you knew Hill in California?"

"Sure. He worked at the wharfs like me. Came in 1910 when the IWW local was formed and was secretary for a couple of years."

She vaguely remembered that in 1911 the Mexican Liberal Party, bent on overthrowing Díaz, had headquartered in Los Angeles and from there had tried to take Baja California with the aid of IWW members and others. "Did you go to Mexico with Hill?"

He nodded. "We took Mexicali in January, and another little town, but in June the Porfiristas ran us out. That winter we went to Hawaii and worked as longshoremen, loading raw sugar. Next year we got beat up in Oceanside when we were headed for a free-speech fight in San Diego—"

"What's a free-speech fight?"

"Lots of cities forbid speaking in the street. IWWs would come in strong and all get up on soapboxes, urging the workers to join and stand up for their rights. The speakers would get hauled off to jail, but there'd be so many they'd overcrowd the jails and bog down the courts, be such an expense that usually the city fathers repealed the law against street speeches and organizing and let the jailed lot go. But we didn't always get it all our way. I've been stripped, beaten and left for dead, pistol-whipped a couple of times, and run out of more towns than I expect you've even seen, pretty lady." Softly, remembering, he went on. "Joe and I left California the summer of 1913, heading for Chicago. We got as far as Salt Lake City. Later Joe did get to Chicago. He was buried there, after Utah killed him."

"And he had one funeral in Salt Lake City and another in Chicago, didn't he?"

"Yes. Over five thousand came to the one in Chicago. We sang his songs on the way out to Graceland Cemetery, and late into the night, after words were said over him in Swedish, Russian, Spanish, Italian, Polish, German, Hungarian, Yiddish, and Lithuanian—languages of the workers he'd spent his life trying to help."

"But wasn't he cremated? There was something about lots of envelopes . . ."

"The funeral was on Thanksgiving and he was cremated next day, November 26, 1915. Some ashes were sent to locals in every state except Utah, and to Asia, South America, Europe, New Zealand, Australia, and South Africa. On May 1, the workers' international holiday, he wanted his ashes to be scattered, and they were. All over the world."

"And you've come here."

"Yes."

"I don't think the Union of Mine, Mill, and Smelter Workers will like that."

"Too bad."

"If you find poor conditions, you could talk to the management."

"I will."

She stared at him, thought of a man she'd never known jerking in a Utah prison yard as bullets ripped his heart. "Don't," she pleaded. "Johnny, don't!"

He came to lay his head in her lap, arms embracing her about the hips. His breath warmed her thighs. She stroked the hair that tried to curl, winced at scars revealed by her touch. She bent to kiss his cheek, but he raised up to meet her lips with his mouth.

He came to her almost every night before he went to work. Through the day she'd think of all the reasons she shouldn't let herself care about him, even reciting them aloud to a bored Nicodemus who would bat her face with his paws till she paid attention to *him.* At night, as soon as Johnny smiled at her or touched her with his hands, she wanted only to comfort and be comforted by his body, give all she could to this one who could love with such sweet wildness though there seemed to be little enough love in his past.

Often he brought his guitar and played for her, sometimes leaving it at her house. Mostly, he sang folk songs, but always he sang something of Hill's. The hours with him were when she felt alive. The rest of the time, even with the children, seemed unreal.

Of course, that late spring and early summer had been past belief. War had been declared April 6 against Germany, and on May 19 Gen. John J. Pershing and 30,000 troops had been ordered to France. Chinese refugees who'd followed Pershing out of Mexico after almost a year's fruitless pursuit of Pancho Villa, had gone to San Antonio, where they were enlisted in the quartermaster's department.

Villa, once a conscientious mule packer for Sonora mines, had become one of the most famous revolutionary generals and in March of 1916 had led fifteen hundred guerrillas into Columbus, New Mexico, where they killed seventeen Americans. Pursuing U.S. troops had killed over a hundred of the raiders, and Pershing had been sent south of the border to try to capture Villa. He met with the same success that earlier commanders had when sent after Apaches.

The strike at Cananea was now sometimes called the

start of the Mexican Revolution. Several of the strike leaders who'd been condemned to the awful prison of San Juan de Ulúa were now generals, and the dead *huelguistas* were considered martyrs. It had been 1911 before the rebels actually took over Cananea. Colonel Greene had barely lived to see it. The 1907–08 panic all but ruined him with the sharp, sudden drop in copper prices, but he'd salvaged what he could. On August 5, 1911, he lost the reins of the horses pulling his buggy and was thrown from it, smashing bones and puncturing a lung. He died of the pneumonia that set in.

Fayte, so far as Chris knew, was operating a mine south of Cananea, one owned independently of Greene. Her young girl's admiring adoration for him was dead, crushed by the bullet he'd sent into Cruz, though that wasn't all of it. She could never have lived as an ornament in his house, a rare trophy, guarded, protected, but a *thing*.

It must be precarious for a gringo in Mexico; it was dangerous for anyone. Carranza was now president, following the murder of Francisco Madero, the idealistic reformer who had been the first president after Porfirio Díaz was overthrown in 1910. Victoriano Huerta, who had conspired to kill Madero, had succeeded him, but Carranza, Villa, Obregon, Zapata, and other revolutionary chiefs refused to accept him and kept fighting the *federales*. Some U.S. Marines, landing at Tampico in 1914 for supplies, were arrested and held for an hour and a half. They were released with apologies, but Huerta refused to salute the American flag in reparation, and President Wilson had ordered a fleet to Tampico Bay. It seized the customshouse at Vera Cruz in April of 1914 and sent a detachment to Huerta, demanding an apology for the arrest of some Navy men. Mexico severed diplomatic relations with the U.S., but more serious trouble was warded off by the offer of Brazil, Chile, and Argentina to arbitrate the dispute. The advancing revolutionary armies forced Huerta's resignation in July. He sailed for Spain. During the ensuing chaos, Venustiano Carranza emerged as president, but it would be a long time before the volcano that was the revolution stopped erupting.

To Chris, there was strangeness in finding accounts in the *Bisbee Daily Review* of aerial battles over Europe fought at 6,000 to 19,000 feet, while across the border in Agua Prieta, Villistas were being shot against the wall.

Congress had passed a Selective Service bill May 18, and when a government agent had entered the Navajo reservation to register men for the draft, he'd been run off. In Phoenix thirty-seven Russian conscientious objectors had gone to prison. In a raid over London German planes killed ninety-seven people and wounded more than four hundred. On June 20, 1917, England finally gave women the vote. The next day in Washington, a mob tore down suffragette flags.

Ladies were wearing Paul Revere tricorns with insignia of the Signal Corps and martially styled coats. *20,000 Leagues Under the Sea* played at the Orpheum, following Fox's best production, *A Tale of Two Cities*. Doug Fairbanks thrilled fans in *The Americans*, and Theda Bara, for ten and fifteen cents, could be seen at the Central in *Her Greatest Love*. Fatima cigarettes were an elegant smoke and gas-fired water heaters and ranges brought clean convenience to the home.

War fever was mounting. The agitators at Jerome were called traitors and saboteurs because copper was a basic need in munitions. Trouble raged in the mines at Butte, Montana, climaxing in a walkout June 21. There was unrest at the Globe mines, but the *Review* complacently reported that all was peace in Bisbee.

When Chris mentioned Jerome or Butte or Globe to Johnny, he just smiled, turned back to his guitar, or took her in his arms. She'd heard of no real difficulties, though there were rumors that the existing union resented the infiltration of IWWs. Miners moved around so much, especially young, unmarried ones, that new men were constantly being hired, and under pressure for increased war production, screening for radicals wasn't as thorough as it had been during the slump years.

Sometimes, after Johnny had left for his night shift and she lay restless in the bed they'd shared physically though he wouldn't share his thoughts, Chris felt a great need to talk with Sant, or simply be with him.

Why was that when she felt she couldn't marry him? He had first asked her when he finished medical school three years ago. She had refused him with almost as much shock as if a brother had made the proposal, a younger brother she'd taken care of when he was little and shy.

Not that the four-year-old orphan Patrick had brought home looked much like the tall young man with Apache-black hair and eyes the color of a blue thundercloud just before it rains. Talitha had said to him once, "Watching you is just like seeing James, my brother, the way he'd have been if the times hadn't torn him between being white and Apache."

Sant had laughed. "My Apache blood couldn't have come from a man who'd have given me more credit with them. They still remember Fierro—and the white woman who died with him."

This heritage had smoothed Sant's way as a doctor on the San Carlos agency. He had inherited his father's healing hands and instinctive method of diagnosis. He also got the Indian medicine men to help with treatment.

"Apaches are just like whites in that many of their ills are caused by a sad or angry or frightened heart," he had told Chris on his first visit home. "To know that people are praying and singing for you to get well, appealing to the great powers, has to give hope, help the body to heal itself."

"Teresita brought back my sight just by speaking."

"She had great power. Much of it was hypnotism, I'm sure, but she must have also been a conductor of tremendous energy. I have some of that in my fingers, but nothing like hers." His eyes changed and he'd reached for her hands. "Chris, you can't hide at Socorro all your life! You have to get out in the world and live in it, decide to trust a man."

She had tried to pull free. He held her implacably, his face as grim as Fierro's must have been when he prepared for battle.

"I teach school here!" she retorted defensively.

"And visit the sick and help Talitha and Sewa look after the aging and newborns!" He gave her a little shake. "Face it, Chris! You're living just as you did before you married Riordan, sleeping in the room you had as a child, safe with a family and people who love you."

"What's wrong with that?"

"You aren't living your own life, loving your love." This shake was rougher. "Christina Revier, you seem perfectly ready to stay here till the day you die, never try again for anything of your own, never risk anything!"

She had loved and she had risked, but the blood had been Cruz's. Would she never feel clean of that? Tears stung her eyes. Averting her face when she couldn't wrench away from those determined hands, she said in a tight whisper, "Sant, can't you leave me in peace?"

She felt and heard his breath catch. "Chris, I've always loved you. Why won't you marry me?"

"I've told you before! You're like a brother to me."

He set his hand behind her head, brought her close with his other arm, and kissed her long and sweetly and savagely. In spite of her scarred memories of Fayte, her deliberate blocking of any sensual hungers that tried to stir in her, Sant's hard yet tender mouth sent her stilled blood racing, swirled spreading fire through her. He touched her breast. She moaned, twisted away from him.

"Sant! That wasn't fair!"

His eyes seemed almost black. "Could a brother do that?"

Retreating, she raised her fingers to her lips and gazed at him reproachfully, till a new thought struck, a way to make him stop tormenting her—and, not so incidentally, to assuage the roused desire that coursed tumultuously through her whole body.

"Would you like to come to my room?" she asked.

His face colored violently, then drained. Rising, he clenched his hands behind him. "No, I won't come to your little girl's room! I won't take you while your blood's up so you can despise and forget me."

He had read her even better than she knew herself. Sobered, ashamed of what she would have done to their long, special bond, she put out her hand to him. "Sant—"

"I want to live with you," he said, each word heavy. "I want to live with you my whole life, see your face the last thing in this world, lie next to you up on the hill after we are dead. I won't have you, Christina, till you feel that way, too."

He'd gone back to the reservation. What he'd said festered; she could no longer sink herself in teaching in the little ranch schoolhouse or in sharing the life of the family, dear as they all were. At the end of the week she had begun to look for a job. She found one in Bisbee.

That had been two years ago. Sant's response to that had been, "Well, at least you're breaking out of your nice, warm cocoon. But it'll be a wonder if you don't marry some mining tycoon or engineer. Trophies have such a nice, safe life. They just ornament a house."

She laughed at him. "Sant, I think whatever I do, you'll say I'm not facing life till I decide to marry you!"

After a moment's surprise, he chuckled, too, but the way his eyes touched her throat and mouth stilled her laughter. "You're right. I am what you have to face up to, Chris. Soon or late."

It was hard for him to force that issue, though, tied down by his work at the reservation. She'd seen him at Christmas when they both went home to Socorro, and he'd come by at Easter, staying at the Copper Queen Hotel, though he was with her every waking moment.

"All right," he said on their last evening. "You've proved you can live away from home. Now, when are you going to prove that you can live with love?"

Holding Nicodemus, stroking his soft coat, she said, "I don't have to jump hurdles, Sant. I'm doing useful work, I enjoy the children, and—"

"You're shutting out your life as a woman."

She yawned wickedly. "Suppose I told you I have a half dozen strong, stalwart miners?"

"I'd know you lied."

"Heckle me enough and I may try it!" She sprang to her feet, scowling. "Sant, can't you get it through your head that I feel incestuous with you? I care far too much about you, even when you're being a stubborn mule, to use you for a convenience."

"I'm not that convenient." He got to his feet, strong, clean, beautiful in a masculine way. He *did* appeal to her, and he sensed it. "Give me a night, even an hour, and we'd have no more of this incest and little-brother nonsense."

She watched him, gripped by the desire that radiated from him with real physical impact. "You can have me, Sant."

He took a long stride then checked himself. "Not like that. Not till you mean it for more than a way to get rid of me and cool any fever you've worked up!"

She hadn't seen him since. As she waited in the twilight for Johnny, she wondered what Sant would think about them. Strangely, she felt guilt, as if she'd been deceiving someone with a claim on her.

That was crazy. She'd been honest with Sant. In fact, if he stood by his tiresomely repeated convictions, he ought to applaud her for taking a lover, one who was certainly not safe.

Toward the end of June, Johnny said he wouldn't be able to see her for a while. The evening of the twenty-sixth he played his guitar in the park, attracting a crowd to listen to six leaders exhort the miners to strike till the company agreed to seven demands.

On June 28 the Citizens' Protective League, made up of about a thousand businessmen and residents, condemned the IWW as a treasonous group conspiring against the government. Cochise County Sheriff Harry Wheeler was down from Tombstone to keep order. He was the last commander of the Arizona Rangers, which had been disbanded by the legislature in 1909.

In spite of pickets, about half the miners were still at work. As the town seethed, Wheeler swore in two hundred deputies. Officials claimed that most of the pickets were foreigners. Except for snatching a few hours' sleep, Johnny was constantly on the picket line now, playing his guitar, singing Joe Hill's songs.

The union demands sounded fair enough to Chris, though not serious enough for a strike till more negotiation had been tried. She knew of Johnny's dream world without classes, wages, or bosses, a society where everyone worked and received enough for a good life. The idea appealed to her sense of justice, but she strongly doubted that it would work.

All the same, though of two minds about the strike, Chris decided to bring Johnny milk and sandwiches. Her action would mark her as a radical and shock the mineowners who were friends of her father, but she felt she must stand in the daylight beside the man who had given her such joy at night. Johnny smiled and thanked her, then wolfed down the food.

Next morning only Sulev joined her for a nature walk. "My da's on strike," he said proudly, "but the others aren't. The kids would like to come, Miss

Christina, but their folks are scared to let them keep you company."

She and the Lithuanian boy had a stroll beyond Chihuahua Hill, watched a pair of red-tailed hawks soar and plummet, found a wolf spider's hole, scared a rattlesnake away from a curved-bull thrasher's nest. After parting with Sulev, Chris walked slowly homeward.

Several members of the school board were waiting on her porch. They came to the point at once. Was she keeping company with an IWW, an outsider come to stir up the workers and make trouble?

"I'm Johnny Chance's friend." She glanced from one board member to another, sad at their closed faces but not blaming them.

"We don't want a person like you teaching our children," said an angry woman who was wearing one of the Paul Revere tricorns.

An elderly storekeeper, who'd tried more than once to squeeze Chris's arm, coughed gently. "As the father of daughters, Miss Revier, let me remind you what grief your conduct would bring to your father, the senator. Would you want him to lose his place among the honored lawmakers of this state because of your folly?"

"My father can't be blamed for what I do," Chris said curtly. The thought of how quickly he'd have dispersed these puny souls helped her control her hurt and humiliation. "Very well. You've discharged me. Please stop trespassing and go about your business."

"You're renting from my brother," hissed the big blond woman. "He asked me to tell you to move."

"My rent's paid till the end of July."

"He'll give you a refund."

"I prefer to stay here."

"Brazen!"

"If you don't leave," said Chris, opening the door, "I believe I'll have to call the sheriff."

After much mumbling and spiteful, curious stares, the group went down Opera Drive, full of righteousness but deflated at her acceptance of their edict.

Finally, it was no sacrifice. Chris lived on a tithe of her income, a good portion of which went to send promising young people to college and help support a children's home her mother had started in Phoenix. The pain was in caring about the children, trying to find a way to interest each one in learning, and now realizing that she wouldn't see them in the fall, wouldn't know how they were doing.

Too, it hurt to be spoken to like that.

Nicodemus rubbed against her leg as she stared sightlessly out the window. Picking him up, she pressed her face against him and let herself cry.

The mayor banned street gatherings. On July 3 the mines in Globe were shut down by strikers, and on the next day five carloads of cavalry reached that embattled town to keep order. In Bisbee's July 4 parade the Workmen's Loyalty League, miners who weren't striking, joined the procession in Tombstone Cañon and marched with it through Brewery Gulch.

There were burro races, pushmobile races, and ball games, but Chris went out only to take Johnny his lunch. She hadn't told him that she had lost her job or that the children, except for Sulev, no longer walked with her. He wouldn't want to know it. He was totally absorbed in the strike, encouraging the pickets with stories of other hard-won union victories, cheering them with his music.

What was he to her?

A lover in the darkness, conquering because of his youth and vulnerability, and some matching of their bodies that drove them to stay part of each other as long as it was possible, feel bereft when that primal joining failed them though they still lay in each other's arms? A man who was hungry, whom she fed? Someone fated and strange to whom she wanted to give such rest and happiness as she could?

She couldn't imagine spending a life with Johnny, or what he'd be like without the cause to which he so utterly gave himself. For this time and place, she felt the need to be a refuge for him, a solid ledge for legs trembling from the cliff they were scaling. She gave him peace. He gave her ecstasy.

As she started home an auto speeded past, then squealed to a stop in front of her. It was Fayte. He climbed out of the gleaming vehicle and in two long strides confronted her. A bit heavier, a little gray in the brown-gold hair, grooves at mouth, and eyes deeper.

"Chris! What are you doing out here so close to these damn red-flag Wobblies?"

"I brought lunch to one of them." She threw back her head, knowing that his tawny eyes were devouring the way the wind blew her clothes against her body.

He towered over her, eyes blazing. "Have you gotten yourself mixed up with that gang of scummy traitors?"

"What I do and with whom is none of your business, Fayte."

She started past him. He caught her wrist, bruising it when she tried to twist free. "Chris, for God's sake, keep away from those Wobblies! You could get yourself killed or hurt if trouble breaks loose!"

"Did you come to start it?"

"I'll back Douglas any way I can. He helped me at Cananea."

"Why aren't you at your own mine?"

"Villistas took it over last week." He grinned, and she felt a moment's liking for him. "Good for a man to start over every now and then. Keeps him interested."

"Good luck," she said. But he still held her.

"I don't suppose you'd invite me to your place for something to eat and a cup of coffee?"

"That wouldn't be a good idea."

"Let's stop at a restaurant, then."

"Fayte, we've got nothing to talk about."

His hand slid caressingly up her arm. "We don't have to talk. At least, let me drive you home."

So you'll know where to find me? "Thank you, no," she said.

His smile died. He let go of her wrist, but his gaze held her even more inescapably. "Chris, I want you back."

Mutely, she shook her head. His eyes hooded. She knew he was remembering having her, how they had made love. She had to remember, too, writhe inwardly as she recalled how she'd tried to placate and please and humor this man who'd treated her like his possession.

His mouth twisted. "Do you think you're in love with one of these damned radicals? Or is your heart just bleeding for the downtrodden?"

"That's none of your business." Turning away, she walked up the hill but didn't go to her house till after his auto had blasted away.

He could easily find out where she lived, of course, but she counted on his pride to keep him from hounding her. She hoped his pride would also keep him from asking around about her involvement with the strikers. If he knew about Johnny—

Fear twined about her heart like a strangler's cord. Why had she blurted out that she'd taken one of the IWWs his lunch? Throughout the rest of that long day she was taut with apprehension.

Afraid that Fayte might strike at Johnny if he saw her with him, she got Sulev to take Johnny's lunch to him next day. The boy came back with untouched food, his snub nose wrinkling in perplexity.

"Mr. Chance says he needs to see you more'n he needs something to eat. They're really upset, all the strikers, my da, too. The union took away the Bisbee local's charter."

"The Union of Mine, Mill, and Smelter Workers?"

"I guess. Said the men here had shown treachery to

union principles." The boy frowned. "That's not true, is it, Miss Revier?"

"I don't think you can pay much attention to anything you hear about treachery the next few days." Forcing a laugh, Chris gave him milk and cookies before he went home, then stared at the rejected lunch.

What a lot of trouble men let themselves in for with their stubbornness! She'd take Johnny his meal, but he had to understand that she couldn't go on jeopardizing him.

He understood nothing of the sort. Refusing to accept the food, he said coldly, "Don't bother, if you're so scared of what your once-was husband is going to think."

"It's not what he thinks! It's what he might do! Listen, I saw him kill a man at Cananea—"

"You think I haven't seen men killed? That I don't expect it for myself during a strike like this?"

"That's still no reason to invite trouble. If Fayte sees us . . ."

Johnny looked at her with the cynical, hopeful eyes of a waif. "I'd rather he saw us, pretty lady, than that you wouldn't come to me."

The strike had absorbed him till anything outside it was hazy, unreal. What mattered to him about her now was that she stand beside him in front of Fayte and the town, that a member of the privileged sided with the strikers.

And that wasn't it at all. She cared for Johnny, the man, the wanderer, not for his obsession. If the workers' demands had been negotiated privately, without fanfare, she believed, Phelps-Dodge would have acceded to most of them. What was going on wasn't a battle for improved pay and conditions as much as it was a showdown between management and labor. Who was to have the whip hand in the mines, the men who owned them or those who worked there?

Chris didn't see how that question could ever produce anything but strife. A successful answer must be to the benefit of both sides. Maybe if the workers had shares in the company, a fair voice in management . . . But she wasn't a negotiator, a striker, or a manager. If Johnny, knowing the risk, wanted her to come to him on the picket line, she would.

XXV

On July 10 Phelps-Dodge held its first annual picnic. There were prizes, races, and free food, but only two hundred and twenty-five people attended. On July 11 sixty-seven IWWs were rounded up and shipped out of Jerome in cattle cars. With water but no food, they were turned loose at Jerome Junction, twenty-seven miles away, and warned not to come back.

Next day the headlines of the *Bisbee Review* screamed: WOMEN AND CHILDREN KEEP OFF STREETS TODAY. Beneath, down the center of the page, ran a letter from Sheriff Harry Wheeler announcing that a posse of twenty-two hundred Douglas and Bisbee citizens were going to arrest all strange men on charges of vagrancy. The park was closed to public meetings. Workers who didn't return to their jobs would be dropped from the employed list. The paper said most of the strikers were Wobblies or foreigners, Austrians who were trying to sabotage the war effort because their loyalties were with the Kaiser.

Chris stared at the incredible words, scarcely able to believe them. Then, remembering Cananea, the marching workers with their dead, Cruz falling under Fayte's gun, she realized the same thing, only much worse, could happen here.

With trembling hands, she picked up the telephone and phoned her father in Phoenix. He promised to call the governor at once and see what could be done, though he grimly added that he thought the strike was unjustified and that the Wobblies were begging to be martyred.

"They don't just want a fair wage, Chris. They want an end to the wage system, a classless society; and though that sounds utopian, people being what they are, it won't work."

"I don't know about that, Dad, but I do know most of the strikers live here and many have families. That posse's going to be armed. It could be a small war."

"I'll do what I can," he assured her. His tone sharpened. "Chris, you stay out of this, hear? You've been blind twice in your life. Isn't that enough?"

"Third time's the charm." She hung up and went down the streets, where no other women walked, in search of Sheriff Wheeler. She found him outside the Pythian Castle, not far from the jail. He was a good-looking, strong-jawed young man who took off his hat at her approach and asked if he could help her. Surely she knew it wasn't safe today to be outside.

"It's safer for me than for the strikers." His face hardened, but she went on, pleading. "Sheriff, the workers have a right not to work. They have a right to ask for better wages and conditions."

"They can leave if they don't like it," he said brusquely. "We think they have dynamite and weapons. It's my duty to protect property and law-abiding citizens."

"Especially property?"

His weather-browned face flushed. "Ma'am, you better go home. Right now."

They stared at each other. His eyes were implacable, his jaw firmly set. He believed he was doing the right thing, protecting the town from rabble-rousers who might explode into a looting, pillaging mob.

"I've called my father, Senator Revier—"

Wheeler's eyes flickered with recognition. He cut in

brutally. "Did you tell him, ma'am, what sort of company you're keeping? I don't care who you call! I'm here to keep order., and I will."

She hadn't heard steps behind her and whirled at Fayte's voice. "I know this lady, Sheriff. I'll see her home."

"Good." The sheriff looked relieved. "See if you can't talk sense into her, Mr. Riordan."

If she objected, she thought, Wheeler would turn a blind eye to any force Fayte might use, or even help him. In angry silence, she walked till they were out of Wheeler's sight past Brewery Gulch.

"You don't need to come any farther," she said.

He smiled. "I told the sheriff I'd take you home."

His tone was pleasant, yet something in it chilled her. She glanced desperately around, but no one was near. If anyone had been, who'd interfere with a deputy enforcing the sheriff's order to keep off the streets? He set his hand under her elbow, moving her forward. She had to either walk or struggle. The latter would only make a public spectacle for those watching from behind curtained windows.

He turned into Opera Drive. So he'd found out where she lived. As they approached her house, dread seized her, a physical horror of this man.

"Fayte, please—"

He drew her inexorably up the steps, opened the door, brought her inside her own house. As she pushed frantically at his binding arms, he swept her up and carried her back to her bedroom.

She fought him then, but he only laughed.

When at last he pulled on his clothes, Chris kept her eyes shut. Soiled by his sweat and smell, she felt she could never get them off her. Fayte sat down heavily by her and lifted her head between his hands.

"I still want you, Chris. I'd like to marry you again."

"You can say that—after what you've done?" Twisting from him, she turned and retched. "I wonder if there's any chance Wheeler would arrest you for rape?"

"Not after you've been carrying on with that damned Wobblie."

"My father—"

"The senator can't shoot half as well as I can. You know that. You'll keep your mouth shut for his sake." His eyes traveled deliberately over her. "I'll be back."

"If you are, I'll kill you!"

"Got a gun? How ferocious you've gotten, sweetheart."

She moved for the bedside table in the same instant he did, but his arm blocked her as he opened the drawer and slipped her revolver into his pocket. His teeth showed in a white flash.

"If you don't want to see me, you can always leave town. I understand that's what you've been invited to do."

"I'm staying right here. And I'll make sure your posse gets the credit for whatever it does."

"Thanks," he said mockingly.

When he was gone, she filled the tub. Sobbing, desperate to get the memory of him off her, she washed herself, rinsed, and washed again, but her nostrils still detected his faint acrid odor. She longed for Sant but knew she mustn't call him. He'd want to take her away; if he stayed for her sake, he could get hurt.

She was certainly not going to be in this house when Fayte came back. Putting overnight necessities into a shopping bag, she called Nicodemus, but he was lying on a neighbor's garage roof and loftily pretended not to hear. She put out fresh water and food for him, then went to the Silver King Hotel and took a room.

"I'd like one near a fire escape," she told the clerk, who fortunately didn't know her, so she registered as O'Shea. "I'm nervous of fires."

He smiled indulgently and handed her a key. "Here

you are, ma'am. Better stay in today. There may be trouble with the Wobblies."

"What kind of trouble?"

"Oh, the word is Sheriff Wheeler's going to round them all up and ship them out of here on the train. They're supposed to have weapons and dynamite, so it could be quite a fracas."

At least Wheeler didn't intend mass lynching. Chris was sure Johnny didn't have a gun, but some of the other strikers might. She wanted to go see him on the picket line but knew that any woman would be turned back.

Any woman.

She laughed out loud as she saw a way to be with Johnny, to elude Fayte. Going downstairs, she smiled prettily at the clerk and explained that her younger brother wanted her to buy him some clothes. Since it wasn't safe for women to be out, could he send someone to do the errand for her? She'd make it worth their time.

"Jed'll be glad to do it," said the clerk heartily, motioning over a boy of thirteen or fourteen who was polishing the windows. "Just tell him what you want, ma'am."

An hour later Jed was happily conscious of the dollar in his pocket, while a youngster in stiff new Levi's, boots, and blue work shirt was climbing down the fire escape.

Knots of volunteers guarded the city park and clustered around saloons and rooming houses. Chris didn't see Fayte or Wheeler. The tension of a storm waiting to break charged the heat of the afternoon.

Chris's head felt light and strange without the hair she'd cropped with shears Jed had purchased. She wore a straw hat pulled low and believed that to a casual eye she'd pass for a rather girlish boy.

Johnny knew her at once, though. As she trudged up

the slope to the mine, he left the pickets and hurried forward. "Chris! What on earth—"

"Women aren't supposed to be out today." With difficulty she kept from catching his hands or reaching up to touch that curly red-brown hair. "Johnny, they're going to ship you all out tomorrow. Why don't you go now?"

His gray eyes were incredulous. "I helped start this. Got to stay with the men. You know that."

She was ashamed. "Then I'm staying with you," she said.

"You can't!"

"Why do you think I cut off my hair?"

"Oh, pretty lady!" He gazed at her, between distress and mockery, before he completely sobered. "Chris, there may be killing. This isn't for you. Why, you're not even sure the strike's justified! Go along home." He put his hand on her shoulder and grinned coaxingly. "Maybe by the time your hair grows, I'll be back."

She shook her head. "I'm staying with you."

"Why?"

"Because I can't bear to wait behind a door while that posse does whatever it's going to do."

His mouth quirked. "You could if you didn't know me."

"But I do know you."

He sighed, but his thin body seemed to grow more substantial, become more firmly put together. "All right. Let's find a picket sign just your size."

Most of the pickets went home at dusk, but a few stayed on, including Johnny and Chris. When shifts changed at midnight, there was jeering back and forth between the strikers and men who'd gone on working. "Call me scab all you want," shouted one burly miner. "Scabbed is what you're gonna be when Wheeler gets through with you! Goddamn sabotaging Wobblies!"

Soon it was still again. Only a few lights burned in town. Chris huddled close to Johnny; at that altitude nights were cool even in July. He didn't talk to her, but off and on he played softly, sometimes sang a little. Not IWW songs, but "Swing Low, Sweet Chariot," "Bonnie Annie Laurie," "The Gypsy Laddie," and the one he'd sung when they'd first met, when he'd asked for food.

"Who's goin' to be your man tonight . . ."

She shivered and stayed close to him. Now and then she drowsed; but when she jerked awake, Johnny was always sitting up, either playing or gazing into the night.

The gray fingers of dawn appeared on the horizon, changed to peach, and rose as the darkness shrank away. Johnny got up, went over to the other pickets, and began to sing "Joe Hill."

"'Joe Hill ain't dead,' he says to me,
'Joe Hill ain't never died.
Where workingmen are out on strike
Joe Hill is at their side.
Joe Hill is at their side.'"

The pickets began to sing with him, softly, then with fervor. "Look!" called someone. "They're coming! Wheeler's men!"

"What'll we do?" whispered a young miner next to Chris.

"Let them arrest us," Johnny said. "Don't give them an excuse to use those guns."

"Come on, you Wobs!" shouted the leader. "We're gonna give you a free ride out of Arizona!"

Gesturing with rifles and pistols, the deputies hustled the pickets along the railroad track toward Warren, a mile away, and herded them into the fenced, board-sided baseball diamond where other prisoners were being cooped. Chris managed to slip in among the confused crowd without being spotted by the deputies.

A few miners stared at her in momentary surprise, but they were too worried about their own fates to trouble about a rich man's daughter.

The whole scene was nightmarishly unbelievable. The posse had seven machine guns in addition to their smaller weapons. Several times, Chris saw Fayte bringing in strikers and turned so he wouldn't see her face.

There was the sound of a distant shot, then several more. In a few minutes word buzzed through guards and prisoners that a deputy named McRae had been shot by a miner named Chew, who'd been instantly killed. As well as searching for strikers, the posse was hunting for the arms and ammunition they thought the IWW had cached, but nothing was found.

"My wife's going to have a baby!" one boyish miner protested. "Who's going to take care of her if they send me away?"

"My old mother depends on me," muttered another.

An older man seemed to be dazed and kept shaking his graying head. "It ain't fair! This is America! They can't do this!"

A Ford parked at the corner, and the driver got out and stood for a long time watching the prisoners. Sant! Chris almost shouted his name, then remembered where she was and swallowed her outcry. He could get her out of the bullpen, but she could do that herself just by revealing her identity. Sant couldn't stop this deportation, though. No use getting him mixed up in it.

Her father must have phoned him, and Sant had driven down to look after her. He'd worry when he couldn't find her, but eventually she'd be on a boxcar with Johnny, the train would take them somewhere, and she could let her family know she was safe.

Still, when Sant got back in his car and drove toward town, she felt abandoned and had to fight back tears.

Armed deputies formed two rows through which strikers were made to pass as they were loaded into waiting cattle cars and boxcars. They were asked if they'd go back to work. Those who agreed were released. The others were herded into cars that smelled of dung.

Johnny played his guitar and sang till the waiting men and those on the boxcars joined in fervently.

"You will eat, bye and bye,
In that glorious land above the sky;
Work and pray, live on hay,
You'll get pie in the sky when you die."

Fayte came through the prisoners to Johnny. Chris faded behind some men. "We don't want you on this train," Fayte said. "Come on, songbird. Sheriff Wheeler's told me to give you a ride out of town."

"I want to go with my friends."

"So you can keep them stirred up?" Fayte prodded Johnny with a pistol. "Get moving, Wob."

Slowly, Johnny moved through the prisoners. Chris followed, though she kept out of Fayte's view. Sant's Ford was back. He was scanning the crowd in the diamond. Someone must have told him she'd been seeing one of the strikers. As they cleared the fringe of strikers, Johnny turned around.

"Let me stay with the others."

"No. You're the head of the snake, maybe its heart. Without you, it won't rattle long!"

"They'll think I made some deal with you." Johnny's voice rose. Chris had never seen him afraid, but he felt fear now. "They'll think I sold out."

Fayte chuckled. "That's exactly what we'll tell 'em, songbird. Maybe next time they won't listen to you damn Wobblies." He nudged Johnny with the gun. "Get going."

Johnny walked a few steps. Then he turned suddenly, dropping his guitar as he sprang for Fayte. Fayte's gun and another guard's roared at the same time.

Slammed backward, Johnny put his hands over his side. Blood poured between his fingers, pumped from the wound in his throat, as he fell.

Chris ran toward him, hat dropping off as she fell on her knees to lift him. His eyes opened.

"Pretty lady."

He coughed. Blood poured from his mouth as he died in her arms.

Tomochic. Cananea. Blood. Darkness. The blue of the sky went black as she felt Fayte's hands gripping her. But as he called her name, there was Sheriff Wheeler's angry voice demanding what Fayte was trying to do, and there were Sant's hands and Sant's voice.

It was late September. Chris, Nicodemus in her lap, had been sitting on the porch with Talitha when the baby stirred, tugging at her vitals. Johnny's baby, the stranger's seed, rooted in her as any drifting seed will try to find a warm rich place to nestle and rest and produce its kind.

"The babe?" asked Talitha. Her eyes were bright blue at seventy-seven and, for all they had looked on, were still unwavering.

Chris nodded.

"When are you going to marry Sant?"

"I can't, Grande."

"Why? Because another man got you with child? That child's going to need a father. Sant would be a good one."

"It wouldn't be fair."

"Fair, fiddlesticks!" Talitha leaned forward. "That boy loves you, always has, always will. And you love him. Or haven't you realized that?"

"I know I love him." Whatever she'd had for Johnny had been transformed into tenderness for his baby, the will to make sure part of him lived on and loved and laughed, grew up strong and well. "But I—I've been married once. And now there's this baby. Sant should have someone young and fresh and new—"

Talitha seized her coffee cup and hurled it at the wall.

"Christina Revier, you plumb turn my stomach with that sort of talk! Sant loves you! Of course you don't deserve his patience, but I didn't deserve your blessed grandfather's either! I still think he was a sight happier with me than he'd have been without!"

Chris blinked. Her grandparents had just seemed to belong with each other, but when she thought, she remembered old stories and knew it hadn't always been so. Talitha had loved Shea for many years, and had married Judah Frost. She'd been as old as Chris was now when she found her peace with Marc.

Taken aback, Chris put down her cat and picked up the broken cup. "I'm going for a walk," she said, "before you heave something at me."

"Well, try to think a little while you're at it," Talitha scolded. "Sant's coming this weekend. It's high time you stopped wearing him out with running back and forth."

"I don't know, Grande. It's so soon—"

"It's always soon!" Talitha's voice softened at the shock that must have shown on Chris's face. "Life's that way, my dear. Johnny's dead, but he left a child. It's out of struggle and death that new life, new hope, come."

Chris looked at her uncertainly, stirred yet troubled. Talitha's hand closed over hers. "Sometimes when I sit on the porch and watch the mountains, do you know who comes to sit with me?"

"Who?"

"Socorro. Your great-grandmother."

"Oh, Grande, really!"

"I don't see her." Talitha's eyes twinkled. "But I feel her. And we *think* together. We don't have to say anything."

"And what do you think?" inquired Chris skeptically.

"That it's amazing how the ones we love live on—how a denied love may at last find fulfillment generations later. I have seen a lot of death, Chris, and a lot of life, and more and more I know they flow into each other as each harvest leads to a new crop."

An awesome thought. One Chris needed to ponder. Rising, she said, "Can I bring you anything?"

"I can get whatever I need." Talitha's chin rose testily. "Except a granddaughter with plain common sense!" Catching Chris's hand, she gave it a squeeze. "Don't be a redhead burro like your great-grandfather!"

Smiling down at her grandmother, Chris had a moment of marveling at all this woman had weathered and seen. An Apache captive till ransomed by Shea, she had lost her beloved brother to his Indian blood when he became the dreaded Fierro. She had loved Shea and lost him; married the scalp hunter Frost to save the ranch; seen the United States move in and subdue the Indians. In the span of Talitha's life, she'd seen Arizona change from a no-man's-land to full statehood.

Mighty events. Yet Talitha, small and indomitable, seemed greater than all of them. "You know," said Chris, bending to kiss her grandmother's cheek, "you really are *grande! Muy, muy grande!*"

Followed by Talitha's snort, Chris went around the house past the corrals and new barns. To the west grazed the Herefords which were now the only kind of cattle raised on the ranch; to the east ranged the blooded horses Patrick had been breeding, though the descendants of the first horses brought here far outnumbered the newcomers and were preferred for work by the vaqueros, themselves the children of Sanchezes, Vasquezes, and their relations.

Climbing the hill where crosses showed against the sky, Chris thought of Johnny and what had happened to the other prisoners. Shuttled about the Arizona and New Mexico desert, the strikers had finally been marooned near Columbus, New Mexico. The army had been ordered to feed them and house them temporarily in a stockade for Mexican refugees. A tent city sprang up, and the men, though told they could go wherever they liked, decided to stay where they were till the government could assure their safety.

Newcomers to Bisbee were investigated before they were given a card, and without one they wouldn't be hired. Investigators from the State Federation of Labor were turned back, and though President Wilson had ordered an investigation into the deportation, there was almost no chance that Wheeler and his deputies would be punished, especially since Wheeler had joined the armed forces.

Of the 1200 deported men, 312 had draft registration cards and 142 subscribed to the Liberty Loan. They had offered to form a regiment and go fight in Europe, as they waited in the tent city.

Gradually, the camp melted. Workers found jobs in New Mexico or Texas or drifted back to Arizona, staying clear of Bisbee. Some sent for their families and started life in another camp.

Johnny?

He was buried there, on the other side of Lonnie, another young stranger, who long ago had died to protect Talitha. Here rested Belen, Santiago, Marc, and Socorro. There were crosses for Shea, Caterina, and James, who lay in other soil.

Surrounded by her dead, those who had given her their blood, flesh, and spirit, Chris knelt among the graves and then stood tall, reaching her arms toward the sun, pledging herself to life.

I am Judith who died in a strange land; Talitha who raised her brother to lose him and adored Shea, that Don Patricio of the double brand who so loved Socorro. I am that lady of compassion who found water in the desert; Marc, who was faithful; Santiago; Sewa. They all loved, in spite of death and terror. Shall I be afraid to?

She gave a laugh of strength and joy, exulting in what was past and what was yet to be. Then she heard a voice call her name. Sant was coming toward her.

With a glad cry, she ran to him.